CHARLOTTE TIER[...] Wessex Downs. She was e[...] studied Philosophy and Theology at Oxford University. She has lived in London, Lisbon and on Dartmoor.

Her writing has appeared in *Conjunctions*, *The London Magazine*, *New England Review*, *Best British Short Stories 2024* and The Galley Beggar Short Story Prize.

She has also written for screen and audio.

THE
CAT
BRIDE

CHARLOTTE TIERNEY

S
SALT

CROMER

PUBLISHED BY SALT PUBLISHING 2025

2 4 6 8 10 9 7 5 3 1

First published in Great Britain in 2025 by
Salt Publishing Ltd
12 Norwich Road, Cromer, NR27 0AX United Kingdom

www.saltpublishing.com

Salt Publishing Limited Reg. No. 5293401

A CIP catalogue record for this book is available from the British Library

ISBN 978 1 78463 362 2 (Paperback edition)
ISBN 978 1 78463 363 9 (Electronic edition)

Typeset in Neacademia by Salt Publishing

Printed and bound in Great Britain by Clays Ltd, Elcograf S.p.A

To Ben

Cats will watch creatures, activities, actions unfamiliar to them, for hours. The making of a bed, the sweeping of a floor, packing or unpacking a case, sewing, knitting - anything, they will watch. But what are they seeing?

—DORIS LESSING, *Particularly Cats*

THE
CAT
BRIDE

◊

INSIDE THE WIRE of the lynx enclosure Mumma is almost my age, sixteen. She sits on a low platform in the arm of a beech tree wearing a long deep-red velvet dress over a pair of wellington boots. She tightens a chaplet of flowers upon her thick head of dark hair, and flicks a veil dulled with dry mud wide behind her slim shoulders.

Outside the fence, at a safe distance, tourists crowd onto rough log benches to watch the show. Men in flared trousers and tight T-shirts, women with head scarves and big seventies sunglasses. Babies bounce on hips and children slop ice cream. Everyone swats wasps. A wooden information sign has fallen from its post and is propped against the wire in front of them.

Mumma drops into the overgrown paddock. She skips through with awkward pantomime fear, leaving a crease of crushed grass. She looks this way and that, a dramatic hand held lightly at her brow, in the green light of a midsummer jungle. Ferns nearly as tall as she is. The wind at this altitude always keeps the landscape waving, but that day she pauses and the moor waits too, stiff and shiny as an oil painting. The lynx are so still you could miss the four eyes. Their fine amber rings. Sitting under a beech, grey pelts dappled with shadows, they are two elegant statues. Sleek lines. Triangular faces. Big, for lynx. But not as big as the other one.

The audience hesitates as Mumma swoons upon a convenient rock. Her long hair swings behind her. She is close to the audience at the fence. Closer, still, to two lynx. Then, someone stands.

A third animal – unnoticed, until now – sits up, out of the long grass, in the far corner of the cage. It is the sort of thing preserved for thousands of years in the earliest forms of art. Worshipped and feared. The sort of thing people told stories about before they even realised they were telling stories. A thing of poetry, and religion. A thing.

The audience points one another towards the animal, nervous this is not part of the show. People take leaflets from back pockets and dark armpits. They unfold zoo site maps and scan flyers, confused about what should be happening. Everyone shifts, looking to each other, to strangers, for reassurance. It is possible, for a moment, not a single person is looking at Mumma. They all worry. What if a mistake has been made? What if this animal, that some have come especially to see, should be somewhere else? In a larger enclosure? – on a different continent? – different world?

It has the shape of a lynx. It has the mottle of a lynx. It has the horned ears, yellow eyes and puffed paws of a lynx. It is, infamously, lynx-like.

But it is the size of a tiger.

The two smaller lynx rise, haunches spiking through the leaves towards the girl. Then Mumma stands, hand to her mouth, like a real fairytale princess, eyes so wide her eyebrows must quiver with effort. She prances though the trees, skirts gathered in one hand, veil lifting behind her. The lynx lope after her, nothing less like predators. The tourists all want someone else to do something, as Mumma's pets lie down. Roll onto their backs. The camera tracks Mumma slowly, bumpily. She hurdles the lynx, arrowhead teeth lazily snapping at her velvet train.

Behind Mumma, the other animal remains at the edge of things. Perhaps it knows it is different to the other cats. Perhaps it knows it is an exact replica of its mother, but for its size. Perhaps it knows it is the true Beast, brutish and unlovable in this form. It yawns. Stares into the mid-distance. The mid-distance is also the enclosure's gate.

Mumma shins a tree as if to escape from her lynx. She clings to a branch, reaching a balletic hand out, to anyone, anywhere, in horror. A lurching close-up as the lynx slide along the trunk after her. The grey heads bob among the leaves as they cram onto the branch.

The chaplet catches on a twig as she swings to the ground. A curtain of hair unfurls but the headdress stays in the tree. The lynx follow.

The other thing rises. It walks slowly, huge head low and heavy, along the back fence, towards the enclosure gate. It's half-hidden in the moor's jungle, but its ears are surely flicking at the flies.

People stand from the benches, freshly alert. Mumma does a lap of victory, with a small, embarrassed wave, flapping her skirts with one hand, close to the thin chicken wire.

The visitors probably wonder what exactly they are applauding when the smallest lynx rears behind her, thudding a paw onto each shoulder for the grand finale. Hands drop, limp and forgotten mid-clap, as Mumma collapses to the ground, carefully, on to her side, extending her neck. The lynx presses large pads to her breast, crouched close, jaw wide and stiff, inches from her throat.

The visitors watch *something else* behind the girl. It raises its nose to sniff the gate. It lifts one mallet of a paw and gently taps the handle shaft.

Mumma takes the lynx by its ruff, pouts her lips and leans up to kiss it, like Beauty did the Beast. Like it might transform. But her eyes flash around the audience. She tries to look behind her, straining under the weight of her lynx. She pushes it off to sit up. She doesn't understand why the clapping has stopped.

The camera stops moving, abandoned. The audience is leaving. Some quicker than others. Babies with round, scarlet mouths are held high. The benches are tipped and hurdled.

Mumma's smile falls.

The smallest lynx draws up sharp, its nose a dart cocked to the sky.

Mumma pushes up to run after the huge cat. You can only see the back of her head, the shining flick of her hair, but she's probably shouting. The monster has managed to open the pulley-and-weight

3

gate with one paw – clever cats can always open doors – and whatever the gate weighs, it is nothing to 400 kilograms of furry, electrified muscle.

Tourists shout silently. Arms fly.

The monster doesn't disappear into the woods beyond the enclosure. It follows familiar smells. Takes paths it is used to. The ones leading to the visitors. Its head is raised now. Its paws lift high off the ground, skipping because it is out of the cage.

Before the two lynx reach the gate, it slams shut.

People pull at one another. Push each other. Mumma, struggling to run in her long dress, almost catches the animal, when someone jolts the camera.

A little girl stumbles and falls, crushing her ice cream cone, face puckering at the sight of splintered wafer. A large man in a cagoule trips over her. He throws the child behind him, turning to face the animal. He snatches the discarded information board, and holds it in front of him, fingers flexing and unflexing around it.

The monster weaves its enormous body to one side, still skipping. It almost avoids the man, when Mumma jumps with wide arms. Grabs the animal by its neck. Knocks it off course. Mumma is riding it, hair in front of her face. It rears to buck her off, and when it stretches high, the full bowl of its belly does not disappear as it should do – it has overeaten – or it's stuffed with rocks. It's swollen with disease, or malignant growth. There's something inside it. Mumma slides off, stumbles backwards. The monster drops to the man's feet.

The man swings the information board and brings it down hard on the animal's head. The animal seems to melt quietly into blood. Mumma throws her body into the red pool of it. To protect it – to protect something. The man staggers backwards. He stares at what he's done, but then Mumma is thrown back again.

The monster is in flight. Dark blood-clogged fur. Black lips curled. Yellow teeth. Its tail, a whip. It lands on the man, drags him around, jaw buried in his shoulder with primal instinct. Mumma

4

grabs handfuls of its soaking coat, tries to pull the animal off as the man carries it. The three of them spin into the camera which falls to the ground. It continues to run, sinking into the mud, as Mumma crawls forward, her face a rising, red moon of blood, to place her wet hands around the animal's belly, while the so-called 'tynx' eats a man –

JULY, 1995

DAY 1

'FIRST TIMES ARE tiny deaths wrapped up with pretty bows.' Mumma shouted over the wind roaring through the taxi. She sat in front of me, her cropped hair a black halo, hand gripping the open window. In the wing mirror, I watched her try to catch the driver's eye, to share a half-smile, but he turned up the radio and stared ahead.

'Batleigh hasn't been a zoo since before you were born. It'll be a boring house with a garden now. If that. Don't get excited.' Mumma was an old-fashioned doll, stiff-limbed but smile painted bright and firmly life-like. Pull the string in her back and she repeated plenty of reassuring mottos and sayings, but she didn't enjoy talking about the zoo she had grown up in. Not unless she was drunk.

The driver sucked his cigarette and the car crossed a cattle grid to a track trimming the fat of the moor. The radio cut in and out – *something about drought – something about lower crop yields – higher temperatures – something about boom boom boo –*

'*Higher* temperatures?' Mumma called back to me. 'Someone must have made trouble in hell.'

The driver, not used to her side-splitting sense of humour, ignored her. White ash from his cigarette whirled out through his window. He crushed the stub into the ashtray.

Something about my booty being so round, something about looking me up and down –

The moor was vast, rolling in every direction. A notched spine of land rose up in a billowing blur next to us. Nothing broke up the hot wind rushing over it. Sheep drifted below two huge tables

9

of granite that rose to sharp tips at either end. It looked exactly like the pictures I'd received.

'Great Bat Tor,' I called, cupping my fingers and thumbs to frame it. 'Formed when the hare-witches turned the bat-witch to stone for—'

'Loveday. Facts only, please,' Mumma warned me.

'Great Bat Tor. Four hundred and twenty-two metres above sea level,' I muttered, to myself. 'Formed by intense weathering over millions of years.'

My feet slid on my sweaty flip-flops, toes stretched to grip the ends. The heat felt like being trapped in a witch's stove. I could hardly see through the lob of wind. I thought I felt my hair lashing across my face. But the doctor had told me it was not possible. Phantom sensations, painful or otherwise, can exist in a limb, tooth, eye or breast, whereas hair has no nerve endings. Whether it exists, or not. Hair is, essentially, a dead thing. It could not be in my mouth, tickling my tongue, flossing my teeth. Not now I was bald.

– something hosepipe ban – something dogs suffocate in cars – something he's never known a girl like me before –

'You don't enjoy a moor.' Mumma watched it fly past, straining her voice – not louder, just harder – to make sure I heard. 'You survive it. In any inhospitable landscape, the sun and the rain never know when they've gone too far.'

Mumma wasn't happy about returning to Batleigh. She had taken me away from Batleigh Zoo as a baby, when her mother put me in a cage 'for safekeeping'. She had never planned to take me back. She was gloomy, I was delighted. Open space everywhere. No doors, no walls, no flat. No Temperance School for Boys. No boys at all. I was free of them.

– someone's a-knock knocking on his door –

We slowed to pass two ponies. The driver nodded to the rider of a grey, stubby one. The girl wore short, hacked jeans, boots caked in mud and manure, with a bunch of curly orange hair bundled on her head, messily, like she didn't appreciate it. She rode bareback, a narrow, white piece of paper rolled between her lips. When she looked in through the car window and smiled, I pretended not to see. Behind her, a proud, chestnut pony tugged at its reins and feinted, sidestepping, as the car overtook it. Its rider pulled in the reins. She had black handfuls of hair, like mine had been, pulled into a ponytail so high it wobbled like a paper crown on top of her head. Her grubby boiler suit was rolled up to her calves, arms tied around her tiny body, and the thin straps of her vest had been tucked under her armpits. She ate a soft, twisting lolly. Sticking her tongue out, creaming it with green and yellow ice, then snapping it back into her mouth, as she watched us pass.

We entered the woods surrounding the old zoo. The driver took out the car's cigarette lighter from below the radio. It was neon with heat and smoke clouded the car. The sunken lane was hemmed in by drystone walls and trees. Everything was pine-black after the sun.

– never, he says, never –

I was blinded by the sudden lack of light, eyes still on the pocket sun of the lighter, when a large, dark animal streaked across the road.

'Shit.' The driver stopped suddenly. The car squealed and threw itself against me, hitting me with the back of Mumma's seat.

– sounds like he's definitely never known a girl like me before –

The driver switched the radio off. 'Shit.' He patted his trousers where he'd dropped the lighter. 'Shit.'

I sat up and grabbed the door handle, to get out, to get a look at the animal, but Mumma's hand shot past me and slammed down the lock.

'What was that?' I said. 'Where's it gone?'

Through the window, the black bars of the trees were webbed with lades and rides cutting down from the high moor to the river. In between them, staring at me, was a boy. His hair was mulched like he'd been pulled out of the earth. His grubby white T-shirt said OASIS, and his shorts were long, to his knees, with a pocket for everything. He lifted a camera from around his neck and aimed it at me. I slid low, into my seat, hoping Mumma hadn't noticed me notice him. When I peeked out again, thank goodness, he was gone.

'You can get out here.' The taxi-driver fixed his eyes on the mid-distance, hands clenching and unclenching the steering wheel. 'I'm not going up there.'

Ahead was a steep gravel drive, yellow with weeds and riddled with nettles taller than me. In the overgrown verge beside it, a big, faded sign in looping hand-written font had collapsed from one of its posts. The corner plunged into the ground. *Batleigh House & Zoo*. A painted hand, severely wristless, pointed into the sky. Another hand pointed into the ground, advertising the car park. Below them both, sitting upright like a pet – fluffy muzzle but mouth yawning wide and toothy – was a cartoon of a tiger. Although Batleigh Zoo had never had a tiger, not exactly.

❧

Mumma walked so fast towards the drive, she nearly trotted into a run. Suitcase in one hand, handbag in the other. Head reeling left and right, scanning the trees either side of the road.

'What was that?' I called.

'What was what?' she said, very, very brightly. 'Keep up.'

'That thing in the road?'

'What thing in the road?' She stopped next to the sign, and dropped the suitcase to stretch her hand.

'It was massive. It was the size of a—'

'It was nothing. It was a black fox. It was a badger. You see them sometimes in the early evenings.'

'But it was huge. It was like a massive – cat.' I jogged to join her.

'Lowdy.' She spoke warmly, tweaked my T-shirt at my shoulders. 'You didn't see anything. We've been up all night. Packing. Cleaning. I made difficult decisions very quickly. I'm not blaming you, but we're both tired and I can't have this nonsense on top of everything else.'

'The driver was too scared to keep going—'

'The driver stopped to let us out, darling. Because we'd arrived.'

12

She flicked a hand towards the sign, but her eyes were behind me, to the side of me. 'You're still recovering, Lowdy-Loo. No monsters or witches.'

'Oh,' I said, remembering my illness, disappointed. 'Yes. Sorry. But I wasn't talking about monsters or—'

'Last night was horrible, but the important thing is to stay focused. Don't let it set you back. No fibbing.' She lowered her head and looked at me seriously. 'It's been sixteen years since there were animals at Batleigh, no matter what anyone says.' She sighed and picked up the suitcase, glancing behind me again. 'If we'd had anywhere else to go, anywhere at all – But at least here you'll have a bit of space.' Beyond her, a calico cat with a dusty black bib strolled into the middle of the drive and sat down, one raised leg ticking like the hand of a clock as it cleaned its hidden parts.

'Yes, Mumma,' I said, happily.

She winked at me, then turned, saw the cat, and startled backwards. 'Oh. *Shoo*.' The cat galloped up the drive and out of sight, but Mumma didn't move. She did not like cats. 'It'll be from one of the farms. You're fine. Are you fine?'

I wasn't entirely sure she was speaking to me. 'I'm – fine. Why wouldn't I be fi—'

Without waiting for me, she picked up the suitcase again, and marched up the hill.

At the top of the drive was a large, dirty white house built in the late nineteenth century by an artist only Mumma had heard of. No one had trained roses to climb the drains, or planted pretty flowerbeds in front of it, so it was a tall, pale box on a hill, hazy in the dusty air. Moss grew on the black slate roof and saplings had sprouted with grass in the guttering like thick eyebrows above the closed eyes of blank windows. The wood of the window frames creaking in the heat made it seem as if the house was snoring.

Gravel lapped up to the walls of the house and, in front of the small, pillared porch, an ancient, scratched Land Rover sat heavily on four flat tyres. An old wasp's nest sagged from the ceiling of the porch and a blunt axe, propped on its head, leaned next to the front door, attached by cobwebs to a large pair of mud-crusted, steel-toed boots.

Mumma stared at the ground, before picking her way around small, buttery sausages of dry scat. 'What is all this?' She checked the drive again, suspiciously.

I accidentally stepped on the dried remains of a dead mouse.

'See? The place is a wreck. And that thing is about to collapse.'

She pointed to the spired roof rising from the southern corner of the house like a tower. It was a spit, skewering the greasy sky on its tip.

At the north end of the house, a tall, industrial gate rusted between fat, untended hedges. It was locked with a padlock and chain. A small sign reading *Fingers Are Food* poked from the long grass on the other side of the gate, so faded you could barely see it. It was general advice but apparently most applicable to the goat. Mumma was adamant big cats were fussy eaters.

The small, homemade zoo had once clung tight to Batleigh House. Through the gate bars, you could still see splintering fence posts and ruined paths across the sloping hillside. Old feed baskets and water troughs. Half-sunken railings – ghosts of cages – collapsed by the wind. Bits of old chickenwire bound low by grass. Immediately through the gates, down one side of the house, was the petting pen for the sheep and goat. On the other side of the house, beyond the tower, out of sight from the gates, would be the butterfly glasshouse. The front of the house looked over the large deer park. It stretched down the hill, replacing the original lawns of the garden. Here and there, pieces of old mirror, objects covered in foil, and even old cans, were scattered across the grass, shining white, catching the sun.

Beyond the old petting pen and the deer park, halfway down the hill, looked like what was once a long, low hedge of rhododendrons. It had unravelled, out and up, exploding into a mad wall spun through with brambles. It blocked the view down into the valley and hid the site of the old lynx enclosure, in the woods below, from the house. A small break in the leaves was the only sign anything was down there. A tunnel so sly you would need to bend to get through. Although, the path was well-trodden and clear of weeds. Kept open, I supposed, by someone or something.

Above the zoo, the house teetered, looking like it might trip and bounce in circles through the old zoo, gathering enough speed to crash through the river and the woods in the valley, roll back up the other side and hit Great Bat Tor itself, scattering the rocks like marbles where, bleary in the heat haze, the great moor shivered.

Perfect, I thought, taking everything in. One tiny, beautiful death at a time. There were places to run. Places to climb. Places to hide. Here, reality left nothing to fantasize about. There really *were* paths not to stray from and a great, scheming forest like in proper fairy tales. We liked them rude and feral and grim, Mumma and I, before I got ill. We pulled faces at the posters advertising the cartoons outside the cinema. 'Fairy tales don't sing and dance,' Mumma would say. 'They're riddles and mazes and survival.' I was the prince stumbling across the extraordinary castle in The White Cat. I could almost believe the little cat queen rode a monkey here, I could believe the house might truly have a staff of disembodied hands, because I could see her court of many cats dozing and rolling about on the grass in the sun.

The cats were everywhere. On the grass. On the paths. Tabbies, calicos, gingers. Some with black bibs, some with white. Juvenile cats, elderly cats. It was like an illustration from a children's picture book.

'Come on,' Mumma called, still inspecting the porch.

I tiptoed away, trying not to disturb the cats, lest Mumma realise they were there.

In the porch, the corners of Mumma's lips pulled away from each other. 'Told you it'd be awful and we'd hate it.' She peeled a finger of paint from a pillar, raising her eyebrows at the cracked flagstones and ivy creeping towards the door. 'But there is, if nothing else, peace and quiet. Fresh air. You'll just have to make the best of it, you poor thing. As I always say, 'close your eyes at night and you never notice the dark!"

I shrugged a little, to seem willing.

Mumma straightened, always bearing her weight equally. With a quick look behind her, as if we might have been followed up the drive by someone, she knocked, rang the wheezy bell, then, unable to wait any longer, opened the door herself anyway. Two cats jumped out of the house. Mumma shouted 'shoo' once they had sprinted past us and eased me inside, closing the door quickly to shut us in.

Inside, the warm, grassy smell of the drive dissolved into leathery air. Smoked, sulphurous, and still.

'Why are there so many cats?' I said.

'There aren't so many cats.' She sing-songed, amused, grabbing my cheeks, one in each hand to make a tunnel between our faces. 'There are three. Three is only one more than two, and two is barely more than one. We could round down and say, basically, there are none. See?'

'Yes,' I said, though I didn't. She seemed reluctant to drop her hands, reluctant to look around.

The hallway was dim, all brown lines and corners, with nicked, scratched panelling running around the walls. A rifle was propped in the corner beneath a row of Victorian illustrations. Lynx, caracals, servals, ocelots. I wrote my initials on a dusty bureau next to the front door and slipped off my flip-flops to stand on the dark, dulled parquet floor. My feet did not fit within the slim lines of the boards. When I stood on tiptoes in front of the grandfather clock, my face was reflected in its face. The second hand feverishly counted the seconds on my temple, my cheek, my chin, my cheek, my temple, my hair, my hair, my –

'Don't touch anything.' Mumma pushed my flip-flops towards me with the side of her foot. 'Put these back on.' She looked at a trail of desiccated cat stools. 'What has happened here?' She coiled around delicately, trying not to step on anything. 'You never know with toxoplasmosis. No need to panic though. Relax.'

I raised my fists above my head, so she could trust I wouldn't touch anything. So she knew I was relaxed.

The disrepair everywhere was almost deliberate, like the cobwebs had been carefully positioned with a needle and tweezers, and the dust sponged on by a painter.

The door next to the clock was ajar, I opened it with an elbow. It creaked, loudly. A cat yelped and ran between my legs. Inside the room, intricate patterns of purple wallpaper were like anatomical drawings from a textbook. The walls were covered in glinting oil paintings of determined landscapes. A swollen blood-red Chesterfield and two stiff wingback chairs lounged at a fireplace. Through the room, over a curved roll-top desk and out of the window on the other side of the house, a roe lifted its head from grazing in the old deer park.

'Four,' I said. 'Four cats *inside* the house.'

'Stop it,' Mumma said, to me, or the cat ambling up the stairs. She shut the door, plunging the hallway back into darkness, and picked up a large waxed jacket from the floor. She hung it over the door knob, to hide it.

'Oh God.' A stiff, nibbled rat lay in a large animal trap next to the front door. Its eyes were half-closed but its jaw lolled gormlessly. Its innards were glossy but dry. Mumma covered her mouth and nose with one hand, and with the other pushed an ashtray full of old tobacco strands and burnt matches towards an empty, yellowed glass tumbler on the bureau. 'How is this place even worse than it was?' She spoke through her fingers, and flicked a cat hair from where it was cradled in the dust.

I opened another door, further down the hallway, into a room filled with empty shelves. The books had been stacked up into one corner, because in the opposite there was a leak. The wet ceiling had soured to brimstone yellow and the wall was daubed with black mould. A projector of some sort stood in the middle.

'I don't want you in there.' Mumma appeared, stuck her head into the room, checked behind the door, then shut it. 'Absolutely no stories, remember? Don't get any ideas about reading those books,' she said, stroking my cheek. 'Come on.'

'Is it you?' A low voice croaked somewhere upstairs. 'I'll know if it's not you. If it's something unseelie I've horseshoes aplenty.'

'Why exactly have you got four feral cats?' Mumma shouted. *Cats* the house shouted back. 'Clean hands, clean mind.' Mumma led me to a cloak room. On the floor, a pair of muddied overalls were hollowed into a bowl lined with cat hair. Mumma kicked them to one side, and ran the tap to swill a rime of black soil from around the sink. I let her wash my arms and hands under the water. 'I never wanted anything to do with cats ever again, you know?'

'I do know,' I said.

'They literally send you mad, Lowdy.'

'Yes. Toxoplasmosis, Mumma.' Mumma had provided me with a long list of reasons we couldn't have a cat when I was desperate for one as a little child.

She picked at errant hairs that had found their way to me. As an only child it is probably normal to feel precious in an intense, tiring way. I was always polished until I shone. Mumma and I watched each other in the mirror. The hot walk had slicked the scalp at her patchy temples. Her hair had once been thick, like mine, but was thinning. Otherwise, we looked so unlike one another, people sometimes doubted we were related. I might have thought her astonishingly beautiful, if I was not so used to her face.

She rubbed her hands through my few millimetres of hair, exactly as I was not supposed to. The doctor had encouraged her to leave my hair as I liked it, splitting and thinning at my hips. 'Carry on as normal,' he said, but Mumma insisted on cutting it. 'If I don't,' she'd said, soaping my head sadly, eyes loose and dribbley, 'every time I look at you, I'll remember.'

'Is this heat rash – or—' she ran her fingers over new pimples on my forehead and kissed me on my phantom parting. 'You'll live,' she murmured, distracted by the mess, seeming incredibly tired after our sleepless night.

As she checked the floor for stools and bones and hairs, I grinned at the mirror, peeling my lips back until I saw nothing but teeth. I was in such a good mood, so grateful she'd taken me away from the Temperance School for Boys, that I did not want to pull a single hair out. This, I thought, must be what happiness looks like.

༄

At the top of the staircase, overlooking the hallway, was a large print of a dark Dutch still life painting. A falling urn, spilling water and flowers, and the arched cat who'd knocked it over watching on, fur in spikes, with its uncannily human face. It was so beautiful. I couldn't look away from it, not even for Mumma's sake.

'Urgh.' Mumma crunched her nose at it as we passed. She picked her way upstairs, watching her step, clapping at random to scare away anything unwelcome.

At one end of the landing a door was open to a large bedroom, air-choked and glowering. In it, as well as a bed fuzzed with fur, was a long, low coffee table covered in newspapers, books, empty bottles, mugs, dirty ashtrays and one ancient, full, litter tray. Next to that, was a chaise. Two round-handled sticks leaned against it. On it, in a yellowing linen suit squaring out a stick-like body, and a bulldog pipe hanging from her lips, lay Grandma.

She rolled a tobacco tamper between two fingers. Her scalp had dragon plates from her treatment and her short hair was a wreath of ashes. She had thick white whiskers in her chin and blinked at us through folds of skin, shiny with heat. She seemed stiff like she'd been lying there for weeks, but there was grass on her trouser cuffs, and a prickle of gorse perching on one shoulder.

I had never met Grandma before. I had received postcards from her and once suggested replying, because the doctor had encouraged socialising, but Mumma said she wouldn't be a good influence. 'What do doctors know,' she grumbled whenever I raised it, all because they'd initially suspected I had a tumour – which I both had, and hadn't had – and if I ever complained to Mumma that I never saw anyone locked away in our rooms all day, she would tell me to stop showing off. 'You don't know how lucky you are,' she'd say, but she'd changed her mind about bad influences last night in the flat. 'What's the worst a deluded septuagenarian can do? And we can't stay here now,' she told me. Shortly afterwards, she was tearing up a roll of bin bags and throwing everything away.

'Well, this is all very unexpected.' Grandma chuckled.

'Don't be dramatic. I called you an hour ago from the train station.' Mumma was at the bed, cuffing pillows for body, stripping sheets. Fine scales filled the air.

'I haven't seen you for sixteen years. And you told me to check myself into a hospice last month.' Grandma looked from my eyes to my feet in one slow blink, and up again in an even slower one. She offered her hand for me to shake, but her grip was weak.

'Hello,' I said.

'Call that a handshake.' She tossed my hand back at me. I looked at it, confused. 'We'll work on it,' she said, picking up a packet of matches and snatching one alight.

'Things change. Lowdy wasn't well. But we're here now, and she's easily overwhelmed, so let's have no silly stories,' Mumma said, always moving, never looking, yet somehow passing close enough to blow out Grandma's match. 'How can you live like this? Why have you got those disgusting cats?'

'For the future, naturally.' Grandma spoke to me, baring a row of gravelly teeth. 'To reclaim our heritage, Loveday.'

'They'll have to go.' Mumma held her nose and walked past Grandma to tie back the faded drapes. She hit her hand against the frames to open the windows. 'All four of them.' She leaned out, inhaling deeply but stopped mid-breath taking in the deer park below her. Her hands gripped the window frame. It sounded like she was gargling her own saliva. 'What?' she said. 'What—' She had finally seen the clowder of cats idling on the grass.

'I'm either upstairs, or I'm downstairs.' Grandma swung a walking stick at the ceiling, smacked it on the floor, ignoring Mumma opening and closing her mouth like a wind-up toy. 'I can't be up and down any more. My days of jumping out of the window are over.' She tilted her head and winked. 'I can hardly make it up the stairs, but now you're better, I'll teach you my little tricks, Loveday. You need to know what to do and when to do it, for when I'm gone.' Grandma shut her teeth and reached for my shoulder to pull herself up, spine creaking under a film of skin. 'Are you old enough for whiskey?'

I passed her the sticks. It was as if she wasn't worried about what Mumma would do if she didn't behave nicely. Grandma was the most interesting person I had ever met and I couldn't wait to live with her, if only for a little while until she died. She was, at least, someone other than Mumma. She, perhaps, would not treat me like a child.

While Mumma was distracted, unable to look away from the cats, leaning further and further out of the window for different angles and perspectives, Grandma beckoned to me and trip-trapped from the room. So, I followed.

The kitchen was a dingy room at the back of the house cooled by the pantry. The black tiles chilled my bare feet and it had a musk of ammonia. A row of medication crammed into a spice rack on the wall and tiny flies dithered between a draining board of fat, hard teabags and a row of over-used litter trays. I brushed off a crumbed foot.

At a dresser, Grandma reached for two squat glasses. 'From now on, Loveday, you must think *cat*. You must breathe *cat*, like I do. We'll start immediately. I'll see you in the library each morning for an hour's theory. Physiology and communication. By the time I've finished with you, you'll practically be a qualified felinologist.' Grandma raised her eyebrows. 'We must encourage the cats to mate. We need cats everywhere. More cats than you have ever seen. Because we need the little ones, for the bigger ones.'

With one finger, she pushed plates to make space at one end of the large kitchen table. At the opposite end, a cup smashed on the floor, making me laugh. 'Oops,' she said, pouring two measures from a grimy bottle. 'We'll train them properly this time. We'll train *you*. They answer to us – to me and, soon, to you – because we're family. I'd like to see the men in the village try and tell me how to do things when we can call them to heel.' She lifted her nose, looking a little cat-like herself, and raised her glass. 'Down it,' she said, 'show me what you're made of.' She threw back her drink. 'Miaow! I shall have the last laugh.'

'No one's had a first laugh.' Mumma appeared and gave me a quick, plastic smile. She had obviously recovered herself by collecting the dirty bed linen. She threw it to the floor, cringing as she took stock of the filthy room, and silently eased the bottle from Grandma's hand, emptying the glass into the sink.

Grandma's hands emptily cupped the air. She jiggled them, looking behind her, as if she had no idea where the drink had gone.

'What have you touched?' Mumma asked me.

'Nothing—' I said, as she took hold of my wrists and pulled me to the sink.

She flicked the tap on using only one finger, and ran the water over my hands, rubbing at my palms and index fingers. She shook off her hands and took a bunch of keys from a hook next to the kettle.

'I knew you were ill, mother,' Mumma said, 'but I didn't know you'd be raving like a lunatic.'

'In the afternoons, we'll focus on the practical, Loveday, because cats won't take care of themselves.' Grandma was speaking to me, but staring at Mumma.

The bones of both their jaws suddenly appeared.

'Taking care of themselves is *all* cats do. If you want me to stay, get rid of the cats and leave Lowdy alone.'

'Why? Where else would you go?'

Neither Mumma nor Grandma blinked.

I looked at the floor, saying nothing, causing no trouble.

'Lowdy is recuperating.' Mumma cleared her throat. 'Doctor's orders.' The doctor's orders had been to get back to normal as soon as possible, which perhaps, in a sense, we had. 'She must rest in a relaxing, hygienic environment. If you would like me to stay and help you die with dignity, you will have no cats, you will have no Lowdy. Do you understand?'

'Do you plan to look after the tynx yourself, then?' said Grandma.

Mumma brought the bunch of keys close to her face, appraising one, then another. 'Go and play, darling girl,' she told me.

❧

It is a bright and manic midnight, bouncing perkily around us like the day, as we thoroughly hoover and disinfect our glaring, two-roomed, strip-lit flat at the top of the boarding house.

The boys I woke have been put back to bed in their dormitories, but not by Mumma. They must get used to being without her. From tomorrow, someone else will feed and muck them out. I imagine them sleeping, deep, or troubled, while we straighten appliances and tweak furniture to sharp angles. The flat is small, clearing up is quick and, eventually, the rooms we have lived in all these years above the boys' heads is pristine.

'Yes,' Mumma says, a little taut, 'we must leave it exactly as we found it.'

Packing is also easy. We don't own much. We always use cardboard plates and disposable pots of salt and pepper. 'Our lives are one big teddy bear's picnic,' Mumma often said, to make living without belongings feel more fun than it truly was. Now, she empties our paper napkins and plastic cutlery out of a drawer and straight into a black bin bag.

'There must be nothing left behind.' She rubs open another bag and nods to a box I have retrieved from under our bed and placed next to the suitcase. She shakes the bin bag at me, but I don't move. I want to bring the box.

'Are you ready to tell me what you were doing in the boys' dormitory this evening?' she asks, voice lowered, arms stiffened, bin bag a black hole between us.

'I can't remember.' I clear my throat a little longer than necessary, to remind her I need sympathy, not punishment. That I am, perhaps, still not well.

'You're not allowed in there. You haven't been allowed in there for three years.'

'I know.'

'Was it the first time you've woken up there?' she said.

'Yes.' My eyes bulge like a baby's with pure, white truth.

Her arms drop a little. 'Well,' she says, 'I'm going to miss this place. It wasn't the job I'd dreamed of, but at least we had this flat. It was all I ever wanted. I loved it here.'

She looks at the blank walls, at the mantelpiece as bare as ever. The chairs are the same uncomfortable metal frames and plywood they use across the campus in the class rooms, but she smiles at them, pained. I look at the grey, curling squares of carpet I toed at, day after day. The bald grey face of the TV, where I sat each morning, waiting for the first video lesson of the day. What it is she sees?

'I always knew exactly where you were.' She sniffs, trying to control something.

'Sorry,' I say, trying to mean it.

She flicks the black bag at me again as I hug my box. 'We can't take everything in one suitcase.'

I reach into the box and, one by one, throw my books into the bin bag. The Red, Yellow and Blue Fairy books, gilt covers winking at the bottom. Joan Aiken's fairy tales, spiky with their filigreed silhouettes. The complete Grimm's. A treasury of Hans Christian Anderson. Ruth Manning-Saunders' ghosts and goblins, charms and changelings, giants, dwarves, dragons, witches, wizards and the rest. Mumma ties up the first bag, and together we roll it into another bag, and another, and another, knotting and reknotting each layer until the plastic is thick enough to dump the weight of so many stories.

Now, it is me who sniffs a little.

'You silly, silly billy.' Mumma puts an arm around me, but it is a pinch, not a squeeze. 'You're too old for all this. You aren't a princess trapped in a tower, and you never were. Facts, facts, facts, from now on,' she reminds me.

I am allowed to pack the hand-stapled scrapbooks of my projects. As part of home-schooling, each term Mumma allowed a project of my own choosing because 'idle heads drop off necks'. I'd done Britain's Oldest Trees, the Privet Hawk-Moth, Animal Ethics and Non-Human Rights, Animal Brides and Grooms, Lost Bodies of the Peat Bogs, and many, many more. I also used to write stories. Nowadays I have to stick to facts. But facts are a million times worse, I think, looking at my project on bog bodies, remembering the horrible statistics.

I place each homemade scrapbook into the suitcase carefully, so my *other* homemade scrapbooks hidden inside, remain hidden inside.

It is already hot at six o'clock in the morning when we walk through the medieval cloisters, between the Grade II-listed chapel with its world-famous organ and the outdoor Greek theatre. We loop around the statue of the founder in the quadrangle, and cross the Palladian Bridge to leave the Temperance School for Boys by the front gatehouse.

'Where are we going?' I ask Mumma.

'Home, I suppose,' she says, and I grin.

We take turns carrying the suitcase, as the sun rolls up like a coach taking us to the ball.

Batleigh House had so many bedrooms, I hoped to have my own, unlike in the school flat. Here, Mumma would surely stay in a different room. In a different bed.

Each bedroom along the landing had a large window over the

deer park, where the cats frisked, and out to the high moor above the valley, but the valley itself was hidden by trees.

The first bedroom was filled with a huge wooden bed, one wall covered with a delicate forest tapestry, a shining silk rug on the floor. The second bedroom was smaller, full of boxes, dining chairs stacked upon one another. But the third was bright and cosy, with just enough room to cartwheel, if I wanted to. A bed tucked under the window, a small wooden wardrobe, songbirds hiding on the floral wallpaper, and sunlight caught in the soft curtains. I ran my hand along the wall, stroking the birds and skimmed a bare foot over the floorboards. I touched everything, making the room familiar to me.

I opened the wardrobe. In it, hung a chaplet of silk flowers and a burgundy velvet dress, all full of holes. Moth larvae ate silk and velvet. They ate anything containing keratin, even human hair and hairballs. I plucked some fibres to taste but spat them out quickly, scratching them from my tongue. Mumma said modern clothes were too obvious, so she could not entirely disapprove of the traditional floor-length gown. Despite the heat, I pulled it over my T-shirt, balanced the chaplet on my head, and went to the window.

I pushed up on the sill, long skirts tickling my calves, to look out at the zoo, to the moor.

I was born here. On a night when the river was all wind and the air flooded and the sky was solid as peat, I sank up, out of Mumma and into this world. That's what she'd told me. Perhaps she didn't use those exact words. 'What was I doing?' she'd cringe whenever I asked. 'Running around outside in a storm, giving birth in the grass like a crazed animal. Why didn't my mother take me to a hospital when my waters broke?'

My nose squeaked against the glass of the window as I turned slowly, following the line of rhododendrons along the edge of the deer park below. I had never been happier. Here, I had a lovely room I could come and go from. Outside, by myself, no boys. Free as the buzzards and toads and lichens. I wanted my arteries to ooze sap.

My bones to crystallize with feldspar. Same as any other sixteen-year-old girl, I supposed.

I rubbed my neck, itched my chest, worrying that everything might, somehow, be ruined. That I might, accidentally, ruin it. That I was, perhaps, sicker than we thought.

But then I was distracted, the deer park was stippled with crouching cats, and more glinting mirror and tin and foil. There was no avoiding the cats, no matter what Mumma said, so I smoothed my prickles, tightened the chaplet and gathered my skirts into one hand. I was ready to go out, and help Grandma. Ready to become a practically qualified felinologist.

Mumma was in the hallway, wearing an apron, rubbing a bin bag between her fingers to open it. She smelled like the old flat, of spiky disinfectant and bleach. I used to pretend I was Hansel and Gretel in a forest, inhaling the fake pine fumes, a cold toilet bowl between my hands. Mumma loathed soil under her fingernails, hated leaves stuck to her heels. 'Hygiene separates us from beasts,' she would cry. 'Try opening a safety cap with talons, darling!'

She tipped a basketful of old, grassy tin cans and foil into the bag and watched with surprise as I passed her. The velvet dress sleeves puffed into little windsocks as I ran. It was big for me, but I was still growing. Even this afternoon, I had noticed my shorts tighter at my hips, digging in after fitting loosely for years.

'I'm going outside.' I flung the back door open. The cat-flap in it was now held shut with two rusted meat hooks, and there was a new pile of bin bags on the doorstep. Beyond that, was a grisly collection of mice carcasses, bird bodies, a shiny half-eaten slow worm and other cat offerings.

Mumma tugged me inside by the skirts of the gown. 'Don't touch anything,' she said. 'Zoonotic diseases.' She pushed me behind her, into the house, looking one way to the petting pen, poking her head out further to look towards the deer park. 'Shoo,' she called weakly. 'These bloody cats. We've got to do something about them.' As if summoned, several cats – a tortoiseshell, two tabbies, one black-and-white – milling on the path to the lynx enclosure, slalomed through the long, dry meadow grass towards the back door. Mumma shut it on them.

'Shoo, shoo.' Mumma pulled off one rubber glove and waved me backwards to the hallway. 'What are you wearing? You look like a Tudor wife about to be beheaded.' I was hugely flattered. She unrolled one white, rubber-pruned finger to an inch from my nose. 'You can't go outside. It's not just the disgusting cats. It's dangerous on the moor. There are old mine shafts and falling rocks. When the fog comes in you can't find your own feet. You mustn't get lost. Stay inside. Do you understand, sweetie sausage?'

I nodded. I could not bear to say yes out loud.

'And no dressing up. You're not a princess. It's for your own good, remember?' She pulled the dress over my head, then flipped open another bin bag with one graceful hand. She folded the gown in half across her knees and slid it in, then held out her hand for the chaplet. She knotted the bin bag tightly and threw it at the back door. Outside the window, two cats dashed away. 'We're sticking to serious, sensible past-times,' she said. 'You've got to grow up, darling heart.' She tried to cheer me by taking my cheeks and pulling them out. 'It's time for beddy-byes. I'll tuck you in.'

I did not cheer up. I wanted to scream for being sixteen years-old, heading to beddy-byes with pinched cheeks. But, of course, she only wanted the best for me.

'Yes, Mumma.' I tried to feel as grateful as I knew I should be. 'Thank you.'

She unpinched me and knelt to empty knives from a block into a cardboard box. She sealed it quickly with tape because I was not allowed to touch knives any more, either.

⁂

Upstairs, Mumma did not turn towards the door, still open, to the lovely room where I'd found the dress. She headed, instead, for a narrow twisting staircase at the other end of the landing.

'Lowdy? Come and see me?' Grandma called, deep and faint, from her bedroom.

'Coming—' I shouted back, but Mumma was in front of me.

'Sh.' She span me around, pushing me up the curl of steps. 'I'll deal with Grandma,' she huffed under her breath.

'But I want to help.' Halfway up the spiral, I tried to turn. One way, then the other. Only walls and Mumma in every direction.

'You must understand, Grandma's losing her mind, darling.' Below me, Mumma spoke to my thighs. The parting of her hair looked a little pruned from above. 'She wasn't all there before the diagnosis. Why do you think I left? Even when you were a baby, I couldn't trust her not to chop you up at feeding time. But now look at the cats. There's no knowing what she's caught from them. You heard her earlier, ranting on about taking care of the tynxes.'

'The tynx,' I corrected.

'There's no tynx.' Mumma brushed some invisible disease off the point of each shoulder. 'It doesn't matter. She'll be gone soon. This will be over and we'll finally have some money. We'll start again somewhere. A lovely all-girls school. Don't let Grandma bother you. You're still recovering. Ignore her.' She pushed me on, I clipped the top step and tripped into a tiny room, with an army cot, a small chest of drawers, an empty wardrobe and unsanded floorboards. There were no windows, but a row of dirty glass doors looking out to the turreted wooden balcony. Mumma rattled them, checking the lock was fast. 'God knows where the keys are now. Most of the ones I've found are rusted out of shape,' she said to herself.

'Is this – the attic?' I asked, catching my foot on a nail poking from a plank.

'Focus on rest and relaxation. There's plenty of it here. Because there's absolutely nothing to do!' She stood in the door, staring at the empty crown of my head. 'I loved playing here as a little girl. I wished I'd stayed up here, locked away, nice and safe, playing by myself all day long.' She nodded into the room so hard she looked like she was on fast-forward. Something caught her eye, and she stopped, smile fixed hard in place.

I followed her eye to two rolls of part-rusted chicken wire leaning against the drawers.

'Lovely, lovely, lovely,' she said. 'Can I trust you to be a big girl, Lowdy-loo?' Mumma asked. 'Do you promise never to open the doors to that stinky-winky balcony?'

'I suppose so – ,' I said.

'The balcony could collapse at any time,' she said, a little grim. 'If you were on it, you'd break your neck and be paralysed and I'd have to spoon-feed you in your bed for the rest of your life. What a horrid thought.'

'Yes,' I said, because it was, but I'd also noticed her tone.

There was a long pause as she stared at me. 'You couldn't open the doors anyway,' she said. 'Goodnight darling. What a good girl you are.' She ran her hands across her thighs, into the pockets of her apron and pulled out an old brown key that clearly had held its shape.

I stared at it. Heart yowling. Blood standing on end. 'Mumma, can't I sleep downstairs? In one of the spare rooms?'

She looked incredibly sad. 'I wish you could, but I can't find all the keys, and we don't want you wandering around a strange place while you're asleep, do we? What if you got out again? I couldn't bear it if anything happened to you. The boys' dormitory is the least of our problems. *Here*, you could drown in a mire. You know about the Vaults, don't you?'

'Yes.' She'd forgotten about the project on peat bogs I had done when I was fourteen. My diagrams explaining the waterlogging of dead plant material in Vault Mires, sometimes to a depth of 6 metres. My illustrations of red sphagnum mosses and spindly, carnivorous sundews. My world map annotated with mummified bog people discoveries. 'But the Vaults are right out on the moor—' My voice was light as pink wafers for her.

She smiled. 'Exactly. Aren't you lucky? Having me to worry about you. Don't unpack now,' she said, pointing to my scrapbooks and few clothes on the drawers. 'We both need an early night after last night's drama.' She balled her hands into two fists for me. 'And don't forget, no fiddle-faddling.'

She shut the door and turned the key so quickly it sounded like the door spat.

I stared at the keyhole.

Since I was thirteen, I had stayed in our small flat because Mumma said I was not allowed to wander around the Temperance School for Boys. In The White Cat fairy tale, the little white cat queen had been sold, while she was still a girl, by her own mother to fairies who locked her in a tower with only a high window. In Mumma's defence, she had often hung me from the flat window, clinging to my waist, chanting things like, 'if you keep a fish in a bowl of sand, how will it grow fins for the river?'

I couldn't believe I had escaped one tower, to find myself in an even smaller one, but Mumma made better choices for me than I did for myself. It might be a box room with bare floorboards and empty walls, but it was all mine and I would enjoy my first night in my own room. Why would I care about being locked in when I was fast asleep? I was *relieved* to be locked in. I would be forced to get the rest and relaxation Mumma knew I needed, after all, I had hardly slept last night what with all the humiliation and cleaning. Tonight, there was no way I'd get carried away with ideas of escaping like a fairy tale princess. Because why would I want to sneak out when I had this room all to myself?

'Thank you, Mumma.' I spoke through the keyhole, understanding I was actually very grateful.

A moment later, there were voices below me. A slow, deliberate interchange. They got louder. Grandma shouted something. Mumma's reply was a quiet murmur. Something knocked against the floor. Grandma's stick, perhaps. A door slammed and everything was quiet.

I stood still for a long time, ears pricked.

Floorboards stretched. Pipes popped. Something with a

beak scratched at the roof and outside there was a lonely miaow.

Poor Mumma, I thought, having to look after everyone.

⁂

The doctor had told me to keep busy, not to dwell on any unhelpful feelings, but instead to enjoy pastimes and pursue hobbies. Although I felt nothing but delighted about Mumma's love for me and the prospect of my full recovery, I leafed through my scrapbooks on the desk, to take out the hidden books inside, needing a distraction, somehow. The paper of the secret books was thinner, more delicate, because my hobby was collecting pictures of women from newspapers and magazines.

I slid under the cot, on my back, and tucked them behind the springs. It was between slats of a bed at the Temperance School for Boys that I saw my first picture, years ago when I first started to go out at night while Mumma was asleep. I had collected my most recent picture the night before last. Now, I made adjustments, so the newest was framed nicely between the metal.

Next to my belongings, on the chest of drawers, was a small tabletop book rack stuffed with educational pamphlets written by Grandma. I flicked through the titles. It seemed like Grandma was an expert on many topics, not only big cats but butterflies, clapper bridges, stone circles, birds of prey, wildflowers, stone rows, rocks, high altitude forests, stone cists, ponies, piskies, mining, the Bog Hover fly, the Ash Black slug, West Country Shamanism. I was glad of new reading material. They were factual pamphlets, after all.

I was distracted by movement at the balcony doors.

A buff ermine moth fluttered on to the glass.

Beyond the doors, the warped balcony floor had a skin of moss and lichen. The beams of its roof were splitting and flaky. Condensation had trailed down the doors, pooling at the sills for so long the door jambs were swollen. Cracks in the wooden frames were wide enough to fit the tip of a finger inside but Mumma said Grandma preferred the things she couldn't mend herself to remain as they were. You could just about see whittled garlands of honeysuckle and leaves wrapped around the weather-greyed spindles and balustrade. The balcony faced the moor and, outside, the sun spilled like juice across the valley to where Great Bat Tor dragged its dark wings wide.

I could open the doors, I thought. If I wasn't so pleased with this tiny, sweltering room, I could open the doors. I could see a slight hummock, so it wasn't a huge fall from the balcony to the ground. In an emergency, in case of a fire, I could do it. Like I used to, at the school. I rattled the doors gently, testing the join. Preparing for an emergency.

If I kicked the join until the doors flew open, the deadbolt of the lock would stick out, maybe a rusted hinge clink to the floor. One door would swing uneasily at an angle when I leaned over the balustrade into cracking peat and burning rock and thirsty ferns. I could watch and listen and drop over the side, and if Mumma was in the library, or the dining room, or the drawing room, well, I was used to creeping below bright windows. Hiding in coffers. Behind pillars. Beneath the bell tower.

My breath misted the glass. It misted the deer park, the woods and the path to the lynx enclosure. I wiped a perfect square on the window with one finger.

In the middle of it, where the trees looked up and the sky looked down, something appeared walking slowly, beyond the deer park, jolting with each step. It had long, thin forelegs like branches, then a short body and stubbed back legs. In the chalky dusk, it was a grey, made-up monster. I rubbed the window clean and pressed one brow against the glass.

Grandma, in her suit, lurched like the goddess Bastet along the path towards the rhododendrons. Cats emerged from the long grass, from behind bushes, to weave in and out of her sticks. Bunting her legs, tipping their bottoms to her. All she was missing was a lion's head. She reached the tree line, and tipped her face to one side, to the tower. For a moment, I imagined a hideous face swivelled towards me. An oversized set of teeth. A flattened nose, perhaps.

Sometimes I confused what was real with what I had made up. Mumma would tell me it was only Grandma. I was almost sure it was Grandma. I could hardly see from this distance. Whatever it was, I couldn't believe *it* could see *me* at the window, but it inclined its head towards the wood and carried on out of sight.

When it was gone, there were no cats and everything was nice and calm and relaxing in my tiny, simple bedroom. Nothing moved, inside or out, except my hands twisting and untwisting a pamphlet entitled *The Tynx: hybrid cat or evolutionary joke?*

The subject of this text, Nella, is the only known extant example of a tiger-lynx hybrid, or 'tynx'.

The specimen is female, approximately 3 metres long, with markings similar to those of a tiger, but different, one might say 'lynx-like', colouring.

Her mother is, without doubt, a Eurasian lynx. She was bred in captivity, although the circumstances are currently unknown. The habitats of lynx and tiger do not overlap in the wild and, in addition to it being (theoretically) impossible for two parents of different genus' to mate, there is also no historical suggestion of the tynx existing naturally. There is no notable local lore, historical references nor native word that seem applicable from any possible natural habitats. Based on this lack of documented evidence, it is possible Nella is not only the first known extant example of the 'tynx' hybrid, but possibly the only example, ever.

If we dismiss suggestions of 'anomalous gigantism' and other coincidental abnormalities which might arguably account for the animal, and instead assume the 'tynx' as a hybrid does exist, we must also assume it is crossed between a lynx and a tiger. It must have had parents of two different genus' albeit, theoretically at least, impossible. But how to account for the mixture of behavioural traits? Should a tynx chuff like a tiger, or bark like a lynx? Furthermore, broadly-speaking, Siberian tigers eat ungulates (deer, pigs) but will also hunt fish, birds and, if necessary, other predators, like lynx. Is a tynx likely to eat its own mother?

DAY 2

The animal's ears prick. It wonders where it is. It smells something good and jumps.

When it lands, hard, its muscles tighten. It stretches its toes. Digs its claws into the grass. It pulls back, holds, waits, then shivers the stretch off. It takes in the good scent. It brings a paw to its nose, to comb with its tongue.

It stops. It purrs. Its fur ripples. It takes to its toes. Follows the scent, down the slope into the trees.

Trees move in the dark. It reaches. Buries its claws in a trunk and sits on its haunches. When it drags its claws down, the bark disintegrates. Fine strands scud away.

It paces near the strong, rich scent, buried under the leaves.

It leaps to the perfect branch, rolls onto its belly, curls its hindlegs and reaches out its forepaws, head sunk into its neck, eyes slitted to doze.

There is a movement, under the leaves.

The animal's eyes snap wide open. They lock onto the boy.

'Oh. Shit.'

The animal inhales, rests its head to its forepaws, content.

Something mewed. Long, high, pathetic.

I sat up from the tower room floor. Shocked to be awake.

A thin, grey tabby, little more than a kitten, sat on the balcony watching me through the open glass doors. Its wispy tail, still glossy and new, tickled the air. It lifted black lips and mewed again, tongue pink through two small fangs.

The balcony doors were wide open. Deadbolt sticking out. Rusted hinge on the floor. One door hanging uneasy, at an angle. I didn't know how or why, but they were open, exactly as I had imagined they might last night.

I was too exhausted to worry about it. A full body tiredness. I could hardly move. Like I had barely slept, for the second night in a row.

I wrapped the bedsheet around myself to get up, no memory of stripping off my pyjamas during the night. The bedroom door was still locked, so neither Mumma nor Grandma had opened the glass doors.

Beyond the balcony, blackbirds fluted in a mallow dawn and a low mist over the valley was cool relief. A buzzard hung in the air unmoving. The tabby cat coiled backwards to lick its leg. I waved it away. 'Stupid cat.' It hopped to the balustrade, jumped, span in the air and hit the ground to walk away. It was a true fact that cat spines are twice as flexible as human spines. Humans can seem inhumanly flexible if they spend hours a day stretching – but who has hours a day to stretch?

I closed the doors, watching the cat walk to the deer park through the glass.

There was a brown flash. A squeak, and the cat was gone. The buzzard shot into the sky, a rag of grey fur scrabbling in its grip.

꩜

Later, I woke again to the key turning gently in the lock, but Mumma did not come in.

We always slept late, Mumma and I. I never knew a bedtime because once upon a time, not so long ago, when Mumma's work was done, she would tell me her stories. Stories she could not face in the glare of day would come to her once her thin fingers with their pristine, docked nails were clinging to a glass, late into the night.

The house was quiet, the room hot. I remembered my strange early morning and felt for my head, for a thinned patch. The balcony doors were shut now, so it seemed less likely they were ever open. I had probably dreamed it. And the monster in the deer park.

On the landing, there was no sound. I opened Mumma's door. She was back in bed after unlocking me, and did not rouse. She was a statue, draped in sheets and trapped white in plaster, like the ones in the arches of the refectory at the Temperance School for Boys. Through the closed curtains, a shard of sunlight pressed its point to her throat. It must have been a very late night. She wouldn't remember any of it.

Whenever I stared at Mumma for too long I stopped recognising her, as if she was not my mother at all. Not even real. When I was very little indeed, I secretly believed she was truly a big cat herself. Fur plump with leaf skeletons. Scrap of yellowed fat hooked on an incisor. She told me so many stories about growing up with the lynx, I thought she was one. A skin-changer, like in fairy tales. Like the bear who turns into a man each night, I thought she waited until I fell asleep to take her true form.

I shook my head. Boredom was dangerous. After being so ill, Mumma had told me, 'incubate your eggs with boredom, and you'll hatch vipers, not wrens.' I couldn't fall into bad habits, telling stories. I needed something real to do, so I closed the door and crept along the landing to see Grandma.

Her bedding was rumpled, the curtains still closed, but Grandma was gone. The room was no longer lined with litter trays, empty glasses and mouldering tea cups. Now letters were piled with other letters, books organized by size, sticks leaning against the wall. I flicked through everything, and took an old, yellowed newspaper.

Downstairs, warm air stirred the hallway. The back door was propped open. Outside, the sky was soft, birds floating like bunting. The petting pen no longer dazzled with tin lids and foil, and the cats were already out and snoozing.

There was fresh kill, a mouse, still whole, on the doorstep and the bags of rubbish next to it were sour and cheesy with heat. The bin bag with the red gown in it was on top of the pile, the black plastic ears of its knot slithering in the breeze.

Lying on my stomach I reached the bag without leaving the house, as Mumma would prefer. I dragged it towards me, took out the beautiful dress and put it on. Grandma's dirty old overalls had been washed and hung in the cloakroom so I bundled them into the empty bin bag, and dropped it back onto the heap of rubbish.

In the other bags, I found an old film reel, and a collection of torn photographs. I pieced some into a picture of Grandma, about Mumma's age, long hair in shining curls. She looked completely different, balanced up a tree in what I supposed was the lynx enclosure. Her flouncy, flowery dress was hiked to her knees as she wedged a pig's head into the fork of a branch, two fingers hooked into the snout. There was one of Mumma as a child, a lynx tugging a dead chick from her fingers. Then, me. A newly born baby, wrapped up so tight you could see nothing but a bundle of blankets, in the crook of Grandma's arm as Mumma stood at a distance, staring at me, like she'd never seen a baby before. From Mumma's late night reminiscences, I recognised a photograph of the lynx, Sofia and Koshka. They drank from the river in an early morning mist. Mumma said there was no attention to security and the lynx were often unsupervised like this. Something she didn't approve of in retrospect, but thought nothing of at the time. The two lynx had long, swirling tongues half sunk into the water while Grandma stood nearby, in another floral dress, arm around her head to stop her hair flying, big smile. In the background, Nella was huge. Nose furrowed high, teeth bare, hooded eyes fixed on the photographer, while her mother and aunt ignored her.

A shadow fell over me, blocking the sunlight for a moment. Then the shadows shifted and the photograph lit up again. There was a noise beyond the quiet of the house. A soft, circling rumble.

A low, warning growl.

I looked up, expecting to see Grandma at the door, or a cat trotting away, perhaps a crooning buzzard cruising low across the grass of the petting pen.

But Mumma was right, Batleigh Zoo was perfectly peaceful – the petting pen was completely empty and there wasn't a cloud in the sky.

🐝

Objects are important in fairy tales. Often, common, ordinary-seeming things – boots, peas, mirrors, pumpkins, harps – turn out to be powerfully magical treasures. So I tidied the film reel, the photographs, the gown, and the old newspaper properly – fast, before Mumma saw – up both sets of stairs, to hide in my room, just in case. Once it was all safely beneath my mattress with my other ordinary-seeming things, I heard the phone ringing in the kitchen. I must have been too slow because by the time I answered, the caller hung up.

The kitchen smelled crisp with acid. Yesterday Mumma had worked hard. Nothing clung to my feet and there were no plates of fur to tempt me. I lifted the lid of a large stewing pot on the stove, releasing a fetid smell of leaf and stalk, as Mumma entered the kitchen in her dressing gown carrying a pile of towels.

'Yuck—' I said, and when she saw me, she dropped the towels and ran across the room to push me from the stove. She snatched the lid from me, and slammed it back on the pot, chest heaving.

'That's not for you. How are you feeling? Good sleep? No silly thoughts?' She clutched the hot pot, steam licking her face, speaking extra fast to distract me.

'Good. Great. Fine.' I was thrown by Mumma's jumpiness, and trying not to look at the stewing pot. 'Resting and relaxing. I've only just got out of bed.' I poured myself a glass of milk, and she turned away from it.

'Put the kettle on will you.' She opened and shut cupboards, emptying out jars and ancient tins, then inhaled sharply. 'Where's the coffee?' she shouted.

'Piskie's took it.' Grandma either laughed or coughed as she limped down the hallway, smart and suited. Her trouser cuffs were grey with dew and her sticks left pocks of mud on the floor.

'Go back upstairs. I said I'd come to you,' Mumma said, sniffing an old tea caddy.

'It's nearly midday. Are you trying to starve me to death?' Grandma winked at me and straightened a lapel, but her smile did not reach all the way. 'Hoping to get your hands on my zoo all the sooner?' She swayed from stick to stick.

Mumma deflated into a chair at the clean kitchen table as I poured her a cup of tea. It stewed black as a potion in her mug. 'Everything was either rotten, or junk. It had to go. Viennetta and Pop Tarts are worse for you than the cancer,' she said smoothly. 'Do you honestly think anyone would want this vile place? I'd rather be absolutely anywhere else.'

'Then it's a shame you had nowhere else to go. Be a bit more grateful.'

'In a hospice,' Mumma said, 'breakfast would be served on time.'

They stared at each other.

'Give Lowdy a shopping list.' Grandma reached out a stick and dragged Mumma's tea towards her. The tea slopped and she flicked the steaming teabag onto the table.

'Lowdy can't go into the village.' Mumma watched the teabag stain the wood.

'I can.' I stood to show commitment and enthusiasm.

'Are you worried about the tynx?' Grandma said, slightly disbelieving. 'They won't bother her. They'll know she's family. They'll smell it—'

Mumma smiled, kindly, to me. 'See? She's ga-ga. This is what happens when you are so unpleasant no one will speak to you. You become alienated and confused. If she wasn't dying, I'd have her sectioned.' Then, she spoke loudly and slowly to Grandma, like she was speaking a different language. 'They'll chuck rotten eggs at Lowdy in the village. Do they still leave dead livestock at your front door?'

'It was a silly game.' Grandma threw a hand in the air, but it trembled. 'It was only a couple of lambs heads. It might have been a ritual sacrifice.' She rolled her eyes to their corners, looking at me with intrigue. 'They were probably trying to appease me. I'm a VIP around here.'

'You go, if you're so popular. Even you can see Lowdy hasn't been well.'

Grandma spluttered with laughter taking in too much boiling tea. 'She's got short hair, not an extra head.'

I looked from Mumma, to Grandma, and back again.

'She'll take a wrong turn and drown in the mires and then you'll be sorry.' Mumma stood, winced and put both hands to her head as she went to the kettle.

'You know there isn't a road to the mires. She's here now. There's no squeezing her back in—' Grandma said, prodding a stick at Mumma's belly. Mumma doubled over and pushed it away. 'Shall we dip her in gold and keep her on the mantelpiece instead? She's not a child. She is my heir apparent!'

'I am a sixteen-year-old woman,' I said. 'Indubitably,' I added, reminding Mumma I knew many long words and was not afraid to use them. 'I can help.'

Grandma lifted her head and inclined it to me, like a king.

'You are not going outside,' Mumma shouted suddenly, then seemed to regret it. 'We've got to take good care of you until you're well again, Lowdy.' She quietly appealed to Grandma, as if I couldn't hear. 'She can be very immature. And around here things can be unpredictable.'

'Nothing will happen to her on the road in the middle of the day.' Grandma shook with the effort of standing firm. 'And if she can hold her own in a busy dormitory in the middle of the night—'

'She was sleepwalking.' Mumma poured boiling water from the kettle, high, into a teapot. 'It was an accident.'

My eyes fell to think of wetting myself in the boys' dormitory the night before last.

'It was a rebellion. A revolt! A mutiny! She pissed on her oppressors! She's a hero.'

'She's nobody's business but mine.' Mumma took a ladle from a drawer then slammed it shut.

'Why are you cossetting her like this? You had all the freedom in the—'

'Freedom is negligence covered in buttercream and sprinkled with chocolate drops.' Mumma sloshed soup from a pot on the stove into a mug. 'Drink this.'

'What is it?' Grandma looked into the mug.

Mumma turned her back on us to pour her tea. 'Broth.'

'If that's all you've got—' Grandma ran a glistening tongue around her rusted lips, '—then, I suppose when we're hungry enough, we'll have to eat you.'

Mumma tried to smile easily, like there was no problem.

There was a long silence.

I couldn't wait to see what happened next, but there were three loud raps at the front door. Three knocks, like in a fairy tale. One knock you might have imagined. The second, you could ignore. But a third knock and your visitor is not going away.

Mumma straightened immediately. She looked at me, then Grandma.

I stood as Grandma staggered from the room. Mumma followed, spilling her tea. We both passed Grandma in the hallway. I pulled in front, but then Mumma blocked me with her arm. She reached the door first but Grandma nudged in front of her and opened the door so fast Mumma tottered back.

A hot wind blew into the house. The pictures on the wall shook

43

in the corner of the hallway and the rifle clattered to the floor. I jumped, Grandma wobbled to her heels and Mumma dropped her cup, smashing it to pieces. Black tea ran towards the doorstep.

The boy in the porch wore the same shorts, the same OASIS T-shirt, he'd been in yesterday. A mangy, ginger cat squirmed in his arms. 'Whoah,' he said as it kept almost jumping away. 'Whoah.'

'Who are you?' The skin on Grandma's face shot behind her head, and her nose and mouth sharpened to a point.

'Um. Digger.'

'That's not a name. It's a machine. What you want, *Digger*?'

I thought I might pass out. I disliked all boys. Watching the cat trying to get out of this one's grip, I felt hotter and hotter. My chest felt full again, on the inside, but now it also bulged out below my eyes, hairs pricking through the skin. I tried to itch it with my forearms.

'Is there something wrong with your cat?' he said.

Either it leapt, or he threw it, but it hit me in the stomach, claws out, scratching me as it bounced off my hip and fell to the floor where Mumma kicked it back out of the door.

Digger turned to watch the cat scamper down the drive. 'She shoots, she scores—' he said, awkwardly half-raising both fists into the air.

'Are you OK, Lowdy?' Mumma said, flustered. 'Go and lie down.'

'I thought it was yours.' Digger gave a half-laugh. 'I saw a note in the newsagents. Is the job cash and that? I've got my own bucket—' He stretched his neck, to look as if he wasn't craning to see behind us into the house. 'If you think you might need it—'

I gave a tiny cough, to clear the skipping in my throat, putting a hand up to hide it.

'Lowdy, go and rest.' Mumma spoke across her shoulder to me.

I went red, not with embarrassment, with panic. I wanted him to leave my new home.

'Did you hear me, darling?' Mumma knelt to collect up the sharp pieces of her mug.

'I can probably borrow a rake, if that sweetens anything—' The boy's head slid this way and that, looking behind us like he expected to see someone else in the hallway.

Mumma shut the door on him.

I did not go and rest. I walked loudly up the main stairs as Mumma and Grandma whispered fretfully at the door, but I stopped, out of sight, in the tower staircase. Even from this distance, I believed I could smell the rotting fruit of his sweaty palms. The sharp, melted sugar on his tongue. The sleepy, sour perfume behind his knees, inside his elbows, under his shoulders, and –

I slid down the wall. The sound of Grandma and Mumma bickering faded into a sharp ringing in my ears. The cat's scratch at my side was like a knife wound. There was a weight in my chest. My rib cage was swelling, like my breasts were finally arriving – like all my missing hair was bunching up in my chest. It kept rising. A clot in my throat. I couldn't breathe.

My hands were at my throat, cinching it like it was Mumma's waist. I clucked, wordless. A drowning chicken. I kicked at the stairs, to get Mumma's attention. So she could tell me to breathe. So she could get her hand in my mouth. So her fingers could scrape the back of my throat, but find nothing. She would grab both sides of my face, hands still wet with my saliva, to shout, 'There's nothing there, Lowdy. *There's nothing there.* Breathe.'

There was nothing there. I wiped my own hand on my shorts, breathing again, and pulled up my T-shirt to look at the scratch. It was a small, red scratch. Nothing like a knife wound. I could hardly feel it. I slid back up the wall, wiping water from my eyes, relieved Mumma had not, in the event, seen me. If she had thought I was not ignoring the boy – and that I was not recovering well – who knew what she might be driven to.

I peeped around the spiral of the staircase.

At the front door, the hump of Grandma's back turned on Mumma. 'Whatever makes you happy, dear. I couldn't care less.' She chewed the words out then hobbled up the stairs.

When Grandma's bedroom door slammed, Mumma called Digger in from the drive.

I crouched on the landing, watching him enter the house. Watching him trip over the door sill then looking back at it, surprised.

'Who put that there?' he said, grinning. 'I love cleaning. Mopping, and cleaning – I'll do anything that's dirty really.' He leaned forward a little to look into the cloakroom.

'I don't know what you've heard, but none of it's true.' Mumma counted on her fingers. 'Firstly, no one ever let that animal out deliberately. So if there were any mishaps, they weren't intentional. Secondly, there have not been exotic animals at Batleigh Zoo in sixteen years. Thirdly, you may not tell people the place is in this state. It's only like this while we sort it out. Things get messier before they get tidier. I've got some jobs in the house, and outside, but only for today.' She spoke louder. 'So can we trust your discretion?'

'OK,' he shrugged. Something in his pocket beeped. Mumma stared in surprise at his shorts. 'I'm cooked,' he joked, splaying his hands out either side of him. 'Like – in an oven.'

'We need some shopping,' Mumma said.

His arms sank like they were drowning.

A muffled shout came from behind Grandma's bedroom door. 'Get cat food.'

'Do not, under any circumstances, get cat food. In fact, later, you can get rid of the cats,' Mumma said briskly. 'Take the short cut through the zoo.'

❧

I knocked quietly on Grandma's door so Mumma wouldn't hear. Grandma wheezed, coughed and inhaled, all three at once. She was grey and moist on her chaise in the heat, and did not open her eyes.

'What is Mumma doing?' I said, to Grandma's window, scanning the deer park for Digger on his way to the village. 'With that clown?' I was desperate. I would have done all the chores Mumma asked, had she allowed me into any of the rooms. had promised me – and herself – no more boys. And here she was, trusting the boy, not me, with my own home.

In The White Cat, by chance, a prince identical to the one the white cat queen had fallen in love with came upon the enchanted cat-castle, in dire need of a beautiful woman – the *most* beautiful woman – to be his bride. This was the exact opposite of that. Digger looked exactly the same as all the other boys I had ever hated, and now I also hated him.

I pressed against the glass, checking the blind spot below the window, annoyed to miss him leave. There was a horrible, sour smell. Me. I had never known anything like it. My T-shirt pulled damp and heavy from my armpits. I sniffed one, wondering if I was rotting at only sixteen.

Something squeaked plaintively. I could have sworn it was coming from the walls. I imagined mouse pups, slow, blind, crawling over one another. The incessant crying. The bitter smell of vulnerability. I slammed a fist against the wall and Grandma rolled her head towards me, opening her eyes. The squeaking stopped. There was only the distant sound of Mumma banging cupboards in the kitchen.

'What is Mumma doing with that boy?' I raised my shoulders and eyelids, worried.

'She was more fun before she grew up.' Grandma sat up, flicked her jacket from her hips. 'But if it makes her happy to bleach the toilets. Dust the trinkets.' She waved her hand, casually, but her mouth fired statement after statement. 'It gives her something to do. It doesn't bother me. It's still my place. Let her fuss, but if you don't like the boy, get rid of him. You'll be in charge when this is all yours.'

I was substantially cheered.

She leaned to reach her pipe, to rest her elbows on her wide knees. She pressed a pinch of tobacco into the pipe bowl, threw the tobacco packet across the coffee table and pointed her tamper at me. 'No one took me seriously until I took myself seriously. Make eye contact. Talk loudly, and slowly. Lower your voice. Don't sound whiny. Say only what you need to. Don't babble. Get their respect.' One of her feet bounced very fast.

'Whose respect?' I asked.

She struck a match. 'His.' Crossing her eyes to light the pipe, she spoke between inhales. 'Your mother's. A tynx. We respect whoever's got the power. If you're not the alpha, you're a beta. Always let a cat know who's in charge.' Her lips popped around the wooden stem as she drew the flame through the tobacco. She threw the dead match to the floor. 'I'm finding it hard to get down and feed them, Lowdy. And the tynx.'

'Mumma hates cats,' I said, carefully changing the subject, in case Mumma overheard.

'Nonsense. How could she?' Grandma almost shouted at me. 'Cat is in her blood, whether she likes it or not. See? *You* even look like a cat. Those ferocious eyebrows could be whiskers.' She struggled to breathe, barrelling her chest like an ape. 'She didn't used to hate them. She used to be one. She didn't have a word until she'd turned five. People kept coming to assess her development when she started school. But kids're animals.' She waggled her hands, dismissively. 'It's a food chain. And the class didn't like her.' She sat up excited, puffing out smoke, slashing through it with a jittery finger. 'But she knew how it worked – the alpha takes the best meat. They're either accepted, or challenged. So, one day, when they'd lined up to collect their lunch boxes, she took the lunch box of – I don't know – the girl she thought was the alpha. She took a bite of everything.' Grandma chuckled. 'This other girl grabbed her hair. So Aster jumped onto the lunch table, showing her teeth, swiping at anyone who came near.' Grandma couldn't speak from trying to contain her laughter. 'It took three adults to restrain her. When I got there the entire class was still crying.' She collapsed and whistled. Slapping her pipe to her chest. Spilling hot ash on herself. 'She wasn't allowed back.'

I grinned. Mumma had told me so much about her childhood, but never this.

'I was excluded for bad behaviour too,' I said, and felt my face drop. 'The parents complained about me. Then I had to do lessons on my own in the flat. Mumma was so cross.'

I'd been pretty cross too. So cross, Mumma had been forced to lock me in a cupboard for my own safety. 'Any mother would have done the same,' she'd insisted.

'She's a hypocrite.' Grandma lifted one shoulder, not interested. 'Your mother spent too much time with the animals in the enclosure here. And if you behave like an animal for long enough, you alter your own state of consciousness. Full transformation. Shamans do it. Same as witches. Because if you want to understand an animal, you must live as one.' She nodded, knowingly. 'If you can do it, you can harness the power of a universe even more mysterious than this one. The raw animal psyche is more unknowable than space. Deeper than the sea.' She laughed one minute, then was serious the next. 'It's not all burning sage and crawling around in the mud. It's actually very hard work.' She was obviously joking. She fell back, tired, and coughed.

'You're not supposed to be in here, Loveday.' Mumma entered the room, holding a mug. She went to Grandma. 'Stop filling her head with this rubbish.'

'She talks like a baby in a silly high voice whenever you're around. It's an act. You clearly don't know her at all,' Grandma told her.

'Go and *rest*, Lowdy.'

'But Lowdy and I must start work.' Grandma's own voice went higher. 'We may not have long. Everyone wanted to see her, Lowdy. She was a star! People came from all over. She made the village rich. Locals were always at the door asking for favours and advice. We were at the centre of everything – because *we* had the power. The animals' power.'

Mumma put a hand on my shoulder and turned me towards the door.

'Who was a star, Grandma? The tynx?' I said, because when people were delusional, it was important not to patronise them, otherwise they also get cross.

Mumma span me around to face the door. 'Stop talking about cats.'

'I didn't say cat, I said tynx.'

'A tynx is a type of a cat,' Mumma said.

'—or is it?' Grandma wiggled her eyebrows.

'If I find you in here again, there'll be a great deal of trouble.' Mumma told me, and held the drink out to Grandma without looking at her. 'Drink this.'

⁂

I wander the grounds of the Temperance School for Boys at night, the shadows all long rulers and set squares under a cricket ball moon.

For the last three years, I am so bored of my days that I wait for Mumma to drink and sleep, then escape the flat to make my nights more interesting. Tonight, I check the staff pigeon holes for private notes and eat a biscuit stolen from the kitchen. I fill time until I am sure all the boys are asleep.

I had plenty of friends when I was younger, when running and climbing and hiding were the games children played. My friends were boys, because the school was for boys – and one girl, as a charity to one of the boarding house matrons, Mumma. 'It's an opportunity,' Mumma would say when I complained of knowing no girls, 'so much is put into a boy's education. And, here, it will be put into you.' I joined my year group during classes, but when my friends went to their boarding houses together, or to play sports on the fields, I stayed in the rooms we lived in, waiting, out of sight, for Mumma to finish her duties. I read a lot of stories and found everything else very dull. So, at night, I often escaped to visit my friends in their dormitories, until I was found there once.

Afterwards, I had cried on Mumma's knee, not understanding how I was to blame. 'You are a disruptive influence,' Mumma said, stroking my long, long hair. 'You distract the boys. The school has never been co-educational. It's not what the parents want for the boys. You have to learn elsewhere.'

Elsewhere was our flat at the top of the boarding house. It did not go well at first, but after a while, there was nothing left for me to break.

Now I have to stay away from everyone during the day, leaving the flat through the window at night is even more important. With no friends left, I learn how to hide. How to be quiet on my feet. I keep to corners and avoid being seen. I keep all senses alert. I know how, sometimes, you smell someone before you see or hear them. I know, most of all, if people aren't expecting someone to be there – under beds, behind doors – they simply assume no one is. They never stoop to look, never turn quite far enough. They never hear you breathing.

In one dormitory, the boys are teddy bears in neat rows of beds, some still sucking their thumbs. The older ones have thin shower curtains around their cubicles. Each has exactly the same cupboard. I am jealous of these boys, their privacy, a space of their own they used to share with me. I resent how they turned on me. I haven't changed, they have. I come to haunt them, to take small, petty revenges - tonight, I lie on top of a wardrobe to flick droplets of water onto someone's sleeping face. The boy rouses. He pulls the covers to his chin, looking around at the other boys. He is desperate to wake someone, but can't bear the humiliation of telling anyone he's scared. He told on me three years ago though –

In another dormitory, they sleep soundly. I tuck someone's Tazmanian Devil duvet so tight around them, they'll wake hardly able to breathe. The boys barely stir when I rearrange their posters, turn them upside down, back to front. The Pamela Andersons, the tennis girls without underpants, the HELLO BOYS, the Jurassic Parks. I leave the Blu Tak on someone's cupboard, press some of it, as evidence, under his nails. I have brought a witch-bottle I brewed with stomach bile, nail clippings, a teabag-aged curse, and a secret ingredient. I pull up a floorboard so someone will trip and find it under a bed. In each dormitory, I torment one boy at a time, so news of my tricks passes through the boarding house slowly. These incidents only add up when the boys share their strange experiences. Only after they've had their unease confirmed by another boy will they each feel comfortable enough to go to bed miserable and afraid. I take my time, because I have so much of it.

It pleases me every time Mumma comes home complaining the dormitories stink of urine. I am delighted to be responsible for these boys being shamed for foul habits.

The back door slammed, the house gulped, and the staircase puffed hot air into the tower. Digger was in my house. His heavy boots sounded in every corner. I slid, quick and slow, down the stairs, across the hallway. I was flat to the wall, peeping into the drawing room.

The keys hung in a limp hand at his thigh. He stared through the window at the cats in the deer park – or perhaps beyond, to the path into the lynx enclosure – the path into the woods. He had not even taken off his boots, but he was trusted with the keys, while I was not.

From the crack in the door, I saw only his solid, square back. A bead of sweat bobbed below his ear. The hair closest to his neck dripping into soft stalactites. I felt overwhelmingly thirsty and my scalp was wet. I closed my eyes. A single hair brushed my lips. But it could not have been one of mine. Even if phantom sensations could be exacerbated by stress and anxiety, hair cannot carry the same repressed memories as flesh. I cradled my fists and blew out, trying to float it away, so I wouldn't inhale it and choke. There was a stabbing at the cat scratch on my hip, a rush of blood to the head and I held the hallway panelling for stability.

I thumbed the roof of my mouth for the second time that morning, just in case. I hoped I was not sickening again, and tried to relax, rubbing my prickling chest gently. Through my T-shirt, I felt something hiding under the newly swelling buds of my breasts. A tiny black deer tick on my sternum so small you might mistake it for a freckle, unless you were up close. I plucked it off and stepped on it, quickly, before Mumma could shriek about Lyme Disease. Digger must have heard something, because he turned towards the door.

I flattened myself behind the grandfather clock as he left the drawing room. He stopped in the hallway, back to me, and looked down towards the kitchen. If he turned, clockwise, towards the cloakroom, he would not fail to see me. My T-shirt melted with sweat. I closed my eyes, unbreathing, wishing I was at the very least flat against the clock itself, instead of the wall. He turned back into the drawing room.

My muscles relaxed. I half-smiled. I hadn't lost my old tricks during the recovery.

But Digger used damp cloths without rinsing them, streaking surfaces in dusty waves across the room, as his shorts gave tiny beeps. He rammed the hoover at the skirting-boards, denting the wood, without bothering to lift the curtains. He stacked glassware into a box, clashing dram glasses together, chipping a decanter in his hurry. He chanted to himself about packing it up, packing it in, about letting him begin, going through my magnificent home like it was jumble. - *he came to win, battle him, it's a sin* - It was painful to watch. I almost bruised every time he poked the mop into a corner. I felt raw when he scrubbed the window sills.

Mumma, too, kept an eye on him, making excuses every time she came back. 'Cream cleanser,' she cried at one point, waving the bottle at him, 'just in case.' Why did Mumma care more that I was *not* in these rooms, than that he *was*? Who, I thought, was tearing their hair out now? Then, she brought him a cup of tea. A hand shading her eyes to look out at the deer park - one way, then the other - before remembering to offer him the mug. 'Here.' 'Cup of tea,' he said, taking the boiling mug easily with insensitive fingertips. 'Classic.' His lips ribboned around the pale steam on the sweltering day like he had never drunk a cup of tea before in his life.

'Round up the cats,' Mumma said. 'Tap saucers at the back door. Don't go into the trees. Did you hear me? Not into the trees.'

'Why can't I go into the trees?' He finally met her eye.

'If you tap the saucers, they'll come to you. You won't *need* to go into the trees.'

I heard her trying to smile, but I wasn't smiling.

He left room after room unlocked, spinning the keys like they were a toy. Dipping in and out of rooms at random. Exactly as Mumma had told him not to.

He was too careless to notice me. He wasn't aware of cracks between doors, or inches below sofas. He looked to bigger spaces. Every so often, he went to the window, checking, like Mumma, left and right. He sniffed at furnishings. He touched the floor, then checked his fingertips. He did not love cleaning. He was looking for something.

I wouldn't be able to rest or relax or recover until he was gone, but I knew how to scare a boy, and I needed to scare this one so he never came back.

❧

When Digger left the dining room, I crept in. I found an old chess set and when I heard his footsteps returning in the hallway, scattered the pieces across the floor, setting a few spinning spookily and scrambled into a cupboard, before he entered the room. I was thinking about attaching strings to slam some doors and move curtains as he got on his knees. He collected up the chess pieces, then looked at the cupboard. He stood and opened the door to me.

'Are you OK?' he said. 'I'm not saying it's weird, but what are you doing?'

'Sh,' I said. 'Sh.' I went to close the door, but he held it open with his arm. The arm looked good enough to rub a cheek against, but at the same time I wanted to sink teeth into it. I prayed Mumma hadn't heard him. On the other hand, it took the stiffening of my mouth into a hole to stop myself screaming for her. At night, in the school, I never, ever let them see me anymore. Except for that one bad time.

Digger stared at me for too long and I became conscious of my bald head. I pulled the cupboard door closed on myself. My fingers crawled over my skull, and I ground my eyes into my knees. He opened the door again.

'Just chilling out and that?' he said. 'That's your prerogative.' He hadn't, until then, struck me as the sort of person who would know the word 'prerogative'. He looked at the floor. Perhaps a little pink, but he had been cleaning in the heat. 'Can I check, are you going to tell?'

'What have you stolen?' I was aware of baring my teeth at the villain.

'Nothing.' He showed me his hands, eyes big like a stupid fish. 'I was just – looking. I'm interested in the old zoo, cause I'm gonna take a photo of the cat. For a competition. It's five grand and you go in an exhibition in London.'

'Which cat?' I wondered why a London exhibition would want photographs of them.

'The man-eating one. The tynx.' He was quiet, looking behind him in case someone heard. 'The tiger that's a lynx.'

'Nella?' I was, for a moment, too confused to whisper. 'Nella died sixteen years ago.'

'The one that eats the sheep. I saw it last night. Loads of people *pretend* they see it, but I did actually see it. Down in the enclosure.' The boy's voice was higher. 'Last night. I saw it. I did. Does it live here?' The childish fizz and spurt of him made me nervous.

'It was a black fox,' I hissed, as firmly as Mumma had been when she'd told me this. 'Or a badger.' As I carried on, I sounded less sure of what I was saying. 'You see them sometimes – in the early evenings.'

'But a massive cat is nothing like a sheep or a dog.' He moved close. 'We've had a pony with its stomach clawed open. Throat latch to tail. It was actually, like, gross.'

'If there really were moor cats, everyone would see them. All the time,' I said, as Mumma had often told me. I remembered Grandma limping into the woods the previous evening. He might have mistaken her for something beastly in the wrong light.

'You get pictures of them in The Sun and The Mirror. So it's definitely true.'

'If those photos were real, someone would have proved it by now.'

'But that's why Angela Browning's done that report in Cornwall. Moor cats are clever,' he said, excited. 'You don't see them if they don't want you to. But I'm gonna make a hide and track it every night 'til I find it.' He stretched over me. His eyes buzzing like strip-lights. His brackish breath hanging in the air after all the whispering. Mumma would not be pleased. 'Please don't tell anyone the cat's around here, or someone else'll find it first.'

His shorts beeped. He took out a small electronic device, and checked it, frustrated. 'My mum keeps paging. She didn't want me to come. She thinks Mrs Cat's a psycho.'

'Who's Mrs Cat?'

'The old cat lady.'

'Lowdy, darling? Where are you?' Mumma called again.

'It's a joke. Everyone says after Mrs Cat's husband left, she was so desperate she did it with the tynx and had all these tynx babies and that's why we have all these moor cats.'

'That's not funny—'

'It's banter,' he said, almost warmly. 'A woman having sex with a cat is classic.'

'*Lowdy?*' Mumma's voice was trill, and far away in the house.

'When you say 'classic' do you mean of timeless high quality, or are you too lazy to learn a more appropriate word?' I was almost hoarse with whisper-shouting. 'This zoo only ever had females. Did you do biology?'

'You're funny.' He smiled and put his head on one side, like my doctor had whenever he was trying not to frighten me. All boys are friendly, fun, laid-back. 'Meet me tonight at the old enclosure.' He was suddenly serious. 'But I can't meet if you tell.'

'*Lowdy, darling? Where are you?*' Mumma called again.

'There's nothing to tell,' I shrieked quietly. 'There was only ever one tynx and she's dead. Stay away from the zoo.'

'*Loveday, do I have to come and find you?*'

I shot out of the cupboard, into the hallway, before Mumma saw where I'd come from.

'Where have you been?' she said, as I met her at the bottom of the stairs. She saw my red face, my throbbing chest, my fist at the scratch above my hip, and she went to the dining room door.

Inside, Digger was on his knees, rolling up a rug. Force-feeding it to itself, his black eyes cauled with boredom, still shaking his head slowly from the end of our conversation.

She held out her hand. 'I need the keys.'

⊱⊰

Mumma beckoned me in to the pantry. It was narrow and windowless. It smelled of brisk citrus and old cat, and was full of near-empty shelves, covered with new mice traps.

'She's stocked up for the apocalypse. No wonder she never goes out. It's all out of date, of course. Except the red wine, which I suppose improves with age if you spend enough on it.' Mumma checked two antique jars of jam for sell-by dates like she checked me for pimples and grazes. 'Stay away from that boy. Let's have a break from boys now we're here, shall we? You need to rest and relax.' She put the jars in a box. 'What must you do?'

'You invited him in—'

'Where have these bad tempers come from, Cloudy Lowdy? You were so sunny until we came here. What must you do?'

'Stay away from that boy,' I said, perhaps a little too flat. 'Rest and relax.'

She smiled at me. 'Show me those fists and open your mouth.'

I stretched out my arms as she looked inside my mouth, one side, and the other, then tapped my chin up to shut it.

She picked up the box. 'Can you hold this?' She rested it onto my outstretched arms, and continued to fill the box with jars of pickled vegetables and preserved fruit.

'Oh,' she said, too lightly, seeing my arms tremble. 'Oh. Is that too much?'

'Nope.' I looked ahead. She was right. Digger had distracted me with his classic jokes.

'OK,' she said. 'Wait here. I'll be back in a moment.'

She shut the door, locking it behind her, went into the kitchen and boiled the kettle. There was the clang of iron as she put the heavy stewing pot on the stove. The vicious run of a knife over herbs or leaves. The growl of a spoon against the lip of a mug as she stirred tea. The spritz of cleaning spray as she disinfected her space.

I wished Mumma had not let Digger into the house. I wished she had not wanted the house to be improved. Why, I thought, is she not happy with everything exactly as we'd found it, like she usually was? I concentrated on my breathing, knowing I could do it. Knowing I could separate pain from body. Thankful to Mumma for teaching me another important lesson.

I closed my eyes on the ache, and distracted myself with the real, true power of hate. Earlier, I'd watched Digger from the corner of a window, cursing him creatively as he rinsed a scrubbing brush under an outside tap, T-shirt tucked into his back pocket. Shoulder blades blinding with sweat, I'd wished them to knot behind him until he couldn't lift his arms from his sides. Water frothing on the gravel, like the saliva behind my teeth, I wanted it, water and grit, to fill his lungs and drown him slowly. He stroked the bristles of the brush with the solid, round head of his thumb, bending them over. One by one they sprang free, flinging themselves up, spraying water into the air, all I could think was –

Mumma unlocked the pantry.

'Great.' She took the box and dropped it loudly, breaking all the glass. 'They'll be rotten inside. I'll bin it all instead.' She stroked my face and kissed my head. 'You'll have to stay in your room while the boy is here. It'll only be a day or so, but better not risk it.'

'I'm going to lie down anyway,' I said. 'My belly hurts.'

I floated out of the pantry, head lowered, not needing to see the droop of her face as she stared at the box of broken glass on the floor, unable to be sure I was lying.

The phone rang and she answered, wedging it between shoulder and chin, watching me pass by, into the hallway. She listened for a moment, then hung up, without a word.

❧

I was lying on my bed, facing the wall, when Mumma locked my door softly, to keep Digger safe.

But, as she liked to say, 'better to be swimming in milk you can churn into butter, than drowning in water.' She would stop worrying when she saw me staying away from mires and rocks and shafts. I'd never be found in the boys' dormitory at night again, because there were no dormitories. She would probably not lock me up tomorrow, or the next evening. She wanted me to rest, and when my hair was grown again, she would see I was well.

I went to the balcony. The sky curtseyed and the sun blushed, as Digger stood in the deer park, a yowling wicker cat basket full of cats at his feet. Cats darted away, tumbling across the grass and into the trees. He held a scrawny, spitting, scratching cat under one elbow and opened the wire door of the basket carefully, trying not to let the cats already inside, out. He managed to get the cat in, and the door shut quickly. He looked up, saw me, and shot his fist into the air. '*Boom shak-a-lak*,' he shouted, swinging the basket of gurning cats around his head. I backed away from the balcony window, scratch burning.

When he had gone, I was invited downstairs for supper. I hid most of it in the bin.

Afterwards, walking through the house, he was everywhere. Everything he had touched almost glowed. I tried to cover it, to place my scent over his. With aching arms, I re-rolled the rug. I emptied the chess set and boxed it again. I regreased the door handles with sweat from my own hands. Licked the bureau so I could write my initials on it again. I pushed a sofa in the drawing room from one wall to another until the blood in my ears was staccato with phantom pocket beeps. Still, the house seemed less mine than it had yesterday.

In the cupboard I had hidden in, I found a folded piece of paper and a book.

Back in my room, I opened the paper to a quick, rough pencil drawing. A dappled thick-coated animal, wide slanting eyes, and a light mane rising to two sharp ears with thin, delicate points. Next to it, for scale, Digger had drawn a man. On all fours, the tynx came to his shoulders. It was beautiful and horrifying. *See you in the enclosure*, Digger had written.

The book was called *British Lions and British Tigers and British Bears, Oh My!* by David Fowler. It was oversized, the pages thicker than in most books. The title was too large across the cover, and below it were three small photos of a lion, a tiger and a bear. No tynx.

I folded the paper up, and rubbed hard at my hip, to irritate the scratch, to remind myself to do something to keep the boy – his thick unfeeling fingers, his steaming face, the lazy long lift of his arms – away from the zoo.

I imagined the lynx enclosure. The thick, mossy air hanging in the trees. The hum of the river at dusk. Digger secretly draped in loam and leaves, waiting for something 'classic' to happen. I imagined it so clearly, it was like I was there. I raised my fingers, stopping myself falling into a vivid daydream, but all was the same on my head, as far as I could tell.

I piled the newspaper I'd taken from Grandma's room together with her pamphlet, the old photographs and my *Macmillan Illustrated*

Animal Encyclopaedia, surrounding myself with healthy facts, deter-mined this would not become a paracosm.

I was so relieved I never had to see Digger again I collapsed onto the books and papers with my pillow wrapped around my head and screamed so long my hair would have dropped out, if I'd had any.

BATLEIGH ZOO CLOSED AFTER MAN KILLED IN CAT ATTACK

Batleigh Zoo has closed on council orders due to public safety concerns. After a recent escape of the zoo's main attraction, the so-called 'tynx', locals formally petitioned the council, referencing the previous years of complaints. The animal escaped during a dangerous performance involving a young girl dancing in its cage. It went on to attack a forty-six year-old father of two, who later bled to death.

A 'tynx' is not a recognised genus of big cat, but the owner's term. In the zoo advertising material, it is described as a unique hybrid of tiger and lynx, but experts agree it is more likely to be an 'anomalous' case of gigantism.

The animal was put down by vet Paul Harris, at council insistence. He said, 'Whatever it was, it was incredibly dangerous. Everyone knows the zoo was run by amateurs, so this was an accident waiting to happen.'

A council spokesperson commented of the owner, 'She is not fit to be in control of dangerous animals and has been cautioned for bringing a lynx to a council meeting with her.'

Local Batleigh publican, Frank Mortimer, claims the animals were often seen around the village and on the moor. 'They weren't kept in their cages like they should have been. She let them out whenever you went near the place. The pub's been much quieter since the incident but now the zoo's closed hopefully people will feel able to visit the village again,' he said.

The council has given the zoo's owner a month to re-home or euthanise the remaining lynx.

The animal's hide is damp. Its long, rough tongue flicks in the heat.

It lies back, reaching its toes over its heavy head. It rolls over, springs out.

The scent is outside again. It hangs in the heat under a white moon, settles on thorns, leaves, gravel. A gentle, teasing mist. The boy has been here. He's not here now.

It pads through the trees, slow and light, nudges the leaves where he was hidden, but he is not there either. It finds only woodlice, earwigs, and other tiny, startled, creeping things. A bat lunges low. It jumps for it. It drinks long and cool from the river, glimpses itself and pauses. But then it catches his scent again.

❧

The animal crosses a field. It butts at apples and plums, sour and hard and straining.

The boy is here. The animal circles the building. There is no way in. The openings in the walls are too high, too small. It finds ledges, jumps from stone to stone, finally onto straw above the boy. It tugs its claws through the straw, but it's bound tight. It crouches at the edge of the roof and extends its neck. Dips its nose.

The animal sits, haunches to the thatch. It licks a paw, washes an ear.

There is a faint beep.

DAY 3

SOMEONE WAS BANGING at the front door. Banging, not knocking, loud and urgent.

When Mumma left her room, I was on the landing, pulling up my shorts. I had woken, again, naked and exhausted, on the balcony, staring at a toilet-block blue sky. I had been able to leave the tower, so maybe Mumma had decided not to lock me in after I'd gone to bed. Perhaps she was less concerned about me once Digger had gone home. Perhaps she was waiting to see if my bellyache developed into something more serious. Or perhaps she was drunk and forgetful. It seemed, regardless, a good portent.

She smoothed her hair and tightened her dressing gown as she reached the front door. The noise stopped when the heavy bolt was drawn and the door was cracked open. She checked at ankle level for cats, then opened the door wide. I slid down the stairs, to join her. She placed a hand flat against the doorframe, across me.

'Oh – hullo.' The man in the porch had shoulder-length grey hair and spectacles on a cord. He wore walking shorts and a polo shirt that said *The Moorland Gazette*. He looked twice at me and I backed away, running a hand over my bald head trying to hide it.

Mumma didn't reply, but leaned her head against the door.

'A'right. Can you tell the lady Peter Carter's here?' The man looked to the drive, waiting for Mumma to do this.

'I'm afraid not—'

Peter Carter's cheeks puffed red. 'We've got photos of that cat on the loose.'

'That cat?' Mumma frowned like she was concerned for Peter Carter.

'That damn big tynx or whathaveyou. Miriam Mortimer saw it outside Bat Farm last night. Staring at the house. She says it's the size of a car,' Peter Carter said, threateningly.

Tiny hairs stood up on the back of my head and kept going, along my neck, down my spine until they reached around niggling the little scratch at my hip. I gave it a rub.

'Mimi's getting the photos printed. In Okie. They do it in an hour. I'll have them exclusive.' Peter Carter took out a notepad like it was a weapon. 'So the old lady'll need to tell me what's going on.'

'Goodness.' Mumma leaned more heavily into the door, waiting to hear a long story.

Peter Carter repeatedly made dots with his pen at the start of a line, like he hoped a sentence would begin at any second. 'All this,' he flicked the pen behind him to the drive, still peppered with scat and entrails, 'it's not normal.'

Mumma was very good at silences.

'We've got proper evidence now.' He tapped the pen against the notepad. 'So them government wildlife advisors'll be here next, once they've finished over on Bodmin. Angela Browning's gonna hear about it. It's probably the same cat! Over here, over there! Picking off lambs. Lurking around. You can't walk home from the pub without watching your back! We know the old lady let it loose. So, what's she going to do about it now?'

'I'll ask her.' Mumma stared past him, into the air. 'When she's not so busy dying.'

Peter Carter looked at Mumma properly for the first time, then at me. He clicked the pen at Mumma, slowly, thinking. 'Are you the kid who was locked in a—'

'Excuse me.' Mumma shut the door on Peter Carter's shocked face. 'Too early.' She fake-yawned, stroking a finger around my collarbone, half-smiling as if she'd already forgotten Peter Carter, but I saw the gleam in her eyes. She was cross. 'Yet another fake photo. And I was never locked in with the lynx. I could come and go as I pleased.'

'I understand,' I said gravely, behaving perfectly and hoping to hear more.

'Open up?'

I opened up. Her eyes circled the inside of my mouth.

'OK,' she said, finding nothing. 'Stay inside, understand?' She shouldered off her dressing gown as she walked upstairs, pausing to look at the drive from the window at the top of the stairs – one way, the other – then her bedroom door clicked shut behind her, making clear I was not to follow.

I was annoyed. After this supposed sighting, I worried Digger would still be poking around the old zoo, hoping to bump into a tynx. But as long as he stayed away from the house, Mumma wouldn't make me fold myself up in my room all day. Again.

'Eh?' Outside, Peter Carter hit the front door again but with my head against the thick wood, I supported it. 'I'll come back, you know? We're sick of it. Everyone lives in fear of that bloody animal, and now we've got evidence. You can't keep it here. We won't have it.'

The noise shook my skull, but the door did not give.

Peter Carter's footsteps had dwindled out of hearing, when there was a noise from the other side of the house. Someone was shouting. The rooms overlooking the deer park on the ground floor were locked so I went straight to the window in the back door.

Grandma crawled, with difficulty, through the petting pen. Ripped and muddied pyjamas clinging to her slight body. Twigs and leaves caught in her hair. Walking sticks whirling like spokes on a bicycle. 'Where are all the bloody cats?' she called. 'I need the bloody cats.'

She caught sight of me at the window, and pulled herself up with her sticks. 'Thank god.' She smoothed her fine hair back with relief. 'Help me, Lowdy. The old girl's not herself. I've been out all night. Come and help. Quickly.'

'I can't.' I rattled the back door handle, to show it was locked.

66

It was easier than explaining I was too scared of Mumma to leave the house.

'Get my keys. From my room.' She came to the window, cheeks sucking in and out with breath. She slapped a hand over her chest to support it. 'Get a can of food. A saucer. Something to tap it. Quick as you like. She needs something to eat. She's not well.'

Grandma did not seem confused. She was calm. She was serious. I had great sympathy for her. It was natural to tell stories. To believe in more exciting worlds. As she weakened and died, it seemed Grandma escaped her painful days by reliving the strongest, most vital version of herself. She was the famed keeper of a near-mythical predator. But no one could hear her speaking like this, or it might get back Peter Carter, Miriam Mortimer, Angela Browning or, even worse, Digger. Digger would get the wrong idea. He might think there was something in it. He wouldn't realise how ill Grandma was. He would come back.

'Look alive, Lowdy. What are you staring at?' She waved a hand in front of my face, then rapped the glass between us with a stick. 'Get out here. I can't keep racing up and down this hill. I need help.'

I backed away from the glass. I had to stop her.

Mumma was a hump of sleep in her dim bedroom.

'I understand I can't go outside' I said, very polite, 'but Grandma's in the petting pen shouting about the tynx.'

Mumma rose from the bed like there was a string pulling the top of her head. 'Please don't bellow at me like that, darling. But thank you for telling me,' she said. 'Please, put the broth on the heat.'

From Grandma's bedroom window, I watched Grandma clock Mumma at the back door and make a break, limping as fast as she could – which was incredibly slowly – towards the path through the rhododendrons into the woods.

Mumma dashed across the grass, came up behind Grandma and grabbed her in a hug, holding Grandma's arms tight to her sides so she couldn't keep walking. They argued very quietly, Mumma speaking directly into Grandma's ear, as she led them both up and away from the rhododendrons. Mumma never took her eyes from the treeline behind her, probably worrying that more little cats were hiding there with their exotic buffet of diseases.

Mumma and Grandma tussled their way into Grandma's bedroom, and as they entered Grandma stared at me with stones in her eyes.

'Are you feeling better, Grandma?' I said, really, really meaning it.

She did not answer me, and she did not look away.

'The old girl needs something to eat,' Mumma said, in the manner of an impression. Without looking at me, she put a hand out for the mug of broth I had poured. 'Thank you, Lowdy,' she said. 'Now, please go out.'

'Sorry,' I mouthed to Grandma, but her expression was hard as granite.

⁂

I am very small, not yet at school, and my favourite stories are about Mumma performing as Beauty, with her Beasts.

Sometimes we pretend to perform together, in the zoo's show – she is Beauty, I am the Beast. Then, afterwards, moving the books from the shelf, or perching on the narrow kitchen surface, I am a lynx, asleep on the sunning platform in the enclosure she told me about. I run around the school grounds on all fours, refusing to listen when staff called me. Refusing to come when they say I am scaring the younger boys. Sometimes when Mumma catches me I behave beautifully, like I am well-trained, and she calls me her 'little familiar'. Other times I nip and squeal and she says I am the devil's pet.

When I am little she doesn't mind so much, but I get older and older, and so do the boys, and she must keep me inside. If I am restless, she trails around after me, stroking my hair, distracting me with a toy, only letting go when it is black and frigid outside and she has a drink in her hand. The older I get, the less she wants to play this game with me.

꩜

The deer park was quiet without the cats and Grandma. I couldn't enjoy the grass, white and prickly beneath my feet, nor the hot fat of the sun spitting in my eyes. Leaves twitched and a woodpecker rapped and I raced to get under the trees before Mumma saw me on the path to the old lynx enclosure. Before she realised.

I hadn't even waited to eavesdrop. Mumma had specifically told me to go outside and I had specifically found the back door unlocked. Mumma had to believe I was nothing if not, more or less, obedient.

The thin little tabby from my balcony leaped out of a bush, hopped ahead, then jogged back to join me, twisted little face grimacing and whining.

'Sh.' I checked behind me, for Mumma, just in case.

The cat followed me into the rhododendrons, ducking and hopping the nettles and brambles my flip-flops flicked at it. There was heaving, untamed growth everywhere, but the path was well-trodden. Soil-raw and splitting dry. Sinking out of the heat into the brown and green trees felt like sliding into peat. For the first time in three days, I felt a little cool. I couldn't believe I was finally out. Free at last, for as long as it took Mumma to realise.

The cat mewed at my heel.

'Shoo,' I said. It didn't.

It butted my legs, tipping its head to look at me. I had wanted a cat so badly, once. I would have taken any pet, for the company. I couldn't see the house through the trees so, surely, the house could see me even less – I picked the cat up. One hand cupped its tail. Fingers laced into its ribs.

'Hello, hello, hello.' I clicked my tongue. 'Will you be my secret pet?'

It purred and nudged me with its pointy chin. Its paws expanded and contracted. Fur fell out in clumps, under my slight stroke. I shook the hair away – stepping on it, so I didn't get ideas – and cradled the cat like a baby as I walked into the old lynx enclosure.

The boundaries of the enclosure were sketched out by a narrow ditch, just visible, where the fence would have been. The zoo's paths ran along two sides of the enclosure, and the river and woods along the others. Bits of chicken wire were still sunk into the ground here and there. It was a tiny zoo, but the lynx enclosure was the size of a tennis court. In the corner, near the riverbank, was an oak tree. The sunning platform – some mismatched planks hammered between two branches – was still there. The cat scrabbled out of my arms. It followed me on foot, sniffing saplings.

As a little child, I had imagined the platform as a glossy, orange perch, but here it was, black and dripping with Old Man's Beard just above my head. I jumped and grabbed the planks, crumbling away a bit of dry, rotted wood.

I ran down one side of the pond in the middle of the enclosure, and up the other. No cool clear water, in the drought it was a concrete scoop stained brown with algae. Or possibly cat faeces. But I danced around, like Mumma must have done when she pretended to be Beauty with her lynx beasts. I imagined my skirts billowing. But only once. Then I did fists and recalled some bog body statistics.

Below the enclosure, the river dawdled, hoarse and low, across black stones, so low in places the bed was exposed. Mud cracked and crusted. Nothing like how Mumma described the rush and heave of its winter weight.

On the path along the river, an ash trunk was shredded at chest height. My fingers slipped into the pale slits. The pith and splinter felt familiar. I sucked a fingerful of soil, sandy and silted, but heard a noise in the trees, so spat it out again to listen carefully.

The trees dipped and stretched. There was only the occasional tick and click of twigs and leaves falling from the canopy into the berry-black belly of the valley. Then something rustled. Rippled the light. Crunched softly into dry leaves.

The little cat shot past me towards the house and out of sight. I caught a scent. A sound that didn't belong.

'Grandma – ?' I whispered, nervous. After all, she was probably still cross with me. I waited for the comforting sound of her sticks dragging down the path through the rhododendrons. For the smell of tobacco to hit the air. The noise stopped. If Grandma was there, she did not reply. It suddenly didn't seem likely that Grandma was already recovered from her earlier distress, at least not enough to be up and out again.

What if the long-forelegs that night had not been Grandma's sticks? What if the squat body belonged to something unhunched?

I stepped behind a large fir tree, then inched around the trunk to look out. Something moved a few metres away, among the trees at the river's edge.

But there was rustling everywhere. In the branches. At my feet. The leaves were skittish and sentient. My hands were pinned to the bark of the trunk. Sweat thumbed my neck, ran down my ribs. I couldn't move. I didn't know what monster might be creeping around me – creeping through the trees it lived in, where I had appeared, thoughtlessly, for the first time.

A doe broke cover.

It crashed through a low sleeve of shrubs near the river, its eyes rolling towards me. It suddenly changed direction, forced within an arm's length of me, by something. I felt its brown draught and tripped backwards over a piece of varnished pine wrapped in weeds. I stumbled and snatched it up. A weapon. I swung it in one direction. In another.

But there was only the breeze caught in the treetops. The mutter of the water. The parched swallow of the too-hot afternoon. There was nothing there, I was simply not used to the noises of the moor.

I loosened my grip on the plank to see it etched with writing. *Koshka and Sofia are sisters. Siberian lynx are nocturnal and live in very small groups in high altitude forests. Their thick fur keeps them warm in freezing climates and they live in dens or caves. They can* grow larger than 70cm to the shoulder, and jump up to 10 feet high. Like many big cats, they are solitary, secretive animals. They come together only to mate, although mothers and offspring often remain close as the female raises the litter. They can go unnoticed for years as they do not hunt, but instead lie in wait, disguised, waiting for prey to pass them.

Although Petrosinella's fraternal lineage is unclear, she is Sofia's daughter. She is an unusual case of gigantism, or she was bred with a much larger cat. She was, unusually, a litter of one, as lynx commonly have two to four kits.

After Nella was put down, Grandma told everyone she'd sold Sofia and Koshka to a wildlife park in Northumberland. I suppose, at some point, they also died.

While I read the piece of wood, something moved in the corner of my eye. Something long, dark, and bigger than Grandma emerged from the trees. I was too scared to move in case whatever it was noticed me.

But when I raised my eyes over the plank, it was Digger. Cat basket in one hand, open tin of Go-Cat in the other. He sucked loudly on the air, calling for cats as he scuffed through the leaves stopping to bend and turn one over, to pick something up, to look at it on his palm.

As he walked past, the wire door of the cat basket swung towards me. The friendly little tabby I'd held was behind the bars. It hit one side of the basket, then the other. As Digger sauntered along the path, he threw the cage up into the air and caught it again. 'Alrighty then,' he shouted, looking all the time for evidence of the tynx he wanted to photograph.

I slumped against the trunk, relieved, in one sense. Incredibly disappointed in some others. Mumma had said Digger would be here one day only, so what was he doing back? My scratch was very irritated indeed.

I crouched behind the old butterfly glasshouse on the other side of the zoo. Its panes of glass, broken and jagged, glinted in the fierce sunshine. The wrought iron door was rusted permanently ajar. Vines grew in coils, each fresh acid-green shoot jarring with the solemn, sickly greens of the moor around it.

When I twitched my T-shirt to look at my scratch, it was redder, thicker, more inflamed than when it had first happened.

Digger took the cat basket into the old meat room where Grandma had stored and prepared the lynx food. He opened the heavy door only enough to squeeze himself inside. A moment later he left without the basket, passing the glasshouse, and me hidden behind it.

Howls and snarls were muted by the thick walls of the outhouse. There was a small, high window. I stood on tiptoes, spat on my hand and cleaned a patch of glass to look through. The cats were crammed into a room with a solid concrete floor, stained brown, gutters to either side – now peppered with a few little black stools – and a sink. The wicker basket was on an old unplugged chest freezer at the back. The cats leapt over and crawled under each other, moving like water in all directions. A spat broke out and a small space cleared as two cats went stiff with aggression.

I thought about being trapped in the flat in the boarding house. The strong, animal desire to be free. I wanted to release the cats. I wanted them trilling and prancing through my legs in a cheerful furry stream. I could wave on any who sat to groom themselves, and march them below Grandma's window in a parade, to make up for letting her down.

I couldn't risk it. I couldn't risk Mumma locking me in the tower all day, as well as all night. I would let them out later, when she thought I was in bed, and then blame Digger's sloppiness.

I dropped from the window, turned and found Digger stood behind me. I immediately wanted to shuck my own skin.

'Your mum's looking for you.' He jiggled a rake from hand to hand, so casual he seemed nervous. 'Did you find my book? Someone got a photo of the tynx. Told you.'

'Not *another* fake,' I said, grabbing my scratch where it gnawed at my hip. Why had I inhabited a different body since I'd seen him? Swelling, heavy flesh, with fluids and irritations I had never known before the last two days. I would not survive being so close to him with my new sweats and itches. I'd had enough.

I jogged away, up the hill.

'My dad's gonna shoot it.'

I stopped, looked over my shoulder at him.

'Him and his mates've laid badger traps in their fields, 'cause it's never come so close to the houses as it did last night. Not since he was a kid. When the zoo was still open, Mrs Cat used to set them on people. He says he'd see them on the road and the moor. The park ranger was at ours this morning. Look.'

He moved towards me, holding out a flat hand and I waited, because in fairytales, gifts were given. Roses, shoes, skins, grace, apples, the fur of a hundred cats. Although, the gifts were not always welcome.

Digger looked around like he was being watched by his saboteur from the dense spaghetti of rhododendron branches. I did the same, thinking of Mumma.

The thing on his palm looked like a curled shell in the low light but, close up, it was clearly a claw. Cats sometimes dropped their sheaths, when new, sharper claws grew in beneath the old. But this was a huge arch, the size of a domestic cat's paw. With a thick base where it might once have emerged from a toe, it was pale and stained from use, not too sharp. Dog claws grew and grew, and were ground down by hard surfaces as they walked, but cat claws grew sharp, then stopped. Claws were made from keratin, like hair. They had no nerve endings, no memories, unless you got close to the quick.

'It's fake,' I said, crossly. 'You can buy those. For traditional medicines. For shamanic rituals.' I had now read Grandma's pamphlets. More than once. This fact was in *'Illegal trading – cruelty or conservation?'*

'Well, I found it, in a tree. Down there.' The breeze turned with him, flattening the leaves of the rhododendrons, as his eyes went to the trees hiding the enclosure. 'I've gotta find the tynx before they kill it, 'cause they want it gone before lambing season.'

'Can a lamb be the same size as a cat?' I remembered the buzzard snatching the kitten, wondering if local raptors were stealing lambs.

'It's for you. So if you find anything, you show me, OK? You can't tell.' He still had his hand out, sheath offered to me.

'There's nothing to tell. It doesn't exist. My Mumma says so.'

'She's only just got here. I told you, I saw it.'

'Sometimes,' I said, 'if you imagine something enough you believe you've seen it.'

'Am I imagining that tree?' Digger pointed at one with great seriousness, then grinned like a protractor. His world was so solid, it was a joke to him that it could be anything other than exactly how it looked. 'You come out with some classic banter. You're Pamela Banterson.'

I said nothing.

He stepped closer, skidded on something, almost fell over, then looked around for whatever had destabilised him. 'Whoah. This is no time for dancing.' His grin clung to his face against all odds, waiting for something. 'Eh?' he said, hopefully.

'There is no tynx.' I was suddenly aware of my balding head rushing away from my brow. Without hair my face was frameless and unpretty. So unlike how a lady should look. 'I don't know what you've seen, but our tynx died years ago. Leave us alone. Stop coming here.'

'Alright, alright.' He tried to nod and shrug at the same time. Now, his smile was stiff. 'Well, there's a photo. You'll get it when you see the photo. A photo is *scientific evidence*.'

My scratch itched. I wanted to gouge it with the claw. I wanted to gouge Digger with the claw – could almost feel the flesh sponging around it. I could slip in through the wound. Swim through him. Make myself so small he wouldn't notice me inside him.

I snatched the claw from him.

'Yeah,' he said, a little weakly, like he was running out of words, 'you have it. We should – meet up and that. If you want?'

'*Digger?*' It was the girl I'd seen from the taxi riding a pony out on the road. The girl with my old black hair. She pushed her way through the rhododendrons. For a second, I thought she was me. She was in wellies and cut-off jeans, an old shirt tied at her naval, drawing her tiny waist in tight with a knot like a fist. '*Digger?*'

'Oh my god,' Digger looked at me. 'See? Everyone's looking for it. I'll get rid of her.'

He jogged towards her, grinning back at me, before grabbing her by the shoulder, mumbling into her ear and pushing her back into the trees.

I ran through the deer park and the petting pen – sadly cat-free again – the angry tug of my scratch dragging me home.

❧

Mumma sat at the kitchen table. The light had gone and the dark room smelled of soup and peaches. There was a bottle of Archer's next to her yellow gloves, but no glass.

'How many times did I tell you to stay inside?' She stared blankly ahead of her. She was a lot less happy than she had been when I was telling tales on Grandma.

'You told me to go out.' I frowned, believably. 'You wanted to speak to Grandma so you told me to go outside. I thought you wanted me to get some vitamin D. For my recovery. You haven't hung me from any windows recently. Why is the boy back? Why did you let him come back?'

Mumma closed her eyes, thinking, then opened them. 'I don't like these outbursts, Loveday. You've been irritable since we got here. I knew Grandma would be a bad influence. Have you been into the woods?'

'Surely it doesn't matter now all the cats are shut up, unless it's true there's a ty—'

76

'Have you been into the woods?'

'No. I was resting and relaxing in the sun. Getting some vitamin D—'

'Have you spoken to that boy?'

'He said you were looking for me, so I came to find you. Ask him.' If I made up sayings, like Mumma did, one of mine would be 'a knob of honesty greases a pan of lies'.

Mumma looked at me. 'Have you been crying? Why have you been crying?'

'No,' I said, touching my cheeks, realising I had been crying and seeing an opportunity. 'Not really, I mean. I wasn't feeling well, but I'm better after some fresh air.'

She nodded, tired. 'Fine. You've had the fresh air now. Repeat after me. I stay in the house. I stay away from the boy. I stay away from Grandma. Like you mean it.'

'I stay in the house,' I said. 'I stay away from the boy. I stay away from Grandma. Like you mean it.'

Mumma ignored my hilarious joke. 'If it happens again there'll be real trouble.'

She believed me, and her gullibility made me suddenly fond of her.

'Send the boy away. I'll do the cleaning.'

She craned back, to see me from a distance. 'The cleaning's not your business. Is it?'

If she suspected I hated Digger, she would be worried about the consequences – for him. I took her head in my fingers, to press my forehead against hers, to distract her.

'Why do people think there's a tynx in the woods?'

'What people?' She snapped.

'The man at the door.' I snapped.

She tried to look away, holding the table for support, but I held fast to her head. 'Lowdy.' She peeled off my hands. 'It's an historical issue. They don't like her here on her own. They don't like not knowing her business. They blame her for Batleigh going down the pan after Nella attacked that man and the zoo closed. But before that, they complained about the tourists clogging the roads and frightening the wild ponies. They don't like her. She's too weird. People used to come from the village, bring flowers and things, asking how she ran the place, out here on her own. They'd get cross, sometimes, when she didn't want to talk, and she'd let Nella out, herd her at them. Nella did nothing, of course. It just kept everyone on their toes. But now they point a finger at her every time they lose a sheep to a dog off the lead.'

'So, it isn't Nella?' I thought of the sounds in the trees. The weight and pad to them. Before the deer ran.

'Nella was put down.' She tried to push me back, but I held tight. 'You know that.'

'Are you *sure*?'

'How could Grandma hide something the size of a tiger all these years? This is exactly the rubbish I don't want you thinking about.'

'Well, why don't you want anyone in the woods?'

'Who's been telling you about the woods?'

'Telling me what about the woods?'

'Grandma is cuckoo.' She stared into my face intently. 'She always has been. But throughout history, groups make monsters to have something in common. It improves social cohesion. It's how gossip works. 'A shared foe makes firm friends', if you like. There is no tynx, only the village's idea of a tynx. I don't want to hear you talking about the tynx again. It's more make-believe you can't handle.'

She pushed me off, swigged from the schnapps, stretched her gloves, finger by yellow rubber finger bouncing back into their proper shape.

'The good news,' she said, brightly, 'is the house is clean and the cats are gone. There's only Grandma left to deal with.' She looked at me with a smile. 'So, stay in your room and now we've got a bit of paid help, we'll be out of here sooner than we thought. Quick as the flick of a whip. Open your mouth, please, darling.'

Later that night, while Mumma snored in the drawing room, cradling her schnapps bottle, I went to Grandma, to apologise, so I could still be the heir.

I turned on her bedside lamp, but she stayed asleep, the handle of her empty broth mug in the crook of one hand. Mumma had changed her, because Grandma's twiggy hands now poked from the frilled sleeves of a laced nightdress. I pulled up the collar until only her nose showed. She looked like grandmother-wolf in Red Riding Hood.

'Oh, hello. Why do I feel like this?' she said, waking. She blinked a few times to focus, spat the collar away from her mouth. 'Am I asleep, or am I awake?'

'I'm not allowed to talk about the tynx.' I whispered, watching the door. You could never be too careful with someone as stealthy as Mumma. 'But how do they fake the photographs? Can you tell me exactly how they do it?'

I needed to explain the fake photo to Digger, so he would believe there was no tynx, and would never come back to work for Mumma.

'I feel awful.' She smacked her lips a few times. She shuffled her shoulders, trying to sit higher. 'What the hell have you done to me?'

'Not me, Grandma,' I stammered a little. 'It was Mumma. She's helping you.'

Grandma ripped the dress at the neck. Weak, as she was, she tore the thin material from her. Half-naked, she was the wrong shape, like an animal with flat, wet fur.

'It was you. I thought *you* were different,' she said.

'*Grandma*. Whisper. You'll wake Mumma.'

I couldn't look away from her tiny, pointed mushroom-cap breasts. Nothing like Mumma's soft, spongy old mounds. Nor like my pictures, with breasts so moon-plump and oddly shiny they were a little like babies themselves. Instead, Grandma's breasts were like mine.

'I'm sorry,' I said. 'I want to help, but I have to behave. If Mumma thinks I'm ill again, she'll worry. She'll make me stay in my room so everyone's safe, and then you'll never be able to teach me how to be a practically qualified felinologist.'

The stones in Grandma's eyes fell away. 'We need to keep cross-breeding. We need another even *better* tynx. We've almost done it and, when we do, they'll all wish they'd done it first, because that animal kept the whole village in work at one point.'

'Is this one of your funny jokes?' I said, a little frustrated.

'Stop listening to your mother. She hides everything. Do you know she never even told me she was pregnant? Let alone that she'd given birth. She hid it so well. Then I found you one day, in a spare cage! Just like that, a little baby in a cage!'

This was not the story I'd heard many times from Mumma. It was the opposite of that. Grandma sounded coherent. I knew people didn't always look like they're struggling to know what's true and what isn't, but if Mumma *was* wrong about the tynx, it wouldn't be the first time she'd ever been wrong.

Grandma saw me thinking. 'It's your mother who's nutty, not me,' she said, more slowly. 'Are you actually even ill, Loveday?'

I ran my hands slowly over my spiky head.

'If you want the zoo, prove it.' Grandma reached under her pillow and pulled out a set of keys. 'As I keep saying, we need to feed the tynx.'

⁂

'They'll thank me when Batleigh's full of tourists again,' Grandma said, in the petting pen. She leaned on me with one arm, and lit our way with a torch with the other. I'd helped her into fresh pyjamas, with trousers so long they couldn't have been hers. They dragged through the grass. Her pipe was unlit and hung from her mouth like a dummy. I had to indulge Grandma a little, even if it was a stupid decision to come out. I knew there was no tynx. Even if

Nella hadn't been put down, the life expectancy of a big cat in the wild wouldn't be much more than fifteen years, plus she'd been reared in captivity which would make her less resilient. I knew my facts.

'Sh,' I said.

'When you've reopened the zoo.' Grandma's feet shuffled quickly, anxiously, in the dark. 'You'll name it after me. The zoo, but also the tynx. Get a memorial statue made. Bronze. In the town square. My hand on its shoulder—'

'Whisper, Grandma.'

The drawing room windows beamed with light. I tried to keep Grandma stable, while stopping the plastic bag in my hand from rustling as it swung back and forth. Inside were a half-scraped pat of butter and an unopened packet of cheddar. It was all I could find.

'The visitors didn't come every summer to pat the sheep. The tynx was the star. That's why they came. Men used to knock on the door offering me flowers. But it was *her* they wanted. She was a beauty, and a man would marry a cat if he could. That's how the story goes. A man met a lovely young cat with thick, sleek fur and wished to marry it.'

'I don't think so.' I shuffled backwards through the rhododendrons to support Grandma. 'In The White Cat, the cat promises the prince she's the beautiful princess he wants, if only he will cut off her little white cat head,' I said, as we straightened up next to the old enclosure. 'So he chops it off, and the cat is grateful to turn back into a woman for him. No one wants to marry a cat, Grandma. Princes want to marry princesses.'

My favourite type of fairy tale was when someone has two different skins. The skin they came in, and the skin they're cursed with. The happy ending – unless there's a twist – is when they get to pick a skin, like Swan Maidens and Frog Wives, but they don't usually choose their animal skin.

Grandma swung the torch before us and caught a fox in the

light, stopped dead still in surprise. It lowered its head and dashed into the leaves.

'I'm not talking about The White Cat. I'm talking about The Cat Bride. It's a fable, not a fairy tale. There's a difference.' Grandma stopped walking. Her voice was so throaty and gruff it was almost lost in the noise of the river next to us. 'A fable,' she said, 'has a moral. It's instructional. *Educational.* A man met a lovely young cat with thick, sleek fur and wished to marry it. Venus saw the man loved the cat, so changed it into a beautiful woman for him. That's what happened.'

Because I loved skin-changers, one of my home-schooling projects had been animal brides and grooms. Like many fairy tales, folk tales and fables, The Cat Bride had a few different endings, but none of them ended happily ever after for the cat. Usually, on the wedding night, the cat hears a mouse in the room and, forgetting she is a woman now, springs to catch it like a cat. It's fairly consistent across the tellings that the husband isn't pleased to realise that however beautiful she looks, his new wife is essentially still an animal.

'I'm a cat bride, you're a cat bride,' Grandma said. 'It's a woman's lot. We're never what anyone really wants. The beautiful woman is a fairytale. It's not the same for men. They can be any old shape.'

'Alright.' I wasn't listening. I looked in the bag again. 'Let's leave the food here—' I wanted to nip to the meat room and let all the cats out, but needed to be back inside before Mumma woke and checked on me in the tower.

'For the cats and rats to get at? Are you an idiot?'

Grandma stumbled from the enclosure, and me. I followed her, a black will-o-the-wisp, torch flickering on a slim path hugging the river.

'Venus changes us into beautiful women,' she said. 'But when we marry, our husband realises we still catch mice with our hands and teeth. He's horrified. And Venus is angry with us. But we never *asked* to be turned into beautiful women. We *want* to be cats.'

I would like to be a beautiful woman, I thought. If I was beautiful, with hair in the right places, the boys wouldn't be distracted by everything wrong with me, they would see straight through to who I was on the inside.

We arrived at an old stone pump house. There were empty cans and packets and dirty bowls outside the entrance. Tins were rusting, paper labels half-degraded and buried beneath the leaves. 'We need to stock up. Use cans in an emergency. Fresh meat's better.' She looked around, a little distressed. 'Where *are* all the cats?'

The heavy-planked pump house door, streaked with green algae, was half-open.

'Let the dog see the rabbit?' Grandma laughed, uneasily, at her own joke and pointed her stick at the bag in my hand. 'She might be asleep now, of course. Be careful. Move slowly. She hasn't been well. It makes her tetchy.' The heavy-planked pump house door was slimed green. Grandma rapped it with her stick. It opened a few inches with a soft, socking sound and a rotting, meaty smell crept out. 'Get to it,' she told me, so I unwrapped the butter and the cheese with clumsy hands, unable to believe what was happening.

'Is it really in there?' My heart hopped at the black crack of the door, for a second, I believed Grandma, despite myself. 'What do I do?'

'Just throw it to her. Don't worry. She probably wouldn't hurt a fly.' Grandma took a step backwards, and handed me the torch.

I stretched my arm out then used my single, longest finger to push the door open. I edged around it, eyes readjusting to the black inside, keeping a distance. Ready to run.

Then, I baulked, finally seeing the horrible, horrible head.

I pushed the door open, appalled.

Stinking meat and cat food sludged across the floor. Presiding over it stiffly on all fours, tiny marble eyes wild and skewed in slightly different directions, brows too high, ears too low and flattened sideways, unevenly-stuffed body thinning from skinny shoulders to too-round rump – was an enormous, taxidermied tynx. Some of the cats might have used the old model as a lair because one side was crushed in, and there was a carpet of shed long, grey fur.

Grandma poked me with her stick, worried. 'How's she looking? Better?'

'She's fine.' I took Grandma by the arm and led her quickly to the path. 'Let's go before Mumma misses us.'

Grandma was cheerful on the walk back. She squeezed my arm and leaned in to my face. 'We need to get a couple of the toms in there, don't we? Let's see what she makes of them, eh?' She winked. One eyelid crushing down, closing out the real world, the other filmed over with madness, exactly as Mumma had warned me.

I was so shocked, I completely forgot to let the cats back out.

Chapter 6: The Cat-leigh Mystery

Since the closing of the zoo in 1979, rumours of a mysterious big cat have circulated in the village of Batleigh. The owner of the zoo was variously accused of animal cruelty and child abuse (never officially) but the zoo was most famous for its tiger-sized lynx, whose origins remain murky. The owner believed the animal was a hitherto unknown hybrid. The rest of us agree it was probably a freak of nature, in the nicest possible way. During an unfortunate incident in 1979, the so-called 'tynx' broke out of its cage, mauled a man to death and was put down shortly after, so what is the mysterious cat so many claim to see around Batleigh?

An important piece of background information is that the village has never recovered from the loss of tourism after the zoo closed. Please see the photograph in appendix 12.1. Note the two queues of people running from the ticket office! The smiles on all the faces! It's like they had no idea there was a very real possibility one of them might get eaten! People who knew the owner and the zoo, personally, suggested it was business incompetency and poor living conditions that led to the animal 1) escaping in the first place, and 2) being hungry enough to attack a man

Descriptions of the mysterious animal haunting Batleigh and surrounds have varied over the years. Sometimes it's stripey! Sometimes it's grey! Sometimes it's like a shadow! The animal has also grown physically, increasing in reported size over time. But is it the snowball effect of exaggeration, after all, doesn't everyone love to spin a good story?

There is the usual messy collection of debunkable penumbral photographs taken at a distance. These are common in all regions staking claims to mystery cats. As ever, witnesses report being too afraid to take out cameras on the occasions they even happen to be carrying such a thing. The photographs may or may not be authentic, but if there is a resident big cat we would also expect regular paw prints, which could be snapped at closer range and without fear of attack. Perhaps it is the case that people walking dogs aren't so aware of paw prints, or paw prints are more easily lost in the natural moorland environment than they could be by the sides of pavements and roads. Let's not forget the moor's elevation and pattern of relief. It receives one of the highest levels of rainfall in Britain: very helpful for washing evidence away.

Local farmers insist the monster cat is responsible for a regular loss of lambs each spring, but there is natural mortality during lambing everywhere that can account for a 10-15% loss per flock. Furthermore, what would a big cat eat outside the spring? The exact prey of the mystery cat all boils down to theoretical DNA. For example, if the cat were indeed the impossible hybrid tiger-lynx, we cannot assume it has received in that genetic combination the appetite of a tiger (killing deer once a week). It might have received the appetite of a lynx and graze, if you will, on smaller mammals but with greater frequency. Despite suggestions of attacks made by village residents, none of them cite a glut of deer carcasses, or domestic cat carcasses (the preferred meal of the Catamount of yore).

Many people claim to have seen the creature at night. Witnesses described a 'feeling' of being followed, and then a confrontation with a shadowy presence. So far, so fairly standard 'bogeyman' fare. What remote rural habitation doesn't like something living in the woods to threaten the children with? Many Batleigh kids grew up with the legend of the owner of the zoo being able to turn into a cat, herself. This story probably grew like many rural legends, branching off from another story, specifically, the rumour she set her big cats on unwanted visitors.

Nonetheless, it must also be acknowledged that a wild animal of this nature is unlikely to be coming so close to human habitations when it has a whole moor full of prey. This behaviour suggests a domestication of sorts. Plus, if there was a big cat on the prowl, it is indeed likely to be more active at dawn and dusk, especially as the village is then quieter. On the other hand, people who are out at night are often under some influence or another, and under these circumstances they are perhaps more than averagely suggestible. Batleigh is home to any number of livestock, working dogs, wild ponies, foxes and badgers so the possibilities for mistaken identity are endless.

If we look for other explanations of the sightings in Batleigh, we might recognise indicators of 'thoughtforms'. The village's communal preoccupation with the animal might have led to collective visualisations, or manifesting imaginations. There are a number of ley lines, and dark ones, running across the moor. Who knows what stew of negative energies might have been brewed by an intense resentment of the zoo, and owner?

And while we're on alternative explanations – what about a ghost? After all, a cat, as well as a man, was murdered in 1979.

There is no doubt that something is happening in Batleigh, but is it really a big cat? Or do locals want a scapegoat for the village's decline so much their psyches have done it for them, without them even knowing? There isn't currently enough evidence for this expert to call it one way or another, but regardless, I'm glad I don't live in Batleigh.

The door isn't locked and, besides, the animal has always been able to open doors.

The other animals surge through its legs. Some run, frightened. Some wait, friendly.

It bounces through the trees, twisting and spritzing. Some of the animals follow, but they get distracted by other scents and hungers, until it races alone, chasing one scent.

His scent.

❧

The animal follows him and follows him, all the way back to the field of apples and plums.

He's in the building. The animal still can't reach high enough, but this time it finds another opening and pushes in, narrowing and lengthening itself.

Once it is in the building, it will find him.

Except there is someone else. It snuffles at its own bars. The animal can't let it make a noise. The animal shuts the little thing away – it's always been able to close doors, too.

The little thing wails, and new noises start, elsewhere in the building.

'I'll go, Penny.'

Lights come on, and the room is lit up, but the animal is already gone.

'What the – ? Penny! Leo's out of his cot. He's in the wardrobe – Something's opened the window. Something's opened the damn window.'

DAY 4

MUMMA SAID THE purr was a perfect lullaby, set to the metronome of a deep, downy chest. She slept long nights between paws as a child. Some evenings, when she felt wistful, she would try to explain the sweet, sweeping glissade of a tail. Can there be any surprise that bored and excitable as a child, I took these cat stories to heart, blinking quickly, trying to catch her shapeshifting between the lifting and lowering of an eyelid? I never did catch her. She changed too fast. I was wonderfully imaginative. She should have done a better job of crushing it out of me.

There was a distant rumbling as fine hair brushed my skin, soft as breath.

Then I woke in the lynx enclosure. In the stiff air, each blackbird, robin and thrush tuned up to the first light. A squirrel helter-skeltered around its messy nest high above me in the branches. I felt for my head and disturbed a number of cats crammed next to me on to the damp platform. One sat tall. Another relaxed on its back, purring. Two jumped into the enclosure below.

I sat up, my arms crossing my chest, and found two little deer ticks. I flicked them off. I was naked, and someone else had let the cats back out.

I sprinted through the trees, into the grey light – through an ankle mist of dewy spider's webs. Prowling cats leaped away, scattering over the grass.

Cats waited at the back door, nosing at the blocked-up cat flap. I stepped over the large carcass of a deer to get to the step. It was intact, not leftovers. I was surprised to find it lying there among the mice and other gifts and tributes. A fly cleaned its legs on one sticky eyeball.

The door was locked so I kicked the cat flap. The meat-hooks gave way easily, but I could only squeeze my head, one arm and one shoulder through.

At the other end of the house, it took a few leaps to catch hold of the balcony. I pulled myself over the balustrade and stayed low, leaning out, to check no one had witnessed – anything. But there were only the cats stalking the garden.

The balcony doors were wide open, again, so I shut them, again, and checked the join looked long-locked. I pulled on my pyjamas, and got into bed, wound in a ball, knees to my chest, shivering with panic. Panic about sleepwalking into a bog or a mine. Panic about being in the woods if the village hated us so much it was producing monstrous supernatural entities. Panic about Mumma missing me during the night. Panic about my head. Trying to remember what had happened before I went to sleep. Trying to remember anything at all.

❧

'Lowdy.' Mumma's feet rattled on my stairs. 'Lowdy. Lowdy. Lowdy.'

I woke dizzy. The heat was roaring. Nauseous with fatigue, I remembered waking naked in the lynx enclosure. But was it a memory? I had never actually been a sleepwalker, despite what Mumma had assumed. The details of the morning felt true, not imagined, but I couldn't focus. Thought after thought flaked from my brain.

I stopped breathing, to touch the top of my stubby head and calm down, but dozens of heartbeats galloped in my ears – faster than mine, out of synch. The heartbeats of cats, I thought. I clapped one ear, then the other, realising I couldn't be hearing anything but my abundant, cursed imagination. But the hearts beat louder and louder –

Mumma missed the lock more than once, too hasty in the dim

light of the staircase. 'Lowdy,' she panted. She hadn't even bothered to tie her dressing gown.

'You locked me in again.' I stared at the key in her hands, brain still dry and itchy.

'They're everywhere.' She shoved a pair of yellow rubber gloves at me. 'And I'd finally finished cleaning.' Mumma's eyes fluffed, her chin crinkled. She couldn't see where she was pushing her fingers into her gloves. She was about to cry. 'I'd even disinfected the walls.'

'Why did you lock me in again?' I said, louder. 'Why don't you trust me?' I shouted, loudest of all.

'I don't have time for more bad moods, Loveday. Help me with the cats. Someone kicked the cat flap open. We'll talk about this later.' She threw disbelieving hands everywhere all at once.

I was strangely excited for Mumma to be disappointed by Digger's failure to lock the cats up properly. Strangely excited for his large moony smile floating before her, as she told him he need never come back. The strange excitement tipped into something else, as I no longer thought of Mumma, but instead I thought of he and I. Standing very, very close together –

'I can't help you with the *cats*.' I used Grandma's low, firm voice, and lay back on the bed, arms behind my head. 'Because I have to stay in my room, remember?'

⁂

I stood at the top of the main stairs. The air was wired with urea. My muzzle sweated under the heavy winter scarf Mumma had tied around my face.

Behind me, Mumma snivelled, her open mouth covered with yellow, sterile, rubber fingers. As Grandma said, she did seem a little out of control, losing her usual poise, with her arms wide, knees slightly bent to fend something off. Although Grandma, herself, had proved to be a little out of control last night with the stuffed tynx.

'Try not to inhale,' she whispered from under her own scarf. 'We need to get them out, but be careful—' She squeezed my arm, rubber hands squeaking on my damp skin. 'It's not only psychosis. There's hookworm, ringworm, rabies, catscratch fever—'

I shook her off. She had asked for help, and she was going to get it.

There were cats everywhere.

Proud on the stairs. Long across the floor of the hallway. On top of the bureau. Standing in the doorways. Weaving between themselves towards the kitchen. Folded up with eyes closed. Watching, waiting. Purring, mewing, hissing. The click of incisors hooking in to scratch. The rasp of tongue on fur. There was even a cat on top of the grandfather clock, one paw raised elegantly, staring back at me, mid-thought.

In return for helping with the cats Mumma agreed she would no longer lock me in. 'Toxoplasmosis,' she had wept, fastening the scarf behind my head. 'As if we don't know it's why Grandma's ill. The litter boxes were ancient. There were faeces on the stove. In the sink. It's bio-hazardous waste. It causes schizophrenia.' Mumma shook me, like I was not taking it seriously enough to put on the rubber gloves, although I was. 'No wonder she's in this state.'

I walked down the stairs, slowly, so as not to startle anyone. The cats were drawn to my movement. Sitting up, paying attention. They jumped from their perches, stretching their hips. They lifted off forepaws, butted little heads against my shins, mewing in greeting, friendly and welcoming. I reached for the little tabby. My hand slipped into the soft, warm puddle of it. I closed my eyes, like it had, picked it up and rubbed its body across my cheek, wanting to purr myself. When I purred really loudly, I made my whole body thrum. Sometimes, when I was little more than a baby, if I had been dreaming hard, when I woke, I believed I saw two chubby, silky paws pulsing in front of me - of course, Mumma said, really, I was still asleep - but now I could see why I had been charmed by cats. Their beauty, their independence, their self-assertion, and indifference. When the zoo was mine, I would make a lovely enclosure near the butterfly house for them. I would keep a choice few in the house, as company.

'Lowdy.' Mumma didn't like whatever she saw on my face. 'Get on with it.'

The soft tufting of the tabby's throat rattled in pleasure under my thumb. 'Do you want them out, or not?' I said.

The cats crowded close to my ankles. Mumma waved a large bedsheet in the hallway, so they couldn't lap back up the stairs. We funnelled them towards the back door.

Upstairs, Grandma's sticks and feet sounded on the landing. 'You've got to get the cats to her,' she collapsed over her words in urgency. 'You've got to get the cats to her, Lowdy.'

Mumma jogged up the stairs. 'Go back to bed, you batty old hag—' There was muffled tussling, as Mumma led Grandma back to her room.

I pushed the last cat out of the back door, and went to follow, but Mumma appeared, sheet bundled under her arm, putting her hand on the door handle, holding it shut. There was no need. The door had latched with a thunk and I had replaced the meat hooks. Outside, the cats congregated around the doorstep.

'Did you let the cats in?' Mumma's scarf ghosted in and out of her mouth.

'No.' I was truthfully indignant and pushed up the top of my bald head to show it.

'Did you let them *out*?' Mumma said.

'Out of where?' I said, wearily. 'You locked me in my room. It was obviously the boy.'

She went outside, closed the door and stared at me – worried – through the window. She took something from her pocket. It glinted like a jewel. She inserted the key she had cleaned into the back door, and locked me inside with it.

'You promised,' I said, angrily, through the glass.

'Go wherever you like, in the house.' She wiped the sweat from her forehead up into her hair. 'Darling.' She no longer seemed like Mumma. Was Mumma, herself, unwell?

She took a step, then noticed the dead deer at her feet. She backed up, watching it, until she hit the wall of the house. She scanned the petting pen for something – something other than the cats mincing across her path. But what did she think might be lurking there? Did she know about thoughtforms? She dashed, zigzagging and waving her arms to herd the cats across the deer park. She sprinted and threw the sheet over one.

'Get in the sheet,' she shouted at the cats. 'Get in the bloody sheet.'

I pulled the scarf from my face, and dropped it to the floor. Alone, locked in, I decided to release the cats again. Even if Grandma was too ill to reopen the zoo, I wasn't, and I would take my petty, little revenges on Mumma, now Digger would no longer be coming back.

There were hairs, here and there, in the hallway. I licked my fingertips to pick them up. Startled by my own thoughtlessness, I wiped them on my shorts, cross for not balling my fists to avoid the temptation – for not being more careful when Mumma could return at any moment.

⁂

Mumma didn't like it when I wouldn't eat. I was afraid to feel full, nervous of what I might be full of. It was the weight loss, and cramps, and sickness, that first made Mumma aware I was ill, but when she entered the kitchen she didn't even notice me pretending to eat a slice of toast for her benefit.

Her hair fell from behind her ears in a splintering frame for her face. Her dressing gown was soiled and her rubber gloves were shredded.

'Wow,' I said. 'Those cats do not like the meat room.'

'What?' She looked down at herself. 'Oh. Yes. The cats.'

She sagged over the table, head in arms, mumbling into her elbows. 'I've got to disinfect the whole place again.'

'So will you be telling the boy to stay away now—'

There was a brief knock at the front door. So quick, I thought I'd made it up.

Mumma sat up. We looked at each other. There was another, stronger knock.

I ran into the hallway. Mumma chased me down, catching me by the arm as I reached the front door.

'We've got to get rid of the cats.' She whispered into my ear. 'They can't see us like this, Loveday. The state of this place.' I put my hand on the latch and she spoke even quicker. 'The state of Grandma. She's a liability now. God knows what she'd say. But we haven't done anything wrong. We can't let them win.' Her forehead was wet. She sucked in great mouthfuls of her scarf then pulled them out with her ribboned yellow fingers.

I dropped my hand from the door. 'Who?'

'The village. The whole village is against us. One of them released the damned cats.'

'No,' I said. 'No. The village loves Grandma. It was the careless boy—'

'Don't be stupid. It's a threat. We can't let it look like we're in bed with this tynx.' Mumma eased the key from the door and into her pocket, then noticed the look on my face. '—this tynx that doesn't exist,' she added quickly. She tightened the scarf around her head, and crouched next to the door. 'Stay quiet. Rest and relax. They'll be gone in a minute.'

Someone hit the door again.

'It'll be fine,' she breathed. 'They'll go away.'

'You get out here,' a man shouted. 'And tell me why that bloody cat was in our house last night.'

Mumma raised her eyebrows and twizzled a finger at her temple. 'Crazy—'

The door was pummelled.

'My toddler could have suffocated. Or been eaten. It turned over his cot and trapped him in a cupboard.'

Mumma shook her head, face sweaty, eyes too amused. 'A cat,' she whispered, pityingly, reddening by the second, 'does not use a cupboard.'

'Digger's told me you've got all them cats in there. Haven't you, Digger?'

There was a brief scuff of gravel. I imagined Digger nod-shrugging.

'You're up to something. You've got to start taking responsibility, madam. I'm coming back with Angela Browning and the rest of them. We keep telling the police dangerous animals are being reared here. If something happens, you'll be liable. Don't think my son's gonna keep helping you. Are you, Digger? What do you think about them letting lose some animal that nearly killed your brother?'

Mumma shook her head, forcing out a silent laugh. 'The parents are covering something up. It's *always* the parents,' she tried to mouth gleefully. 'Some poor children have *terrible* parents.'

The door handle rattled again, and she shot out both hands to steady herself on the floor.

'We're coming back with the police. They'll get a search warrant.' He thumped the door so we didn't miss a single one of his final words. 'We're - coming - back.'

As the footsteps dwindled from the porch down the drive, the nerves at either end of Mumma's smile twitched. 'They won't come back. The police know there's nothing to find here,' she told me, reassuringly. 'If they could have proved anything, they'd have done it *years* ago. That's how we know it's all in their silly heads.'

She closed her eyes, stayed still, her breathing calming. I thought she'd also gathered her fingers into fists, but then she stretched them out either side of her.

I went to the window at the top of the stairs. The drive stretched further than I remembered, and came in too close to the porch. Digger, still in the same T-shirt and shorts, was pushed along by what I guessed was his father in a checked shirt and farm-dirty jeans. His father spat on my drive, and kicked at a sapling in the gravel. Even I knew, now I'd seen old Nella in the zoo, they were making it all up.

The drive stretched wider and wider, like a rubber band. Even though Digger was still on the drive he seemed further away than that. I had never had the satisfaction of him being sent away. I prayed the rubber-band-drive would snap and Digger would be flung back at me, faster, harder than ever. Hitting me and driving me through wall after wall with the speed and weight of his body, across the deer park, down through the trees, to land next to the pump house. Next to Nella's patchworked muzzle. And he would startle, his hopes of a tynx collapsing, just as the model of Nella had. He would realise his father was lying, and then we would –

There was a crash from Grandma's room.

Suddenly, the drive looked exactly as it always had. Real. Unchangeable. Digger and his father were gone. I did my fists, warning myself not to get carried away.

Still crouched at the front door, Mumma rolled her eyes to herself, then stood and cricked her neck. 'Grandma probably needs helping to the loo,' she called up to me. 'Go and see. I'll get her something to eat.' She strode towards the kitchen, seeming much more herself.

⚜

Grandma's room was a warm, dark sea, the air wet with salt. I flung the curtains open and she winced as sunlight fell on her. She had knocked her lamp to the floor.

'Get me out,' she growled. 'Someone's huffing and puffing at my door.'

I thumped the window open to let in the clean air. 'It's OK, Grandma. They've gone.'

'She's bound me up so tight, I can't jimmy myself out.' Grandma's face was pink, her eyes slits in the bright light. She was wrapped like a mummy. She shuffled from side to side and made a gargling noise. I loosened her sheet. She tore it off and stood, panting. Her striped pyjamas were soaked in grey streaks across her chest and under her arms. She jerked herself, without sticks, to the wardrobe.

'She'd put me in a pie, you know?' She wiped the sweat from her face. 'Always ask her where the meat's from.' She was not smiling, but I did a single, quick laugh in case she wanted me to.

She opened the wardrobe door so fast it hit her on the nose, but she emptied the wardrobe regardless, flinging blousy floral dresses left and right. She tossed shoeboxes of strappy sandals across the room and kicked out bags of silky scarves. A jewellery box flew open and spilled shed claws across the floor.

'What is all this—' I picked up a large hair bow and a handful of claws, as she emerged with another air rifle.

'Another bloody activist at the door. Didn't you hear the banging? I'm sick of them.'

I dropped everything to free up my hands and edged towards her, head back, arms out. 'Careful, Grandma. Put that down. You'll hurt yourself.' She shouldered me away.

'Time for school. Time to learn your lessons. This is how we deal with trespassers.'

'Give me the gun.' I said loudly. *'Mumma?'*

I put my arms around her, to grab the butt, but she span around. I ducked the gun.

'You show them who's boss, Lowdy. Be prepared for this shit when you take over the zoo, because none of them will like it. They'll sniff around you like you're a dog's arse, girl.' She rested the gun's snout on the open window sill, pointed it left and right across the drive. *'Where are you?'*

'It wasn't an activist,' I shouted. *'Mumma—'*

'Where is he? Where is the self-righteous bastard? Knocking on the door. Creeping around the woods, bothering the animals. Turning my daughter against me.' She turned inside, waved the gun up and down. 'We need the cats. Do you understand?'

'Mumma—' I screamed as loud as I could. *'She's got a gun.'*

Grandma balanced the gun on the sill again, leaned out and shouted. *'If it weren't for the beef industry, cows would be extinct, you little turd.'*

'There's no one out there.' I grabbed her around her waist, and pulled her back into the room. 'They were at the front door—'

'Where are all the cats—' Grandma shouldered me off. 'Where's the foil? I broke up a mirror to leave in the grass – She needs the cats—'

'Put the gun down. It was a man saying a tynx was in a house last night—'

'Why on earth would it be in a house, for God's sake? Is a tynx a pet? They want to get in here and see how I do it. They want my zoo but they're not having it. It's mine.'

'But they're gone now, Grandma.' I gave her my most delighted smile, so that she might feel how good the news was. 'The boy is gone.'

Grandma growled, aiming in one direction, then another, expecting intruders in all corners of her own bedroom. 'Let me at them.'

Mumma burst into the room with a steaming mug. She raced through, trying not to spill the hot drink, and batting the barrel of the gun to the ceiling as it went off. The ceiling collapsed above us as we wrestled Grandma. Plaster and dust fell like dirty confetti and a chunk of something hit her on the head. Mumma prised the gun from her hands. We gulped in the rot and paint and sawdust and blinked quickly at the wood exposed above us. Soft, wet, and black.

Grandma rubbed her temple, pyjamas and dressing gown now stippled black. 'Why would a tynx be in a house? Unless it's desperate. Put out more foil. Anything shiny.'

I waited for Mumma to tell Grandma how stupid she was, but she was staring at the ceiling. 'Is that black mould?' She sounded like she hoped someone would say no. 'Is that black mould?' She nudged Grandma to notice it.

But Grandma was confused. 'I was trapped.' She knotted her shaking hands to show the struggle. 'I couldn't get up.'

Finally noticing Grandma, Mumma twisted her hands around the gun, and leaned forward to shout at her very slowly indeed.

'You aren't supposed to get up.' Then she tipped her head back up towards the ceiling.

I collected the claws into the jewellery box and showed Grandma. 'What are these?'

She took the box and threw it at the mirror on her wardrobe door. The mirror smashed, pieces falling among the claws scattered across the floor once more. She tried to pry off a piece of mirror still stuck to the door. 'You need this,' she said. Her fingertips were sliced open, blood smearing the glass as she managed to pull it off. 'Here.'

She offered it to Mumma, point first, who realised just in time to step out of reach. 'Let's keep calm,' Mumma said warmly, now very much focused on Grandma.

Grandma swung the piece of mirror at me. 'Put it in the grass to blind the buzzards. It'll stop the buzzards taking the cats.'

I leaned back from the shard, seeing the reflection of the wet, black hole of house above us, and took the piece of glass carefully. I looked at Mumma.

'Loveday will throw it onto the grass,' she said. 'If you get back into bed.'

I held the shard, fingertips pressed hard to the glass, avoiding the edges.

Mumma wrapped Grandma's hands in a towel and settled her back into bed. With a flannel, I pried the remaining pieces of mirror off the wardrobe door and frisbeed them through the window to fall onto the grass below. Mumma picked the mug of broth up from the floor, flicked some black bits out of it, then handed it to Grandma.

'You're poisoning me.' Grandma coughed, spraying something yellow across her torso. Poor Grandma, she has gone mad, I thought, as Mumma half-retched and led me from the room. Mad, and a bit dangerous with it. No wonder Mumma can't trust her in public.

On the landing, I swallowed as Mumma closed Grandma's door firmly.

'Do you know about manifesting imaginations, Mumma? I read in a book the Batleigh tynx might be a collective visualisation.'

'The Batleigh tynx is an excuse for a bitter group of parochial fanatics to harass a loopy, old woman.' She smoothed her skirt and stroked my face, checking my pallor, taking me by the chin. 'Are you here? With me, Lowdy? Nice and real? With your fists, and your thoughts? You're not – self-suggesting? Not when, there's all that—' she gestured to the narrow attic stairs, voice petering out, '—to enjoy.'

'I am not self-suggesting. But you're absolutely sure there isn't a man-eating tynx on the loose?'

'Don't be a moron.' Mumma booped my nose with her finger. 'Last chance.'

'She wasn't a man-eater,' Grandma bellowed from inside her room. 'Eating one man, doesn't make you a man-eater.'

After her broth, Grandma slept, which was a huge relief.

⁂

I must have slept too. When I ran down to the kitchen for a drink of water, the musk of anti-bacterial spray caught in my throat, the sting of alcohol in my eyes. The kitchen gleamed, again. There was no sign of even a single cat, let alone dozens.

I turned the tap on, and Mumma called out, 'There is a drought.'

She was at the desk in the library, licking a finger and racing it through a wad of papers. She span around, and the chair squealed.

'We need to keep her topped up with broth. It's a detoxifying recipe.' She dropped the papers into a box on the floor. 'It's a bit grim. But pure nutrition. She's addicted to sugar and additives and red wine. She keeps wandering out of the house. God knows what might happen to her now she's so weak. She couldn't defend herself if—' Mumma spoke in her most matronly manner. 'She needs a cleanse. Her body has to be healthy, so it can focus.'

'If you're so worried, be nicer to her and stop locking her cats away.' I leaned my head against the door, careful to look weak and tired.

'Don't be taken in, darling. My mother doesn't care about you.'

Mumma leaned back taking a glass from the desk. She sighed, sadly. She had been drinking. 'I have told you she wouldn't even drive me to hospital when I was in labour.'

'She says she didn't know you were pregnant. Or that you'd had me. She says she found me in a cage.'

Mumma, taken aback by this suggestion, finished her drink in one go. 'Gosh,' she said, a little stunned. 'Golly gosh. Does that sound likely? Given how my life revolves around you? How everything I do, I do for you?'

'No,' I said, realising it didn't sound likely at all.

'I was in the woods, trying to survive contractions while she was in the zoo, euthanising Nella. Real pain, you know, it folds you up into tiny, individual parts. You can't multitask when you're in labour. You need someone to take care of you. You can't make good decisions. You can only be one tiny part of yourself, the part in pain.' Mumma ran the knuckles of one hand across her lips, watching me, concerned. 'Have I ever told you about my mother and the horse head?'

'No,' I said, as I always did when she asked this question. I slid down the door, suddenly fatigued, no energy to stand, lolling my head a little.

'She had no interest in me, my mother. But it was only the two of us, so I used to wait. Wait and wait. Outside the meat room. When I was older, I made daisy chains in the picnic grounds.' She rolled her eyes a little, something you might mistake for fondness. 'But when you're very young – it's so hard to wait, isn't it?'

I curled my hands into fists at my lap.

'There were these thuds, and scrapings. Oh, the curses. It was terrifying. I opened the door and she was sitting on the carcass of a shire horse like she was riding it. Wellies and dress covered with blood. Tugging a cleaver she'd wedged in its neck. She jumped up, lifted the cleaver above her head.' Mumma dropped her glass to the desk to lift her hands together above her head. 'She was so fit.' She slammed her hands down in front of her.

'Blood exploded, over the walls, the floor, the ceiling. She didn't notice. Just wiped her hair out of her eyes. I hated blood when I was little. She sprayed it everywhere, all over herself until, finally, she kicked the head away from the body. It slid across the floor and stopped right here.' She pointed to her feet and, also, beyond them to another place entirely.

'Its neck emptied itself into the gutter. You'd think I would have screamed. Its beautiful mane was matted with its own blood – and it looked out with one calm, brown eye. I knew that old horse. You saw it in the village sometimes. And she was splitting its stomach, filling buckets of entrails for the offal bin. After that she stood up, panting.' Mumma sank the rest of her drink, and laughed like a whip.

'When she saw me, she grinned and I screamed. Her teeth were so white in her red face. 'Would you like a go, Aster?' she asked me, offering me this cleaver that was almost the same size as I was.' Mumma stood, tossing her glass from hand to hand, running an eye over what was left on the desk, always thorough. 'I nearly passed out. She found me in the glasshouse. She'd hosed herself down until she was pink as a ballerina, and she offered me a piece of raw horse meat to eat.'

The details of this story never changed in all the times I had heard it. It might even have been true.

'She'd hide food for the cats, to keep them hunting. She let them out at night. She tried to keep them wild. They weren't pets, but they weren't wild either. They were something in between, which was awful.' Mumma turned off the light in the library.

I followed her into the hallway, dark from the sun setting on the other side of the house. She unlocked the kitchen.

'We left the day I found you in that cage. She told me it was for your own safety, because the cats were out. But I couldn't be a hundred percent sure she wasn't going to feed you to them. Imagine,' she frowned, hands folded neatly across her skirt, 'thinking your own mother is a monster. Because that is what Grandma is. I'll bet that horse she chopped up wasn't even ill, just cheap. You saw the condition she kept the cats in. It's inhumane. And now I have to get rid of them. Because of you. Because I can't risk your recovery.'

I had never heard this before.

'If I have to choose between you and Grandma, darling, I'll choose you. I promise, I will always choose you. That's why we're here. And it won't be long now. But you cannot trust a word Grandma says, and that's why, if you cannot stay away from Grandma, you will stay in the tower all day, because, for the very last time, there is no tynx. You must trust me.' Something occurred to her as she appraised me. 'Have you grown?' She dropped her hand from my face and looked at me askance.

'I don't think so,' I said, very light, very careful.

'No.' She sighed. 'Well, what can I make you to eat, darling? Is there anything you fancy?'

She raked her fingers through her hair, they caught in the tangle of it and she held them, stuck to her head like a huge pair of ears. Looking exactly like the batty old hag herself.

Mumma did not lock me in, which was either a gesture of trust, or she was drunk. Either way, I was so relieved that when I saw, from the balcony windows, in the half-light, poor, loopy Grandma in the deer park, crawling slowly into the trees on all fours. I didn't bother Mumma with it.

I didn't bother myself with it, either, I simply pretended I had not seen anything.

After all, it was quite dark, so at least possible I actually hadn't seen anything.

I cracked open the balcony doors for a little wind. There was a distant sound of thumping, barely louder than my own heartbeat, from somewhere along the valley.

I lay back, to rest and relax.

That Digger would never return made me feel hollow inside and raw on the outside, which was probably how real pleasure should feel.

Throughout the house, all the mouse pups seemed to wake and wail at the same time. I stood and thumped the low ceiling. Touching something real. Touching it hard.

I did not get carried away by my extravagant imagination. I was not in the fairy tale where a man could hear the grass grow, and I could not hear a nest of mice pups.

My scratch was not itching, throbbing, stinging or aching.

The animal wakes. It hears a noise. Loud. Low and thrusting. The noise lifts the animal's tail.

❧

It stalks the shadows of rocks along the lake shore. The lights – red, yellow, orange – flash in time with the pulse. It smells him, but the music is too loud. Its ears flick and flap. It paces, agitated. There are too many bodies at the party.

Then he appears, in the trees. He slides down a tree trunk, runs his hands through his hair. So salty, the animal can almost taste him.

The boy turns, and the animal hides its eyes. It lowers its nose, and whisks its tongue in and out of its claws.

When it opens its eyes again, someone puts their hands over the boy's face.

'Guess who.' The girl whickers and sticks out her tongue. Her tiny waist. Her long, oily black hair, so high.

The animal backs away, blood-hungry but tooth-shy.

DAY 5

LIKE A LITTLE bald Goldilocks, I stole perfect things by making them up. If my daydreams had been rightfully mine, I wouldn't need to. You don't need an imagination if you have everything you want.

The sun was high, the room boiling, even with the balcony doors wide open and I stole scents of deodorant, sugar, alcohol, sweat, excitement, before remembering it was not good for me to imagine the party I'd heard last night. It was not good to imagine it so precisely I could almost believe I was there. It confused things.

There were a couple of black, shiny nubs irritating the side of my breast. More ticks. Hooks caught in my skin. Barbed tongues buried inside me. My chest was getting bigger. It felt so different since we'd arrived in Batleigh, that for a moment I didn't recognise my own body. In the last five days, I was itchy and swollen and cross for absolutely no reason whatsoever. Perhaps the ticks were causing an infection. I pulled them out, wondering where they'd come from now the cats had gone. The pain was real, my nerves knew something was truly happening. I went to the balcony doors, and threw the ticks outside.

We had been to many doctors many times since I had turned sixteen, but the first doctor reassured us a normal delay in development often runs in families. 'Nothing around the chest,' he noted, marking a form. 'But have you been itchy at all? The pubis? Moody? No blemishes? Even a girl's voice should lower a little? You'd be getting even hairier.' I was weighed and encouraged to eat more. 'Talk to me about any changes. It's perfectly normal.' Mumma used words lifted from a book of cartoons about puberty the doctor had given her. I was not allowed to read it. Instead, in the books I read, all the girls were preoccupied with being married off to beasts, or besting evil stepmothers. When I had most recently seen a doctor, no one cared about my developmental delay, they were more concerned about my tail.

'Lowdy.' Mumma was on the stairs to the tower. 'Lowdy!

I pulled the balcony doors shut just before she entered the room – the door was unlocked, as she had promised. Everything was finally turning out as I'd hoped.

'Has Grandma been up here?' she said, eyes quickly taking in the room. She was neat – straightened – but for a piece of hair rainbowing from her head.

'No.' Everything was turning out as I'd hoped, and yet I was in a mutinous mood. Tired. Sad. Wouldn't she know, if Grandma was up here? Wouldn't she know, if only she didn't drink until she was comatose each night?

'This bloody, rotten house.' She went to the balcony doors, looked left, then right. 'At least it's clean again. Bunk in with me, join civilization on the first floor.' She pulled up a rug to inspect the floorboards beneath. 'There's a crack in the ceiling of the library. Have you seen Grandma?'

'No.' I kept the panic out of my voice, folded my arms across my chest, wishing I was wearing clothes, suddenly wanting to keep my attic room. Now my door was unlocked and I could move freely around it, the house itself was smaller than it had been. Mumma's hands were around it, squeezing the rooms together, but I could splurge up and out of my attic room, through the balcony doors, and onto the open hand of the zoo.

'Well, the crack wasn't there the other night,' she said. 'What are you doing up here?'

'I'm sleeping up here.'

'I'm not blaming you. I'm blaming the house.' I could tell she meant it because she picked at the stubble above my ear, gently, and without horror. 'That stupid balcony's collapsing, and it's pulling the tower down with it.'

'Maybe it's a ghost.' I was exhausted and defensive.

'There's no such thing as ghosts,' she said. 'And please stop helping yourself to the fridge. That salmon was for both of us. I can't find Grandma. Looking after her is more hassle than it's worth. The sooner she dies the better.' She caught the look on my face. 'I'm *joking*—' she said, looking very serious indeed.

'I don't even like salmon.' Or, I thought, any food.

'Well, who's eaten it all then?' she asked as she left the room.

'Grandma?' I shouted after her, dressing as I followed.

The interior doors of the house were unlocked. Cupboards and wardrobes were also opened. Chairs were pulled out from under desks and tables. Inconceivably small spaces were searched, as if Grandma might be Thumbelina-ing in a drawer or a jam pot, but she was not in the house.

'Grandma?' I was shouting when I found Mumma, her forehead against the window in the back door.

'All right then,' she said.

A huge, grey, furry body lay on the path outside.

⁂

The tynx was dead. It looked nothing like Nella in the pump house. The skin wasn't stuffed to bursting. It managed to be scraggy and skinny, but massive at the same time. Even I couldn't have made it up.

'What is this?' I said, following Mumma outside. 'Nella's dead. So what is this?'

The sun was in our eyes like we were being interrogated.

Mumma stopped, and put a hand out to stop me. 'Wait.'

We stood in the unkempt grass, looking at the body of the animal. The grey and black of its fur, its sandy nose and dirty gold eyes, its whiskers, the pink of its tongue falling over its brown, broken teeth. It was all vivid and shocking against the blanched day. Its stripes and markings weren't camouflaging it. It didn't belong there, in the dry grass of the petting pen. It belonged in a different place. Amongst trees and shadows and black snow and dark suns. It looked ill and very, very old. Its ribs were nocked, its muzzle covered with scars. Its hide was as stiff and unmoving as the granite watching us from across the valley. It had curled in on itself, faced the earth, like Beauty's Beast when his heart broke, but dew, not snow, rested upon its hairs. If I placed my body over it, like Beauty would, and whispered my love into its ear, might it revive? I thought.

Mumma dropped her hand. 'The tynx is dead.' Her whole body relaxed and she half-clapped her hands. 'Thank God, it's finally dead. We'll be left alone, now it's dead. There'll be no more incidents or sightings.' She reached out and squeezed my arm.

I looked at her, something in me had also died. There is a lot of lying in traditional tales. It rarely turns out well, not for the boys crying wolf, nor the stepmothers trying to cover up child murder with cannibalism.

'But there is no tynx,' I reminded her. 'Stop saying tynx, you said. There's only a bitter group of fanatics.'

'I was almost certain.' She spoke like I was a much younger child who needed to concentrate. 'I was almost certain there couldn't be a tynx. But Nella must have given birth.'

'What else are you almost certain about?' I asked. I had ignored Grandma, who had offered me everything she had, and believed Mumma, who always took everything away from me. 'Is this why you put me in a cupboard, again? Because you suspected Nella had given birth?'

'It's a bedroom, not a cupboard. It was only *ever* for your own good, darling,' Mumma said. 'I wish I didn't have to treat you like a child, but you wouldn't understand how complicated this is. Worrying about a tynx would have distracted you, when you need to get well. I couldn't have you excited about cats again. If you hadn't caused all those problems, we wouldn't even be here, having to handle this situation. But we have to get rid of this body, now. Ideally, we'd throw it in the mire, but we're never going to get it there without anyone noticing. Perhaps we can sink it in the river. We'll need to chop it into pieces, wrap them in a sheet and weigh them down—'

There was a noise inside the house. Someone was banging on the front door. Neither of us moved. We could only stare at the dead tynx on the grass.

Digger, I thought, he's back. I'll show him, I thought. I can show him this real dead tynx. Once it's out there and everyone's seen it, that's when it'll be over. That's when no one will ever come back.

'We can show everyone, then they'll know -,' I said, and Mumma clapped her hand over my mouth and shook her head.

'No one can see it,' she breathed. 'No one would believe this old thing made it into that house last night. Look at the state of it. They'll see *one* tynx and think there are more. Why would there only be *one* tynx?'

'Because there *is* only one tynx. Isn't there?'

'Of course—'

'It's Peter Carter, madam.' We heard shouting from around the side of the house. 'Half the kids on the moor saw your cat last night at a party down the reservoir. The park rangers are involved now, so you're going to have to be helpful.'

Mumma grabbed me by the shoulders. Breathed into my ear. 'Get it to the meat room - it's empty. If anyone sees it, Grandma'll be in real trouble. Go.'

'What trouble?' I said. 'Where are the cats? What about Grandma's breeding programme—'

But she leaped into the house and the next moment I heard her at the front door. I hoped she'd ask Peter Carter whether anyone had seen Grandma at the party last night.

'*Who did you say you were? As you can see, we don't keep pussy cats any more—*'

I am thirteen. I am not yet home-schooled. I am not yet trapped all day in a tower.

Some of the older boys say I am an animal. They laugh at my hair. I can't be a girl, they say. I don't look like one. They shout *Get a comb, Cousin It! Where are your drums, Animal?* because of my armpits, and my upper lip, and my legs – which look more and more like theirs – but they never notice the hair on my head. My incredibly long, shiny locks, black as a moonless night, as a fairy tale would say.

In the posters on the dormitory walls, the ones next to the beds of my thirteen-year-old friends, the names – Pamela Anderson, Madonna, Jessica Rabbit – appear to one side in large cursive, like signatures from a legal document. But while their hair is thick and healthy, like mine, their bodies are greasy, oiled. Plucked, like the women are waiting to be grilled.

'Don't be silly,' Mumma says, when I ask to use tweezers on my body. 'If you don't like it, don't look at it.'

Then, some older boys stop me one day when I am with someone from my class. They are friendly. 'Don't go to the little kids tonight. Meet us instead,' one of them says. 'Let's have a midnight feast.' He smiles and pushes my friend so he trips backwards.

Afterwards, the boy from my class doesn't think I should go, but he's been tripped up, so he's pretty cross. Boys my age seem young, so like children, so unlike the princes from fairy tales who inherit kingdoms and go on quests, nonetheless I like them.

I don't want to meet the older boys, but unfortunately one of them has pressed a folded piece of paper into my hand. A picture of a woman.

The older boys meet me in their common room. They look more at each other, than me. They seem nervous, excited, until a grinning boy appears, holding a plate of sausages at his waist.

'Meat,' one of them shouts.

'Hot dog?' the boy with the plate asks, politely. Then, he jabs his plate at me, not so politely. His trousers are unzipped. They slide down his thighs.

'What do you mean?' I am confused.

The boys laugh, but for a second I don't recognise it, disguised as a pale finger pointing at me from between the two cold sausages.

'Eat it,' one of them says. 'Animals love meat.'

'God,' says another when I don't move. 'I said this was a waste of time.'

No one laughs so much now, and I wish I had not come here.

The older boys want to know why I'm not eating the meat. They tell me they know what I get up to, in the dormitories at night, with the younger boys. They know I'm stealing their most precious belongings. They want to know why I do it, if I don't want the meat.

'I'll give them all back,' I say, wanting to return all the pictures. Wanting this moment to be over. 'I'm sorry.'

But they don't want them back. 'Keep them,' one of them says, and I know it is because the pictures are easily replaced.

A teacher arrives, stepping into the room, as if not expecting anyone to be there, even though he has been told what is happening by the child who witnessed the invitation earlier that day. The plate is dropped and the boy bends to hide himself and pull up his trousers, but the teacher realises something of what has happened.

'We aren't blaming her,' the head teacher tells my mother. 'But this was never intended as a school for girls. She shouldn't have been there. It was only a silly game, but this is why,' he says, 'the parents pay for a single sex environment.'

'Promise me you won't play with the boys anymore,' Mumma says. 'You are not allowed in the school, so if anyone sees you, we'd have to leave and then what would we do?'

I am thirteen and no one calls me animal again, because no one ever sees me again. I stay in our flat at the Temperance School for Boys earning more and more time out of the cupboard by getting less and less cross. By showing I can be trusted.

I suppose the boys think I'm at another school. If they ever think of me at all.

❧

The animal was very clearly dead. A sticky, white fluid had run from its eyes, gathering into stiff little balls next to its nose. It smelled of the woods, of mulch, but sweeter, more rotten. Even if it had been alive, it hadn't been healthy. But its length. The forehead alone was like a rugby ball. Legs like cricket bats. Even malnourished, the fur filled it out. Puffing up fur is one of a cat's survival tricks, making it look bigger and less vulnerable in front of a threat.

I knew it was dead, I knew Peter Carter could easily walk to the end of the house and look through the zoo gates. I knew it was important to hide it, quickly, for Grandma's sake, but still I moved towards it slowly, knees bent, ready to run.

I nudged its plush cushion of a paw with my foot. The paw lifted a little, then rolled back to the grass. I touched my foot to its belly, and flinched, just in case. Nothing happened. I touched it more firmly. Its belly, its ribs.

'*Are kids at a rave 'reliable witnesses' then?*' Mumma's voice drifted from the house.

Crickets sawed in the grass and blackbirds went off like alarms in the trees, as I stepped a foot either side of the animal and grabbed its chest, under its forelegs. Loose skin slid in my hands, so I hugged it tighter. I pulled it up. Its head lolled to its chest, its dry tongue onto my hand. It was the heaviest thing I had ever lifted. The land bore half the weight, as I staggered backwards, dragging it down the hill.

'*This is private property. If you don't leave I will call the police—*' Mumma's voice got fainter.

The forepaws to-ed and fro-ed like fluffy swings and the hind legs traced the lawn like the daintiest ballerina's. It was hot work on a hot day. The sweat in my palms made me feel like the tynx was salivating. Each time the animal slipped down, I squeezed harder, like I was resuscitating it.

By the time I reached the meat room, sweat ran off my head like water over a stone. I pushed the door open with my back and was grateful to be in the dark, out of the sun. The room was dim and stinking and empty of cats. The floor was smeared in faecal matter, crusting to dark peaks in places, and pierced with short hairs. There were a couple of dead bodies, perhaps they had died of dehydration or perhaps as prey, but either way they had been chewed apart, cannibalised. Only swatches of fur, here and there, remained. It was sad to see. I thought I might be sick. I dropped the tynx reluctantly, despite my aching arms.

The body slumped onto the floor, this time onto its back, two paws at its chest, back legs a diamond. It looked, like this, somehow familiar to me. Not quite like the picture Digger had given me, nor the photographs of Nella I'd found. It looked oddly like it was tucked up in bed, taking a little nap. A small snatch of cloth was trapped in the underside of one of its forepaws, hidden behind the pebbles of its pads. When I untangled it, I found a piece of ticking, exactly like Grandma's pyjamas.

'Grandma?' I half-said out loud, then felt very stupid indeed.

I looked for Grandma at the butterfly house. I called across the deer park and in the woods. She wasn't on the front drive, and she wasn't on the path along the river, or at the pump house where Nella still slumped, mad with death. The old zoo felt empty. But near the enclosure, on the river bank, not far from the platform in the tree where the big cats would have sunned themselves, was a collection of branches propped against each other for a tepee. A net woven with twigs and grass and leaves was thrown over the branches, blending it in with the trees. It hadn't been there yesterday.

'Grandma?' I said, but as I got closer, I recognised the cool air of the woods balancing on the same cheap, fruity cordial that lined the dormitories of the Temperance School for Boys when no one opened a window from one summer to the next. A sticky smell in the fluff of pockets and broken seams under the arms. It oozed down his neck and stewed behind his knees. It syruped in the shadow of each vertebra, pooled in the corners of his ears. Digger was in the hide.

The scab along my scratch tore apart and wept a little, thin and watery. I was light-headed. Breathing deeply. Staying calm. Staying real. I was perfectly composed, while rotting, breaking down inside bit by bit, with wet, acid anger. I fisted my hands, trying not to get caught up in a sticky clingfilm of rage.

Digger, whose father had promised he would never come back, had come back. Had he seen me moving the tynx? Would he tell his father? Would they return before we got rid of the body? How dare he?

'Your father said you weren't allowed back.' I tried to kick the pile of sticks, to have authority in my own zoo, but my leg shook. 'How long have you been here? Have you seen my grandmother?'

'No.' The tip of the wigwam shook as he moved. 'My Dad doesn't know I'm here.' His voice muffled by the structure. 'D'you like my hide?'

'Go away.' I kicked out again, for the hide to collapse on him, but it only wobbled. 'Or I'll tell my mother you're down here. There is no tynx.'

'It was at the party out at the reservoir last night,' his voice cracked high. 'Loads of people saw it,' he said, clearing his throat deeply. 'You look – nice—'

The dead tynx had not been at a party last night. It had obviously been dead in the petting pen for hours. It was so old and malnourished it was surely hardly able to walk, like Grandma, let alone walk very far.

'Lynx are shy,' I said. 'Read the old sign over there. It would never go near a party.'

'A'right, Ripley. Where's your alien?' The man standing further down the bank had tiny eyes in a face covered in what looked like mud. He was Mumma's age, perhaps, and made me nervous. A tight cap blunted his big head and he wore green fatigues. The jacket was buttoned to the neck even in the heat, like he'd rather be serious than comfortable. He took a packet from one of his pockets and slid out a cigarette. 'Fowl.' He called behind him.

A whale of a man, also in army trousers, also smeared with mud, rolled along the path, a clipboard of papers in front of him. Mustard-white hair trailed past his shoulders, and a peppery beard tapered to a sharp point threatening his chest.

'Ah, right,' Fowl said, noticing my bald head, then flicking through his notes. 'Ripley. I get it.' He had a crusty voice, slow but precise. He shucked his hair back with one hand, and wrote something. His grey T-shirt, black under the arms and tucked around his belly into his waist band, read I Get Better With Age.

Behind him, more men trickled down the path, dressed in fatigues, faces filthy. A breeze hit them and even from this distance I realised they weren't wearing mud, but scat.

I had never known any men. I had no father, being found under a bush - pulled from a mire - carved out of rock - depending on the day and how much Mumma had drunk. I had been home-schooled since I had stopped attending classes at thirteen. Of course, there had been teachers, ticket collectors, shop assistants, people on the street, boys lying asleep in musty dormitory rows, plates of sausages - and Digger now. But they weren't proper men as I imagined them. When you imagine a dog, you don't imagine its end, or its beginning. You imagine the dog in the middle. The dog, itself. I had never known any men, and now a dozen came along, faces covered in something's crap.

'Talking to yourself?' The first man asked, checking for someone else as smoke fogged his face.

A bird chinked, anxious and invisible, above us. I imagined Grandma crawling from the trees covered in mud and leaves again, but this time in front of these strangers.

'This is private property.' I marched at the first man, looking him in the eye, like Grandma told me. Like an equal. So he would respect me and leave. 'You can't be here.'

'Calm down, sweetheart. *You* shouldn't be here. Here be monsters.' Fowl laughed, beard lifting like it was coyly exposing something. 'And you're a tasty treat. Right, Denny?'

I wished I was wearing more than shorts and a vest, wished Mumma knew where I was.

The other man, Denny, looked at the old enclosure. He wandered around me, towards it. 'No.' I shooed and clapped him like Mumma had the cats. 'Go.'

The men behind him laughed, but they turned back the way they'd come.

Digger lunged from the hide. He slid on some leaves but didn't let it slow him down. It was the fastest I had seen him move.

'You shouldn't be here. Go back.' Digger was in Denny's way. 'Did you let the cats out?' Digger seemed taller when he wasn't shrugging or swaggering or making jokes and ruining everything.

'There are signs everywhere,' I said, holding my scratch together. It was pulling apart. I would drain out through my own hole. 'Go awa—'

But Fowl held up a hand to stop me, and addressed Digger. 'What cats?' said Fowl.

'Old Mrs Cat's cats, day before yesterday? From a shed down there.'

The men looked to where he pointed, at the line of rhododendrons, beyond which was the meat-room and a dead tynx.

'This is private property.' I squeaked. 'Go away- '

'Who're you?' Denny spoke over me, pointing his cigarette at Digger. 'And who is she?' He pointed the cigarette at me. 'Who's Old Mrs Cat? And what,' he said, pointing towards the trees, meat-room and dead tynx, 'is in a shed down there, mate?'

'It's private.' Digger's voice subsided, not threatening, more factual. 'This whole place is private.'

'You're trespassing,' I said.

'I'm a saviour.' Denny tapped his cigarette into the undergrowth. 'I've got enough tranquilisers to bring down an elephant. So when we find this tynx- ' he took a long drag on his cigarette, ' –it's mine, and I'm gonna have a photo like this.' His fingers made a pitchfork, ash from his cigarette dropping onto the dry leaves. 'That's what'll be in the papers next time. Its head in my hand.' He shook the crook of his fingers at me, trying not to raise his voice.

'It doesn't exist.' I pretended I was Mumma.

'Alright Scully, then what did I see at the reservoir last night? When I find it, I'll be on the TV and in The Sun. They'll make a film of me. And I'll sell it to a museum. Or, I'll make it into a rug. I'll be a household name. It's a big deal.'

Dread settled like the smoke around me.

'You wouldn't get close,' I said, not wanting Denny near the zoo, or the tynx, even if it didn't exist. 'All cats are stealthy. A domestic cat can wait for an hour to catch a mouse. Even a lynx can see a mouse 250 feet away,' I cleared my throat, wanting to pop my windpipe back open. '250 feet away, in the dark.'

'I'm not a mouse.' Denny lowered his head like it had a horn on it.

'And a tynx,' I said, 'is not a lynx.

'Jesus.' Denny stuck a finger in his ear and shook his head. 'Lower your voice or you'll upset the dogs.'

'If it is a tynx. After all,' Fowl said, 'does a tynx even exist?'

'Go away.' I pushed the air, showing them what to do. 'Go away. Go away.'

'What else would it be?' Digger hawked the words out.

'I'll tell my mother—'

'Calm down, calm down. We're going,' Fowl said, not looking at me. 'Could be an alien,' he told Digger. 'Could be prehistoric. Could be a thoughtform. Gotta bunch of ley lines around here.' He took a blue leaflet from his clipboard. 'There's even a hideous demon that takes the form of a cat. Very nasty piece of work. So all we can say conclusively, at this point, is that it is a mystery cat. I'd know. I've written a book on 'em.' He handed the leaflet to Digger, and nodded towards the moor. 'You hear anything, leave a note behind the bar at The Crown.' He walked up the path, kicking a sapling aside, crushing hearts of pennywort to nudge through the leaves with his foot.

Denny somehow managed to look down on Digger, even though they were the same height. 'We'll be tracking it at the reservoir tonight. Show us around if you want, little man.' Denny went to ruffle Digger's hair, and laughed as Digger ducked away.

'Trespassers.' I looked Denny in the eye. I did not babble. I tried to stop my chest pumping in and out, then I caught the smell of scat again. 'You stink.'

'Charming.' Denny dropped his cigarette stub and brought a solid boot down on it softly, holding my eye. 'See you around, little man,' he said, without looking at Digger.

Digger, too, was trespassing, but that didn't seem important to him, or me, anymore. The men had gone and so had my hatred for Digger. It had dropped away, thick and heavily like my hair had. I was high as a crop-top because Digger had defended me. He had fought his way through brambles. He had offered me a glass slipper. He had woken me with a kiss.

He watched the men go. Sunlight caught him through the leaves. It moved here and there as he read the leaflet, illuminating him in small parts, like he was made of gold pieces.

'"The Cryptoscience Institute is a non-profit organization dedicated to improving education and research into rare and undiscovered species",' he read aloud. '"We are a global network of professional naturalists choosing to work outside a restrictive academic structure. We conduct our research in the field, achieve incredible results and are well-qualified to provide plenty of evidence for the existence of many unacknowledged species. For more information on the amazing discoveries the world does not want you to know about, you can buy* *the following books - Deathworm and Friends—'* he pulled his face back into his neck with disgust. 'Dickhead and Friends.'

He screwed up the leaflet and shoved it at me. The print on the leaflet was faint, like the photocopier had run out of ink. Where the paper was folded the words disappeared through the cracks completely. There were sketches of the Loch Ness Monster, the Yeti, a fish with a head and a thing like a goat with wings. On the other side were smaller pictures - a humanoid with a lizard's head and a large black cat with red eyes, and the list of books, *Deathworm and Friends, The Complete Land-fish, Mandible Men Diaries* 1 *&* 2 and *British Lions and British Tigers and British Bears, Oh My!*

'Oh. You gave this book - to me—' I said, gently and softly, realising something strong and vigorous. He really liked me.

'Shit,' he said, over me. 'Now they know the zoo's here.' He looked low into the understory along the path, rubbing his hands over his dried lips.

'But everyone knows the zoo's here. They won't come back because they'd be trespassing.' I used Mumma's reassuring tone, pleased to give him something in return for his affection.

'They won't *care*.' He mumbled at the ground. 'They'll know the tynx is drawn to old pheromones here.' He picked a fern, running his fingers along its stem.

'There is no tynx.' I didn't want him to be right. I didn't want them coming back before we'd got rid of the body. I didn't want Grandma to get into trouble. 'Pheromones don't last twenty years anyway. Perhaps they did see an alien. Or something prehistoric.'

'It was the tynx. There's nothing prehistoric about the *nineties*.' He tore the frond into blades, threw them to the ground.

'Yes,' I said. 'Nothing. Except Komodo dragons. And tapirs. And horseshoe crabs. And giant salamanders—'

'They can't find it before me. I spent over half an hour building that hide.'

I wanted Digger to give me his quartered orange of a smile, but suddenly nothing seemed 'classic'. The fern he'd torn was strewn in pieces at my feet.

He followed after the men, stamping up the path like he was splashing in puddles. 'Don't let them come back. Don't tell anyone about the hide,' he called to me. He clipped his elbow on a trunk, but there were no jokes about who'd put the tree there. 'Wanker,' he yelled at it, and then he was gone.

Digger, I wanted to shout. *Dig-urgh*. To summon him was to push and moan at the same time.

There was another body wrapped inside mine, swelling up, ready to split each smiling end of my scratch and tear my old skin open. To drop it, and see it bunch around my ankles on the ground, so the other body could step out. The other body could hear and see and smell better than mine. The other body always knew golden Digger was there before I did.

Of course, I thought, in the fairy tales love often requires a different body.

'*Lowdy?*' Mumma shouted, faintly, from up the hill, inside the house, where she had obviously finished telling her most recent lies.

<hr />

Mumma leaned out of the back door like she was on a boat, one hand clutching the house.

'There you are,' she said. 'Why has it taken so long? Quickly, come inside.'

Dried bits of fur and feathers and bones and cat scat outside the back door were shrinking in the sun, getting smaller until they would eventually be dust to kick away.

'Is it in the meat room?' Mumma said. 'Is it hidden? Did you shut the door properly? Do we need to barricade it until we can think of what to do?'

'Go and have a look,' I told Mumma, my voice sharp and stinging as sherbet. 'Now there's nothing to worry about outside.'

Mumma stepped back, into the shade of the house, and folded her arms.

'I'm not a wicked witch, Lowdy. If it wasn't for you, I wouldn't be here to have people harassing me. Bringing up my childhood. Reminding me of the worst time of my life.'

'Where,' I said, 'is Grandma?'

'Don't know.' She was brusque, trying to bounce me into good behaviour. 'Come in. Let's have breakfast—'

'We have to find Grandma.' The sun, high now, cooked my head like an egg. Sweat ran like melted butter.

'Of course, you're cross,' Mumma said, looking me in the eye. 'But I didn't *know* there was a tynx. Grandma's obsessed with the past. If it hadn't been true, and the tynx had been a symptom of her illness, I'd have frightened you for nothing. And it probably was partly the illness, even though it turned out to be sort of true.'

'It was completely true. And now Grandma is missing, so we need to call the police.'

'Let's play grown-ups, Loveday,' she said, as if she wouldn't have preferred me sucking a thumb and hanging off her every word. 'Grandma's fine. We'll keep an eye out, but she's gone for a walk or something. Remember, last week she didn't have anyone keeping an eye on her. She's used to her independence, and now we're under her feet. She needed some space. She's a fierce old girl. She'd want you to come inside, and rest.'

I felt faint, nauseated by Mumma. Grandma could hardly walk. She didn't need space. She wanted me planning a new zoo with her. She would be devastated by the death of her tynx. I took a step to steady myself.

'You told me yesterday she was weak,' I said.

'I didn't mean *weak* weak. I meant a different sort of weak. A word can mean more than one thing, you know? You're too young to understand.'

'Why don't you care about her?' I said.

'Oh, families are a nightmare. Everyone has their ups and downs.

Come inside.' Mumma reached her hands out, but still didn't step outside. 'At least come and have something to drink. It's so hot. I'm worried about you.'

Everything Mumma said seemed weird and contradictory now, but the soles of my feet were desperate for the cool hallway, the chilled kitchen flagstones. I hadn't slept properly in days. I was dehydrated after a long morning in the heat. Bewildered by my head rolling thoughts like dice.

As soon as I stepped into the house, Mumma locked the door behind me. She checked both ways out of the window and then stopped, catching my look.

'Didn't you hear the man at the door? The village is out for our blood. We've got to be careful. You don't want to get Grandma into more trouble. Stay inside.' She tugged me down to the kitchen. 'It's broth I'm afraid.' She grinned horridly, opening the fridge, to show me an empty, bloodied plate. 'I'd been saving the steak. It was for both of us, not just you. If you want something to eat, I'd prefer you not to skulk about stealing it.'

I didn't know what she was talking about, and didn't care.

She took a bottle of brown liquid from the fridge. 'We won't bother heating it,' she said, pouring it into a large glass, tapping the glass with one nail. Sediment drifted through the dingy water. 'This will perk you up.' She offered it to me.

It smelt like algae and rotting fish. 'No, thank you.'

Behind Mumma, the phone mounted on the kitchen wall rang, but she didn't answer it. The coils of wire hanging from the handset quivered like a tail, as she stared at me, turning redder and redder, speaking louder and louder over the noise, telling me she was impressed with how I'd handled a tricky day. How the broth would make me stronger. How Grandma was loopy from the drugs, the illness, the rotten house. How when she was younger, she had thought Grandma wonderful, but then she realised she was wrong. How Grandma is a mad, sad woman who could do with some fresh air. How I must understand, however, that it was important for *me* to stay inside. How I still didn't know *my* way about. How the mires lay in wait, harmless for decades, only to suck people down when they least expected it. How good it was, at last, to trust me. That I was almost well again, that I needed to hold on for a little longer.

'Now the tynx is dead, this will all blow over. No one's going to turn up here again.'

The broth made my eyes sweat and my armpits weep but eventually I was too tired and hungry to resist her.

☘

I woke with my head on the kitchen table feeling fantastic. Or, at least, more fantastic than I had been. Feelings are all relative, Mumma always said. The broth really must have been pure nutrition, I thought, sitting up.

Outside the kitchen window the sun was running away from the zoo, sky red and out of breath. It was early evening and whether it was the broth, or the nap, I was full of energy.

Grandma was not back in her room. She was not in Mumma's room, or in my room. The other rooms were locked again, except the library where Mumma was working, two air rifles propped against the desk beside her. She drank slowly, steadily, sifting through papers, assuming I was asleep.

Why, I wondered, did Grandma and Mumma hate each other? Would I, too, consider Mumma mad and sad in future?

I threw my plimsolls off the balcony, and followed them, treading lightly, avoiding the square orange spotlight falling from the library window. I ran into the trees, to the dark enclosure, whispering Grandma's name, worrying she might need help with a collective visualization, especially as she might have no idea it was a collective visualisation. Whereas I felt fully qualified to handle a collective visualisation.

The sun was low, the river a bronze ribbon. Midges wisped above it like smoke.

There was no sign of Grandma, but circling Digger's hide were large, shallow cups of dust. Paw prints. They stopped at the river. I hadn't noticed them earlier, and Digger hadn't pointed them out. They were so obvious, Denny and Fowl would have said something if they'd seen them. They were fresh, made recently.

I scanned the ground, looking for more, when, on the path to the moor, there was a movement. The sun caught me in the eyes, and I thought there was a grey figure watching from the trees. Even as I tried to understand what I was looking at, it was gone – dropped low, loping through the trees on all fours. It might have been a woman, I thought. Its skin mottled as stone from some awful disease. Or age. Was it Grandma, pyjamas now hanging grubby, greying her body? Was it a deer, dappled? Or was it bigger than that?

'Grandma?' The river shot past me. The grey flashed ahead. I sprinted up the hill, but the woods were striped and full of rocks. Every time I stopped, chest straining, thinking I'd found her – resting, taking a moment's breath in a glade – I was staring at a granite boulder, or a fallen tree. Then, I'd catch sight of something else out of the corner of my eye and follow again. As the light dwindled, I ducked twigs, parted waves of bilious ferns, trying to keep up but stay quiet. Hidden from whatever it was. Because could it really be Grandma, when she could hardly walk?

༄

At the edge of the woods, the path stopped and the high moor tumbled out and up in the soft, cloudless evening. In the distance, the tor was a pile of grey boxes. Long grass twilled over the hills curling into dancer's buns, pinned by its own midsummer weight.

I stopped, looked behind me. Surely Grandma could not have made it this far? But then there was another movement, out on the moor.

I crossed a cattle grid, bent low. 'Grandma?' I whispered, but I had mistaken her for a large lamb calling for its mothers.

I hid behind trees, crouched in shrubs and flat to boulders. I cut across the moor, following smells and sounds, checking under foot for the grass becoming too mushy, like a mire, hoping for another sight of the grey thing I had chased, until I came to the black satin of the reservoir. The dark shapes of trees were figures leaning, waiting, stirring in the lowland breeze, roots in the water like hands in gathered sleeves.

A path wound thin around the edge. The night was playing games. The sky was navy and calm but hunters watched between the rocks, beneath the gorse. It was the men tracking the mystery cat. Liverworts dried out, tart and smelly, with the low water, but stronger than that, the stench of faeces hovered like BO. I avoided clouds of bracken where torches poked out to pass secret messages. Where the slim end of a rifle nudged grass aside, and the moon glinted on the metal of a trap like a winking eye.

Grandma would not be with them. She would not be with anyone.

Digger was at the edge of the water, folded into the bracken, hiding, like me. I was perfectly concealed, but Digger was too big for small spaces. His T-shirt stretched thin across his broad shoulders. I barrelled my back out, to be like him, but my T-shirt was still large around me.

I liked spending time with people when they didn't know I was there. When they thought they were alone. Know someone alone – like when they were asleep, when they didn't realise they were moaning and breaking wind – and you knew them better than they knew themselves. Loving must be watching, when there is no other way to have it.

Three men with smeared faces led a sheep to a flat patch of grass. It darted forwards, backwards, bleating. They hammered a stake into the ground and left it tied there. They retreated a distance, settling in the grass to watch it circling, calling pointlessly into the night.

I watched the men in the grass, covered in excrement to disguise their smell. For thousands of years, the caves of Lascaux proved, people have pretended to be animals. Because to understand how an animal lives, is to understand how best to hunt it. But these hunters already thought they knew how best to hunt it. It hadn't occurred to them that although they had masked their own scent with cow or sheep, any tynx probably wouldn't be keen on killing a sheep surrounded by a herd of cows or flock of sheep, any more than it would have been keen to kill a sheep surrounded by humans.

It had not occurred to the hunters, no animal is only its body. But they all had bodies, surely they should know? And to be a tynx was to be the only one of its kind. To be entirely alone. If it *had* existed, anyone wanting to catch it might fare best pretending to be a mate. Instead, these hunters had tried basic fairy tale cunning, and as Mumma would say, 'there's no point setting an empty pot beneath a chimney and hoping something will drop in.'

Up the hill, a torch signalled to someone at the party ground.

A few seconds later, the reply came from a torch elsewhere.

A whistling owl fell over our heads in a pair of spread hands.

Something crashed into the water a few metres beyond us.

'Shit,' shouted Fowl.

'Shit,' Digger said quietly, to nobody.

Lights appeared close to us on the path. They moved towards the water. There was a sudden splash, then silence.

In his pocket, Digger's pager gave a delicate, muffled beep.

'Shit.' Denny shouted. Something darted from the reservoir. Squat and low, it raced from the exposed shoreline towards the trees.

'Shit.' Digger stood trying to see.

'Digger?' A girl whispered from beyond Digger. She rose from the grass, the girl with dark hair who could have been me. 'Digger?'

'Eh, who's there?' Fowl's torch flickered across me. I ducked lower.

'*Sh*, Caitlin,' Digger growled.

Denny ran after the animal, his torch swinging madly, hitting trees – bark – grass – a wide face – yellow eyes – as he ran in the wrong direction.

This time I stood. It's Bastet, I thought. It's a cat-shaped demon. It was definitely not Grandma.

'Digger?' whispered the girl, loudly. 'What's going on? Who's that?'

'Eh, who's there?' Fowl's torch flickered across me. 'Eh.' He shouted. 'Eh?'

But I ran. Without thinking. Up the hill, away from the terrifying face.

Fowl called behind me. 'It's kids, Den.'

As I ran, from the corner of my eye, there was black movement. 'It's kids,' Fowl shouted again.

꧅

I was fast, but the thing was faster, coming after me. To one side, trees must have hissed and clicked as it hit them, fast but light. It was all drowned out by a white noise of fear. It caught up, coming closer the faster I ran, until it was abreast of me – so quick, it seemed slow.

Then I left the tree line.

I was on the edge of the high moor. Nowhere to hide. Nothing but the black stack of the tor ahead. I turned circles, trying to guess where the creature might come from next. But nothing streaked out after me. Only Digger panting, jogged up. Camera pounding against him hard as my heart.

'Shit.' He breathed. 'I thought they were following. But they went after the badger.'

'What badger?' I watched for eyes everywhere, anywhere.

'Back there.' He turned to the reservoir.

'So what's in the trees?' I whispered.

'Nothing. It was a badger. At the reservoir.'

'I've got to go. She's not here. She can't be all the way out here.' I was disorientated. Woozy from being outside too long, in air so rich. I was dizzy, looking for the security of walls at the edge of the moor, wanting to find cloisters and buildings penning me in, but there was nothing in every direction.

'Who's out here?' Digger said. 'Where did you come from?'

Had I imagined the thing in the trees? Sometimes, if you're expecting to see something, you see it, and you can see nothing else. I'd forgotten thoughtforms and collective visualisations. 'I need to find my Grandma.' I reminded myself of the real thing, of my own fists and my own head. 'She's fine. She needs space.'

'What?'

How, I thought, shuddering, will I get home safely? What might follow me in the dark? 'I don't know my way,' I said. 'What if I wander onto the mires?'

'What are you talking about?' Digger said. 'The Vaults are miles away.'

'The fog,' I said. 'There might be a fog coming.'

'But there's a drought on. It's been in the news how hot it is. There's never going to be a fog.'

Below the hill, tiny lights clung to the reservoir, and I silently cursed Mumma. I knew the way I'd come, and I knew exactly where the Vaults were – there was part of an ordnance survey map glued into my bog bodies project. I knew that you needed moisture for fog. There was no way I'd end up in the mires. Why did Mumma always have me doubting myself?

'The tynx won't come now,' Digger said. 'Not with all that noise.'

An owl yodelled. Digger stepped near and the land smelt of cooling earth. Bark was softening, releasing arid tension and I was out of breath. Fevered blood rushed to remote parts of me, I was swelling everywhere inside. In my other body.

'Are you doing A Levels?' I said. 'Have you always lived here? Did you know it's a myth that hair grows after death? Did you know there are trees on the moor 500 years old? Do you think it's true that bodies of prehistoric human sacrifices could be perfectly preserved in Vault Mires? Have you ever heard of thoughtforms – ?' I pressed on my scratch so it didn't explode, feeling stretchy and yielding as Digger peeled his rucksack from one shoulder then the other like he was turning the page of a delicate book. I was weirdly aware of every slight and sly movement of him.

In fairy tales, suitors were not often chosen. Couples were usually thrown together by chance and circumstance. Given our very particular circumstances, I could kiss Digger - comfort him, like Mumma did when she kissed the littlest boys goodnight, except I would not gargle with salt afterwards. He could lean me back, my phantom hair swinging below us. I could reach forward over our yellow toes, close my eyes as they did in the illustrations-

There was a slow moan.

'Shit,' Digger lowered his voice. He'd heard it too. 'Shit.' He moved backwards. Back towards Denny and Fowl.

A great dark mass shifted in the grass. I lowered myself quietly into the bedstraw. Digger backed further and further away, torch light flickering, camera drumming his chest.

I caught the scent of dry grass and manure. A herd of ponies grazed on close by. They turned plank faces to us, ears flicking. Probably, I thought, they had been the gallop in the trees - sounding lighter than you'd think - probably, they were the strange creature I'd seen.

'Ponies,' Digger called. 'Those are ponies.'

He jogged to me again and the herd trotted away, ghosting in and out of their own shadows, black manes and tails bobbing.

The shape in the grass lumbered up to follow, white patches luminous under the moon, then stopped. It flicked its tail, looked to its rump, and urinated. Its belly spread out horizontally, too far, like it was bloated. It urinated again.

'Is it ill?' I whispered.

'Definitely,' Digger said, not whispering.

The pony bent one way then the other to its flank, losing fluid from its rump.

Digger went closer. It tried to avoid him, but it was too heavy, in too much pain. He crouched, putting his camera between him and the mare's lifted tail.

The pony nosed at the grass, before dropping to its forelegs, panting and rolling stiffly onto its back. It tautened its shining, wet legs, and threw its nose back, grunting, to see its rump. In the camera flash, there was a white glistening promise under the tail. The pony startled at the light. It shuddered as head and forelegs appeared through the split with slippery force. The pony dragged the ground with its hooves, like it didn't want the foal out.

'Stop it.' I didn't want to see, but Digger's camera flashed again.

The pony lay, pushing the foal out weakly. Small hips slid through. The glairy sack was ripped. Fluid spilt. The foal's coat stuck in wet clumps, half-in, half-out of its sack.

There was a sudden yawn inside my belly. A hurricane had opened up in the middle of me, trying to drag everything into it. Feeding the foal straight into my hole, sack and all, would close it.

Both animals flinched, lit up white with flash yet again. The light sharpened the mild grass. It should have been tender, cupped around the ponies, but flashed metallic and spiky.

'Please.' I looked at Digger, watching from behind the camera. 'Stop showing me it. Stop it.' I took the camera.

'Get off—' He elbowed away from me.

The foal squeaked. It sounded sating and filling. It sounded juicy and satisfying.

It collapsed, nudging its nose over its mother's hindleg. The mare brought its head to its rump and they met there, nose to nose, for the first time, nostrils flaring.

I licked my lips.

The camera caught their four large, black, frightened eyes again. The foal's coat dried into tufts in the warm breeze. Ropy ligaments and tender protein.

The mare twitched its rump where bloodied afterbirth swung. Tendons catching between teeth.

It dropped its nose to push the foal to sit, but its long legs cycled through the grass helplessly. Sweet marrow and salty blood, iron-rich and satisfying.

The mare tapped the foal's breast, urgently, and trotted as Digger's camera flashed and flashed and flashed. I backed away. I was never hungry. I never felt like this.

The foal came to its forelegs, swayed. It shuffled sideways, crossing its feet accidentally, yolk still in its ears, wobbling after its mother. The mare didn't look back. I couldn't watch. I didn't want to know if the foal would be left, not able to catch up with the mare now Digger's camera had scared her away. I didn't know what I might do to it.

'At least I got some photos of it.' Digger crawled after them, camera still flashing. 'I might be able to use them. The others were only chasing badgers. They won't see anything. They don't know what they're doing. They'll think the ponies are the tynx.'

'*Digger?*' Caitlin called from somewhere in the trees.

'Sh,' Digger rasped.

'There is no tynx,' I yelled, running as fast as I could from the foal, and anything else.

❧

In the easing temperature of the night, the house smelt like a bog. Broth simmered on the hob in the kitchen, but my intense hunger had entirely gone.

The library was an inferno. The pad of my feet echoed in the room. Mumma had removed the paintings and desk in preparation, I supposed, for the room being redecorated after the leak. A fire lapped in the grate, feeding on a pile of paper. Mumma turned her head slowly, one arm resting across her torso, the other on a cocked hip. She didn't seem worried, her hand wheeled a tumbler of melting ice about the air. If anything, she was celebrating.

'Let's stop flushing the toilets,' she said. 'Unless we really need to.' She rang the ice cubes in her glass like a bell. 'We need to conserve water for essentials.'

There was a symmetrical pile of her tailored navy and black clothing folded at her feet. Her underwear was foxglove pink. It balanced lightly at her shoulders and hips, reluctant to touch her. One strap drifted down her arm. She vigorously poked some ticking stripe pyjamas deeper into the fire like she was trying to destroy evidence of a crime.

'Why are you burning Grandma's pyjamas?'

'Lice. We should burn everything. It's all infested.' She looked up. 'I thought you were in bed.'

'I had a nightmare,' I said to her rosy profile, trying to sound light as sweat ran down my nose. I went to the window and caught myself in the dark reflection, head shining like a silver coin.

'We'll get the tower checked for mould. It sends people mad. Let's sleep in here. It's nice and warm.' She wrapped her soft skin around mine, my damp body darkening her light silk. We used to sleep in the same bed. When I was a child, I wouldn't be parted from her, and she worried about me having nightmares, suffering, as she had, from nightmares herself as a child. But now I didn't like the idea of waking pressed against the mattress by her arm again.

'I do nothing but dream when I'm here.' She brushed a phantom hair from my forehead. Beneath the gin she smelt of chalky talcum powder. 'When I was small, I dreamed of huge fleas. Brown and shiny. Scurrying under my door, clicking and clacking around the frame, through the cracks in the floorboards, until they were every-where. I tried to cross a carpet of them, hopping and nipping at me. I couldn't balance on their backs.'

She leaned back. 'It was like slipping on marbles. And if I ever reached the door to call for help, I'd open my mouth but all I could do was growl, and then they'd jump in.' She crawled on her hands and knees, to throw more paper onto the fire as it bucked and spat.

'When I came around – properly awake, you know – I'd often be lying in the doorway of my room. So I'd try to find her, my mother, but when I came downstairs I could still hear the clicking, so I would run outside. To the enclosure. The lynx were always awake at night. They seemed so pleased to see me. When I was disorientated and half-asleep, I thought Koshka must be my mother. As she cuddled into me, I thought she was my mother turned into a lynx at night. But, of course, she was probably in here.' She nodded at the desk. 'Typing, typing, typing – God knows what – on her typewriter.' She swung her head, accepting this again, all these years later, her voice low and fast. 'When I interrupted her work during the day, she slammed her hand on her desk. *Out. Now.* She'd be typing again before I'd left the room.'

I had heard this story so many times I could tell it myself.

'Little children can be very trying.' She turned to the fire. 'Eventually, each night I'd wait until the coast was clear and go out, to sleep in the enclosure.' Her lips widened, in memory of a smile. 'My mother was always busy prepping in the meat room first thing so I'd creep back inside. She never even noticed. I shouldn't be bitter. I might never see her again.'

'You told me she was fine,' I said. 'You said she'd gone for a walk.'

'Yes, darling. You mustn't worry. After all, if she had wandered into a mire, it would be a quicker way to go, wouldn't it? Less painful for her?'

She pinched a piece of ash from the eyelash trim of her camisole, and noticed a splash of blood near the hem. She looked up at me. 'Time of the month,' she said, like it was a joke, then threw her own skirt on to the fire.

The woods are dark fur. But, the boy's not here. He's not here, but he was here. He's a sharp tang on the tongue. He's gold breath in the lungs. The animal turns. How did it miss him? He was here.

Branches dragged from the trees lean on each other. Beech, against ash, against oak, made into a new tree. The animal jumps on and slips off. It jumps again. It jumps again and something gives way. The new tree collapses because there was nothing to it. The animal steps on the new tree and the branches roll on the ground unsteadily.

⁂

On the moor, the animal turns from the stone faces. An ancient hum shivers in tussocks of grass.

Something smells good. Fresh and tender.

The foal can't run. It can barely walk. It doesn't struggle. It is too surprised when its thin neck cracks.

The animal's nose is bloodied and then it is done. But there is no muscle to the foal. And the animal has no appetite anyway. It leaves it for the rats.

Somewhere a mother honks with pain.

DAY 6

DAWN WAS BREATHLESS and flattened. The moor bandaged in hot, tight clouds.

I lay on the balcony, staring at the sky. My body was a pulse, stomach churning thick. I knuckled my head a little, naked, shattered, confused. I burped. My tongue tasted of metal like I'd eaten something unpleasant and in one corner of my mouth, my teeth ached. I ran a long nail between them and pulled out something tough and stringy and white. I flicked it away, and felt better without it sitting there, hidden at the back of my throat. Whatever it was.

I rolled over and screamed.

There was the carcass of a foal on the balcony floor. Although, it was more like a spider with its legs hanging long either side, and ribs raised like fangs and palps in the middle. It was covered in flies. There was nothing left of its own in the cavity, only bits of meat rotting in slick rainbows. Below the body was a black stain of blood on the wood. The neck was an empty balloon, deflated and half-severed from the body, but its head still hunkered over its knees, like it had an instinct to protect itself, even at the end. The hooves were pristine, like they'd hardly known ground beneath them.

I pushed it away from me until it hit the balustrade, then I picked it up and rolled it over the side. It dropped to the ground, startling a tynx in the deer park.

Except the tynx was dead and in the meat room.

It was grey, and then it was gone. Into the trees. Before I could properly see it.

'Something's in the zoo.' I ran through the house pulling on clothes. 'In the woods.'

'Stay inside,' Mumma appeared on the landing wrapping up her dressing gown. She was thick-eyed and hoarse-throated.

The back door was locked, so I passed her again as she descended the stairs.

'Stay out of the library,' she called firmly, as I ran into the library.

'It's a tynx,' I shouted, opening a window, climbing onto the sill. 'It's another tynx—'

'It's not another tynx.' She swiped for my shoulder. 'But do not go outside.'

'We've got to catch it before they do,' I said, feet hitting the grass. 'For Grandma.'

'I said no, Lowdy. It's dangerous.' She hit the window frame, trying to scare me. 'Get back in.'

I ran down the deer park, and ducked into the trees where there was the sound of the river, the frenzied kissing of leaves, but also a grunting in the enclosure.

Whatever it was, I had no way of catching it. Nothing to tempt it to the meat room with. No way of approaching it safely. Nothing to defend myself with – no stick, no trick, no quick, cruel insult it would understand. I could only pray that Grandma, not Mumma, was right. That this tynx would recognise me, as family.

I ducked low, but when I came close I straightened up. There was no need to hide from the grey thing, soil-mussed as the cats we'd rounded up, turning in circles beneath the sunning platform. Her hair had collected into thick, dirty bedstraw. Her skin was the colour of my worst mood, my wrongest day. Her pyjamas were torn and stained almost as if mouldy. Grandma did not look good. How could I have mistaken her for a tynx?

'What happened?' She scrabbled at my shins to stand. 'You left me on the Vaults.'

'You went for a walk, Grandma.' I pulled her up, but her legs weren't strong. She rolled to the ground again. 'You needed space. Are you OK? What happened?' I crouched next to her.

She closed her eyes, took a deep breath and when she opened them again, they seemed narrow, wider. Had her irises always been so yellow, or was it the polished morning light in the woods? She gripped the earth and the knuckles of her fingers collapsed, phalanges leaping in high arches like she was dislocating them.

'Did you feed her? She's not in her right mind. She doesn't recognise me.'

'The tynx is dead, Grandma. I'm sorry.' I was sorry, but seeing the state she was in, not liking how tynx-like she looked, I was also glad that once she recovered, this would be over. The tynx was dead. I'd seen it. The sightings would stop. The people would leave us alone and Digger's mother would allow him to come to the house again.

Grandma's throat rattled, low and wild. Probably all her shamanic research. 'She was all I had. The others won't accept me.'

I put an arm around her but she snapped her teeth at me. As I fell heavily to the ground, shocked, someone cleared their throat. A group of men on the path by the river – camouflaged, faces covered in scat – watched Grandma paw at the soil.

Her back heaved. She hacked something painful and solid out.

Digger's whole body – black hair, brown face, red arms, white T-shirt – was loud and crayony next to the muted group of men blending in with the woods. Denny and Fowl were there, next to him. And next to them, was Caitlin, biscuit-faced with make-up, not faeces.

'Gross.' She covered her mouth with her hand, hiding the rest of her feelings, the girl who was almost me.

'Get off my land.' Mumma had arrived quietly, Grandma's old wax jacket over her nightie, a rifle gripped at her hip, scarf around her mouth.

The men at the back muttered between themselves, turned to leave, again, saying sorry to the trees, until only Denny, Fowl, Digger and Caitlin were left.

Mumma raised the rifle at Digger. 'What are you doing here?'

'There's an animal in the woods,' Denny shouted. 'The boy says he's seen it here.'

'She told them I saw it,' Digger called, pointing at Caitlin.

'You saw a black fox, or a badger.' Mumma's voice was long and thin as the barrel of her gun.

'Or a pony,' I said.

Grandma set her rough, grey face to the men. 'Did you hound her to death? Did you kill her?' She tottered towards them, tugging at her pyjamas, like she was trying to release her chest, then she sagged and covered her face with her hands, embarrassed to be crying. 'Now what am I going to do?'

'My mother is ill, as you can see,' Mumma shouted. 'God knows what you've done to her. Get off our land. Or this will be a matter for the police.'

'Who's dead, darlin'?' Fowl shouted to Grandma. 'What's happening here?'

Rifle still raised, Mumma pulled Grandma up the hill and through the trees. 'I will call the police.' She shouted behind her.

'Nice one,' Denny said to Digger, the whites of his eyes shining out of a brown crust.

'It's here,' Digger said. 'I did see it.'

'What a lot the lad has seen,' Fowl scoffed.

'Itchy chinny chin-chin, methinks.' Denny rubbed the crap through his stubble.

'Trespassing,' I shouted at him.

'*Loveday.*' Mumma was up near the house.

Fowl and Denny finally walked away.

Digger turned to follow, head hanging, but Caitlin didn't.

'Help us catch it,' she called to me. 'Then we'd be the ones in the papers. It's good money. Are you sixteen yet? Because it could lead to modelling – you could do a baldy Sinead-O'Connor thing.'

'Shut up.' Digger told her, pulling her arm, tugging her behind him. He was disappointed to leave. But in the fairy tales, love was so often forbidden.

I watched him go, leaving me trapped here, waiting for him, like a real Princess. My eyes on the wide tubes of his shorts stretching with every step. His underwear soaring away from his saggy shorts. At one point, he took his waistband and pulled it up. He was closed as a text book, to me, all the information I needed inside him. I trapped a retch in my mouth.

There was hair in my throat. Fine, floating hair. It could swell and wedge in a throat. But I did fists and remembered everything had been carefully removed. I swallowed back phlegm, relieved I never ate much and knew my stomach must be empty.

The scratch at my hip nipped and snapped.

⚜

I don't only steal pictures from my little friends. I collect pages of newspapers I find lying around, otherwise they would be thrown in the bin.

There are newspapers in the boarding houses, in the staff room, in the headmaster's office, left on the seats on the bus, in waiting rooms. They are easy to find. There are pictures of naked women wherever there are people. Not only holding their breasts and arching their backs, the naked women are also in magazines about normal things. They often look sweaty and ill, or half-asleep, to advertise perfume or alcohol. Shampoo and jeans. But a boys dormitory is the best, most plentiful source of pictures. So I go back night after night.

The older boys, who meet me in their common room, who offer me a sausage, have heard about my collection of pictures from the younger boy, who was tripped up. I'm surprised, as my friend never asked me about it himself. I didn't think he knew about my collection – I didn't think anyone knew about it, safe as it is, hidden inside my other books in our little flat. Anything I took from his dormitory, and the others, I took carefully – never a full calendar, never anything that might be missed.

But things *have* been missed, and I am terrified they will tell Mumma.

'What do you want them for?' one of the older boys asks. 'If you don't want this,' he says, pointing at the not-sausage. 'This,' he says, 'goes with that.'

How to explain it is research. How to explain I can be curious about the formation of rocks, without necessarily being a rock myself. The boys should understand. They also collect these pictures to learn something. To collect pictures of women, is to learn what it is to be a woman – not one at the beginning, like me, nor one at the end, like Mumma – but a woman in the middle. A woman itself.

⚜

The Moorland Gazette was shoved half through the letterbox. I pulled it inside. Someone had scrawled a smiley face in red marker across the front page. Crosses where eyes should have been. I held the page at a distance, then looked at it very closely.

TERROR CAT BACK.

It was a dark photograph, of a dark building, with a large, dark, cat-like creature walking away from it. It didn't look like the skinny dead tynx. It was a different shape – wider, perhaps. It didn't necessarily look like a tynx at all, depending on what you thought of when you looked at it. If you looked at it thinking of a large dog, it looked more like a large dog. Or perhaps a wild pony.

'*Local Batleigh farmer, Ned Spring, said, "This thing has hung around Batleigh for years. This photo proves it. Now we need to find it and get rid of it."*'

The photo was very similar to Digger's sketch. It looked real. Digger would say it was real. It looked fake. Mumma would say it was fake. It looked fake and real. Who decides what is fake and what is real? Mumma, of course, because once upon a time, she had more experience than anyone with a tynx. But perhaps it was real. It might be real, or it might be fake. Even Mumma couldn't say for sure, now.

There was a choking noise upstairs. A mug of broth sailed over the banister and smashed against the opposite wall. I walked slowly up the stairs, listening to the row in Grandma's room.

'I *needed* Poconella and now she's *dead*. Why aren't you more upset?'

'You've all been dead to me for a long time, mother.'

'You can't choose your family.'

'Don't start—'

'I gave you everything I could, under the circumstances.'

'I was feral.'

'We protected you—'

'Don't bring the cats into this.'

'—and you took Loveday away from them.'

'You would have fed her to them.'

'She could have been so special.'

'You are selfish, obsessive, and egotistical. And a terrible, terrible mother.'

Grandma's voice took on a narrow, bitter tone. 'I need help with the new zoo. It's going to be much harder without Poconella—'

'There is no new zoo. There are no more tynx.' Mumma's voice got louder and louder.

'—and you're no help. Taking advantage of me. Living like a princess. Fannying around all day—'

'Do you think I'm enjoying myself here?'

'You're trying to poison me.'

'If only I had the guts. We would never have kept an animal on in this state.'

I stepped into the doorway. Grandma was on the bed, hunkered back, flat and tiny, as Mumma leaned over her, shouting. Grandma saw me.

'Loveday, start your metamorphosis. As soon as possible. Don't come inside. Listen to the birds. Follow the ants. Smell the difference between each tree.'

'Lowdy, please leave.'

'Evolve, Lowdy. Let the cats see you properly.'

'Ignore her, Lowdy. There are no more cats.'

'Enter their world. Gain their trust. You must breed again. We need more. We must start again. Name the new zoo after me. There'll be a statue. Bronze. My hand on its—'

'Lowdy, I'm afraid Grandma is having a delusional episode.'

'Lowdy, tell someone she's killing me—'

'Lowdy, get out.'

⚜

The Nesquik scent of honeysuckle drifted over the balcony. I stared at the ground below it. There was nothing on the grass. I might have dreamed throwing a dead foal to the ground, but for a blood stain so black it looked like a hole in the balcony floor.

I checked in the deer park, and at the butterfly house. There was no foal, but the meat room door was wide open.

The tynx was also gone. There was no sign of it. No sign of anything heavy dragged over the dried slurry of mud and faeces and remains. There were only slight imprints of bare feet in the large reddish-brown floor. Like the body had changed into a person and walked out.

⚜

Mumma was at the fridge. I watched her although, naturally, she couldn't see me.

She moved so fast her greasy hair slapped her cheeks and her face was red and puffy. With her rubber gloves on, she smelled the milk, checked how much there was, then slammed it back into the fridge without her usual care. She did the same with the butter, and the yoghurt, looking for something.

She closed the fridge, knocked her forehead against the fridge door, then turned to open a cupboard of tins. She emptied three tins of tuna in brine into a large mixing bowl on the table. She caught her wrist on a sharp lid but didn't stop to look at it. She shook the bowl, appraising it, bobbing her head as if weighing something up, then went to the stove and took the stewing pot, licking at her bleeding wrist. She spooned the broth onto the tuna, not stopping to clear up spills on the table, or pat away splashes down her top. She stirred the bowl, sloppily, and then leaned over it, inspecting the mixture.

She jogged down the hallway with the bowl. She passed the front door then doubled back, checking the bolt and lock. She locked the back door behind her too, but I knew she was going into the woods.

I never caught up with her. She'd slopped a little of her tuna mixture out of the bowl by the old enclosure, but after that her tracks disappeared. I tried to do as Grandma said, to distinguish the trees by sound, to smell the ants and let the birds be my compass, but I never saw who Mumma was feeding her nutritious broth to.

If anyone had inherited Grandma's ability to access a stealthy inner cat, it was Mumma.

Flesh melts on the animal's tongue. Tender and flaky, greasy with whatever coats it.

The boy watches the animal eat. Or is the animal watching him? It is too dark for the boy to see properly. He does not have the animal's night vision.

The boy steps back though, nervous, feeling the animal draw close.

The animal lies and runs its tongue over its forelegs.

The boy calms. Sits. Gulps.

The animal can smell his body. His sacrum, his hairline, the crooks of his arms, legs.

The boy puts a shaking hand into the dark.

The animal licks it, and feels a bit woozy.

DAY 7

OUTSIDE, THE BLEACHED sky drained towards the plughole of the sun. Inside, the house smelt tart as bowls of unflushed toilets fermented. I swallowed back a mouthful of bile, feeling poisoned, as I crept along the landing towards Grandma's room. There was a sudden, unexpected rattle and the door shook in its frame.

'Jesus Christ.' On the other side of the door, Grandma shouted. 'Let me out—'

'Grandma?' I whispered. 'Can Mumma turn into a cat? Like you? Is that what she's hiding?'

'Lowdy. Let me out. She's taken my keys and I've – made a mistake.' She knocked briskly from the inside.

'Sh, Grandma. I'm not supposed to bother you.' I tried the door handle quietly, ducking an eye to the lock to see the deadbolt drawn across. 'It's locked. It's for your own good. When Mumma's up, she can—'

'I will not be locked up in my own home. Go and get her. Now.'

'Be quiet.' I pleaded. 'I'll find her keys.'

'Get on with it,' she said. I wanted to know the truth too much not to.

I overthought each step, keeping to the balls of my feet so I didn't disturb some long shrunk, or expanded, floorboard. But when I pressed Mumma's door handle, the door opened with a shrill whine.

I stopped.

I tried to gulp. The fug of stale air made me gag. White noise rang through my head. A layer of decoration had been stripped from Mumma's room since I was last in it. The tapestry was folded over the end of the bed now, only the hooks were left behind on the wall, and a rug was rolled up at the skirting board. Our suitcase was open on a chair. Mumma's clothes and wash-bag sat neatly in it. Nothing had been unpacked. Nothing put into drawers. On the bedside table was a glass of water, her rubber gloves and the keys.

Mumma lay on the bed, one leg half-cocked, camisole rucked around her waist. Her hair covered her face, and her lips were slightly parted. She did not look especially like someone who had recently worn fur, not skin, but I supposed this was the trick to it all.

Down the corridor, Grandma shook her door again.

Each time Mumma exhaled, I took a step. I kept my eyes on her as I took the keys. I tried to stop them clinking against one another, and backed away.

'What is taking so long? Tell her to give you the damned key.' Grandma drummed on her door, hard, with her stick.

There was movement behind me on the bed. I froze, hand on handle, almost out. Mumma inhaled loudly. I ran through excuses for being there in my head. I thought you were up. I heard voices – smelled smoke – somebody's at the door –

When I chanced a look, she was screwed up again, asleep.

On the landing, Mumma's door safely shut, I ran to Grandma's room, desperate to learn how Mumma and Grandma could turn into animals.

I unlocked the door and Grandma slammed it open. She pushed me out of the way with her stick. Her neck craned from the collar of her pyjamas and her few hairs were greased high with shock. She was red with heat and the pale ticking of her pyjama bottoms clung tight to one thigh. Wet and yellow.

'No, Grandma.' I pulled her back, but she shuffled fast, tap-dancing along the landing. 'I'm not supposed to—'

'Where are you?' She tried to shout. 'Where the bloody hell are you?'

'Sh. Please. Sh,' I said. 'She's asleep.'

She took her stick to Mumma's door. She had been so frail for the week I'd known her, but she found strength – her animal strength – to beat the door. I got between it and the stick.

'Stop.' I whispered, still hoping that something, whatever it would be, could be avoided. 'Stop, please!'

She lowered her stick, panting, holding me out of the way with it again. I smelled the urine. Her hand shook as she opened the door.

Mumma was now wearing her dressing gown, so only pretending to be asleep.

'You can't lock me up,' Grandma said. 'This is my house until I die. Is that clear?'

'Crystal.' Mumma rose from the bed as if her chest was on a thread. She dropped her feet to the floor, washed out and unwell, exactly how I felt. 'Lowdy. Bring me your things.'

'No—' I looked at Grandma.

'You stay, Lowdy, darling,' she said, far too lightly. 'We'll be fine.'

'Ha! If I left Lowdy here, you'd probably put her in a cage again.'

'I keep telling you, it was for her own good. The lynx were out.'

'Darling, did I ever tell you how I found her feeding you raw meat—'

'—it wasn't raw, it was undercooked—'

'—you were barely six weeks old.' Mumma's tone was even and absolute. 'Bring me your things.'

My mouth filled with dreadful acid.

I went upstairs and lay on my bed, overcome with nausea, clutching and unclutching the sheet beneath me, but the stink of urine followed me. I tried to think of a plan while suffering juddering visions – boys, lined up, staring – the animal in the paper – a light switching on – another stink of urine – Digger's sketch of the cat – *Get a comb, Cousin It! Bang your drums, Animal!* – the dead tynx.

'Lowdy.' Mumma called. 'Hurry.'

From the top of the stairs, I was surprised to see her dressed at the front door. Her white singlet tucked into a navy pencil skirt. Her hair smoothed under. But her eyes were still red beneath blood-heavy lids. If Mumma is part-cat, I thought, surely she would want to stay here?

'Time to go.'

Grandma banged cupboard doors in the kitchen and Mumma flinched.

'I'm not—' I said, wondering how I'd never noticed how cat-like she was before. She had hidden it well in the flat, or perhaps it was being here in the zoo, on the moor, away from the fist of civilisation, that brought it out. No wonder she wanted to leave.

'Where's the damn tea?' Grandma limped towards Mumma.

'Perhaps you've run out,' she said. I was sure we hadn't.

'You can't freeze me out. I'm not dead yet. Where's the tea?' Grandma was not babbling.

Mumma smiled at me. 'Bring your things for the suitcase, please.' The suitcase was open at her feet. Smooth, folded items fitting into one another like squares of cheap carpet.

'I'll change my will. I'll leave it all to the damned cats.' But Grandma wobbled, looking more see-through. Her voice wrinkling up. 'Where's the tea?'

I stared at the suitcase, imagining my secret books hidden within other books with a clumsy tuck of my hand so Mumma didn't notice a thing, but I realised I would do anything, *absolutely anything*, to stay here. With Grandma, with Digger, with the zoo, with the outside – with the real tynx, dead or not – with the truth.

I dropped a step towards Mumma who, just like a cat, couldn't be trusted.

'I'm sick, damn you.' Grandma shuffled away.

Step by step I moved towards Mumma. Hands curling at my sides. I wouldn't leave poor, dying Grandma alone to defend the zoo.

'We're all sick, darling.' Mumma used a theatrical voice, like she was quoting someone. 'Lowdy, if you can't be bothered to pack your things, they'll go in the bin bag.'

Step by step. Hair hackling on top of my head.

Below the kitchen sink, the pipes crunched. 'There's no water,' Grandma shouted.

'Really?' Mumma squatted to rearrange the suitcase. 'Chop, chop, Lowdy. The clock doesn't stop to shake hands.'

One more step and I was above her. Me and my fists. Ready to do something. A Mexican wave of anger, rippling through me.

Behind me, the click of a stick brought Grandma to the kitchen door. 'I'll die without water.'

'You'll die with it,' Mumma said, consoling, pulling the buckles of the suitcase tight.

'Why are you like this?' Grandma slumped against the door. 'I'm so thirsty I could drink the river Dart dry. I want clean sheets. Someone, feed me.'

'Lowdy.' Mumma stood and patted my head. 'Grandma's better now. I'm looking after her. Go back to bed.'

჻

Mumma locked the doors and took all the keys with her.

Before she left, she had come to find me in the tower. 'I've got meetings in town,' she said. 'We'll get a taxi. Have lunch. It'll be fun.' 'I don't feel well,' I burped, rolling away from her. She saw I was telling the truth. She ran a quick finger over the roof of my mouth, then held her hand to my forehead, frowning, then tapped it, reassured. I was not too hot. 'So rest,' she said. 'Relax.'

I watched her taxi pull up from the landing window and watched it leave through the key hole of the front door, before I went to Grandma.

Her bedroom was tidier, cleared of the neatened piles of books and papers, no chaise, no coffee table. It seemed bigger. The light was brighter in the empty room. Her throat, heaving with sleep, much louder.

'Grandma.' I shook her arm gently. 'Grandma.'

Her eyelids half-opened. 'Kitten. My little kitty girl.'

'No, Grandma. Is there another one? Not Nella. Or the dead one. But another one after that? Is there a third tynx? Like the boy says? Or is it Mumma?'

She clicked her tongue, and stroked my head. 'Here she is, kitty girl. Are you hungry?' Her words slid into one another as she closed her eyes. 'Aster gets giblets from the butcher.'

'Where do we take the giblets? Where do you feed the tynx?'

'The zoo,' she said. 'Where you live.' She felt her own face, pulling the skin from the bones. 'What's she given me? What's in that broth?'

My own poisoned head still ached. My temper was short. 'Is there another tynx?' I took Grandma by the shoulders, she groaned and her eyes rolled back. 'Those men will find it, if I don't. If it does exist, they'll kill it, do you understand? Even if it *is* Mumma—'

'We only had those lynx because the council couldn't rehome them. They should've been put down.' She wouldn't open her eyes.

'I'm not talking about the lynx, I'm talking about the tynx,' I said, flat, realising she was not with me.

'The owner died. They were starving. They'd been born in captivity, hand-reared, so they liked people.' Her weak hand stirred the air. 'They knew their names. So we went to see them - they rubbed the wire of their cage when they saw us. I thought—' She scratched her cheeks. 'They'd been pets, you know. Aster was small. I thought it was good to have something a bit vicious-looking around here. Guardcats, sort of thing.' She gave a half-snore.

I nudged her awake. 'They'll kill the tynx. Whatever it is. Do you understand? If you don't teach me about it, how will I ever become a real felinologist?'

'They arrived late, after sunset. I'd hired this farmer with a cattle lorry.' She turned away from me, giving me bad news. 'High winds and sheeting rain, typical autumn here. I directed the lorry over the field with a torch, lined it up with the meat room. Full of meat. The farmer was furious. They'd been gnawing at the wood of his livestock box, spitting and swiping through the gaps in the planks at the other traffic. The lynx were scared - you don't ever want to scare a big cat. Then this farmer opened the lorry and sprinted back to the cab.'

'Can you hear me, Grandma?'

'—lorry wobbling like it might tip over. We grabbed windfall – branches – and waved them, shouting to get the cats out of the lorry into this room, without them making a break for it. Eventually this nose came out. Sofia was big, you know, for a lynx.'

'That's not very big.' I snapped.

'Seems big enough when it's a wolf,' she said, eyeing me, like she was more awake. 'Her head was low. Suspicious. And then I realised – a lynx is not a pet.' Each word came as separately as a sentence. She rubbed her head into her pillow and closed her eyes. 'Sofia went into the barn, but there was no sign of Koshka, Sofia's sister – and, Jesus, she was smaller, but fierce. There was this rumbling. I thought it was the sky. My little Aster went towards it. I was shouting at her to get back when Koshka appeared. She bounces off the fence, across the windshield and over the cab where this farmer was howling, up on top of the lorry. I dropped the torch and when I picked it up, Aster's on the lorry on her fingers and toes. Her nose only a whisker away from this cat's. So I ran over, waving the torch, yelling, and this animal pounced off the box at me. They love to drop on to prey. And she's on me, one paw over my heart, like she knows it's there. Her face is right in at mine.' Her hand was almost touching her face. 'She's got these huge canines, and pupils thin as a piece of paper in the torchlight. Then Aster's here with me – always there one minute, gone the next – and she calls out 'Koshka', and this cat stands proud. Aster walked into that barn and Koshka followed.'

'I told her we couldn't keep them. And she wouldn't come into the house for a week. She slept in the old pump house. So I put up fences for a pen, but all year I found places to rehome them, and every time I told Aster, she disappeared again. She only ever came to me when she had ticks on her back she couldn't reach.' She half-shrugged one shoulder. 'But if you can't beat 'em, they can earn their keep, so a year later I built the cat house with steel lining and lights, and put them on show.'

'So Mumma came home?'

'Your mother was the cat who walked by herself and she walked in the wet wild woods by her wild lone. All places were alike to her and she would not come in.' Grandma looked like Mumma when she was drunk. 'One day she walked away forever.'

Mumma's obsession with hygiene and hand-washing gave her away. Cats didn't wear rubber gloves, but they licked themselves clean constantly.

'The cat who walked by herself did come in. And it killed mice and was kind to babies,' I said, knowing the *Just So Stories* very well. It ends when the cat behaves.

Grandma's lips met each other, thin. 'Then that cat was not your mother. There was a time when the only sound you heard in the valley was the bark of those lynx, and when Aster was messing about in the enclosure with them, visitors would think they'd seen three animals, not two.'

'There *were* three animals, Grandma. There were two lynx and one tynx.'

'Petrosinella had Poconella and, and – One tynx, two tynx, three tynx, four.' Grandma's face sagged into itself. 'Playing cats is your favourite game, Aster. Why do I feel so bad?'

'Was Poconella Nella's daughter? Is she the dead one? How many tynx, Grandma? Are you one? Is Mumma one? How many tynx?' I hit the mattress next to her, to keep her focused. 'How many? How many? How many? '

'Aster.' She called to the door, squirming away from me. 'There's a tynx in the house. Good kitty.' Eyes shut. Mouth long. 'Aster, why is there a tynx in the house—'

I left the room, because poor Grandma didn't realise she was asleep. Poor Grandma, I thought, so tired now.

Downstairs, the phone rang and rang.

The phone stopped ringing, then started, then stopped, then started. Eventually, I answered it.

'Hello?' The receiver slipped through my sweating hand, dreading the giggling, or worse, the silence.

'A'right,' said Digger. 'I can't talk.'

'Oh.' I dropped to the floor, first in surprise, then I stayed, to concentrate. 'You can come over.' I began to shake. 'It's OK. I'm here on my own.'

'My Mum won't let me.' He sped up. 'You need to bring that claw to the village.'

He was pointlessly tracking Nella's dead daughter, Poconella, when he really needed to be tracking Grandma or Mumma. The idea of him had intensified with his absence. The longer he'd been gone, the emptier I'd felt, until I was starving for the slightest piece of him. Now, I could go and help him. The two of us breadcrumbing our way through the woods, over the hills. He would show me careful paths through the Vaults. I would comfort him when we found nothing, pretending all the tynx were dead. Him weeping softly, head on my knee, my hand locked into his hair, promising him a new zoo, a new tynx to photograph, one day. Perhaps we could build a new cage, together, for Mumma.

Somewhere in his home a woman shouted. '*Digger?*'

'I'll meet you there. OK?'

'Yes, please,' I said. Persinette's mother craved parsley so much that her husband stole into the fairy's garden to get it for her. Digger craved the claw, and I would steal into the village for him. I felt something whizzing around in my chest and panicked it was filling up, but then I found three tics clustered together beneath my breast. It was their fat shiny bodies sending my blood spinning, I realised with relief. I teased them off, one by one.

'I mean, yes,' I said, but he'd hung up.

I was upside down, dancing on the white coals of the sky, the claw in the pocket of my shorts. Branches were stiff and leaves were still. Even the birds kept to the shade. I sucked in great powdery breaths of dead briar and yarrow, and ran a hand along the hedgerow for brown blossom to hail like confetti. My eyes lingered on the dark snarl of trees and I felt a little nervous, remembering the dead foal and Mumma with the tuna – two tynx, three tynx, four – but I saw nothing, and reminded myself not to see anything with the flick of two quick fists. After all, hadn't I watched Mumma go off in a taxi to town?

I jumped and kicked off a field gate, just for fun, and skipped down the open road, freer than I'd ever been, thanks to Digger.

A minibus was parked in the village's pot-holed marketplace, next to a tractor. Many of the shops were empty. Windows dusty. To Let signs propped on the sills. Outside the grocer's, under a faded striped awning, a tall woman with a money pouch at her waist emptied apples into a brown box. A lone man sat outside the pub, shirt stripped off, trousers rolled up, bare feet resting on his backpack. He patted a map spread across a picnic table, his yellow drink sparkling like a urine sample.

Trailers were hitched to two quads next to a hand-painted sign. *Batleigh Cat Tours.* Below, a grey T-shirt hung on a broom stick, stuffed with straw to be a headless, limbless torso. The T-shirt said HIGH TYNX and featured a tynx with a moustache smoking a huge cigarette. A £5 sign was stapled to it. Three boys stood over little bikes next to it, talking to the curly red-haired girl I'd seen riding bareback the day we'd arrived.

A group of men, a mixture of Fowls and Dennys, frowned at the brilliant day. Map cases and cameras hung from their necks. Cigarettes pricked their lips. Some held sheets of metal-wire. Parts of a cage, I thought, wondering whether they expected to fit a tynx into it.

Beneath the *Batleigh Cat Tours* sign, stapled newspaper cuttings hung limp in the hot, windless day. The headlines were huge.

MYSTERY CATS LOOSE AGAIN IN DEVON
MOOR BEAST RETURNS
MYSTERY CAT WITH MORE THAN NINE LIVES
VILLAGE GONE TO HELL IN A CAT BASKET

The same photograph from *The Moorland Gazette* was in each article, and on the front page of a national paper. If the photograph hadn't been faked, the animal had been caught there, trapped on thin paper. Looking like this, people would know it as nothing more than an animal to hunt. A cheap, thumb-smudged thrill.

A flyer slid across the ground in the breeze. I put a foot on it, and picked it up.

JOIN THE HUNT

Help catch the Mystery Cat terrorizing Batleigh!!!

In the name of science, a team of Professional Cryptozoologists will track and find the mystery cat threatening the public, and YOU CAN TOO.

- *Do you have eyes???*
- *Do you have ears???*
- *Do you have feet???*

If the answer to all the above is YES, then you are fully qualified to sign up for our assistant cryptid investigation team. You will learn the skills needed to track Mysterious Animals, and rewrite science as you know it.

Assist us in our hunt for Batleigh's Mystery Cat.

For more information, ask for Fowl behind the bar at The Crown.

A man wearing a national park T-shirt set up a picnic table. Gaffer tape shrieked as he attached a huge piece of cardboard to it. CURFEW 7:00PM. Outside the pub, a table was scraped across flagging into the shade. Heavy boots shuffled on tarmac. A zip fastened with a shrill crescendo and a biro was gripped so hard between someone's teeth the plastic fractured. Everywhere, hands were in and out of pockets. All around the busy marketplace, details loomed large, overwhelming and unfamiliar.

Then a quad bike started, and everything was more normal.

Someone in a national park polo shirt rang a handbell and shouted. '*Village curfew tonight at 7:30. There will be fines if you do not have permission to be out. A boy was attacked last night. Sign up here if you want to help the search. Curfew tonight at 7:30. Fines if you do not have permission to be out. Curfew here tonight at 7:30*—'

Mumma wouldn't have attacked anyone. That was the opposite of what she would do. And if the only full tynx was dead, no one could have been attacked. The boy had probably imagined being attacked. Thoughts sprinted through my head, competing, trying to win the race, the ribbon. I tried to stop thinking, remembering the easy bliss of my walk, but my back teeth throbbed. There was a smell. The puncture of a vein. A scissor-slice through muscle.

The butcher's door was open, while the butcher in her brown-stained apron herded wild ponies out of the marketplace, on to the moor road. She hissed and waved her arms. The ponies trotted, swatting flies with their tails. The grocer left her stall, belt of change clanging at her waist, jogged to help her. A quad idled behind the herd of ponies.

'Let's find this bitch.' A passenger shouted and kicked the trailer tailboard.

I jumped. The ponies skittered, hooves sliding on tarmac. The driver nosed the quad between them. The herd scattered onto the pavement, into a shop doorway, brushing past windows. One pushed too close to the butcher, and she slapped its flank. It panicked, and set the others trying to canter through the tight space. The driver revved the engine, and the ponies rolled their eyes, wanting to turn back. The men in the trailer cheered as they got free of the ponies, turned a corner and were lost to sight.

One of the boys on the bikes nodded towards me, and his friends all looked.

'GI Jane,' he called.

'Lad!' the other two shouted, high-fiving him.

'Michael Stipe,' laughed another.

'Lad!'

'Homer!' the final one shouted.

The boys high-fived again, but the red-haired girl smacked their hands out of the air.

'Oh my god, shut up.'

'What? Homer's bald, isn't he –,' someone muttered.

The boys were talking about me. It would be impossible to track each boy down for punishment like at the school. I felt a tickle in my throat and stared at the pavement, wanting to run. My hands, like they were someone else's, inspected the nape of my neck, pulling lightly at the stubble. No, I thought, squaring my shoulders, and looking casually at one fist.

Digger cycled into the marketplace, camera around his neck, rucksack on his back, dirt on his face.

'Lad!' The other boys cheered when they saw him.

I followed Digger through the churchyard's avenue of yew trees and headstones badged with dry lichens. He stopped in front of a cracked granite chest sunk into the grass. At its head a small cherub, face worn away, knelt, hands on its knees, palms up. Two huge wings curved above and below it. Somewhere a drain or guttering was struggling to sluice itself clean in the dry spell.

'Alright,' he said. 'Did you bring it?'

The bell rang, distantly, in the marketplace. 'Curfew tonight! Curfew tonight!'

I offered him the claw. He took it, held it up to the light, then put it into his rucksack.

'Alright, then.' He swung his leg over his bike, ready to go. He hadn't made any jokes, grinned or even shrugged.

'There might be other things to find,' I said, quickly, putting a hand on his handlebars. 'Whiskers. Or carcasses—'

He sagged, looking at his trainers, rocking slightly. Or perhaps that was me. I wanted to touch his back, or his neck, or his arm – anything, anything at all – but when I stepped closer, he edged away.

'Is there something in your house?' he said. 'I heard it. All the weird noises.'

'It's an old house.'

'Houses don't growl. And there was a tynx in the zoo last night. It nearly killed me.'

I was unable to speak. A cold itch prickled wide around my ribs. 'It might have been Mumma,' I said.

'What? It wasn't your mother.' He was disgusted by my doubting him, not like the sweet, friendly boy he had been a few days ago when we'd first met.

'Or an – ornament?' I said. 'It might not have been alive? Did it seem – stuffed? Or, just, dead?'

'It was *alive*. And it was lying down, right next to me, like, submissive, so I touched its back and stuff, but it kept pushing me around, grabbing me by the arm, or the shoulder, with its teeth. It's definitely used to people.'

'But are you sure it was a – *cat*?' I said. 'In the darkness. Someone might have been using a big toy, like a puppet.'

'Who the hell would do that?' He pulled the front of his T-shirt down, tipped his head back. 'It was a fucking tynx.'

There was a single claw mark running around his neck, like the cat had stuck out its forefinger. The graze looked sore – shiny and lickable as a Push Pop. I lost my breath.

'Every time I tried to back away, it smacked me around the head.'

His story was not at all what I would have imagined, and I did spend a lot of time trying not to imagine this stuff. 'So – did you get the photo?' Confused and enthralled, I was still able to think of him and what he wanted.

He faced me, for the first time. 'No, I didn't get a photo.' His voice was high as a child's. 'I couldn't even turn on a torch. I thought it was going to *kill* me.'

'You aren't supposed to be in the zoo. You tracked it. This is what you wanted.' I replied so fast I sounded like Mumma, but I felt sorry for the animal. 'If it's an animal, it can't control itself. Maybe it was being friendly. You just said it was hand-reared.'

'What? No, I didn't. I've gotta catch up or I'll lose 'em.'

'Lose who?' The smell of rotting eggs from the drain hitched my stomach.

He cocked an elbow towards the marketplace. 'They're taking me out proper tracking.' He loosened his rucksack straps until they were long. 'They use shit to cover their scent and wear masks on the back of their heads because tigers only attack from behind. They know what they're doing.' He pumped at one brake, then the other.

I didn't tell Digger that the poor Sundarbans Islanders knew, from experience, that tiger masks on the back of the head were less effective at deterring tigers than, say, a gun.

'I thought you said it almost killed you last night?'

'Exactly. Strength in numbers. We're going to catch it together.'

'What about keeping it a secret? And the competition? If you've found it before anyone else, they need you, you don't need them.' I held onto the angel. 'I can help you.'

'It's not what I thought it was. It *attacked* me.' He straightened. 'If it's gonna attack me, we need to kill it.'

Every hair on my body stood up. What if it wasn't Mumma? My balcony door open, night after night, while there was clearly something in the woods. A thought-form. A cat-shaped demon. But Mumma would say he was lying. 'It's dark in the woods at night,' I said. 'You can't see anything. It might have been my Grandma. You saw her. She's not well.'

'We can't meet again.' He stood on one peddle and looked towards the marketplace. 'I'll get grief from my Mum. Alright?'

'*You* asked *me* to bring you my claw—' My voice rose, but his camera bounced as he cycled away through the yew trees. I felt a searing pain in my scratch and dug my fingers into the crown of moss on the angel's head. Dry lumps fell over its feet. Yellow drifted in the air.

Shortly afterwards, another quad bike started, unsettling the crows in the nests high above. They flew in reluctant circles around the church tower as Digger drove off with the men in the trailers – sitting right at the back, with Caitlin. Her arm draped over his shoulder. Her long hair flying in the wind. She had not smeared her face with anything.

The laughter of the trackers seemed to ring around the churchyard long after the quad passed. Then, a white dropping fell, heavy as my heart, and hit the angel's head and I realised it was only the crows.

Even with the doors open, there was no breeze in the tower. The house was silent, Grandma fast asleep, as I sat on my bed to cut out photos. I had angrily bought all the newspapers I could in the newsagents and was using the same safety scissors Mumma had used to take the weight of my hair, before she took the plastic sheath off the razor and finished the job properly. All the papers had the same vague photo of the mystery cat. I also found new pictures of women. I shoved what was left of the papers under the bed and grouped the photos into two piles on my desk – cats and women – trying not to look outside. Trying not to watch for a sign of the men washing over the moor, the quads dragging them like a current. The white noise of the engines. Caitlin, pony-tail swinging perkily, next to Digger on the trailer, instead of me.

Once, I had cared about my hair deeply. It had been black as a raven's wing, like Snow White's. There was little hair on my round head now, although I had hair elsewhere. Fine and invisible, here and there. Dark and soft as a pelt on my arms and legs. Wired as whiskers in other places. But in that way, as the boys at school had often pointed out, I was hairy like an animal, not like a woman. 'Everyone is hairy,' Mumma reassured me. 'Because we *are* all animals.' But in my pictures the women were glossy and hairless. The ones advertising deodorant and ice cream. Moisturiser and chocolate.

I froze. The desk seemed neater than I'd left it. More symmetrical. Tighter angles. Grandma's stapled books were gone. Had I given Mumma good reason to suspiciously go through my belongings? When had she been up here? And why didn't she trust me? I tried to remember what I'd lied about, and when. If she'd opened my scrapbooks to spy, she might have checked elsewhere too.

The bed was still unmade, the sheets piled together at one end, and, under the mattress, my secret books were where I had left them. I rocked them against my chest, calming down. She had not found them, despite being a sneaky, creepy spy. I crammed them back under the mattress with the film reel I'd taken from the library.

But the old suitcases under the bed were gone, and when I checked the wardrobe, deserted wire hangers edged towards each other with a tinny, nervy sound.

Downstairs, I found a bin bag of old antlers in the kitchen, and a bin bag of curtains in the living room. There was still smoke on the air in the library. The nest Mumma had set alight, night after night, was warm. A fly raged against the window as I poked in the fireplace at the slag and cinders. Nothing of Grandma's pamphlets remained. There was only blackened paper, disintegrating into ashes at a touch. Mumma was getting rid of Grandma.

In the kitchen, I opened a drawer, to run my hands over the knives. I made a mental list of anything Mumma would hate me doing, and remembered the film reel under the bed.

❦

The projector in the library purred loudly. The image jumped and shivered on the closed curtains, colourful, but silent and steady. Like the camera was balanced on something firm. Mumma was my age, sitting in the beech tree, the chaplet and veil on her head.

I was entranced – the tynx, the tourists, the man, the blood. Mumma.

She was thin, tiny. She was pregnant with me around that age, but there was no bulge where her tummy was. When I was ill, she had told me children were more resilient than adults. She had shown me her smooth skin. Her narrow hips. 'Look, see?' she said, 'I had you so young, my body didn't even notice. In fact, if you weren't here now, I'd hardly believe it had ever happened.'

In the film, it was not Mumma who looked pregnant, but Nella.

When the room cut to loud, black silence, Mumma was a shadow in the doorway, holding carrier bags. She stared at where her image had been.

'I told you not to touch anything.' She spoke carefully, controlled. 'What did I say?'

'Don't touch anything,' I said. 'But—'

'What did I tell you?'

'Don't touch anything. But you said you were a child when you did shows with the cats.' I was quick, defensive.

'I *was* a child.'

'No, you weren't. You were my age. And weren't you supposed to be pregn—' I moved towards the projector, to rewind and show her what I meant, in case there was some confusion, but she kicked it over. The film snapped. The reel rolled into the corner of the room. She took me by the arm, forehead butting against mine.

'The thing about the past,' she said, 'is if you're stroking the fur the wrong way, its claws'll take out your eyes.'

'But—'

'You're on a slippery slope.' She dropped my arm, blew a hair from her lips, and went to the door. 'Come on.' She found her keys.

'Yes.' I panicked. 'I will stay in my room. I will leave the door open.'

'Will you?' She stroked the pockets of her skirt to find her keys.

She stood back at the stairs to the tower, allowing me to pass, then followed until I was in my room. I gave her one last chance.

'Please, Mumma,' I said. 'Please. Don't lock it. I promise I'll stay in my room now.'

'Lowdy.' She went to speak, then shook her head. 'I trusted *you*. *You* let *me* down.'

I snapped. 'You weren't pregnant. Nella was. You lie about everything. If there's another tynx, those men will keep tracking it, and when they find it, they'll kill it because it's attacked – someone. So how will Grandma start a new zoo?'

'There is no tynx.' She pulled the door shut, and the key turned in the lock.

'Then what was the massive cat I helped you hide?'

'I don't know what you're talking about.'

'The old, dead tynx in the meat room.'

'There is no old, dead tynx in the meat room.'

'Where's it gone? Was it Grandma? Can she turn herself into a tynx? Or can you—'

'This is very disappointing, Lowdy—'

'Are you trying to kill Grandma?'

'—after all our hard work.'

'What are you hiding?'

'This is very serious, Loveday. Come back to the real world, please.'

'I'm fine. You're the problem.'

'You need something nourishing to eat.'

'Real mothers don't lock their children up.' I shouted and thumped the door, then bent to look through the key hole. 'You are not my real mother. You are a witch.'

Her mouth appeared, her tongue a worm. 'If I am not your

mother, then where is my daughter?' Her lips stayed there for a few moments. But I didn't reply, so she left.

'Knives, knives, knives. Where do they go?'

Mumma sang loudly on the landing below to the tune of *Three Blind Mice*, like it was a big joke. Like she wasn't bothered. But I heard the crush in her throat because I'd also taken the gin and her yellow rubber gloves – and yet I was the one who needed to live in the real world.

I broke the seal on her bottle.

DAY 8

M Y HEAD WAS a slab and my throat so dry I couldn't swallow.

⚘

To spite Mumma, I crouched on my knees and elbows, imagining my whiskers like I had as a child. I did laps of the room, remembering how to be a cat. I had paid careful attention to movement when I was little, studying cat anatomy for accuracy, whenever possible. I'd practiced as if it were ballet, or gymnastics, but I was never a pet – never a lovely, cuddly playful thing to be teased and entertained by. Domestic cats had shiny fur, but my fur had naturally been a protective coat, like a predator develops in hard winters and blinding summers.

I stood up. It was a stupid, childish game.

⚘

Mumma unlocked the tower door, slung a mug of broth at me, and went to my desk. She flicked through a few of my homeschooling scrapbooks, stopping at one page or another, then turned to me and ripped up a project I'd done in my first, sad year of homeschooling. I had written an essay on fairy tales, and composed my own. She gathered the pieces up, along with the rest of the scrapbooks, with both arms, as if I didn't know it all by heart.

167

I rolled to face the wall. Held my belly. Gave a little cough. Cleared my throat.

'Don't give me that,' she said, and locked me in again.

But I was only grateful she hadn't found my women, or my cats, and, after all, the tower was so much better than a cupboard.

There was once a kingdom of towers and boys, and the kingdom had a girl for a pet. They fed her titbits and let her climb trees in the courtyard. When she was little, she looked exactly like the boys and they understood her, but as she got older, her hair grew, and she looked less like the boys and more like the sisters and mothers and aunts they had tried to forget. They didn't like it, so the boys pulled the girl's hair – to pull it out – and each time they did, it grew longer. This became a great game, until they stopped pulling it, and it kept growing and growing anyway and they wished they hadn't started pulling it. Without a sister or a mother or aunt to help it, the hair didn't know how to stop growing and because of all the hair in the way, the boys could never get close enough to the girl to tell her to cut it off.

The girl's hair filled the rooms of the kingdom, until the boys couldn't use their rooms. It filled the roads of the kingdom, so merchant-boys couldn't sell their goods. The fields were full of hair, and the crops and livestock suffocated. The fisherboys worried they would need to fish further and further away, in the deepest places of the sea, to escape the hair. But when they did, they found there were no deepest places of the sea. The hair had filled up the oceanic trenches too. When the towers disappeared under the hair, the boys had to build new towers, on stilts, above it. They were exhausted because every day they had to raise their stilts a little higher to stay ahead of the hair and, eventually, they were so tired of constantly having to raise themselves up they decided to go and destroy the terrible monster at the source of the hair.

The boys armed themselves with matches to burn the hair and scissors to cut it when, luckily, one boy remembered they were only dealing with their little girl pet. The other boys were so relieved about not having to fight a monster, they made the boy with the good memory their king. At which point he shouted bossily, 'Where is the little girl's wicked stepmother or fairy godmother? Whoever finds the person in charge of this little girl will have my firstborn daughter for a wife.'

The whole kingdom searched for someone related to the little girl, and found no one so brought him a witch instead. She magicked the girl's hair short and shut her in the highest tower before anyone could start pulling it again.

At first, the girl was delighted with the tower, having been buried beneath her own hair for so long. In the long dark night of her hair, she was used to telling herself stories, but once in the tower, it was harder to interest herself in stories from her own head, because she could see the whole kingdom from her high window. She complained to the witch, but the witch was busy with her witching business and told her to behave because she was lucky enough to have a lovely tower and if she didn't get over it she would be put back beneath her hair and to remember it was a lot harder when the witch was young and the kingdom wasn't so understanding about things like hair. So the girl watched carefully the witchcraft taking place around her and, at night, when the witch was asleep, magically grew her hair into the pelt of a lovely cat so she could leap from the tower and play happily outside. The boys loved to play with the night cat, and every morning, before the witch woke, the cat would lick her fur off and be a perfectly smooth little girl again. Although it was a bit of a shame she had to change shape twice a day, the girl knew she'd rather be a free cat at night and imprisoned during the day, than suffocate in a shroud of her own hair underneath the kingdom all the time.

I rested my forehead on the balcony doors. The sun went down. The whole village, like me, was curfewed for a second day, trapped inside their homes.

There was nothing for me in the tower. Only the gin I had hidden in my pillowcase, and another night pretending the walls were Digger's skin. Rolled sheets his grip. The musty draughts his hot breath. Holding myself together with a firm pressure either side of my scratch.

Lights flashed, out on the moor.

Someone was ignoring the curfew.

⚜

Fear was a challenge, something to resist until the last possible second. A thing to find ways around. Fear was a hand reaching for you when you're hiding beneath a bed, but it's also you, under the bed. Teeth bared. Ready to bite. Mumma didn't approve of fear. She shuddered and said it was too revealing.

I moved fearfully fast through the zoo, running from what were probably rocks or trees looming dark. It was important to remember what is real, to make fists in the night, with branches whipping past, and the pale underside of leaves leering like faces of tricksome spirits.

The orange light was off the moor path, down in a wooded dell. I crept quietly through the trees, knowing it would be Digger. He couldn't stay away. He wanted a tynx too badly. It would be easier once he knew the truth. His mother wouldn't object to me once she knew the tynx was dead, and whatever was stalking the village was nothing to do with me.

The way to the dell was steep and pocked with granite. I slipped on the dead leaves. My feet sped up and I hit a large boulder, the size of a van. I waited, listening to voices, to laughter drifting through the night. Someone shouted 'Lad!' and was hushed. I edged along the boulder, to look over at the flickering light. A handful of figures hunched around a fire. Yet, every one of them faced me. Pale, freaky, ghoulish faces tipped towards the sky – flat and fiendishly circular – bodies bent in the wrong direction, crabbing towards the fire.

I ducked, not understanding what I'd seen. Wishing I hadn't come.

But when I chanced another look, I saw grey masks. They'd used paper plates, and added huge ears. The eyes were too big, and red, with angry black brows and stripes. The mouths were too wide, and too red, and too toothy. Except one, with a curly grin of human-looking teeth. They were like the pointless masks Sundarban Islanders used to deter the tigers.

I moved to another boulder, lower and closer. The scent of Digger was unmistakable, sliding inside me. Like a finger, somehow, beckoning. He hadn't changed his clothes in the week I'd known him, and his shorts dripped off him. He was talking to someone next to him.

The cat mask on the back of her head hung to one side. Her hair was high, knotted on the top. Dark, like mine. She was my height. She clearly didn't eat, like me. She put her arm around his shoulders and swayed, back and forth. He swayed with her, with me.

She / I turned and I saw my eyelids shimmer. I had drawn stars in gold along my cheek bones. Perhaps Mumma had taken me to the No 17 counter – told me to choose something for my birthday. My vest was knotted, the straps were thin and showed my bra, and my belly sank like a valley into cut-off shorts – still dirty from riding in them all week. My skin was pale as wax next to my black underwear. I felt it was my hands plucking at a strap as we talked. I ran them across my chest, like she did, but when they cinched my hair, I felt nothing.

My high ponytail slipped lower, flopping over the mask, greasy kinked strands escaping. I pulled it over my shoulder, curled the end of it around my finger, then I dragged him towards me. Ran my fingers underneath his mask. Whispered something into his ear, and we both looked around.

It was not me.

Caitlin adjusted her badly-fitting bra, and smiled at me. A small, untrue smile. Digger looked past me, eyes unfocused, not seeing what she was seeing. The other kids smoking and drinking at the fire, stopped to follow their gaze.

I thought I might, simply, die.

I turned – to run home – into three fiendish, round, grey faces behind me.

'Boo,' said one.

'Homer!' shouted another.

'Meowargh.' The third clawed at the air, the can in his paw spitting foam everywhere.

The boys twisted their masks off their faces and pushed them behind their heads like the others. I hardly recognized them without their bikes. They stared at my baldness with the same yellow, gurning cartoony faces they had on their T-shirts.

'She's Sigourney Weaver in Alien 3.' The first one swigged from a can.

'She's Captain Pickard—'

'Gay—' The third meowed and clawed, showering me in cider again.

I gripped the rock behind me, with nowhere to run.

'Was it your Mum who couldn't talk and crawled around like an animal?'

'My dad said their class thought she was a girl, except she had whiskers.'

'If they catch that cat, is it actually going to be your hairy mum?'

'I've caught *your* hairy mum.' The boy put up his elbows as the other two hit him.

'Lad!'

'My grandad says it's Mrs Cat's fault he had to close his souvenir shop.'

'My mum says Mrs Cat should've been done for manslaughter.'

'Sh.' Digger scrambled up the slope towards us, Caitlin followed.

'What are you doing here? What are you telling them?' He shook his can, and drank the dregs. He might have been drinking me. I was thinning into fine, clear bubbles filled with nothing but air.

Behind him, Caitlin's hands were on her hips, adjusting her shorts, the thick, yellow slug of her tongue hanging from her mouth. 'Do you have, like, cancer?'

'*Caitlin.*' The red-haired girl who'd waved at me in the village appeared wearing a head torch. She nudged Caitlin, hard, to one side.

'It was a joke, Rosie.' Caitlin shouted back, kissing Rosie loudly on the cheek.

'*Sh.* She's come for the curfew party. Who's yer little friend?' Rosie smiled and held out her hand. In the light of her torch a tiny spider crawled from my shoulder onto her finger.

Everyone waited for me to speak. I tried not to collapse.

'Tynx.' I could hardly hear myself.

'What? Digger said.

The boys looked at each other, suddenly quiet.

'*Where?*' Caitlin vultured nervously over Digger's shoulder.

'The tynx.' I whispered more than ever. 'I tracked it here—'

I pointed into the trees surrounding the dell on all sides. The three boys were already skidding and tripping back to their fire. 'The tynx,' they whispered, hoarsely to the others. At the fire, people laughed, then stopped. They leaped like cats themselves, collecting their things, holding improvised weapons high above their heads – a spade, a golf club, a hammer. The party jogged in the opposite direction, leaving the fire burning behind them.

But Digger followed me. 'Where?' he said.

There were quiet shouts and calls from behind us. Warnings and explanations, as I moved quickly into the darkness.

'Call the ranger—'

'Get the lads—'

'There,' I said, pointing at random. Then, as if I'd seen something, I ran. I was a slingshot. As fast as desire. Ferns in a tempest. A storm of pine needles. I could hardly believe I wasn't truly chasing something.

'Wait—' It was Digger. He was pulling his camera strap over his head.

I stumbled, remembering my hands under his mask, which weren't my hands at all, but Caitlin's.

'Eh—'

Had Digger ever, I thought, said my name – my awkward, drab, cumbersome caterwaul of a name? 'Eh?'

'Digger—' Caitlin was behind him.

Her hands. His hair.

'Over here—' The hill was gorse. Calves in thorns. Trying to find a path, trying to keep Digger, trying to lose Caitlin. Through the trees to one side of me, something was coming. Something big. With teeth. And eyes.

I tripped onto a track and moved faster than I'd ever moved.

'*Wait*—' Digger called.

The thing kept its distance. It stayed parallel. Was it something, or was it a mask? Had Caitlin somehow got in front of me? Or a pony?

I hurdled bushes, ferns, rocks.

It was pacing me.

Teeth rattling, toes crushed. Limbs lengthening. Spine unfolding. The flash of a tail in the corner of my eye. It was a tynx. There was a real live tynx, hunting me.

Someone was groaning, and it was me.

I burst out next to the river, but the thing had gone. There was no movement until I heard Digger nearby. A hiss of energy left him as he slowed down.

Digger staggered from the trees. 'Eh? Where is it? Did you see something?'

'*Digger*—' Caitlin was lost in the dark somewhere, far behind.

He didn't answer. He was as still as a trophy in a cabinet, listening for me. My name might as well have been etched into him.

'Digger?'

There was a rev of quads and the wail of a whistle somewhere.

'Help? Digger?'

'We've got to tell the others,' Digger said. 'They've got the tranquilisers.'

'Sh.' I watched the trees, and held out my hand to lead him. The tynx would surely stay in the cupboard, out of sight, knowing this wasn't the moment to be itself. Knowing it was less important tonight than Digger. 'Come with me.'

'Help—'

I smiled into the darkness thinking of Caitlin, wandering alone through the woods. Hair catching on twigs. Nothing but berries and crumbs to eat. Waist caught by ivy. Thinking she was being stalked, slowly, carefully, by a tynx.

⁂

The zoo was dark and warm as a mouth.

'Did you really see it, or what?' Digger tapped his fingers against his camera.

'Yes.' I wished he'd stop banging on about the tynx. Reminding me of the apex predator that was almost definitely dead, regardless of what I kept thinking I'd seen. But without the tynx I had nothing. 'I thought it went down here. Just now.' I kept walking.

'It attacked me, remember? I'm going to get the others.'

'They've gone.' I dropped out of his sight. 'They were too scared. They don't know what they're doing. They've never been near a big cat, have they? They've just read some books. Only my family really knows anything about the tynx. No one else.'

A moment later, his feet stumbled along the path behind me.

The river below the enclosure was bright where the trees parted for a glimpse of the moon. 'It's so hot.' I pulled my T-shirt up, damp from the run.

'What are you doing?' He cowered on the bank in the moonlight, pointing his camera in all directions at once. 'Is the tynx here, or not?'

I wanted Digger. I wanted bits he wouldn't miss – his dead hair, his old skin. So much of a person looks sensitive, but exists without feeling. Eating a tiny bit of one boy, doesn't make you a boy-eater. My stomach murmured. It felt like there was a claw inside me, testing my scratch, looking for a weak spot, somewhere it could get a hold, thread itself through.

I took the corner of his T-shirt and tugged it.

'What are you doing?' He braced his elbows against his ribs, held his top down. 'Stop it. We've got to be careful.' He stared into the trees, where there was nothing except more night. 'I'm not scared,' he said, 'but that tynx is dangerous. And I think there's more than one of them.'

I barely heard him. My ribs knocked against his. His lips weren't ready for me, cracking as I pushed in, to shut him up. I licked something caked at the corner of his mouth. I took gulps of his face and neck, places where blood fidgeted below his skin. He tasted very, very bad.

'Don't do that. I need the smell. I told you.' He pushed me an arm's length away, and looked into the lynx enclosure. 'Did you hear something?' He was limp with distraction – yearning for something that did not exist.

The tip of a claw worked itself through my scratch, then another, then another. They were peeling the skin of my hip apart. One puffed paw after another, slipping out.

'No,' I said, although since we'd been in the woods I had heard dog foxes, tawny owls, hundreds of pipistrelles, my usually keen hearing better than ever.

I slipped my arms around his back. I flattened him against a tree trunk, to experience him in two dimensions, smooth as paper. Up close, but at a distance. I wanted to look at the idea of him, so he didn't ruin it by being himself. My fingers sank into the bark behind him. He tried to move. His lips clenched against his teeth, but I kept rubbing at him. He tried to duck under my arms, but they were low and small and tight to the trunk. He was too big to curl under them. 'There's a curfew. I'm not supposed to be out.'

'You said you wanted to meet up,' I said, heavily, into tiny hole of his ear.

'Can you let me go? Please?' There was a toddle in his voice. I drooped, drained of excitement. My fingers tingled at the tip, ached in the knuckles. I pulled them out of the tree, annoyed, catching him on them.

'Shit—' He caught his head on a branch, clutching at his back. 'Why did you do that?' He lifted his T-shirt, twisting to see something. Four nicks ran from the bottom of one shoulder blade to the top of his hip.

'It's nothing.' There was mulch and pink skin under my long fingernails.

'Whatever.' He was indignant, like not taking his injury seriously was insulting. 'I said I heard something.'

I rubbed my shaved head. This was surely not how men on quads felt hunting for the tynx. The ones teaching Digger to disguise himself by wiping scat on his face. Were they scared of the dark? Did they do as their mothers said?

'I wish I hadn't come back here. Now I'll never catch up with the others. You probably didn't even see a tynx—'

I stood and collected my clothes. Slipping a finger into the cup of my bra, feeling a fresh new batch of ticks latched on, disappointed. 'I know what a tynx looks like.'

'Liar.'

A ball unravelled in my stomach. I had not been well, I remembered. I felt it in my throat. I needed to go inside, I realised, and walked up through the lynx enclosure.

'Are you leaving me on my own?' His voice pitched as high as the mouselings.

'There's a curfew.' I called, over my shoulder. Was my nausea was due to Digger, Mumma's gin, or something much worse? 'We're not supposed to be out. You're not scared, are you?'

'Bitch,' he said, leaving the way he'd come.

I had expected something different from my first kiss, based on the stories. A creak on the stairs? Hair spread like a crown, and a bed of feathers? Lips of petals? A cry of joy would have been nice. There was none of that, but then I was no Beauty.

Around me, the rhododendrons slurred into one slick, black obstacle. The mulch snapped dry beneath my feet. The only sound was the gentle buzz of a woodcock and the jeering of the river.

– until a strange echo struck up.

My feet cuffed the compacted soil on the path, and a soft stammer followed.

I emerged into the deer park, dazzled by the moon, twisting, expecting to see Digger behind me. But he hadn't followed. Confused, I tripped and fell to my knees. I thought I heard a low growl – but then a stream of air gushed from my stomach. My tongue was zesty and peeled.

Somewhere on the moor was a stutter of quad bikes.

The ground rolled beneath me as I crawled, retching, through the tough grass. There was a bright piece of mirror Mumma must have missed. A thick, flat nose floated on it. Two narrowed eyes. A huge, broad head crowned with hairy horns. Its mouth opened and its teeth were yellow stars tearing through the night. The tynx had crept up, preferring to attack from behind, like the Sundarban Islanders' tigers.

I went to scream, but vomit came out instead.

The animal had gone when I opened my eyes again. Disturbed, perhaps, by the noise and smell. There was only my head like a silver coin in the mirror's reflection, and pricks of light across the valley on the moor.

I stood up, unsteadily, tonguing the last stringy stalk of broth from my mouth, hacking the algal scald of bile from the back of my throat.

'Ah.' Mumma appeared behind me, arms folded. 'So, you can't handle alcohol either.'

DAY 9

I WAS A twitching flame of panic. I woke thinking Mumma was burning me alive in the library hearth.

There was thunder in my head. My vision fluttered. I was miserable about Digger, but in a foggy, gloopy way. Not a fleshy, bloody one.

I went through the house like one long breath, checking for Mumma. She wasn't in her room, the kitchen, the library. Everywhere else was locked. She had entirely disappeared.

'Grandma?' I tapped lightly on her door, and let myself in using her spare set of keys.

The curtains were half-drawn on the sun. The room was hot and Grandma was a beached fish in the bed, hair gummed to her head.

Her eyes opened stickily, disturbing a fly on her brow. Her cheeks trembled with a smile. 'Hello, darling,' she said. 'Have you finished walking?'

I opened the windows for fresh air and the curtains slapped me.

I found a clean flannel in the bathroom, but the tap didn't come on, so I went back into Grandma's bedroom and softened it in an unfinished mug of broth instead.

'Where's Mumma?' I said. 'We need to teach her a lesson.' I sat on the bed and smoothed the flannel over her face. 'She's trying to hurt you.'

Grandma leaned into the flannel. I felt the heat of her and tried to wipe the green broth sediment from her face.

'She's not trying to hurt me, Aster,' she said. 'She's only an animal.'

'It's Lowdy.' I waited for her to see the difference. 'I hate her.'

'She has to know who's boss.' The knot in her neck struggled as she tried to speak and swallow.

'Exactly,' I said.

'If they won't eat—' she raised her voice, '—get up a tree with their meat. Shove it under the turf. Get them interested in it. We treat them like bloody pets.' She waved her hand, as if this was all obvious. 'This is a business.'

'You're not well.' I rubbed the flannel over her hair, feeling so sorry for her.

I caught sight of my baldness in a shard of mirror still left on the wardrobe. Once upon a time, I could run a brush through my hair until it shone like syrup. But now I looked nothing like Mumma had in the film. My hair had grown a few millimetres. I looked like Hans My Hedgehog from the fairy tale, my head covered in quills. Hans rode a cockerel and bargained with a king for a wife. When the wife came unwillingly – the king's fault, but also Hans' for trying to make such infernal bargains – he stabbed her with his prickles and returned her home, disgraced. When he bargained with a second king for a second wife, she remained true to the deal so he threw away his skin and became a beautiful man for her. No one would do that for me in this state, no wonder Digger had been so horrified.

Grandma looked at me, as if I hadn't been sat next to her, astonished.

'You've come back, darling. Did you have a nice walk? I've got news.' She smoothed the bedclothes, and leaned to whisper. 'Sofia is pregnant. No wonder she's so big.' Grandma popped her arms out. 'Poof. She can hardly walk. We'll have to get the head out, or Sofia's hips will pop apart and she'll need a set of wheels to trundle around on.' Grandma giggled.

'Did they?'

Grandma's face fell. 'Did they what?'

'Did Sofia's hips pop apart when she had Nella?'

Grandma pulled her face to one side, to see me from a different angle. 'Nella was born big but had no birth defects. She's a miracle.

Her ear tufts were so long, she was like a length of rope. Once she hits puberty, she'll be bigger than any male, whatever she is. Her hips didn't pop apart, but yes, Sofia was a bit of a mess, as well you know.' Grandma looked at her hands. 'They don't like the cub. They don't understand her. That's what they don't tell you about cross-breeding. Mothers don't like it when they don't recognise the babe. When it looks like a different species. When it behaves like a different species. Lions are social, but tigers are solitary. Alien traits in offspring are worse than being unrelated. It's an aberration. Confusing and threatening. No wonder Sofia was depressed. The mothers feel like a failure and resent it.'

I knew this. I had read Grandma's books. I was practically a qualified felinologist, but I didn't interrupt.

'Sofia attacks Nella whenever she stares at herself in the river like a tiger. A tiger will hunt from the water, if necessary. Sofia and Koshka don't like it. They always exclude her. They patrol the enclosure, make sure she sticks to her bit of it. Pretends she isn't there. We must breed from her. Who knows what will come out!'

I turned Grandma's head towards me. Her lips squashed between my hands. 'Nella was pregnant when she ate the man. Did she give birth before you put her down?'

Grandma put her hands to my wrists and twisted my arms away. 'How big was the litter?'

'Aster?' She leaned away from me. 'Aster?' Her voice cracked as she failed to shout.

'Don't call her, Grandma. She's killing you,' I said.

'You're a liar,' said Grandma, afraid. 'I don't even know you.'

'I'm the heir. I will bring the tynx home. I promise. All of them.'

'Don't come here again.' Grandma was translucent as jelly, slimy as ice cream. 'Aster—'

Noiselessly, Mumma was in the room. Like she had been standing just outside the whole time. Like I hadn't noticed her, camouflaged against the wall or something.

Like last night, when she appeared from nowhere, exactly where I had imagined the tynx had been.

⚜

'We don't torment the dead, Lowdy. They're tormented enough.' Mumma locked me in the tower. Tidied me up. Cleaned me away.

'Grandma's not dead—' I shouted. 'You're a tynx. I knew you were hiding something. You're always hiding something.'

'Lowdy,' she said through the door. 'Please.'

I lay on the floor, my stomach coiled in on itself and my mouth tasted of Mumma's breath in the mornings. I was beyond tired. I barely slept now. The house was haunted, I thought. The house must be haunted. Every night the moor entered the house and kept me awake. Except I never felt fully awake, either. I was always tired and always dreaming.

When I left the house, I didn't bother to close the balcony doors behind me. Mumma would know I had my own exit now. But I was too unhappy – with Mumma, with Digger, with Grandma – to care.

I walked slowly through the deer park, the skirts of the red gown clinging to my legs. I lay back on the platform in the enclosure and closed my eyes. I would build a cage. I would tempt her in, then keep *her* locked up. Mumma would be the star of the new zoo. I would need wooden posts, chicken wire, meat –

⚜

It was very late and very dark when there was a quiet beep. I woke to Digger stalking low through the sedge beneath me, trying to turn his pager off. Denny followed him.

Even at this distance, camera in one hand, torch in the other, Digger looked twitchy. Hardly able to focus on tracking. And yet, the curfew, the rumours, his mother, the dangerous tynx itself – me – none of it worried him enough because here he was, again, with his camera, bringing the worst type of stranger to my zoo.

How, I thought, had they not seen me? Was I striped by shadows, like a tynx?

Denny rubbed a glowing stub into the grass, and shone his torch across the river. Someone answered with brief flashes.

'Over here. It licked me here – look, someone's destroyed my hide.' Digger showed Denny his collapsed hide. 'It's a threat.' He was excited, bouncing on his feet. 'Someone knew I was close to finding it, because I worked *here*—' He pushed out each word individually, but Denny wasn't listening. Denny had taken the path towards the deer park.

'Yeah.' Digger jogged to join him, trying to get in front of him. 'That's the house—'

Something moved in the trees at the top of the path. They both stopped.

This was the moment, I thought, when I'd finally see it, whoever it was – the tynx.

'*Loveday? Is that you?*'

The men folded themselves over. Switched off their torches.

'*Who's there*—' Mumma's voice was a hoot of air. '*I've got a gun.*'

My fingers dug into the platform. My vision striped into black and white.

'We're helping the ranger find this mystery cat.' Denny stood, switched his torch on. Digger did the same. They shone their torches at Mumma who had no gun, but a face like a spiky bomb. Why wasn't she appearing as a tynx? 'You seen this animal, Madam?'

'We're helping the ranger.' Digger parroted Denny.

'*It's midnight. Get off my land.*'

Why wasn't she threatening them as a tynx? Why wasn't her head lowered, lips raised?

'Unfortunately, the creature's been seen here, Madam.' Denny stepped towards her. 'So we're just doing our job.'

'It's our job—' Digger repeated.

My eyesight twisted in the gloom. From the shadows to a grey ether world, bright as day but with none of the colour.

'You are trespassing on private property.'

Why wasn't she attacking them? Slowly, sliding her hips back to the ground before -

'Where are you guys? Digger?'

Why wasn't she -

'Go back to the quad, Caitlin—'

An ache spread in both directions from my scratch. I slipped the gown off to stretch.

'Is it just you and your daughter at the house?'

'I will call the police—'

Why -

'See? This boy here's very worried, says you're hiding all sorts. Digger, didn't this girl tell you the animal's here somewhere—'

'Yeah. Definitely. She definitely did. I think so.'

'So you see, Madam, unfortunately, I'm in a bit of a predicament. I've got to find this animal. Otherwise, how will this little lad sleep safe at night?'

'Digger? Digger?'

'Shut up, Caitlin.'

A set of claws, sliding through the scratch, peeling me apart -

'I don't know what she's told you, but Loveday is sick. She is a sick, sick child.'

'Sorry to hear that—'

The animal flies, straight and true.

The man goes down, but jumps back up. 'What the fuck?'

The animal's gone. The man runs to the river.

'What's happening down there? I've got a gun. I'll call the police.'

The animal leaps out to chase the man a little – into the water – for fun. Then stops as he splashes away.

The animal smells its mate, and laps back through the dark.

The boy shakes, feeble as a cub. 'Who's there? Caitlin?'

The animal's ears frisk. It hears something else.

'Is someone still down there? Get off this property, now.'

Lights flash. The *man* again. 'Flush it out, Fowl. Flush it out of the woods.'

'That's a woman shouting—'

'Forget her – It's over there—'

'Are you sure it's – an animal?'

'Flush it out. Whatever it is. Shoot—'

'You are trespassing. Do you hear me?'

A star in the leaves. A firework of soil. The animal shrinks. Catches itself on a tree.

The boy runs, away from the animal. The boy abandons the animal, without ever knowing how close the animal was.

A witch appears in the trees. *'Where is my daughter?'*

'The cat was here.' Men cry from the other side of the river. 'Where is the cat?'

'Lowdy?'

'Digger?' shouts the girl. 'Where is Digger?'

'Lowdy?'

The boy runs from the animal to the girl.

'Lowdy?'

The animal is so hungry, it lets the boy go.

'Lowdy?'

Expelled. Undigested. Fur in a green throat. The animal hides in a fold of moor.

DAY 10

IT WAS HARDLY dawn and I was naked near the old pump house, blinking at the twirling violence of branches overhead. No birds sang. No insects flew. They sheltered, somewhere, from the wind.

I rolled over, and met Nella's bossed, glassed eyes.

This is how it used to happen, I thought, struggling to recall why I was here. I always remembered pretending to be a cat, but never pulling my hair out. The doctor said the more you pretend to be a thing, the more you behave like it - eat like it, sleep like it, react like it - the more you become it. You train your brain, convincing it to rewire. Shamanism, like Grandma wrote about. But you can re-train your brain, reverse what has become instinctive, he said. You can stop habitual movement, he said. Push it away whenever it occurs to you, he said. Stop acting on it, he said. You can make an idea taboo. He said. I might have been thinking of the tynx, researching the tynx - telling its stories - but I walked on two legs now, not four. I had matured out of telling my brain I was a cat. I no longer felt like a cat, except -

It was Grandma who was a cat. Or Mumma. But why had I ever thought they were cats?

A branch thudded to the ground near me. My muscles were tender. Joints bruised. I rolled over and my scratch widened into a shocked, red mouth.

I limped through the zoo holding my leg. Clusters of ticks were weights beneath my breasts. Heavy and dragging me down.

In the gale, the pines were gigantic bristles of a broom sweeping the floor of the sky.

My shorts and T-shirt had blown – from somewhere – across the lynx enclosure. I dressed next to the river. A white sheet was caught on water-dipped roots. The current gurgled through it like it was dry-heaving, and the cotton was dragged in every direction.

If you are so used to hiding stories within other stories, I thought, was it possible to hide them even from yourself?

☙

Moss tendrils and frills of old man's beard bobbed across the floor like they were underwater. The rusty hinges of the balcony doors grated. The wind was loud, hissing at the edges of the tower. Firing the hot, grey day in through the doors with me.

'Thank goodness. Oh, thank goodness.' Mumma's voice rain-bowed over the dull thuds and slams below us in the house. In haste to reach me she fell from the bed, knocking an empty gin bottle into her sticky tumbler on my bedside table. 'You've broken those doors, but it doesn't matter! It's nice to get the air flowing through.' When she held me, she was a pneumatic, juddering thing. 'You're OK,' she said. 'I've been up all night looking for you, but you're here now. There were bloody men in the zoo. That horrible boy brought them here.' Her eyes were two thin lines. Her hair millions of insect legs on the move. Her blouse angled like a geometry question. She did not look like she'd been out, transformed into a cat during the night. 'You are OK, aren't you?' She looked to my hands holding my scratch. She plucked tick after tick off my torso. 'Where have you been?'

The room was tidy. Furniture at careful angles. Clothes no longer on the floor. The smell of bicarbonate of soda and lemon. Her body had creased fresh sheets, but the bed could easily have been made without disturbing my private collection. The floor could have been swept without Mumma lying on her back, looking at the slats beneath the mattress.

'I don't know. In the woods.' I was truthful with exhaustion. 'I was cross. You keep locking me up.'

'There were men in the woods. Did anything happen? Are you OK?' She almost shouted.

'I'm fine.' I almost shouted back. 'Don't you keep saying there's nothing to worry about in the woods?'

There was a delicate, glassy silence, each waiting for the other to smash it.

'This is why I have to lock you up. Didn't I tell you to stay inside? Over and again.'

'I'm thirsty,' I said.

'My throat's drier than one of Grandma's pamphlets on cross-breeding.' Despite everything, Mumma tried not to smile to herself.

She found a bit of water pooled in a tap somewhere and swayed from side-to-side, steadying her eyes to wash my cut while I clung to the rolling top of the bath. Every breath she let out stank of the evening before. She pressed the flesh in at the sides, and ran the edge of a clean flannel down the middle. The scratch gleamed like lip balm.

'Will it scar?' I knew I had been naughty. Knew Digger had been there. And Caitlin. Knew how fierce I could be. How betrayed I felt. But, still, I did not know anything more.

'Maybe.'

'Scars show you can fight,' I said.

She winced, braced herself against the sink. 'Scars show you've lost.' She held my eyes, but she was looking at somebody else, locked away from me. 'Oh dear, oh dear.' She tipped my hands towards me. She showed me palms raw, black with dirt. 'Why do you let your fingernails get so long?' She pulled up a filthy foot, to see the sole, swollen and painful to move. 'Are these blisters, or burns?' Mumma sniffed at it. 'Or both?'

I shrugged.

She sponged tiny amounts of water over my hands and feet, plucked out dozens more ticks from my back, and checked inside my mouth. Afterwards, she hung her head. 'Where were you? Were you chasing boys again?'

'No.' I was annoyed. I'd never chased boys. I had spied on them. Punished, observed and scared them. But never chased them. Most of the time, they'd never known I was there.

'You need to be here. With me. Nice and real. With your fists, and your thoughts. You mustn't - self-suggest. Not when, there's all this—' she gestured to the small, near-empty tower room and her voice petered out, '—to enjoy.'

'I am not self-suggesting.'

'Then why,' she was suddenly crisp, 'tell the boy you'd seen a tynx?'

'I did see a tynx.'

'What?' Mumma's lips stiffened to a grey death.

'The tynx you made me move for you.'

'Oh, that tynx.' Mumma's blood returned.

'Mumma, please, tell me the truth. What tynx did you think I meant?' I reached out a hand. She left it hanging in the space between us.

'No tynx,' she said. 'No tynx at all. Stop saying tynx. It's been an awful misunderstanding.' She raked her fingers through her hair, they caught in the tangle of it and she held them, stuck to her head like a huge pair of ears. 'You're fine. That's the important thing. You're safe and sound.'

I dropped my hand, disappointed. She still wouldn't be honest with me.

There was a crash. We both looked towards the balcony, but it clung to the house, squeaking and squeaking, back and forth.

'Is that Grandma?' I said.

'No. She only walks at night. When her head's asleep, her body has no idea it's almost dead.' Mumma clucked, trying to find saliva to swallow. She stuck her tongue in the dirty wound water, then offered me a lick. 'It's almost over now, anyway. And there's no point putting a pig in a hat if you're not taking it to a party. I've worked so hard here. As long as you stay inside now – resting – I can finish the job.' Her head was bobbing, bobbing, bobbing. She licked her pale lips.

'Drink it.' I directed the water back to her.

'No. It'll rain soon. And we need this for your head. We need it nice and smooth, so every time you touch it, or see it, you remember to –,' she took a deep breath, and let it out, floating her arms to either side, giving herself space, 'rest and relax and recover.'

The first time Mumma shaved my head, she cheered me up by listing other bald women – Joan of Arc, Jo March, poor, unbright Princess Melisande with her overbearing, ill-educated mother – but this time she didn't say a word. She concentrated. Eyes wide, like this was a witch hunt, like she was shaving my hair lest anything demonic hid in it. I pulled away each time she lost her light, unsteady grip on the razor. Each time it skidded in the soap. By the end, it was an uneven job with nicks and scratches.

Beyond the doors, the lively forest whooped and applauded.

⁂

There was banging. I was half asleep. I thought it was the wind, or Grandma – but there was shouting at the front door. I got up. Heat had pearled across my chest, prickled on my head. My room was dim. Outside the day whirred like an oven.

Mumma was on the landing, crooked as a broomstick, holding the banister and staring through the window above the stairs. The drive was littered with twigs and moss and lichen like a tide had gone out. A large white van was parked on the gravel. Its sliding side door was open, showing the wires and electrical equipment inside.

'Who is it?' I whispered, and someone hit the front door again, fast. Four times. The door handle swung back and forth in the empty hallway, ghostlike, as someone tried it.

A slim, young man jumped from the van, a navy T-shirt tucked into his long shorts. He flicked a wire, and fixed it into a video camera.

'Hello?' A blunt voice came through the door. 'It's Peter Carter.'

There was more knocking.

The man at the van looked through his camera, swung it around the drive, at the house, and caught sight of us. He whistled and pointed.

There were footsteps on the gravel. I watched over the hook of Mumma's shoulder. Peter Carter appeared, below. A new navy, collared T-shirt puckered below his belly. It had an insignia on the chest, too small to read from the top of the stairs. His long hair was solid in the wind while the beech tree behind him waved wildly. He held a plastic card hanging on a cord around his neck, as if it were a police badge, or a bible.

'I'm working with South-West Now.' He shouted over the roaring trees. 'I've got a few questions for the old lady.'

Mumma didn't move. She probably didn't even blink, because Peter Carter turned to his friend for help. The young man jogged to him, then did nothing.

'South-West Now.' Peter Carter shook his plastic card. 'Can she hear me?' he said, loudly to the young man. 'Something attacked a man last night, on this property.' Peter Carter used his plastic card to point at Mumma, regretfully, like he was disappointed to bring her this news. 'This is serious, my love. So let's get on with it.'

Perhaps Peter Carter saw Mumma inhale, long and slow, because his voice lightened. 'It won't take a minute, madam.' Peter Carter looked at the young man, who looked back at Peter Carter. 'You can be on camera, my love.'

Mumma's head sagged to the side.

'You can't hide away forever, you know? People want answers. If you don't get the facts out there, someone else will and it'll be a whole different story. We've got a claw now. That's evidence. Your daughter gave it to a local boy.'

I lined myself up with Mumma's back, to take on the familiar, sharp lines of her shadow, to feel only what she might feel – to feel nothing of my own. She tipped backwards, tottering to stay on her feet.

'A fully grown man was jumped on last night. Here. In the zoo. Witnesses heard him fall in the river. They chased something through the woods in the valley all night.' His voice was loud and strong again, but Mumma turned and stumbled into her bedroom.

The men stared at me, in the space she'd left. 'South-West Now is the south-west's highest quality early evening news update.' Peter Carter's voice went so high I hoped his friend had caught it on camera. 'And *they* came to *me*.'

I did a tickly cough behind my hand. Mumma had missed a little stray something, surely.

'Are you OK?' The young man called up. 'Is she ill?' he said to Peter Carter.

'Let's go,' Peter Carter said, planting his feet more firmly into the drive. The young man lifted the video camera to film him. 'I'm here at what many consider the source of the Batleigh monster, Batleigh Zoo. The villagers hold the owner of the former zoo personally responsible for whatever is terrifying the area.'

Peter Carter was chopping the air with one hand. I slowly crouched, out of sight, until I was hidden from the camera by the banister.

'A woman known locally as Mrs Cat is said to have released a dangerous feline predator onto the moor after the tragic death of a man closed the zoo suddenly in 1979. The way she cared for the animals she exhibited here in the seventies was always controversial. She allowed her daughter to play in the lynx enclosure and even brought a lynx to the council meeting deciding the zoo's fate. To this day, young children in the village are warned of how the former owner of Batleigh Zoo can turn into a big cat, like a witch, and told to keep away from the house. But is this silly fireside story-telling, or a serious comment on the mental state of someone who might have released an apex predator on a local community—'

I hurried into the bedroom after Mumma.

The windows were open. The curtains boxed in the wind and the tassels of her bedside lamp were frenzied. She crawled across the bed, tucking up small. I followed, tucking up the same behind her on the bed. I shuffled forwards until I covered her back.

'Mumma? Mumma?' I placed my head on hers, ear to ear, until there was no space between us. My phantom hair whirled around. Even Mumma pulled a hank of something invisible out of her mouth. 'Please,' I said. 'If there's a tynx in the woods. We need to make it a new home. Here in the zoo. To stop the men coming back.'

'You're not to talk about thingies, Lowdy. Ignore the village. It's mad.'

'The village isn't mad. I saw it on the old film, Nella was pregnant. She had babies. I think you're feeding them—'

'Even if she was pregnant,' Mumma croaked, 'why would it be with a tynx?'

'Because Nella was a tynx.'

'Was she?' Mumma stared at the wall. 'We only have my mother's word for it that she was Sofia's. I wasn't there when she was born. She could have bought a strange-looking tiger.' Mumma's eyes were unfocused, like she was looking at a Magic Eye poster on the dormitory wall. 'You can't believe a word Grandma says. I warned you, but you never listen to me. This conversation is no good. If you don't stop this obsession, it'll end in tears.'

She lurched to the window, closing it, looking at the moor tremoring above us. The woods raging below in the zoo.

'How are you doing that?' she said to the window.

'What?' I sat up.

'That—' she said, and fell backwards.

Good reflexes can be simple luck. Good reflexes can be genetic. Good reflexes can be the result of constant training. Cats have exceptional reflexes. They can respond to a stimulus in as little as one-hundredth of a second. Because they have sharp eyesight.

Because their whiskers are sensitive to changes in air pressure. Because the discs between their vertebrae are so elastic they twist their spines one hundred and eighty degrees. They probably move before they even know they're moving. Once upon a time I knew an awful lot about cats.

I caught Mumma.

She blinked at me. 'How are you everywhere at once?'

'You're not well,' I said, a little scared. Her eyes were dull, not shiny. Something white split at the corner of her lips and she was so heavy I had to lower her onto the bed.

'I've got a headache,' she said. 'The sort where your eyes glitter and hop.'

I emptied every faucet in the house and held her on the bed, her head in the crook of my arm. She suckled water from a milk jug like a baby.

'We need more water,' I said. 'I'll get it from the village.'

'No. Not the village. Get it from the river.' But her voice was slurred and confused.

The river was stinking and muddied. She needed plastic, see-through bottles of clean, tidy, filtered water. I wanted her well. Making sense, looking after me, telling me the truth about the tynx, so we could bring it home to the zoo, care for it.

She held my shoulders, her head at my chest. 'Please, Lowdy, please. Don't go to the village. Don't leave the house. You're supposed to be resting. You know what's out there.'

'I love you,' I said. 'I really love you and I'm sorry you're ill.'

I went to the window above the stairs. The van had gone.

'No.' Mumma shouted from her bedroom, as I walked down the stairs putting on Grandma's old wax jacket. 'Don't go.' I opened the front door and every window in the house rattled in its frame – 'Don't speak to anyone and stick to the roa—' I slammed the door hard behind me, so I had no choice but to run as fast as I could. Imagining the tynx chasing me.

Cars were parked up the hill into the village, across people's gates, blocking the pavements. I heard the crowd before I saw it.

The sun was gone and the black sky was a lid, lowering towards the ground, forcing the wind in circles, trying to get out.

In the marketplace, I joined the queue for the grocer's stall. Fresh fruit and vegetables shrank and sweated in the heat. The cut on my leg throbbed from running. I pulled the hood up on the jacket, hoping no one would notice my very distinctive head.

The quad bikes were abandoned, and the *Batcombe Farm Cat Tours* sign was now tied to a lamp post, butting against it in the bluster. The newspaper articles had been torn off, perhaps by the wind. The HIGH TYNX T-shirt flapped empty, its straw stuffing skating around the marketplace.

The pub spilled hunters and their drinks from its low-walled terrace onto the road. In their matching fatigues, they rubbed fists and forearms over red faces, guttering like wax in the heat. A pot-cleaner ran out with a tray, collecting empty glasses, filthy apron whipping in the wind. Cars honked to clear paths through. A bottle blew off a picnic table and smashed to the floor. A cheer went out. Then the men stared at the broken glass, and kept talking.

In front of them, a man in a grey suit with a microphone on his lapel talked to the video camera. His hands gripped the air like he was strangling it.

'—farmers regularly report loss of livestock. Local businesses report loss of livelihood. Family cats go missing and walkers are followed by shadows. There's even the occasional photograph for sceptics to dismiss as hoax. But last night, in the grounds of the old zoo that everyone blames for this nightmare, a man was attacked by the animal. Whatever sort of big cat it is, it *is* big, and this incident is the most recent in a week-long frenzy of sightings and near-misses. It's been seen at a farm, out on the moor, even at a party at the reservoir. But why has the mysterious animal become bolder all of a sudden? Is it hungry? Is it looking for a mate? Perhaps we'll never know, but we do know it's out there, and this village is determined to catch it—'

I shuffled along in the queue, holding my hood tight, dreading being served. As I asked for the water, a green national park Land Rover pulled into the marketplace. Whistles blew. Glass rang out, hitting tables, flagstones and other glass in loud toasts. The men moved together, following the vehicle, shouting and slapping the tailgate.

The grocer dropped four bottles into a plastic bag for me, and closed the stall. She didn't even take my coins. The striped awning above her collapsed to flap in the wind. Her arms turned the handle so fast I could barely see it.

I drank half a bottle of water walking home down the hill. People passed me walking up. Men, but also women with children. A toddler with a grey tiger mask on the back of its head. Farmhands still in their muddy boiler suits.

Digger cycled up the road, standing tall on the pedals of his little bike.

I must, I thought watching him, go home now. I must get this water back to Mumma, I thought, scratch whining at my hip. I must stay away from these people.

The plastic bag fluttered nervously in my hand.

※

The trees in the churchyard hit each other as people funnelled through the single door of the village hall opposite.

I followed until I lost sight of Digger.

The small hall was packed. It was loud, even from the entrance. I couldn't tell where the wind ended, and the voices began. Condensation fogged the windows and the air was packed so tight with water it was a damp pillow to the face.

I was half-hidden by a faded red curtain in the frame of a

window. I felt the tickle in my throat and swallowed again, and again.

The hunting men laughed smoke from their cigarettes and map cases hanging from their necks danced over their chests. The farmers had hard faces, arms folded, nodding at each other and staring quietly down at dirty boots. Women frowned, bouncing babies higher and higher on their hips, distracted by tense, whispered conversations. A few smartly-dressed people held notebooks and pens, and a man with misted spectacles collected signatures for something. Rosie leaned against a wall watching the room. An elderly woman wept. Another woman led her out of the hall, past me, and onto the empty road, where thunder murmured softly in the distance. Everyone was pink with heat and I drank the rest of my water.

Everyone parted to let a man wearing a national park T-shirt drag a flip-chart through the hall. Someone had written GOOD NEWS in huge, empty bubble-writing on the first page. A waiter from the pub ran in carrying an empty bottle crate. It was passed over heads, hands reached out of the crowd, to help bear the weight. Everyone wanted to touch it. Everyone wanted to be part of the solution.

Condensation fogged the windows.

The crate went down and a man's head appeared, a foot or so above the rest.

'Can we get a window open in here?' He shouted, patting the grey air. 'A'right. A'right, then. I'm Dan. I'm the area park ranger. Thank you for coming.' His voice strained to be loud. 'We had a load of sightings of this lynx last night. Which is good news.' He smiled widely, but the corner of his lips twitched. 'It's good news because we know what we're after so you can all calm down.'

'It's after the children.' Someone pointed at Digger, who flushed red, standing a head above most of the other men.

'And us.' It was Fowl, hands on his belly, threading and unthreading his fingers. Denny leaned on the wall at his side. 'And it's not a bloody lynx.'

'A'right.' The ranger shouted. 'The good news is we're working together now, and there's no evidence lynx are dangerous.'

'What about our Diggory, then?' A farmer with his hands under his armpits nodded towards Digger. 'He was spying over at the zoo, and he says there's two of 'em. *And* he says they might keep them in the house.'

I pulled the curtain across my mouth, and cleared my throat into it.

'Two what? Two lynx?' said the ranger.

'Two tynx.' The farmer bellowed. 'We've all seen the size of that claw he found there.'

Digger shrugged a nod. 'It's gross,' he muttered. 'That place. There were cats everywhere. They made me clean it up. And I saw it in the woods—'

'He doesn't know, does he?' said Denny. 'No one can see anything in the dark because of the goddamned trees.'

'It's not a bloody lynx,' Fowl said again, louder. 'And you couldn't keep a bloody mystery cat in the house.'

'I do know.' Digger expanded into a rectangle. 'I'm the *only* one who knows what goes on over there.'

No one was interested, but I ground the curtain between my teeth.

'Anyway, we've spoken to some experts—'

'What experts? 'Cause I'm South-West Now, now—' Peter Carter raised his plastic card, but no one was looking and no one was listening.

'Not the mad old cat-lady—' There were quiet sneers.

'The other one's so bossy. She tells you to wash your hands after using the bathroom like you're five or something.' Digger said.

There was a brief, confused silence.

'We've spoken to some experts,' the ranger repeated. 'Proper zoo experts. And there is no evidence lynx are dangerous, unless *threatened*. They're like your little pussy cats at home. They're incredibly shy. This cat has probably lived in the area for a long time with no problems. So - sorry, can we get a window open in here - let's not panic.' The ranger spread his last words out so we did not miss them.

'And what about tynx? Are tynx dangerous? Are *tynx* incredibly shy?'

A murmur rose. People jostled forwards, to ask questions, speaking at once.

'I think you'd know if there were a damned tynx—'

'There's more than one—'

'We do know—'

'The bald girl's a compulsive liar. I know—' Digger shouted.

My heart did its fists. It rested. It relaxed.

'This is bullshit—' Someone belched.

'Whatever it is, leave it alone.' Rosie cupped her hands around her mouth to make herself heard. People laughed.

'Who let Friends Of The Earth in here?'

'She's on the blob. Who let Mrs Blobby in here?'

Someone patted her on the head and she walked quickly, eyes forward, out of the hall.

'Questions at the end, please.' The ranger smiled with only his teeth. 'Last night, these gents—' He pointed towards Denny and Fowl. 'These gents tracked this lynx—'

'We tracked something—'

The ranger took a breath and looked at his notes. 'These gents tracked - whatever it is - towards Many Sisters circle. And they think they got a shot in. So it's probably hidden away somewhere, bleeding to death. Which is great news.'

'Did they *think* they got a shot in, or did they *get* a shot in?'

Voices rose, washing together, frothing and falling.

'Lemme finish.' The ranger patted the air again, waiting for everyone to settle. 'We're still doing up our belt for a proper job. A'right?' He smoothed sweat from his temples across his hair and held a large, unfolded map above his head. 'We've got a few good trackers here, and the fire service'll pitch in, so we'll split the area and get a few teams out to find this thing. The rest of you, stay in tonight.'

Every hair on my body stood up at the same time.

'But first,' the ranger wheezed, '– can we get a bloody window open?'

The villagers, women and children, edged towards the door, hunching as they stepped out, braced against the roaring day. I hid among them. The hall was half empty, but no quieter, if anything the smaller crowd was even louder, everyone speaking at once.

'For the umpteenth time, can I remind everyone to keep away from the bloody Vaults? I could do without grockles going missing in the bogs on top of this.' The ranger shouted and tried to grin and wink. 'A'right, let's get everyone in their zones before the light goes. Quietly, quietly catchy lynx-y. We've got a map here, so if you shout out—'

When I looked back, Fowl and Denny were lost among the farmers, hunters and reporters, but Digger left the group when Caitlin called him. She pulled the straps of his rucksack down and kissed him. The world flashed black and white in front of me. He turned to watch the ranger fix his map to the flip chart as if the kiss had not happened. Caitlin stood behind him, in my floor-length red velvet gown, adjusting a huge Sweet Sixteen birthday badge, finishing off a bottle of Hooch while she waited.

My shoulders broadened. The tip of my head pulled upwards and my teeth squirmed in their gums and my scratch spat at my hip. I ground my fists. I would go home. Let Digger go on his wild tynx chase. It was nothing to do with me. I had to help Mumma look after Grandma.

Someone finally managed to open a window. A gust of wind blew in and flipped the map up like it was a skirt.

༻❀༺

The house felt safe as a cave when I stepped inside. Mumma was right, I thought, I should never, ever leave the zoo. No one could be trusted, especially not Digger who would rather be a little lad with the big lads than loyal to the zoo. It was true – he would say anything.

Mumma was in the kitchen, a little revived, pulling out pans and stewing pots. She dropped one to the table when she saw me, Koosh-ball hair sticking out from her head.

'Thank goodness, you're back. I've imagined terrible things. What else do you think the boy's told people? About the mess? About the kitties? Do you think they laughed? Do they think we live like animals? Do they think my mother's lost her mind? That there's still something wrong with me? That I have fleas? That I'm not house-trained? Oh God, please don't tell me they know about the mess. Or the cats.'

She stopped, eyes swollen, cheeks screwed up, sweaty chest pumping for breath.

'What mess, Mumma?' I looked around the kitchen. 'What mess?'

'Yes.' Her shoulders softened. She gave a small, embarrassed smile. 'Yes. OK. That man's death was nothing to do with me, no matter what they say. If the gate was unlocked, that's not my fault. You believe me, don't you? I always kept everything locked up so tight.'

'They're only interested in the tynx,' I said. 'If there is one, we need to bring it back to the zoo and look after it properly, then they'll never come here again.'

Her smile fixed, and went no further. 'Take this.' She slid a heavy-bottomed casserole dish across the floor to me, too weak to hand it over. 'It's going to rain, Lowdy-Loo.'

I sat her at the table and held the water to her lips. She put her hands around the large bottle, eyes rolling around.

Afterwards, feeling better, she checked the shelves, opened cupboard doors, looked under the sink. I watched from the back door as she went out into the petting pen and deer park, adding the pots and pans, anything she could find, to buckets and bowls as thunder chuntered above her.

'I'm so glad you're better, Mumma,' I said, the crisis washing away with the hope of rain. 'Is there another tynx? Because I'm going to need your help getting the enclosure ready. We can use the old chickenwire and—'

'I'm sorry about earlier.' She flattened her troll hair from where it stood on end in the wind. Her shirt was untucked and unbuttoned, wet emerging under the arms and in a line down her back. 'I've been a bit distracted. What with Grandma. And being back here. And everything else. But we have to keep you on the right track. Once it starts raining, and the water tanks refill, you'll never have to go out again.'

The moor was a silhouette and Great Bat Tor looked like a little upturned staple. The men were out there. Caitlin and Digger were out there.

'Will you come inside now? Shall we lock this door?' I said. 'Shall we close the windows? Shut the curtains?'

Her smile dropped off her face. 'How was the village?'

'Great,' I said. I fought myself and grinned. Mumma appeared to do the same.

'Speak to anyone?' she said.

'Nope,' I said.

'Great.'

'Great.'

⁂

Mumma gave me the key and sent me to Grandma's room with a mug of soup. She was a thick mound of sleep in the bed. I checked she was alive, holding my breath so as not to smell her. She teetered on the edge of the mattress. I swaddled her tight, so she wouldn't fall, and tried to give her water. It dribbled down her chin, through her beard and darkened the sheets. When I hadn't kept such a tight grip on my imagination, I had been foolish enough to believe she was the tynx. That she'd been too good a shaman – too strong a witch. But now, I knew she'd never been anything more than a very ill, very unhappy woman. She really was better locked away.

The curtains billowed into the night. I pulled them inside, shut the windows, then reached under her wardrobe to retrieve the one pair of rubber gloves I hadn't shredded.

At the kitchen table, Mumma stooped over her glass like it was a cauldron. Ice went in with the pop of bones leaving sockets. I placed her gloves on the table. We needed to make peace in order to work together again. 'I'll leave these here,' I said.

She smiled and reached to squeeze my hand. For the first time in a long time, I didn't want to let go. Down the hallway, a door slammed shut.

In the library, Mumma stood in front of the window, one arm draped across her hip, the other swinging her glass like a pendulum. I leaned against the wall opposite, where a sofa had once stood. Through my T-shirt, I felt my tick, bloated beneath my bra.

'You're never too far from a storm here.' Her voice was loud in the empty room. 'It's only ever a matter of time.'

Lightning poked the sky, fizzing at the window, then disappeared.

'See?' Mumma pointed her glass to where the crack in the ceiling had spread down the wall. 'You do your best, but the house still falls apart.'

I didn't know who she was speaking to, or what about, but she stepped away from the window to better look at the crack.

Outside, the garden lit up with a spit of lightning and a few feet from the library window, standing on the lawn, a grey monster watched us.

Mumma must have been speaking because she came towards me. I leaned around her but the windows were black. She clicked her fingers at me. 'Lowdy, are you in there, darling?'

Lightning silently lit the garden again. It was not a tynx, or a lynx, or a cat. It was the size of a person and the shape of a person. It had long arms like a person and stood on two legs like a person, but the ears on the top of its head rose to peaks like horns.

– and the racing wind did not so much as ruffle its fur.

I stepped forwards.

It did the same, except it walked like it hated me.

Then the windows were black again and thunder rolled.

'Close all the windows,' I screamed.

Mumma spilled her drink down her front and dropped her glass.

I stumbled backwards.

'Lowdy,' Mumma shouted, picking up chunks of crystal from the floor. 'What is wrong with you?'

I ran into the hallway. The lights flickered and died.

'Lowdy,' Mumma called. 'Lowdy?'

My feet slid on the floorboards as I slowed to turn. I hit the door frame, unable to see, as I ran into the drawing room. I closed window after window.

'I'll find a torch. Be careful of the glass on the floor.'

Mumma's voice called to me from a long way away. The sound of her sweeping glass in the library carried along the hallway like the tinny music of a pull-string toy.

I dropped below a windowsill in the drawing room, hiding. Sweat bubbled on my cheeks. Above my head, wind piped through the window frames. I thought the floor thudded with footsteps, but it was the heavy tread of my own heart.

Then, above my head, came a slow *tic-tic-tic* on the pane of glass.

'Put your trainers on so you don't cut your feet.' Mumma emptied the dustpan into a bin in the distant kitchen. 'We can't use the hoover while the power's out. It'll be on again soon. Storms always pass fast here.'

I pulled up slowly, and watched the ears rise with me. The triangular, grey face emerged on the other side of the window. It tapped one claw like a fingertip on the glass. *Tic-tic-tic.* It lifted back its lips and soil dribbled from its mouth. Its tongue was furred with moss, running around twinkling rows of granite-grey teeth. It smiled.

'*Mumma*—' I screamed until I couldn't breathe.

She was with me, on the floor, in a second, holding me, staring through the window, looking for what I had seen.

'It's not a big cat.' I shouted into her chest. 'Why didn't you tell me? It's a monster.'

'Calm down.' Mumma had my face in her hands, seeing the tears. 'It's you. It's your reflection, darling.' She pushed me up, to show me. 'There's no monster.'

I went cold, seeing only myself in the window, knowing it was hiding from Mumma.

She plucked my cheek, teasing me. 'There's nothing there.' Her voice rose and fell like a lullaby. I almost believed her. 'Look. See? Just an ordinary girl.' She stuttered, sounding confused herself. 'But remember what the doctor said? You've got to stop this obsession with the stories. With the papers.'

Time stopped while she and I stared at each other.

'What on earth were you doing with all those clippings and books about the tynx? You know it's not good for you,' she said.

I breathed again, knowing my *secret* secrets were still secret. I let her run her hands over my soft, smooth head. I let her slow my heart. I wanted her to be in charge – it was easier that way, believing her – believing I'd misunderstood what I'd seen through the window. It was only my reflection after a very difficult, tiring day.

'If you stop thinking about cats, you'll stop seeing them everywhere. What a lot of ups and downs you're having, darling—'

Something white fell into the doorway, rasping.

We both screamed at the pale outline of a figure.

Grandma yowled in the darkness. 'You bitch.'

'Stop it,' Mumma said.

'You vicious bitch. You think you can tie *me* up—'

The lights came back on and we were blinded. Grandma slipped backwards on Mumma's polished floor. She was like a children's ghost, wrapped in the sheets I had tucked around her so tightly. She was gagging, tugging at the sheets around her neck.

Mumma pulled the sheets from Grandma's shoulder. She stared at them and Grandma, piled at her feet.

'Where is she?' Grandma croaked, thirsty and scared, pointing at me. 'I saw her.'

The lights went out again.

'What were you thinking, Aster?' Grandma's voice was tiny as a pixie's in the dark. 'Why have you let a tynx into the house?'

Outside, thunder and lightning chased each other.

⚜

By the fragile light of a candle, Mumma came to the tower where I lay, melting with sweat, on the bed.

'Let's not tuck her in.' She sat next to me. Her face flickered bright and dark. 'Better she falls out of bed.' She had brought her drink with her. 'She won't be with us much longer.'

'It's me.' I rolled my head onto her lap. 'The monster full of soil. Grandma saw it. When I was younger, did I pretend to be a cat too long, like a shaman?'

'Grandma lives on out-of-date food as a point of pride. And it's not just the ergot, it's the bad fish, the strong cheese, too much caffeine. You tell me something she eats that won't make her hallucinate, there's the real challenge.'

'It's not a hallucination. The men saw it. It's what they're after.'

'Who?' She was quiet, leaning towards me, away from the candle. Her face in shadow.

'The monster hunters. The experts.'

'Never listen to experts, darling, trust me.' She put down her glass to show she was serious. 'They're not after a monster. They're after a real animal. Whatever it is.'

'But I dream – ,' the braided ball in my neck tried to plug the words in, '—I'm an animal. Or maybe I'm possessed. But they're not dreams, because I can't really be asleep.'

But Mumma wasn't listening. 'Mumma?'

'Loveday. This is worse than all the kitten games and stories. Rolling around in ferns pretending to be something, doesn't make you it. It makes you *you* rolling around in ferns pretending to be a thing.' She suddenly returned, lay back next to me and gave a short, tight laugh, pretending to be charmed. Half her face was white, half black. 'Is this that boy? Has he been giving you these silly ideas? He'll be watching silly films and reading silly books. He'll be a liar. They all are.'

'What?' I lay back to watch the candlelight squirming on the ceiling. 'He hasn't said anything.'

'They will say anything, Lowdy. Anything at all. And it's always rubbish.'

    – Caitlin's hands in Digger's hair –

'I've barely spoken to him,' I said. 'But I really, truly feel like a tyn—'

'The doctor said that cat business was all these silly stories we told about the old zoo and the fairy tales. It's always a mother's fault, but I was trying to entertain a lonely child—'

    – her hands pulling the straps of his rucksack –

My fists shivered from side to side at my temples.

'And you're not a child, anymore.' Mumma relaxed my arms to the bed. 'There's no such thing as monsters.'

She twisted her glass between her thumb and forefinger, one slight degree at a time, the rest of her fingers gracefully erect. 'I used to read in the lynx house at night. In winter. Out of tourist season. In my father's old skiing clothes – his hat, big gloves – before Grandma wore it all. I'd take a torch. I was about fifteen, and I saw a black figure, creeping along the path.'

She tipped her chin, eyelids half shut, making a show of frightening me so I would know it was a performance. 'It was so long and thin. For one ridiculous moment I thought it was Death, you know, *Godfather* Death, from the story, come to blow my candle out. So I turned off the torch and ran to hide in the meat room. But when I went through the door this arm grabbed me.' She gripped her own ribs so hard the bed jumped with it.

'He closed the door and pushed me onto my hands and knees. Onto that disgusting, offal-y concrete floor. He had a black head and this huge pair of horns above it. That's what it looked like in the dark. But it was only a pair of wire-cutters.' She smiled and grasped two thick handles out of the air, spilling her drink on me.

'Please remember,' she counted out one finger. 'I didn't go to school.' She counted out another finger. 'There were hardly ever any extra staff at the zoo.' She threw her fingers out. 'I suppose I was a recluse! I wasn't lucky like you, darling, free to be myself. I only knew how to behave for my mother. Everything was a performance. She loved the idea of me as a little cat girl, because it sold her tickets. Can you imagine? Trapped here all the time, in a *zoo*? And she was in the house, through the trees – she and I weren't close, not like you and I, darling – she had no idea where I was. I thought my heart would stop, if this boy didn't snip my head off with the cutters first.' She laughed the high laugh of someone with no sense of humour.

'He had a black scarf over his nose, and a hat pulled over his eyebrows. He told me I'd get hurt because he was letting the cats out. What I'm saying, is these things seem like ghosts and ghoulies, but there's always an explanation. This is the real world, not a fantasy. That boy thought he knew all about big cats, but he didn't know the half of it.'

I knew about the end of the zoo, about Brigid Brophy and Richard Ryder speaking out about the exploitation of animals. I knew Grandma had found this preposterous, given how tame their cats were. Throughout the seventies people had tried to expose illegal practices in vivisection labs, boycotted industrial farming. They were all vegetarian or vegan. And activists often tried to release captive wild animals.

'He thought they'd go to the moor.' Mumma was flat, to the point, 'but they lapped back to the zoo, looking for my mother. He kept coming back and letting them out. He got rather upset about it by the end. Horrible business.' She shrugged a little too late. 'I had to set sweet Nella on him. Unfortunately, she got a taste for it.' I must have looked shocked, wondering exactly what it was she was telling me. 'A taste for being out of her cage, I mean. Time for bed, then.' She ran her hands down her skirt for the keys. 'An animal is an animal. And a poorly girl is a poorly girl. Grandma filling your head with nonsense hasn't helped, but you're not a monster, Lowdy. You've been sick, but you're getting better. You have to take care not to let your imagination run away with you. You'll be even better now we're rid of all the cats. The lights will be back on tomorrow, I'm sure.'

'Mumma, did I help you move a dead tynx to the meat room?'

'What on earth are you talking about?'

I smiled. 'Thank you, Mumma.'

She kissed me on the head and left the room so fast her movement blew the candle out.

⚜

My reflection was a shadow in the dark glass of the balcony doors, disappearing every time lightning struck out on the moor.

I thought of the creature at the window, the thing Mumma said was only me, and my eyes stretched into two ovals, yellow as brimstone. I was not shocked. I was not surprised. I was relieved. I was as sure as my two fists that I was not half-asleep.

Grandma had told the truth. Thank goodness she had prepared me.

But Mumma had lied. Nella had been pregnant – pregnant with me. It was obvious. How could I have thought Mumma was a tynx? Mumma, herself, often told me she'd found me, a little cat, under a rock, stolen me for a changeling. She often told me her body showed no evidence of carrying me. 'Look,' she had said, more than once, of her taut belly, 'how did you ever fit in here? I'm more of a teenager than you.' She took pride in remaining neat and tucked as a child.

She told me she loved having a little pet. She told me she wanted something to comb and groom and delouse. But any real mother would take pride in being a real mother, not hide it.

Nella would have licked the backs of my ears and taught me to hunt, but stupid Mumma had shown me how to squeeze out a mop and offered to French-braid my hair. No wonder I had so little in common with her.

My cheekbones widened. How long would I have believed Mumma, had I not seen the evidence that the animal was me? What else had she lied about?

My nose flattened. How long would I have believed it was all in my head? That the face shifting and blurring in the mirror was an optical illusion. 'You can see anything when there's too little light,' Mumma might say. 'Stop thinking of cats and you won't see cats – have you been eating poppy seeds? Nutmeg? Mulberries? Why didn't you tell me about this black mould above your bed, *darling?*' Perhaps she'd take me to the doctor again. But she would never tell him I was really a cat. 'Loneliness and alienation are deficiencies,' he'd repeat. 'Any hole needs to be filled with something.'

A hair can't feel pain, but it can cause it – knit it into a shirt, gather it into whips. Every shaft on my body was thickening, spinning up and out. Each soft vellus swelling into something like wire, needling through the skin. Tens of thousands at once. Hair was protection from cold and heat and sweat and dust and light. It shielded your most precious organs – eyes, ears, mouth. And so on. Hair proved you were grown-up. That you could protect yourself. That you should be taken seriously, not coddled. Hair was armour. Hair was wisdom. The more you had, the safer you were from contamination, invasion, defilement. The more the better, science said.

The older boys at the school didn't agree. The more I had, the less powerful I was. My heavy eyebrows and weighted lips were a threat, and they knew it. They noticed my legs and armpits, when I hung upside down from the monkey bars with my friends, suspicious and repulsed. *Chewie*, they'd shout then groan – my friends then moving away from me. I was never allowed to shave or pluck, like Mumma did. 'You're too young,' she'd laugh. 'You're a child. Leave it and you'll attract less attention.' But it attracted more attention. The boys who had once been my friends, cocked their chests and battered themselves in impressions of apes when I passed. *O-oo-ooo*. They whooped and gurgled and left me crying. Then they blackmailed me, and offered me things an animal wants to eat. It was better if I stayed at home, the headmaster told my mother. I was too disruptive, he said, it was not, as well we knew, a school for girls. So Mumma locked me up and pretended they were the problem, instead of admitting they were right, and I was an animal.

I didn't have hair, I had fur. I felt it from the inside, everywhere, all over me. I had seen myself, monstrous in the drawing room window, because I was halfway through changing, like now. It only took a few minutes to finish.

I closed my eyes. The room was black and my muscles ground against each other. Electricity forking through fibre and protein and fat. Shoulders swelling. Spine stretching. Things can happen, but not be possible, like when dancers and models strike inconceivable poses for hours. My mouth was crammed with oversized incisors and canines, creaking and splitting into carnassials, as my jaw cracked wider. All bodies transform. What is growth – from infant to adult – if not complete transformation, shifting from one shape to another?

I took one of the sharp knives hidden under my mattress to my scratch, reopening the scar, allowing my own claws to clasp the skin from the inside, tear it open and reach out, leaving the flaccid pink girl of me puddled on the floor. To leave behind the idea of a girl, and be the animal, itself.

Not a primitive ape, fat-fingered and empty-eyed, as the boys said. A tynx, powerful and precise as the electrostatic discharging in the storm outside. As a child, I'd seen my paws clearly – puffy, gentle things right in front of me – and my tail with a will of its own. I was kittenish, out of control, but a mature cat is assertive, deliberate, intrepid. Trees bowed to hold a big cat. For the power of a tiger and the stealth of a lynx, flesh would rip itself apart to become devoted meat. Nature accepts its own authorities.

Rain tambourined across the roof. I opened the balcony doors and closed them behind me. Droplets of rain slid through the fretted trusses of the roof, studding my fur like jewels. My long tongue scooped my nose, rearranging my whiskers.

Mumma could point at her smooth skin all she liked, but she was not powerful, stealthy, supple. She had held me as a kitten, before my paws were weapons. My fur was fine to stroke while it was downy, until it knotted with burrs and soured with spray beneath the tail. When I grew up, Mumma became a true stepmother – a mother stewed and blackened and overcooked, abandoning daughters in forests. Poisoning them. Knocking them out for a hundred years.

I was hardly able to believe how she had locked me up like a cliché – because she had realised how valuable I was, and how cheap she was.

She was not part-tynx. She was thirty-two and a miserable, hygiene-obsessed liar.

Below me, in a net of rain, she limped through the garden – checking behind, checking in front – dragging carrier bags along the path into the woods.

The animal walks through the air like it is descending the staircase for a ball. It smells something nasty.

'Who's there? Is someone there? This zoo is private property. I've got a gun—'

It stops, distracted. Something smells delicious. The rain has wet the scent and refreshed it, but as it keeps falling, heavier and heavier, the scent thins. The wind lifts it, drags it around the trees, diluting the trail.

'Is someone there—'

The animal follows, before the smell is lost forever.

⁂

The animal is in his room. But he is not there.

It is undone by the efforts it has made to get inside, only to find he is gone and the room filled with someone else's scent. Pony dust and Twister juice. The animal sniffs the sheets and gets glitter on its nose.

The animal shreds every scent of him. Sprays everything, everywhere. Lies panting. But it's not enough.

⁂

It is a white, wheeled home and the animal's claws run down it, through the wheels.

He has been here, but the animal can't get in.

It rips anything it can.

It's not enough.

⁂

The animal's hunt is in the air, and on the ground.

They herd together, panicked, maa-ing. Who will answer them? Where are their mothers?

It drops between them.

It is tooth and white of eye.

It is the spatter and plash.

It is groan and yowl.

Water runs with iron.

When they come for the animal with flashing lights, rain drumming their hoods, their feet slop in blood.

'Jesus—'

'What the—'

The animal watches them from a tree. Licking a paw. Flicking its ears.

They walk beneath it, wet with adrenaline.

They never know it's there.

It keeps to trees and stone.

It finds another throat, and another, and another, and –

DAY 11

THE RAIN WAS a milky sheet hiding the moor. It sounded on the grass, the earth, the millions of leaves. A mouth wide open saying ah. The timber griped as I crawled through the balcony doors, covered with blood and mud, belly like a bulb.

Mumma sat on the bed, still wearing the clothes she had worn last night, her arms folded around a bottle of bleach. Her stained shirt retucked and rebuttoned.

'Mumma, I was—' I stopped, remembering she was not my mother.

'I'm not even going to ask,' she said, not looking at me. 'You've got something around your mouth.'

In the bathroom, the tap glugged, and shook, then gushed. The water tanks were refilling as the river rose with rain. I plugged the sink, and looked in the mirror. For a second, I did not recognise myself. The blood made my lips swell across my face. There was a pink, heart-shaped stain around my mouth, pointing to my chin. My face and neck were streaked and peppered with ticks. Blood stiffened brown, caught in the heat of my breasts.

I scrubbed blackened hands, stippled with cuts, and pulled up the soles of my feet to find the same.

'Put some clothes on.' Mumma didn't move when I came to the door.

'I told you,' I said. 'I know now. I know I'm a—'

'You didn't listen to me about the balcony, then.' She spoke loudly over me. 'The thing is, darling, I say these things because I don't want you to get hurt. You have no idea how painful it is to have a child.'

'Nor do you,' I said.

'From the moment you latched on to my breast I've been full of dread.'

'Nope,' I said. 'That never happened.'

'Before you were a baby, you were a terrible case of constipation. But I was so worried about Nella, those cramps were a welcome distraction. They never tell you—,' she said, '—nobody ever explains the agony of growing a person.'

'Your imagination is extremely overactive.' I took pleasure imagining the doctor's head on my shoulders as I tried to imitate his voice.

'Sometimes I dream I'm still pregnant, and my entire body is a puffed, hard knot, and when I wake, I think it's over, but then I remember you're still there, like an infection—'

'Why didn't you tell the doctor I was part-cat? Why didn't you tell me?'

'—it's only ever a matter of time until something happens and I swell into a fever from you again.' She laughed, high. 'We might get on better if you accepted my being concerned you might fall to your death from this rotten house is completely reasonable—'

There was a loud buzzing in my ears. It was what she did, pretended I wasn't speaking, pretended I was nothing and no one, hid me away from herself. My head was full of racing air. I held out my hands. My sore fingers shrank into stubby, furry bean digits. I blinked widely. Forgetting I was upright, I staggered a little, and my forepaws elongated back into human fingers.

'Lowdy.' Mumma dropped the bleach to stand. She put her hands to my head, picking the ticks from my skull. 'Are you alright?

'No.' I could hardly hold my head up, weighed down by my phantom hair.

'But you haven't been fiddle-faddling?'

'No.' My stomach drummed heavily, full, though I didn't remember eating.

'I want to trust you –,' she sounded a little desperate. 'I want you to create your own boundaries. To live here in the real world.' She crawled her hands into my mouth, gripping each jaw. Prising them apart, checking for anything hiding between the teeth. 'But you're not very good at it.'

I burped.

'What have you been eating?'

'Raw meat, I suppose.' I leaned forward and brought up a half-digested red, raw tide.

She stared at the shining puddle of discharge.

'Told you,' I bellowed.

Mumma opened her mouth to speak, then stopped. She shook her head and took the bleach from the bed. 'You have to *want* to get better.' She smoothed one hand across her shirt, not noticing where the soft fabric was stiffened with spilt gin. 'So, are you —' she cleared her throat, eyes skirting the meaty puke, '– happy?'

Something inside me lost its grip, a microscopic seed was disintegrating – breaking up, unknitting itself like the puddle on the floor. I was so tired. When, I thought, did I last sleep properly, all the deep, long night? I was spinning like a top, shoulders circling my hips.

'Let's start again. You and I. You are the most important thing in the world. I need to take better care of you.' She put her arms out to steady me but I stepped out of reach. 'I would do anything for you,' she said, arms slow scissors in the air between us. 'And I need to do better.' She bowed her head. 'Start with simple statements. Repeated clearly, with intent. '*I am only a girl*,' she said. 'And I will get you some delicious, nourishing broth—'

'—better after a bath.'

The rain kept falling, somewhere outside, on a different planet.

The tanks in the attic dripped fast and the temperature had finally dropped, but it was too hard to wake. I stayed asleep, in the luminous black swirl of my eyelids.

'*They that wash on Monday, have all week to dry.*' Mumma rushed a toothbrush around my mouth. '*They that wash on Tuesday, are not so much awry.*' She pulled off my pyjamas, ran a comb over my – nothing. She flopped my hands over her shoulders and pulled me upright. '*They that wash on Wednesday are not so much to blame.*'

The world was a fuzzed line. I passed the bedside table, empty but for the mug of broth she'd fed me. What had Grandma said was in it? I thought, still unawake. Mumma had cleaned the vomit and walked me down to the bathroom.

'*They that wash on Thursday, wash for shame.*' She scrubbed my face with soap, twice, so excited she did not notice new ticks cowering beneath my cloud of breast. They itched, but how to unlatch them without leaving in the mouthparts that cause infection?

'*They that wash on Friday wash for need.*' She slid my limbs into some old tracksuit bottoms and a T-shirt. '*And they that wash on Saturday, oh, they're sluts indeed.* What day is it actually?' She squinted at the ceiling, like a jolly vintage governess with chaos and morals for fun, feral children.

'And who cares? Gosh. What a difference these new chaps make,' she said, brightly, to my hair-filled breasts, before plummeting me through space down many, many stairs.

She left me, curly as a straw, sitting at the kitchen table.

This is not happening. This is the paracosm, I thought, unable to feel the tynx inside at all. How has she done it?

'Look, darling!' Mugs, glasses, jam jars, egg cups, and ice cream tubs full of water fluttered into view on every surface. 'Keep drinking. You'll feel better when you've rehydrated. Have as much as you want. We'll put them out to fill up again. Or even use the taps.'

I took the tea cup Mumma offered with tensed fingers, trying to focus as she clapped her hands, catching excited breaths. I gagged a little on the sweet water. She leaned across the table, weaving her hands through the containers of water to tip the tea cup a little higher. She forced the last dribble of water into my mouth, then took the cup from me and held my hands.

'Are you feeling better, darling?'

I pulled away. Ready to unroll the claws from my paws. Ready to show her how I was everything Digger wanted, and more. How I was the heir, and this would be my zoo. I was dangerous. Not to be underestimated. I threw my arms across the table. Water splatted the walls and trickled off the table. Cups and jars hit cupboards and smashed on the flagstones. But nothing happened. I brought my blunt fingertips close enough to focus on, disappointed.

'Are you alright, darling? You're going a bit red.' Her nose twitched, holding in a smile.

I tried again, putting everything into the furthest ends of my body. Only when my lungs were flapping and my face was black with blood did I scream, long and frustrated.

'Kids.' She rolled her eyes to a side-audience who didn't exist.

'I'm not a kid.' I pushed out my lips, to free my tynx teeth. I shook with the effort, but nothing happened.

'Of course, you're not, sweetheart.' She over-shook her head, patronizing me. 'We'll light the fire. I've found a puzzle. Or we could even start sewing a quilt, if you like?'

'No.' I teared up.

'We don't have to. It was just an idea I had because of the curtains.'

The kitchen windows looked at me, wide and lidless.

'I'll make more soup. Shall I chop an onion? I could sharpen a butter knife on some granite. Or – you could tell me where the knives are?' she said, and I dropped my forehead to the table. I used to steal the knives, when I was little. But I didn't have to any more, now I had my own claws. Mumma even bought me a scratching post to use them on, to stop me damaging the legs of the furniture, to stop me destroying everything whenever I was let out of the cupboard.

I must have slept again, suddenly, like Little Briar Rose, because

I opened thorny eyes and time had hopped. There was a peeled onion in front of Mumma, white and stinging. Outside, rain fell like the knife at the board – chopping and tossing handfuls at the window.

'You'll be back to your old self in no time,' she said, but not to me. 'Try to remember, everything's just a phase with children. Isn't it?'

⚘

The bare walls greyed with premature dusk. The house choked on burning onions and yellow sap. Mumma wrapped me in a blanket next to the fire in the library although it was not quite cold. She lit candles in case we lost power again, and sat with her legs under her, piles of faded fabric on her knees. Her mug of green broth turned up the corners of her mouth, and gave her a clownish smile when I poured mine onto the floor between us.

I hate her, I thought. I hate her, I hate her.

'Stop grinning, Lowdy.' She pulled the fabric out of the way of the spillage and crossed her legs to face me. 'I'm trying my hardest, but I can't do it again. So, alright. You're a cat.'

I stayed very still and very quiet, in case it hadn't happened.

'Can you hear me, darling?' she said. 'You're a cat. That's that. I don't know how it happened, but there we have it. Perhaps you're half and half. Wait – wouldn't it make more sense if we were *all* cats? You, me and Grandma? A family of werecats? But why now? Is it a full moon or something? Perhaps it's all the fresh, moor air—'

I pulled my hand out from under the blanket. There were no claws on it, but as Mumma kept saying, I was not, currently, well. I tucked it away again.

'No? I suppose there isn't heaps of evidence for Grandma and I shapeshifting. But perhaps skin-changing is a rather private matter – you'll know what I mean if you ever get your period. On the other hand, you seem adamant you're related to Nella, so something must have happened. Perhaps a man fell in love with her. Or perhaps

222

they didn't. Either way, I suppose Nella couldn't do anything about it when he impregnated her. There's always drugs or restraints. I don't like to think about it, to be honest, but here we are, thinking about it anyway. But, say you're a cat – or part-cat – whatever you prefer – now what? Has it improved things? Do you feel better? Now I've *admitted* it, do you think we can deal with it a little better? Together? Will you let me help you?'

She waited for me to speak, but I was stunned.

'It is worth bearing in mind, when you are cross with me, I've only wanted the best for you. I think, probably, it is best not to be half-cat. If I *was* actually part-cat, I'd tell you to practice being human, like a cat-shaman, you know, until you forgot your catness. If I *was* actually part-cat, I'd keep it to myself. It's definitely a lot easier being human, but you can lick that mess off the floor if you like.'

Mumma was very convincing when she wanted to be, and more than that, it was possible she did want the best for me. I, myself, had, on occasion, lied to protect her, after all. Perhaps she was not my *worst* enemy.

She tilted herself away from the broth on the floor, to fold the fabric in on itself. Her scissors made a long 'sh' sound running through swathes of material. The noise was creeping around the room, in and out of the empty bookshelves, when someone knocked at the front door.

Mumma pulled back her lips to show me her teeth, but it was not a real smile. 'Pretend we're not home,' she whispered. It was a game. She put a hand across each eye.

Someone shook the door handle, then banged again.

Mumma sighed.

Nothing else happened.

She lifted one hand up, then the other, peeked out, then winked at me, like we'd won.

She drove her scissors through the fabric, faster than before. Pieces of it fell from her lap, sliding to the floor.

The room suddenly glowered. Behind Mumma, a man in a black

waterproof, hood up, zipped to the nose, rapped on the window. Water ran off his coat. I almost didn't recognise him without his flip chart.

'We've been knocking.' The ranger shouted through the glass. 'It's wet out, you know?'

Mumma turned to him in shock. Another man in a red water-proof jogged up behind him.

'We're from the national park authority. There's been a flood. The river's burst its banks at the bottom of your road.'

Mumma stood. The scissors clunked onto the floor.

'This is really a courtesy.' The second man sounded angry. 'There's a right of way across this land. We could've just driven through.'

Mumma went to the window. Her fingertips rested lightly on the sill.

'We need to get through,' the ranger said. 'It's been seen here. I believe your daughter's been telling everyone it lives around here, so we're concentrating our search on this part of the moor. Something killed a load of livestock overnight. It's an emergency. Would the girl like to come out and speak to us?'

He looked at Mumma, and behind him the other man held up a long, slim rifle. 'You've got a lot to answer for. It's ripped some fella's caravan. How would you like it? Eh?'

'Alright.' The ranger waved the other man behind him. 'We need to get through. That's all for now.'

'It's only gone in someone's house and shat everywhere.' The man in the red waterproof reached past the ranger to smack his hand off the window, making me jump. 'Shall I come and shit in your house? Eh? How would you like it?'

'Lowdy,' Mumma spoke under her breath. 'Why did you say you'd seen a tynx here? What have you done?'

In my core, pieces of possibility span away from each other, dissolving into nothing. I felt weaker than I'd ever been. I found myself wanting to do fists. Wanting to say positive statements. Wanting to fiddle-faddle. Wanting to change shape.

'Lowdy.' Mumma redistributed her weight. 'Go and check on Grandma, please.'

'Yes, Mumma,' I said.

⁂

Condensation ran down the inside of Grandma's windows. Behind me, she lay in the bed, asleep, or something like it. I kept my distance from her scaly face, from the curving white feelers of her chin. There was a smell turning my stomach. An oily gutting. A smell a body would rather keep private. Or, perhaps, I'd imagined it. She was probably doing really well.

There was a roar from the garden. I peeped over the windowsill to see the national park Land Rover drive slowly into the deer park and past the house.

'South-West Now and the national park authority coming through.' Peter Carter hung from the window shouting to the empty grass in front, looking back to make sure everyone behind heard.

The Land Rover was followed by a quad with a trailer, and another quad with another trailer. I swallowed, trying to scratch an itch inside my neck. This would be the last one, I thought – each time I thought this quad would be the last, but they kept coming like a cheap magician's hankies.

'D'you know where you're going—' Someone shouted.

'Is that the way?'

'Doesn't matter—'

The car pushed through the narrow path into the rhododendrons. A flock of small birds flew out and branches squeaked along the doors.

Peter Carter leaned out into the rain again, to check the damage. 'Not a scratch,' he shouted to the driver as they disappeared out of sight.

The quads followed where the path had been forced open into a tunnel. In the trailers, the men sat bent over in dark waterproofs, watching the ground, the trees, the sky, through the scrim of rain. One of the quads caught a wheel on something and revved hard to free itself. The air filled with white smoke and the quad jumped free. The men in the trailer behind slid one way then the other, crashing into each other.

'What's happening?' Grandma coughed. It was painful for her to swallow, and even nastier to speak. In Mumma's defence, I thought – unable to look at how gross Grandma was now – it can't be easy looking after a rotting person.

'The river's flooded,' I said. 'There's a right of way.'

'Not through the damned zoo—'

Then, Digger rolled through, behind his Dad on a tractor. Hood down, hair soaked long and stuck to his cheeks. He didn't look at the house, only forwards. I pressed my forehead onto the wet glass.

Then people came on foot holding spades, rakes, a garden fork. What, I thought, will they do with those? I cleared my throat and coughed a little. It's fine, I thought, they're after the tynx, except the tynx is –

The butcher, the grocer, and the man with the petition from the hall were pointing at a map in a waterproof cover. A smart man with a mobile phone rubbed his eyes like a tired child. The three boys skidded around the side of the house on their little bikes. 'Lads,' they shouted, spraying gravel at a sheepdog. The dog barked, but the lads were gone.

A farmer in an agitated conversation walked through Mumma's shrine of pots and pans. They rolled and chimed across the grass. The man looked back, aware something had happened, but kept walking, to finish what he was saying.

Denny walked through, taking broad strides, shoulders dipping from side to side, a cigarette in his mouth. He looked at the house, to me at the window. He took his hat off, soaking his hair, and pulled it on again. I dropped, out of his sight, hanging on to the windowsill with no feeling in my legs. If Denny wanted to see a tynx in a cage, use its skin as a rug, take its head in his hand for photos, what would he ever do if he caught *me?*

When I looked over the sill again, he was gone. The last people were on horseback. I recognised Caitlin, a poisonous berry in a waterproof over my gown. I tensed every muscle to stop myself hurdling Grandma, jumping the banister, and smashing through the back door to kick her from the zoo. Rosie was nowhere to be seen. The ponies walked slowly through the rough passage into the rhododendrons. They stumbled. Slipped in the mud. Pressed brilliant flowers torn from the trees deep into the trenches left by the tractor.

The ponies shied when the quads revved out of sight. Everyone waited. There were whistles and hoots. Men shouted to each other. Cats, I heard them say. Cats. Cats. Cats. Then everyone moved again, as the Land Rover found its way through the woods to the bridle path.

When Fowl jogged past, all that was left on the grass were two deep streaks of mud. His hood fell from his red head. His yellow beard was frilled with water and his compass frisked at his belly. He stopped, resting his hands on his knees, then half-jogged to catch up.

'What am I going to do, Grandma?' I hugged the wall, as they plundered through the enclosure, wrecking our path to the moor, wondering how far the blood-rage of a single apex predator would get me against an entire village. I briefly wished I wasn't part-tynx, after all. I wished I hadn't terrorized the village, then encouraged that same village to look for me at my home. Establishing I was half-cat was not the great achievement I had expected it to be.

Childhood had been a cage. Don'ts and can'ts the bars. The happy ending – the key to the cage door – I had childishly thought, was making your own choices. Mumma always said, 'the best bits of being grown-up look like single stems of roses in individual glass cases'. Each blossoming choice was preserved and held apart. A perfect choice – like deciding to eat nothing but sweets, for example, or living authentically part-girl-part-cat – was unrelated to responsibilities or consequences. Mumma saw the rotting teeth of it all.

Grandma never answered and even through the closed window, the river boomed loud in the valley.

⚓

I reset Mumma's pots and cups, organizing them by size, as she would have done. They quickly refilled with rain. The Fingers Are Food sign was now in three pieces on the grass.

The turf was a sponge as I waded through it. A dirty one. The deer park was an uneven pitch of mud. There was no longer a visible path between it and the petting pen. Any old boundary markers had completely disappeared. It looked like it would be impossible to return it to anything like a flat spread of grass.

The slick, hoof-pocked tunnel through the rhododendrons was studded with cigarette butts. Petrol sat on the air and water ran in muddy culverts, brown as strong tea, down the path. It clung to the back of my skull racing along the gutter of my neck.

The lynx enclosure was now part-river, tyre-tread tributaries everywhere. Water rested lightly on the leaf mould, and gathered among tree roots, looking like it had set the zoo in gelatine. White vapours rested on the river and the rain hit the racing surface of the current so fast it was almost invisible. It was impossible to hear anything over the river, not even the search party.

Something swirled where the water pooled behind a row of boulders – where the sheet had been caught on tree roots. The boulders were hardly visible now, but one jutting out wore something dark and hairy like a wig.

I waded to where the bank dropped into the pool like a continental shelf. The swollen body of a cat whirled around. Another cat popped out of the water, for a second I thought it was alive, but it fell back into the water, a tiny, furry breaching whale. Then another popped up, and another. All dead. More and more appeared. Some face down. Some spinning in the current. Marooned over roots. Half-caught on the bank. I stumbled into the water, hardly able to

228

stay upright in the eddies, pulling them to me. Wrapping my arms around a furry bunch of flowers. A new one popped up every so often, twirling around, butting me for attention, from wherever they'd once been weighed down.

I sobbed for them, my smaller relations. They had welcomed me when I doubted myself. Their tiny mews had called to my huge, hidden tynx heart, now as ragged and half-patched as my real mother in the pump-house. I held the cats tight, drowning them a second time in snot and tears, as I tried not to be pulled under, and looked for my thin little tabby pet.

Who did this? I thought. Who drowned our cats? Would they do the same to me? Was it a threat? To be a tynx, is to be caged or killed. Why hadn't Mumma warned me? Last year, she left a note on my Animal Brides and Grooms project. 'Don't forget, the Greek gods used shapeshifting as a punishment,' she wrote, so perhaps, in her own way, she had.

The animal paces the room.

It touches its nose to the clear walls.

It can see the outside. It can smell the outside.

It can't touch the outside.

The animal cries out. Angry. Then for pity.

❧

She is on the other side of the door, but the animal cannot get through to her either.

'Loveday, why have you locked yourself in? Slip my key under the door. Calm down, darling. Please let me in.'

❧

There is a feeble creature inside it. Trying to make the animal small. Like it is. Small with anxiety, wanting to hide the animal away.

The animal throws itself and the walls fall, sharp, all over it.

Its paws bleed and its head is heavier and heavier, thicker and thicker.

The animal cannot stay awake.

Eventually it lies, and waits for the end.

DAY 12

A TYNX SAT on the balcony. It was my reflection, although at this point the glass was gone, so it was not my reflection as I usually understood reflections to work, but since I was the only tynx, it was, somehow, me. We stared at myself.

In the rain, even with the stripes, I was not so much burning bright as I was biscuit-coloured soggy. Drooping ears and fur flat with water made my head like an open book. Eyes not on fire but ashy cigarette butts. I looked into the room, blankly. Waiting for something. My forelegs were thicker than my girl-thighs. Paws like bath sponges. It was a wardrobe of a body, not something you'd want to fall on you. I wished I'd had it to punish the boys at the school.

I shook myself. My fur puffed out. Me-in-the-tower laughed at my black-ribboned Pierrot ruff, and the tynx lowered my head. Sniffed. Watched. Stooped, legs tense, paws ready. One corner of my black lip lifted to show a little tooth, poking out like Mumma's knee from the slit of her skirt. When I growled, the noise came from such a distance, it might have been the grating of the granite under the moor, a tor doming up out of the Palaeozoic era.

I turned my back on my reflection.

Well, I thought – getting into bed, still able to hear my extravagant growl – I can see why people are nervous.

❧

I woke to knocking at the bedroom door.

Mumma was slumped against the wall outside. She eyed my

stinging, raw head. 'What have you done this time?' Her voice strained as she took my hands. 'We'll need tweezers.' My palms glittered with glass. 'Dear, oh dear.' She was virtually singing to sound unconcerned. 'But as long as you didn't go out -,' then she saw behind me into the room.

Ripped curtains pooled around their poles. The desk and floor boards were striped pale with clawing. A rug, duvet, the pillows and all my books had been shredded.

'Well,' she said. 'You've saved me a job.' She nearly smiled, but she noticed a urine stain on the wall dribbling into a sticky orange puddle at the skirting board, and covered her nose and mouth instead.

I lay back on the bed, turning my face to the wall, head and hands throbbing.

She tweezed and bandaged my hands. She dabbed cool cream into the furrows I'd made in my head with my claws. She pulled on her rubber gloves. She swept up the glass. The ruined clothes and curtains went into a cardboard box. She brought a bucket of soapy water and a scrubbing brush. She removed the curtain pole, bedside table and lamp, and gathered the bits of paper into a binbag.

'I'm sorry about this.' She tied the binbag, looking down the stairs, trying not to see me. 'We need to get out of here, darling,' she muttered.

After she left, I slid under my mattress to check my secret books. Now my facts had gone, pictures were all I had left, but when I lay on them, unable to sleep, they were no comfort.

Rain fell in through the broken glass. Beyond the balcony, the moor stretched out, full of quads and risks. I didn't want to see tynx-me out there now.

It was more complicated than the stories suggest, being part-cat.

Depression in cats was like depression in humans. Mumma once told me Nella was depressed because she had been rejected by her mother. She'd never been interested in eating. Her low weight meant her fur clumped into dry, stiff tufts. She didn't groom knots out, and lay around in plain sight, never bothering to hide. Mumma went to the village for choice cuts of meat and climbed the tree in the enclosure to wedge steaks along branches and into nooks, creating a treasure trail to interest her. Nella never had head bumps for Mumma's hips. She never loped to greet Grandma with the buckets in the morning. She was so unsettled, she would sometimes growl when Mumma approached her, and often chewed her own paws.

Mumma said Grandma always had dull hair too. She was always thin. Always alone. She wasn't exactly a hugger. She made Mumma work in the zoo's ticket office during visitor hours so she could avoid the people and the gossip. So Mumma preferred to spend her spare time outside, away from Grandma and their home, with the animals – who were surprisingly affectionate – or taking long walks across the moor.

But these were hidden stories. Grandma's depression was spoken of in lowered voices, beneath the sheets of our shared bed. 'When my father left her and she started wearing his clothes and smoking his pipe, the village overcharged her for groceries and ignored her when she spoke to them. Of *course* she was depressed, but where else could we go? It only got worse when she opened the zoo and became Mrs Cat. I don't know why she didn't just get rid of those silly old cats.' Mumma's voice glanced with juniper and tonic, as she clung to me, her eyes closed, so she didn't see she was the child then, and I the adult. 'Happiness is overrated anyway,' she would console herself, 'if you laugh out loud, you've missed the joke.'

I reached to the tynx inside – to put on my coat, or unroll my tail – for a little comfort and cheer, but my legs and arms remained limp and gentle. My heart was frail and pitilessly girlish, longing for control of my whole animal self, while not able to move the part I did have.

꧁

Mumma returned in a hurry with a plastic razor and a bowl of brown, jellied meat. 'Cat food. It's not ideal, but miraculously it's in date. I'll put out mouse traps, but for now, where would you like it—,' she half-offered it to me, before placing it on the floor. She pushed it towards me using her toe. 'Come on,' she said. 'I'm in a rush. There's a lot to do and you've got to eat.'

She tapped one foot, while I got on my hands and knees. I forced down mouthful after mouthful, trying to hide gags and brawny belches. I was hardly finished, my belly had never felt so distended, when she dragged me off the floor. 'Are you fully full? Promise me you've no room in there for anything else?'

'I promise,' I said, as she pushed me into the bathroom.

When she had first cut my hair, Mumma even tried to cheer me up with a biography of Lady Jane Grey. By the time she was my age, Lady Jane Grey had been imprisoned, charged with treason, and sentenced to death by burning or beheading – but there was absolutely no reason given for all her hair falling out.

If Mumma was disturbed by the lingering wet, brown odour of my throat she did not mention it. The razor planed away at me until it was flecked with white matter. She was more determined about shaving me, this time. 'Believe me, I loved your beautiful thick hair. No one wants to slaughter their best goat, darling, but sometimes it's that or starve.'

When she finished, she looked around the tower room briefly. 'There's still chickenwire,' she said. 'From the old cages. We talked about making a cage, remember? Might be hard to erect something big enough up here.' She flashed me a smile, and was halfway down the stairs, shouting back. 'But don't worry. I'll keep thinking about it.'

I covered my nose with a sleeve of my tracksuit. Grandma's room was a cist, the walls hard and damp. It was a stage, ready for a performance, nothing but a bed in it. Even the wardrobe was gone. She couldn't have smoked for days, yet there was still a sepia shade to the air.

Grandma lay like a cardboard Halloween skeleton and didn't move when I sat on the bed. Her lips were caked with green dust like she'd been gnawing on bark. I smoothed her bedding, her hair, her hand, trying to wear her away to glass so she could stay here eternally, preparing and training me. I kissed her forehead, hoping to wake her, wanting answers.

I would have guessed that discovering yourself to be transformative, would have *been* transformative, like in the stories. But shapeshifting was being ecstatic one minute, desolate the next. I was beginning to understand why the frogs and swans and hedgehogs wanted to shed their animal skins to become predictably, consistently, boringly human.

'Was Nella all tynx?' I asked Grandma. 'Or was she a bit one thing, a bit another? A bit girl, a bit tynx? Was she like me, Grandma? Could she also be a girl? Grandma? How can I breed for the new zoo? What should I do? And when?' If she heard me, she said nothing. Inside, her blood popped and grumbled.

I watched her sleep, counting the hairs between her eyebrows. I lost count. In Ancient Egypt, when a house cat died, the whole family shaved their eyebrows in grief. After a while, I shook her shoulder. Her breath was shallow and muddied as the river. I leaned and put my ear to her chest, listened to the clank of her organs.

'Who was my father?' I whispered through her ribs into her heart, and unsheathed a razor.

Mumma entered with a mug. 'I never knew my father and I turned out alright.' She pulled me off Grandma, legs first, from where I had straddled her.

'Oh my god Lowdy, why have you shaved her eyebrows?' she said. 'Why have you shaved *your* eyebrows?'

'My household is in mourning,' I said. 'The cats are all dead.'

'Please, calm down. Loveday. Stop crying and meet me in the kitchen.'

'Alright.' Mumma sat opposite me and slid a mug of broth across the table. I slid it back. 'I forgot. I'll check the traps again. Now. The eyebrows will grow back. It's not the end of the world. But we have to let Grandma prepare herself peacefully.' She had the high eyebrows of someone not in mourning at all. 'She could die any day now, darling.'

She tried to give me science. Causes and effects. But I was distracted by the facts and knowledge and history that would die with Grandma.

It was Mumma - whoever she was to me - who first loved fairy tales and named Nella for her long hair. No coincidence, then, that I with my own - formerly - thick mane, was that hairy creature's daughter. In the story, Petrosinella's mother gave her to an ogress who locked her in a tower. The ogress dragged the girl, by her hair, to the tower, then used the same extremely long hair to climb the tower, visit Petrosinella, and teach her magic. A prince, pretending to be the ogress, climbed Petrosinella's hair one day, and despite their dishonest start, the girl and boy met every night. With the prince's help, Petrosinella eventually managed to escape the tower, and ogress, and live happily ever after. It was so simple.

What are the chances I would have lived, like Petrosinella, like Nella, in a tower, a cage, trapped by an ogress? How sad that Digger had not turned out to be the prince I needed. Had I found these stories, or had they found me?

'- she's lived a long life and it's important to focus on the positive. Are you listening, Lowdy? What are you doing? Please, get up off the floor. Don't lie there like that. Stop wailing, I've got so much to do before tomorrow. Go to your room. Go on. Good cat.'

❧

I must have slept. One arm around my belly, the other holding my breasts - full of meat and sore - away from the ticks. I woke when a man in blue overalls dropped a metal toolbox on my bedroom floor.

'This is going to be noisy, sweetheart,' he said, looking at me, in the bed.

I pulled up my blanket and he drilled boards into the door and window frames.

The animal sniffs the moon, a white pin in the wall.

The animal is full of energy, with no place to put it.

The animal wishes, more than anything, that she were, simply, a girl.

DAY 13

A SMALL GREY patch appeared in one corner of the ceiling. Every time a tap ran, the tanks in the attic sloshed to refill.

Shadows moved slowly across the room.

A thread of light shifted over the white walls.

Chunks of the floorboards had been gouged out.

My pillow rasped against my scabby head. My skin was on the inside, nerves on the outside, and all the tick legs tickled my breast as I fed them, against my will.

My nose twitched. The tynx of me smelt Mumma's salty broth on the hob. It smelt my own armpits. The sappy, splintering plywood board over the doors. Fresh, chemical fumes of paint. The quaint perfume of the curtains. Dusty mice faeces. The old, wooden musk of the house. I craved the fake smell of Digger's deodorant. His sweat.

My ears pricked. Rain hit the roof and raced through the gutters. A hunk of plaster dropped from the balcony. A dislodged slate shifted in the wind. Mice panicked in the eaves. Grandma's lungs flapped wearily –

Mumma appeared at the door unexpectedly. I shot back and hit the bedframe. Why hadn't I heard her?

'I suppose it's good to see you up and about. Here's lunch.' She held the trap in her yellow rubber hands. A mouse lay on its side, tail swinging off the end, two grey lumps of fur bulging either side of a wire. When I didn't move, she sat next to me and pulled the trap wire open. The mouse twitched.

'Fresh.' She sounded pleased, but her mouth was a ruler barely measuring a smile.

'I don't feel well.' The mouse's foot was still going, just barely, trying to get a purchase on the air, as if it might yet push off something and make it to safety.

She finally freed it and offered it, by its tail, to me. 'Do you want to open up, or—' Its little tongue was a red drip from its mouth. Two tiny teeth bared at me. 'What about your - claws?' Clear liquid seeped from its nose. 'Hurry. I've got so much to do before tomorrow. You must eat,' she said. 'I can't be worrying about you getting worse. It's already bad enough.' She shook the mouse in front of my nose. My eyes bossed to see it. 'Hmmm, tasty,' she lulled. Something wet flew off it and hit my chin.

She dropped the mouse between us. The tiny foot started again, encouraged by the solidity of the mattress. 'This is what you wanted. Your stomach is designed to digest raw meat, nothing else,' she said, a little weary, standing to leave. 'I'm doing the best I can.'

How could I not believe her?

❧

A red car on the drive shone in the rain. Through the window above the stairs, I watched a man in a suit put a ring-binder under one arm and lock the car carefully. He opened a large green umbrella and balanced it on his shoulder. Stepping away from the car, the man looked back, perhaps to make sure it was still there, waiting for him if he suddenly needed to leave.

He tried to photograph the house with a disposable camera. The ring-binder slipped, and the green umbrella slid down his shoulder until it was a huge bonnet around his head.

I opened the front door. His hair leapt back from his forehead like it was allergic to his large, froggy eyes. He collapsed his umbrella in the porch.

'Nick Smith.' His hand shot out. He was younger and bigger, the closer you got.

I looked at his hand.

240

Mumma appeared, pushing me towards the stairs, and opening the door wide. 'Lowdy. Go to your room.'

'Come in. Tea or coffee?' She led Nick Smith down the hallway. I followed, on all fours. Nick Smith slicked his damp hair back, tighter and tighter to his head. He looked around. 'This could be a nice family space—' His voice disappeared as he noticed me.

'Stop growling, Loveday. Go to your room.' Mumma pushed me again towards the stairs with a leg. 'She's going through a stage.'

Nick Smith attempted to smile.

I waited on the stairs, licking one hand.

'Is this an original feature?' Nick Smith asked, of something in the cloakroom.

He lowered his voice in the library, speaking slowly to soften the impact. 'I'm sorry to tell you but there is a crack in your ceiling.'

In the drawing room, he inspected the rain-dimmed view across to the Bat, hands on hips. 'You wanna get rid of all this. Maybe think about walls,' he said, of the deer park sloping to the woods. 'You need to break it up.' He waved his hand from one side of the moor, to the other. 'The view's too exposed. You can all but see the Vaults.'

He turned his back on the landscape. 'You wanna separate the house from the zoo.' He clapped one hand into the other with each word. 'No one wants a home that comes with a zoo.' He turned away. 'Turn it into a tennis court or something.'

When they came into the hallway, I hissed and arched my back. Mumma was determined not to meet my eyes as Nick Smith tried to impress her by using words such as 'yourself' and 'consequently' and doing most of the talking. I wanted to scream.

I waited with my nose to the front door, willing it to open for Nick Smith, but they went upstairs.

'What do you think it's worth?' Mumma said, when they finally made it to the front door.

'What?' I said to her.

'Go and play,' she said, not looking at me.

Nick Smith opened his ring-binder, flipped a page backwards

then forwards, adjusted his trousers at the belt, and looked around the hallway, again. Looking for something he might have missed. He filled his chest with air and expelled it, slowly.

'Do you wanna know what I'd put it on for? Or what you could expect to get?' he said.

'No.' Mumma sighed. 'Thank you so much for coming.' She opened the front door and waved him out of it. He stepped out, confused. As he turned around, she shut the door.

'Lock everything up, darling.' She went to the kitchen.

The cat yawned in the picture at the top of the stairs, and I tried to place the source of my nausea.

I walked into the drawing room to look around. It was almost empty. The room had been stripped, exposed as only walls and ceiling. I went to the library, where, of course, the shelves were empty. There was only the desk left and when I panted, suddenly short of breath, that small sound was flung around the bare walls like a cough.

There was nothing in the dining room but the table and chairs. No pictures on the walls, not even curtains at the windows. I ran back to the hallway, to check for my initials on the dusty bureau by the front door, but the bureau was gone.

A tiny black egg, fat with my blood, dropped from under my T-shirt onto the floor, finally finished with me. Then another, and another. How dare you, I thought as they kept falling. I trod on one after another, bursting them. Tiny, single splashes of blood hitting the floorboard, but mostly the sole of my own foot.

I ran out, into the rain, and down the hill in front of the house, past the new tunnel through the trees. The brume hung along the rhododendrons so you couldn't even see where the hill dropped away, let alone the zoo, or the moor.

I circled the ticket office, the roof more ivy than plank. Trees grew from it. Inside was the bureau, a mirror, and some boxes of books. Chopped legs of chairs, and doors from cupboards were stacked, for the fire. Everything else was gone.

Mumma had been too good at clearing up.

I took hold of the bureau and pulled it from the log pile.

⚜

It was hard, dragging the bureau through the steep, moss-tufted grass, but I had apex strength. The legs left two furrows in the earth which quickly filled with water, like the tracks left by the search party. I was soaked through, and hot. I tipped the bureau onto its back and tugged it by two of its legs. Eventually, I was at the back door.

I pushed the bureau in front of me into the hallway where it shrieked and left gashes in the floor. Mumma came out from the kitchen.

'What are you doing?' she shouted.

I shoved the bureau hard against the wall, and bent forwards, hands on my knees to recover. The water ran off me.

'Oh, darling.' Mumma spoke more softly, appeasing whatever she saw. 'It's the house, you can't trust it. Look at Grandma. It sends people mad. You're up and down all over the place since we got here. Where's my sunny baby girl?'

'You can't sell the house.' I stood over her. 'We're opening a new zoo.'

'Oh god, Lowdy.' Mumma tried to stifle a laugh. 'Come on, now.'

'It's our home.'

'No, darling. It's not your home.' She licked her lips, nervous, knowing I disliked having things explained to me in simple words like I was a child. '*You* never lived here.'

'Grandma.' I shouted as loud as I could, staring at her.

'It's not just the mould.' She stepped forward, her hands braced, pushing nothing towards me. 'There's radon in the air. Asbestos in the walls. Lead from the water pipes. And that's only what I happen to know about. The house is poisonous. It always has been. No wonder you're in this state. We must get out—'

I took the stairs two at a time. The cat screamed in the painting at the top of the stairs. What could it see, out of sight, that I couldn't?

Mumma rushed to reach the painting before me, stretching her arms wide for it. 'Oh no, you don't. Something else I should have thrown out before you saw it. Although if drowning *dozens* of cats didn't prevent this from happening—'

Her words sounded over and over in my head. I couldn't believe it. 'Grandma loved those cats. She'll never forgive you.'

Mumma looked around her, like she didn't understand the conversation. 'What are you talking about? They weren't pets, Loveday. The cats were food. She was feeding them to—' she stopped.

'She was feeding them to - what?'

We looked at each other. I reached out, took the painting from her, turning it sideways to carry it along the landing. 'It's mine. This is all mine,' I cried to the cat, showing it the blank wall of the landing.

'One day you'll realise I did my best.' She hurried to catch up. 'You'll realise.'

'Grandma, get up.' I shouted.

But her bedroom door was locked. I shook the handle, shook it again, and then rammed it hard with the back of my body to protect my painting until the thing flew open.

'Get up.' I dropped my painting to rip back the curtains, letting the grey day in.

'Lowdy. Stop it. Stop it.' Mumma followed me trying to take hold of my arms, but I shook her off.

Grandma didn't move.

'Wake up.' I pulled back the sheets and blankets.

Grandma's eyes watched the ceiling, unblinking.

Mumma tucked Grandma's legs back in, frenzied to begin with, then she slowed, and stopped. She touched Grandma's cheek, leaned close to her face. 'Mother?' she said.

'She's taken everything, Grandma. She's taken our stuff. She wants to sell it. Get up.' I pulled Grandma by one arm and her body edged stiffly towards me.

'Leave her.' Mumma raised her voice, fearful. 'Leave her alone now.' She put her arms around me, tight, like she used to when I was little and I got so cross I would shake. 'She's gone, Lowdy. There's so much to do now. I need to make a list. To register the death. Call the funeral directors. Transfer the assets.'

'You've got to get up, Grandma.' I took Mumma's wrists and pulled her off me. She stumbled backwards on to the floor.

I waited for Grandma to sit up, to intervene and swear, and tell me exactly how a tynx crossbred with a man sired a tynx-child – how it was an anomaly, never a hoax, how the zoo was rightfully mine – but she stared at the ceiling. Skin emptied of whatever had stuffed her, like Nella in the pump house.

'She's dead, Lowdy.'

I left Mumma on the floor, checking her wrists for damage.

The mice had gone, maybe migrating to somewhere dry, but the balcony wheezed with wind and rain. Water filled the old plaster, bloating it. Mumma was downstairs, flicking papers, making notes, arrangements, having a stiff drink. I shut off the sound and smell of her. Instead, I accepted into myself the anger and focus Grandma no longer needed.

My picture was propped opposite the bed, against the wall. 'How did Mumma weigh down the cats?' I asked it. 'How could she crush them together? She must have lost her mind. Stay inside,' I told my picture. 'There's a monster out there.' The painted cat cowered.

Blood ran thin down the inside of my thigh. It kept coming and coming from between my legs, tangy and rich, like someone was committing a murder inside me.

I pulled off the boards Mumma had put up for me, and climbed onto the balustrade.

I leaped off because

Cats always land on their feet.

DAY 14

PAIN FLOWS HEAVILY, but I have blood on my lips, and I like it.

※

Dogs bark in the dark. Rain clumps their fur, runs off their lowered ears. I can't fold up and stick to the shadows tonight. I can't creep inside again.

The dogs aim their muzzles, but I get their throats and leave them bubbling in the puddles. I take control with claw and jaw. They were put in my path.

I smell his family all over these fields.

I hurdle the hedge and shatter a flock. I do not stop until each one is finished. I hope he realises how much he's hurt me.

The last sheep hiccups back and forth around the bodies, trying to find another to follow.

It does follow.

※

I breathe easier now. There is shouting behind me, back at the house.

'It's killed the fucking dogs, Penny. It's killed the fucking dogs. Where's Digger? Page him. Get him home. Now.'

Where is Digger? Get him home. Now.

'The Batleigh woman's on the phone. She's looking for the bald girl. Is he with her?'

'It's killed the dogs. Get Digger home. Get him off the moor. Get inside. Get inside, Penny. Call the ranger—'

⚕

I pass cows.

It takes time. There's girth to them. But all necks leak with a claw in the pipes.

⚕

I am low, but I'm not tired. Fighting the heavy weight dragging inside is an instinct.

I could go all night.

What is stopping me?

Where is Digger?

⚕

I am on the pony before it startles. The thrill of the kill is nothing now, but takes stamina with something so big.

I keep going. I get it in different grips, try new positions, feeling emptier and emptier.

The herd scatters.

⚕

The high moor is quiet.

Until I find more sheep.

⚕

The sky is chalky as a blackboard when I sink my paws into the

248

mire, relieved nothing lives in the mulch. Everything here is already dead. I don't need to prove myself.

The crust cracks. I tread carefully. I wipe my nose across the peat, anoint myself in tannins. I am concealed, brown and ruined as the land.

A pool on a bed of sphagnum. Rain stipples my grey reflection. My eyes swell, unblinking, numbed by everything I've done.

The weight inside dips my muzzle into the water until I can't breathe. I want to sink deep, dreaming.

I back away, spraying bog water from my nose.

My power seeps out of me.

I shouldn't be here.

If you linger on the Vaults, you never leave.

༺

I doze on my platform, in my tree. Something wakes me. A familiar voice calls from the house beyond the woods.

'Please, Loveday. Please. There's a tynx out there. It's killing everything. You've got to come inside. It's dangerous. You're not safe out here. You must come in.'

It's painful to hear. I feel the pinch of my weaker other, unsure. I wait.

'Please, Loveday. Please come inside.'

The voice gets fainter.

'Loveday, you must come back. Grandma wouldn't want this—'

I growl so I can't hear what she's saying and eventually she's gone.

I lift a paw to run my tongue over, and inside she calms down. Gives in.

DAY 15

I T RAINS.
The witch paces the woods all night and all day. Grandma's gun before her. Shouting for me. Her drowning in snot and tears now. Me camouflaged, ignoring her.

'*I know you're here somewhere. I know you've been sleeping in the skins in the pump house. You must get inside. They're coming for Grandma's body. Come and say goodbye,*' she begs at the burrows and sets.

'*The tynx is vicious. It's a man-eater, like its mother. It's in the DNA,*' she warns the sticklebacks and the herons.

'*I'm sorry I didn't tell you the truth. I wasn't sure. I thought the one we found was it, but she must have been breeding. Something's been killing the livestock. The men are out, trying to find it,*' she shouts at the moss and the leaves and the hairy boulders and the savage sky.

'*They're idiots. You must come home, Lowdy. Those animals are capable of anything if they're threatened—*'

She falters. Finally, she goes home.

I leave my tree and wander until I don't know where I am.
– what I am.
White air walls the land in. I can't see my hills or woods.
I cannot return to the collar.
Damp wuther combs my fur like a mother. A thoughtless force of nature.

DAY 16

I T IS EASY to hide from them. The rain covers my tracks.
   I watch the engines pass, hanging above them.

I am the hot air they breathe.

They try to move quietly, but they skin the land wherever they go. They slosh through mud, heavy and loud. They never learned to carry their own weight lightly.

The scent of petrol and sweat, more powerful than anything else in the wind.

I am gone before they think to look up.

❦

Something thunders.

A giant black bird claps through the sky.

No.

A helicopter.

❦

I am so heavy now I can only lie in my tree. Listening. Watching water trickle amongst the grass below me.

I stop cleaning between my legs. The blood gathers into the rain and runs through the planks onto the soaked sedge and washes away.

My tongue darts out.

My ears flick, track movement outside.

My nose can't help itself.

It follows the fervor, frustration and, later, towards dusk, the disappointment.

※

A sick, wet night. A covered moon. I go out. There are fewer of them on the hills. They are less sure.

'That might be a paw—'

'Or a foot—'

'This bloody rain—'

Rain and wind bring branches down. They jump at falling twigs and leaves.

I stay away.

I take my pleasures – are they pleasures? – the chase, the kill, elsewhere. I take up small spaces. I can wait. I have all the time in the world.

※

I return and he's at my tree. He shouldn't have come. He hurts me and I don't like it.

The girl is with him. She pulls him backwards.

They can't see me watching from the darkness between the trees, but I see them clearly, in colour. The red gown.

'Get off, Caitlin.' He twists from her. 'Stay back,' he says.

'We've gotta tell someone.' She points his torch at my piles in the tree roots. An inch further and they'd see my claws lying there. 'That's not an animal—'

The bones are one side, skins on the other.

'It's so - organised,' Digger says, and I feel proud.

I straightened. I tweaked.

She within me is pleased he has noticed, but she is glad he hasn't come any further. That he can't see her disorder, inside.

I am on my haunches, but the inside me won't let me move.

Energy burns. Acid nips my legs.

I growl.

'Did you hear that?' The girl wisps the torch around the trees.

My hackles rise. Every follicle is a pain. My throat is a warning.

'Digger, where is it—'

'Sh.' He scans the darkness, one arm reaching out, swinging in front of him. 'Don't move—'

He offers his hand. The scent is overwhelming, intoxicatingly painful. Inside me, she shudders. Inside me is a fool. The hand he offers is not submission, or an apology. It's a move. Her own fear distracts her. She loses control and I am on him.

'Shit—'

Caitlin screams. I let her run.

Digger runs too, but he trips up. Obviously. He fights the claws. But soon he is quiet.

He's more fragile than he looks, but he will grow me strong.

I know what he's made of.

I will take the parts that nourish, and get rid of the rest. The crap.

Saliva slides from my tongue.

A roar. Lights in the woods. The army.

A jolt of panic within.

The girl has led them back to me.

I pause, then roll him into the river.

The piles of bones and skins follow.

The rain will clean the rest.

'Digger? Digger? He was right here, I swear. And there were these bones. Something moved, over there—'

– but I am gone.

DAY 17

THE DAY STEAMS. Water falls up as well as down.
Caitlin follows Peter Carter and the young man with the
video camera into the dell, to the remains of a fire. A grey homemade
plate-mask in her hand turns to mush in the rain. She has washed
my dress. Her hair is down, but also half up. Two tendrils, either
side of her face. A black ribbon choker at her neck.

'This is where you first saw the animal that attacked your
boyfriend?'

'Yes, Peter.' She pouts at the camera, looking sad because her
boyfriend has been badly injured. 'He wanted me to help find the
tynx. He'd seen it a few times. It was over there, watching me.'

She points loosely, without turning around, in a completely
random direction that happens to be towards me.

I back away slowly.

'It wasn't a coincidence. It was hunting me. It has a whole moor,
but it was down the zoo when I was. It was the size of a bus. When
it went for us, I couldn't see anything but teeth. If it hadn't been
for Diggory protecting me, I wouldn't be here today.'

⚜

My tree is theirs now. The enclosure is bound with red and white
striped tape to keep people out. Men in uniforms come to look for
things, but the rain keeps falling and the river keeps rising. Whatever
was there, is no longer there.

Always a familiar, desperate voice. '*Have you found my daughter?*'

'There's a boy in hospital.'

'Did he tell you where my daughter is?'

'He can't tell us anything at the moment, but a local girl said there was a pile of bones.'

'There're always people trespassing here. Doing God knows what. They used to leave lamb's heads on the doorstep to intimidate my mother. The bones are theirs.'

'Madam, I'll ask you again, was a dangerous animal released into these woods?'

'Sir, I've only been here two weeks. Help me find my daughter.'

'As we've already said, she's sixteen. She's allowed to leave home.'

When the police leave, their tape lifts in the wind and catches, whistling and waving, in the branches above the platform.

I must keep moving through the high branches. I see them below, and I backtrack to avoid them. But they always lap around again. They will not stop coming.

This land has no loyalty. No matter how lightly I step.

I stay awake and awake and awake. It's no life for a cat – we sleep and we sleep and we sleep. We are tender and mild, restful and delicate.

When we're not hungry. When we're not threatened.

Light eases, eventually.

My vision clears back to black and white, and red. It's such a relief.

I keep going, slowly, but now I lose my footing.

They have to shout over the river.

'There's something up that tree.'

'Take a shot—'

'Is it the cat?'

'I need more light—'

'This fucking rain—'

'It looks like—'

'Take the bloody shot—'

'No, wait—'

'Knock it out. We don't have to kill it—'

'Who's got binoculars?'

'Drive it to the river.'

They know so little. Cats are not afraid of water. They drink water. They can not live without water. They are made of water. All animals are.

I beat them to the river.

But there is so much water. The banks have collapsed with the weight. The water struggles to direct itself and rushes among the roots of trees, into the grass. Drowning it, instead of feeding it.

It overreaches, and so have I.

'Take the shot—'

'It's more useful alive—'

'We don't know what it might do—'

'It'll fall in the river.'

'Are you sure it's a—'

'It won't wash far.'

'Wait - that's not a—'

We have not slept for a long time. She does not want control anymore. She cannot handle it.

'Someone get a shot.'

'Don't damage the skin.'

'If it crosses the river we'll lose it.'

'Quickly. Before it—'

A gun cracks. I jump.

'What the fuck was that—'

❧

I walk slowly, no longer flush with the shadows, but sloppy like the ground.

Stopping occasionally for breath.

I need to find a new tree. But wherever I go, hunters are never far away.

I can always hear them.

DAY 18

D AY BREAKS LIKE a heart.
   Red and sticky.

❧

I lie in the open, too tired to hide.

There is a pony, and a rider. She stops, keeps her distance.

I know the smoke on her lips. The curl of her hair.

She whoops for my attention and the air fills with cantrips and mischiefs.

The other, inside, reaches towards her. I feel calmer. Less alone.

In the distance, engines roar.

'Jesus Christ.' She claps at me – snaps at me. 'Can you hear me, toots? Those dickheads are heading this way. I'd get gone.'

I stretch my hindlegs, and my forepaws, and my neck.

'Bloody, bloody hell.' She licks a finger and puts the cigarette out on it.

'Come on, Pudding. Come on.' She kicks the pony. It trots, then canters. It gathers speed, cantering at me.

'Can you hear me?' She shouts, waves an arm. 'Let's go.'

We race with them. Into the wind, into the rain, into the heather. Hooves chime on granite. Paws pound on turf.

My other rides with her knuckles white, eyes streaming, and when I run out of energy, she gives me hers.

Pony-girl-cat-girl. Our hairs flatten to skins, our muscles tremble. We are all only animals.

Then, the pony slows.

'Go on.' Rosie waves me on and trots back, towards the hunt. 'I'll lead them away.'

⊕

I keep going. My other me herds me easily, now I am too tired.

I move through the trees.

I wade through the watery tomb of cats.

I walk the old paths to the enclosure, then I see her.

She leans against a tree, sheltered by the platform. Her arms wrapped around her legs. Rain dripping down her face.

Her hands cross her mouth when she sees me.

I walk towards her, and she pulls herself up, clinging to the trunk of the tree.

I collapse

at Mumma's feet.

The stain on the ceiling reached towards my bed. Water gathered and dropped to the floor. *Putt-putt-putt*. Stoney light peered through the cracks in the boards, which had been reattached, but haphazardly, with gaps, like Mumma had done it herself.

My leg stung. My belly ground. My head ached. I was in a pair of Grandma's husband's old pyjamas. They were sticky and damp in two red wings between my legs.

There was a glass of water on the bedside table. I drank it, and wanted more. I dropped my legs over the side of the bed and winced. My leg was bound tight.

I remembered a gun shot. Falling through the air. Flood. Water. Not grass and moss.

I held the leg, to take one big step and open the door. It was locked. I looked for the spare keys, but there was nowhere to look. The room was almost empty.

The painted cat leered at me from the floor, appalled and streaked with water.

I went to the plyboard and put an eye to a narrow gap.

A tynx sat on the balcony. Her stripes sparkled in the pouring rain. She lifted one leg, and licked a hand.

I stepped back from the boards quickly, pushing my breath out, to take control of the pain in my leg, and when I looked again, she had gone.

⁂

I hit the bedroom door and shouted and shouted until I heard the clip of Mumma's heel somewhere on the ground floor. 'Mumma, I need to go.'

She unlocked the door, and entered, waist poured into her skirt, not a hair out of place, but her eyes small and hooded. She was poised with relief, but wired on no sleep. She carried a tray. A mug of broth, a saucepan, a glass of water and four white pills.

'What's that?' I asked as she offered me the saucepan.

'For emergencies.'

'What are those?' I pointed to the pills.

'Broth first, then those.' She cleared her throat, nervous. 'How are you feeling?' She saw the red pyjama bottoms. 'Oh,' she said. 'Oh. Right. That explains the grumping. And your new—' She cupped her hands in front of her chest and twisted, one way, then the other.

'Mumma—' Hairs whisked around my throat as I tried not to cry.

'None of that, Loveday.' She came no closer, holding the tray out to me instead. 'Broth first, then medicine.'

I sipped the broth. The liquid bounced. My neck sank and stretched to keep it down.

'Come on.' She tried to sound kind.

'Mumma.' I wanted her to sit beside me, to hold me. 'Don't shut me up again. Help me. I need to recover.'

'You'll feel better after the painkillers. It's only your period. Darling.' She added the last word, like an afterthought.

'My period,' I said.

'Your period.' She held the tray further away, her arms stretched so her muscles twitched, showing me she could separate pain from her body. Teaching me a lesson. 'No wonder you're out of sorts. Your hormones are all over the place for the first time. You get used to it.'

I drank the rest of the broth, retched, then took two of the pills with water.

'All of them,' she said.

'Are they Grandma's?'

'It doesn't matter. They all work the same. It's not like she needs them anymore,' she snapped. 'I haven't slept in four days so be a good girl. For once.'

I took them, then squatted over the saucepan. Between my legs, urine and blood diluted into something orange.

'Now,' Mumma said, 'lie down.'

'I'm the tynx, Mumma. Grandma said I was the tynx.' My voice snapped in half.

'I wish you were, Lowdy. There are worse things than being a cat, after all.'

I suddenly felt incredibly tired. 'Grandma said I was a - a -,' I bunched my face together, trying to remember the hard, angular, made-up word. 'She told me—'

'Grandma was very ill. It's bedtime, Lowdy.'

'But, Mumma, did I hurt someone—'

'You're asleep.'

⁂

The dormitory is hot and smells of mud and socks. Someone turns on a long, rectangular ceiling light. It flickers and hums, growing into a custard glow over thin carpet.

The cubicle curtains pull back in a single, loud zip. Some of the boys in bed half-hang, sleepily, from their curtains. Some stand by their beds, wide awake, ready to defend their cupboards. Others sit, faces like crumpled crisp packets, with their sheets and blankets clutched to their necks, to shield themselves from whatever is making one of them scream.

I am completely still, my claws dangling from the tips of my paws and we, the whole dormitory of boys and I, are one stiff, messy papier mâché scene - except for the last sparkling drops running down my leg.

I stay away from everyone during the day. But all cats patrol their territory. They mark corners and spray borders. When a cat moves to a new home its paws must be buttered so it can't run back to its old, imprinted home. Unlike dogs, cats do not give up easily. Cats affect superiority and indifference but if you look, you see their obsession - the compulsion and neurosis in their flinch and skitter. It is why we love them. Cats are so human. It's why we hate them.

The boys are my territory, even if they don't know it. How else will I learn about them? I watch them, learning, always learning how to change myself into the thing they think I am, while they get on with simply being boys.

I push my nightie between my crossed legs, and the boys all move at once, staring at my bald head, shouting for their teacher, pushing each other out of the way to get through a small door with a green emergency exit sign propped to one side.

It seems like the whole school is awake when I am led to the headmaster's office. Younger boys, and older ones, come to doors and windows in their dressing gowns. They do not recognise me from all the nights I have hung over their beds to smell their unbrushed teeth, thinking, tut-tut, Mumma, standards are dropping.

The headmaster is dishevelled, also in dressing gown and pyjamas, at his desk.

Mumma has put on her uniform and brushed her hair. She accepts a chair while I shift my feet behind her.

'She will apologise.' The headmaster is clear about this. 'For scaring the boys.'

Mumma laughs, unexpectedly, especially to her, then meets the headmaster's eye. 'She was sleepwalking.' Mumma seems confused. 'She was obviously scared. She hasn't been well.'

'I dread to think what she was planning.' The headmaster lowers his chin into his neck, and spreads his hands to show Mumma my claws on the desk. 'How does she even have knives?' The headmaster stares at Mumma and I am not the only one in trouble.

'Those aren't hers,' Mumma says. 'They're from the kitchens.'

'The boys are not allowed knives in the dormitories,' he says, and I realise he knows nothing of what the boys have in the dormitories. In fact, it's like he doesn't know the boys at all. 'How could you,' the headmaster speaks to me, 'soil the boys' dormitory like that?'

'She had an accident.' Mumma leans into the headmaster's eye line. She's reaching her limit.

'Those boys are harmless and she threatened them with knives.'

'Lowdy.' The bow of Mumma's lips flattens. 'Did you threaten the boys?'

Having claws doesn't make you aggressive. Although you might be a bit aggressive, if you have claws, because why else have them? Is it correlative, or is it causative?

'No,' I say, holding my head high. The caves of Lascaux contain paintings thousands and thousands of years old – as well as shamans, its feline diverticulum features a cat spraying. 'I was marking my territory.'

'See? It was a *game*.' Mumma says this like it's a secret code word only she and the headmaster understand which will end the conversation. A *game* is also what the boys were playing, years ago, when they offered me the sausage.

'This is black and white,' the headmaster says, and I think of the new colourful picture I've stolen from under the bed and hidden, under my paw, in one slipper. 'She was supposed to stay away from the boys.'

In our flat, Mumma checks my throat, takes out the razor. 'No knives. No claws. No eating your hair. No marking your territory. You wee in a loo. You are not a cat. Or you would you rather stay in a cupboard for the rest of your life?'

I would rather not. Once I am perfectly bald again, we clean our flat and pack our suitcase so that Mumma can take me away from the school, as the headmaster has requested.

DAY 19

THE PHONE RANG and rang. It would pause, then start again, until eventually, it stopped altogether. Or Mumma answered.

Cracks ran through the glossy black stain above my head.

I bent my knee to my chest, and dropped it to the mattress. It felt fine. When I unwrapped the bandages, there was only the pink, pursed lips of a cut. I stood and stretched, fuggy and confused, shook the stiff leg and squatted to test it. My back and belly were mine again. I pulled the waistband of my underwear. The pad was clean and itchy. It tore easily from the cotton it was stuck to. Even my scratch seemed to be scabbing nicely into a thin brown smirk.

Through the gap in the boards the balcony bobbed like a boat on the mist.

I moved the painting of the cat, wiping water from the oil with a sleeve, and hung it on a hook above the bed. I wondered where Digger was. I no longer hated him. I missed him. He couldn't help being clumsy.

I went to the door, knocked, shouted for Mumma.

She came quickly, white and thin, holding the tray in the doorway.

'Hello.' I stood opposite her, the tray between us. She was surprised to see me up.

'Hello,' she said, mirroring my tone.

'I'm alright.' I threw back the cup of broth, and flicked the pills across the tray. They rolled about, hitting a small bowl of warm water. 'Look.' I took off my pyjamas to show her my leg, spinning to give her all the angles.

'Yes,' she said, like she was trying to think. 'I'm organising a funeral.'

'I'll help.' I tried to slide past, out of the room, but she put the tray in my way.

'Please, rest.'

'I'm fine.' I was fine. The red pain had oozed out of me, and now I was fine. I could almost not imagine how I had been feeling. I had been like a different person.

'Please, the pills will help you sleep.'

'I'm not tired,' I wanted to start again, to build something new. 'I want to go through Grandma's things. They're mine now. She said she was giving me everything.'

'You have to stay inside.' Her eyes were blank. 'It's for your own good.'

'Is it Digger?' I said. 'Is he here? Have you spoken to him?'

'Lowdy.' She offered the tray again. 'Have you done something?'

'Tell me how you killed my father,' I said, to lighten the mood. 'How you chopped off his head before you pushed him into the mire?'

'What? Where do you get these *horrible* ideas?' Her voice rose. 'What have you done?' The pills rolled across the tray and hit a razor.

'Mumma,' I said. 'Please, don't. Mumma.'

'Take the medicine.' She left the tray on the bed and dipped her fingers into the bowl of water. She lathered them with soap, to shave my head.

⁂

The boys at school were quite particular about girls' hair, but so were fairy tales. Between the boys and stories, it got confusing.

There was a fairy tale of two sisters, one grows stinking weeds and rushes from her head, and the other finds flowers and jewels in hers. I had hair of flowers and jewels. Hair to swing from towers on. Hair a toad could weave a nest from. Hair so fine, the devil's grandmother would have plucked it from the devil's head. It was

267

hair to write fairy tales about and, when I was young, I wanted to be in such a fairy tale, so I never let Mumma cut it, in case I'd miss the opportunity if it ever came around.

Except for our palms, humans are covered in hair. Although we can remove it, hair is more robust than the edible flesh of us. Maybe we became furless because we were incredibly hot at the time, or because being hairless was attractive – you could see clearly a healthy body free of disease or parasite – but we kept our hair, coarsest and thickest, in our most precious areas. Areas needing protection and privacy. What happens to those parts, when we remove the hair, like the women in the newspapers, the calendars, on the boys' dormitory walls? Without their husks, shell, cocoons, bark, they are exposed and vulnerable.

Occasionally, I would pluck a strand from my glorious head to use in my various curses, but sadly, once my head was shaved, I could no longer use magic to punish people. Every time Mumma shaved my head I was drained of power.

DAY 20

WHEN MUMMA CAME in with my tray, I was sitting nice and straight.

'It's terrible weather,' I said, as she slid the food and medicine on to the bed next to me. 'Shall we light the fire and make soup? Or we could work on the quilt?'

I offered my hand. She took it without looking at me.

'Have we got an onion?' I leaned into her eye line. 'Or I could cut up the curtains?'

Mumma let go of my hand. I tried to grab hers again, but was too slow, swiped the air.

'Would you like it if I wore pink?' I said. 'Like a real girl?'

'People who wear pink might as well be naked.' She almost smiled.

'It was obviously a *joke*,' I said, swallowing my pills, slowly, one by one.

'What was?'

'The cat thing.'

She patted me on the smooth head, but as she left, she locked the door behind her.

'Is Digger coming? Because I really don't care.' I shouted very brightly. 'I don't believe a word he says.'

If I wanted to leave the tower, I would have to change my approach.

🙐

Fairy tales are famous for happy endings, but fairy tales also have twists. Living a boring life, locked in the bedsit, I adored twists. Twists can mean surprising turns of events, or surprising turns of bodies – good reflexes.

A twist could refer to a cat moving deftly mid-air, in free-fall, to avoid a seemingly inevitable fatal end, or it could mean that a cat, like many animals, can change its anticipated shape. Because a cat's shoulders are attached to its body by muscle, not bone, it can collapse its shoulders into nothing and twist itself into a tiny box, should it choose to.

The twist was a dance Mumma sometimes did, if she'd drunk enough.

Oliver Twist was an orphan, with no mother at all.

A Twister was a lemon and lime ice lolly Caitlin liked.

If you twist someone's words, you deliberately misunderstand them.

If you twist someone's arm, you force them into acting against their will.

If you go round the twist, you have gone mad.

If you've got your knickers in a twist, you should probably calm down.

DAY 21

M UMMA ENTERED AND I slammed the door shut behind her. Shocked, she threw the tray, spilling the broth and pills across the bed clothes.

'Now look,' she shouted. 'Now look what you've done.' She sat on the floor to catch her breath. I was surprised to see her defenceless beneath me. I needed to be gentle if I was to build up her trust again.

'If I'm staying here, we can both stay here,' I said.

'I wish I could stay here.' She shoved the pills at me. 'I wish I could take pills and never worry about you again.' She backed out of the room, and locked the door, leaving the soiled tray on the floor.

'I love you,' I said.

'I love you too.' Her voice, outside, fell away to nothing.

There were four tiny white pills. I would have to take them every day of the month, every month of the year, forever, to stop being myself.

I swallowed them anyway.

❧

I swallowed all sorts of things, actually.

It runs in the family. When Mumma was pregnant with me, she had pica. It was perfectly normal, she told me, to want to drink blood and chew granite. 'Anything for the iron.' Many pregnant women craved non-foods. Clay and chalk. Ashes and eggshells. Faeces and soap. Hair. 'You get it from me,' she said, pulling grass from my mouth as a child.

Cats eat grass because a cat diet includes fur, feathers and bones, none of which are easily digested. For a cat, grass might have a laxative effect, or clear out anything indigestible through vomiting. Or they might just like the taste of it.

When it doesn't pass through the digestive system, cats also clear out the hair they swallow grooming, by vomiting when it builds into a hairball, or, a trichobezoar. Because of the shape of the oesophagus, the hair rolls into a tube when it is expelled. So, a hairball is not really a ball. It's not much like hair, either, by the end. All sorts of animals develop hairballs – cows, sheep, deer, humans – and sometimes they can cause serious illness.

Unlike in cats, in humans, eating hair is not considered part of good grooming.

It is considered pica, and also a compulsive psychological disorder.

DAY 22

T HERE WAS A bowl of porridge, fresh water and four pills
on the floor. I ate the porridge, and drank the water. I crushed
the pills against the side of the sink, and washed the powder away,
then lay quietly, so Mumma would think I was sleeping.

Later, I let her take the tray and leave another one.

I don't think she believed I was sleeping. I had pretended to
sleep a million times before sneaking out at night to go and find
the changing rooms edging rugby pitches. Back entrances to science
labs. Desks cleared. Lights off. Perhaps she had never believed I was
sleeping. Do pillows and bunched clothes truly look like a body
under a duvet? Can you feel the sly draught through a window set
against its frame to look as if it is still closed?

Isn't it obvious there are two sides to every girl – the idea of a
girl, and the animal, itself?

꠹

Mumma came to my room late that night, without a tray.

'Are you really asleep?' She sat on my bed, putting a hand on
my back, where it faced away from her. She had been drinking. Her
words relaxed into each other.

I didn't say anything.

'Did I ever tell you, your father was a local boy,' she said. 'From
around here?'

Yes, I thought, yes, a million times you have told me.

'There was all this new talk about cruelty to animals at the time, and he thought he knew best. I told him over and over again they'd been rescued in the first place, those lynx. That it was too late for them - Nella was born in captivity. We worked so hard to rehabilitate them - we all but taught them how to have claws. But he didn't believe me. He told me it didn't matter. I had never known someone so sure about anything. He said they would remember their nature if I stopped showing them affection. Stopped treating them like pets. He told me we were confusing them, and I should be ashamed. We needed to make them understand they were wild. Part of the natural world. I think he was probably more interested in Nella than he was in me.'

I rolled over to face her, bored of this subject.

'Will you read to me?'

'Angel girl.' She rubbed my bare head, like I was a lamp and she was making a wish. 'Of course not.'

꙰

Fairy tales, Mumma once told me, expressed things people couldn't tell the truth about. They were preposterous, losing stretches of time and significant events. It was never clear who was the goodie and who the baddie, except the skin-changers who were both. I never knew who to pity - the dead mothers, the stepmothers, the absent fathers. Fairy tales were unpredictable, a mess, and, unlike my life in the flat, I never saw what was coming next. No wonder I was obsessed.

But fairy tales are also often unsatisfyingly. They are asymmetrical, confusing and obtuse. They leave out an awful lot and they can end suddenly, without tying up the loose ends. They split and fray, leaving questions drifting into the future, where you can only assume they are answered.

DAY 23

I WASHED AWAY my medicine, but I ate until I was full and bursting, knowing it wasn't dangerous, this time.

⚜

My other symptoms of Rapunzel Syndrome – common only in young and adolescent girls – had been standard. Bloating, nausea, weight loss, pain, vomiting. A full stomach was my first symptom, but the doctor constantly referred to my tail – the thing that gave my trichobezoar, my hairball, away. It wagged at Mumma from the back of my throat when, after one choking fit too many, she finally held me to take a look. 'I'm making you sound like a dog,' the doctor joked, laughing out loud, 'but I assure you, you're not!'

It wasn't usual for the tail of the hairy growth to travel from the stomach up the oesophagus. 'But anything is possible,' the doctor said, 'you've proved that!' On each visit he stuck a gold star on my chest, and I was embarrassed, feeling too old for it at sixteen.

It was more usual for the tail to slip in the other direction, into the bowels, where it causes the most harm. Good news for me. Like cats, the gastrointestinal tract cannot digest human hair, so it just curled up, more and more of it, until it was an obstruction. When the doctor failed to break it up by endoscopy, it was removed with keyhole surgery, and I was taught to fist my hands whenever I was tempted to eat my hair. But, from the beginning, I told everyone, truthfully, I had never pulled out nor eaten my own hair. I *loved* my fairy tale hair.

The doctor said hair-plucking was usually due to anxiety.

'What,' Mumma asked me in the flat, holding my face in concern, 'can possibly have caused you such anxiety?'

'Nothing,' I said, smoothing my phantom hair and going to the window to watch the boys run in plump, happy crowds to the playing fields. 'Maybe he's wrong and it's not anxiety.'

Mumma nodded, thinking. 'Well, he was certainly wrong in the first instance, about it being a tumour.'

⚜

In the afternoon, I thought I heard a purr.

There was a yellow eye at the gap in the boards across the balcony doors. I put a finger behind one of the plywood sheets, to pull it back, to get a better look.

Outside, the tynx sat tall, stripey back to me, staring at the cloudy wall beyond the garden. It lifted a paw, took its pads between its teeth to relieve an itch. It turned to me, bulbed chest rising and falling, fur thrown about in the wind.

In one smooth movement it leapt to the balustrade. The balcony seemed to bow down so it could jump to the lawn. It walked slowly across the deer park to the woods.

I could follow, I thought. If I tried, I could pull the boards off and follow.

It disappeared from sight. I dropped the board and slid to the floor.

I wanted to be a good girl, and I wanted to know what was real, and I wanted to know what wasn't. What is the difference between a fact and its interpretation? Can you push the two so closely together you cannot know where one ends and the other begins?

⚜

'Tell him,' I say, distressed, to Mumma, at our post-surgery doctor appointment. 'Tell him I'm not eating my hair. It's grooming. It's what cats do.'

The doctor gently suggests I needed more social interaction. 'Too many stories and too little community allows the imagination to plug the gap between desire and reality. Dissociative daydreaming is often used as a retreat from abuse or excessive alienation.'

'None of which applies here,' Mumma says, picking and choosing from his diagnosis, once we are back in the flat.

But, shortly afterwards, she puts my story books in a box under the bed, and lines our shelves with encyclopaedias.

DAY 24

MUMMA WOKE ME turning on the lights.
  'It's Grandma's funeral.' She smoothed a black shift dress
of hers across my legs on the bed. 'Wear this. You're doing a reading.'
  When she went downstairs, she left the tower door wide open.
I sat up and plaited my phantom hair tidily.

꙰

The taxi followed the hearse across the cattle grid and along the
track over the moor to the village. The rain was light, drifting one
way, then the other, not wanting to fall down. A herd of ponies
grazed the track, shining manes across their eyes, heads pressed to
one another.

  We pulled over to let a quad and trailer pass. Mumma stared at
the driver's head-rest in front of her. The quad stalled, then guffed
black smoke to restart. The men in the trailer stared at the hearse
from under their hoods, rain gathering on their noses to drip.

  In the marketplace, the grocer's awning was folded away. The
flagstones glistened with steel sky, and two tractors were parked
outside the newsagents. The national park Land Rover was wedged
onto the pavement outside the village hall.

  We stopped when a group of men ran, anoraks clapping, in front
of the hearse to the pub. The pub window glowed yellow. Inside, it
was rammed with people. We could hear them through the windows
of the hearse. Mumma looked at her feet. I watched for Digger, out
of habit. He was not there.

On the pavement, people smoked and talked in the rain, drinks and cigarettes balanced in one hand to leave the other free to gesture firmly. Fingers took shape like hooks, palms flying through the air. Heads shook as waterproofs dribbled onto faces and down necks. There was a flash of deep red among them, that of a girl who'd strayed too far from her path. Someone nodded to the hearse, and Caitlin turned with the men to watch us pass.

❧

A man in a black suit held an umbrella over our heads as we walked through the churchyard. My feet were soaked in the court shoes Mumma had given me to wear. The church bells rang but the crows kept warring. The stone angel still waited, hands open, for someone to give her something.

The door of the empty church closed like a capstone behind us.

We followed six men carrying the coffin up the centre aisle.

'Who are they?' I whispered to Mumma.

She looked at me, blankly, like she didn't understand the question.

Shoes shuffled on flagstones, and somewhere a leak dropped quickly.

The coffin knocked against the rack as it was set down. The sound carried around the church.

The six men left the church again and while the priest prayed, I stared at the dull embroidery of the kneelers. Lambs with halos. Lambs waving flags. Lambs reading books. Lambs nestled in lions' paws. Tasty, tasty lambs.

I stood at the lectern. My voice ran through a microphone, so Mumma, alone, could hear it louder than it had any right to be.

'Hear and attend and listen; for this is what befell and be-happened and became and was, O my Best Beloved, when the Tame animals were wild. The Dog was wild, and the Horse was wild, and the Cow was wild, and the Sheep was wild, and the Pig was wild – as wild as wild could be – and they walked in the Wet Wild Woods by their *wild lones. But the wildest of all the wild animals was the Cat. He walked by himself and all places were alike to him.'*

I smiled at Mumma. She tried to smile back.

The priest frowned at his hands.

***

We stood at the grave someone else had dug. Lines and angles crumbled from the earth. The vicar spoke loudly over slurred shouts from the marketplace.

A quad and trailer stopped out on the road as Mumma pinched soil between her fingers and sprinkled it like salt on to the coffin. She nudged me, and I scooped the earth in two hands, grabbing as much as I could. I threw it hard onto the coffin, then turned to watch the hordes from the pub stumble past the churchyard, into the village hall.

Mumma thanked the vicar while I ran along the path, and through the kissing gate to see the village hall full of people again.

A woman rushed along the road with a pushchair, where a child cried underneath the plastic rain cover.

From the entrance, they were even louder than before. Everyone had brought their drinks this time. Shouting across each other. Sliding over and around each other, trying to get the attention of the ranger at the microphone, face boiled white, trying to settle them.

'Most likely the shot killed the lynx.' The ranger smoothed the air, to lower the volume of the room. 'It's over.'

'Then show me the body,' someone shouted. 'It's been a week.'

'It's not a bloody lynx.' Fowl bellowed. 'It's a mystery cat.'

'We're still checking the river lower down,' the ranger said.

'—and that body's mine.' Fowl pushed to get to the microphone.

Denny followed, shaking his head, folding his arms. 'It was my shot.'

'What the hell is a mystery cat?'

Fowl looked around him, like he was taking care to find the

correct words, but no one could wait. Everyone was bored of listening to the same conversations.

'Has it got magical powers?'

'Does a mystery cat climb the outside of a house to take a shit on the floor inside? Don't sound very mysterious.'

'What are you boys even doing here?'

'—wasting our bloody time.'

'Until we've got the body we don't know what it is.'

Mumma called my name from the churchyard.

'The body's mine.' Fowl said again.

'There's been no sign of it for days, so most likely the shot killed it.' The ranger heaved his chest and pointed at a woman with her hand politely raised to speak.

'A child's in hospital,' she said.

The hall went quiet.

'Let's make no assumptions until he's on the mend.' The ranger had flared red.

'He's gone mad, poor lad.'

'Lowdy.' Mumma's voice shook softly behind me, the gate creaking as she stepped out of the churchyard.

'Well, you lot need to find it.' A different woman took hold of the microphone. 'Because what about this.' She picked up a surprised toddler in one strong arm, and I recognized her from the road. The child wrapped its arms around its mother's neck. 'This'd be a nice little snack.' The mother snapped her mouth at the toddler's face to demonstrate, and the child folded into tears again.

'You lot don't seem to know what you're doing.' An elderly woman took the microphone carefully, not noticing a smart man in a jacket drawing breath to speak. 'Whatever it is, it's a dangerous animal.'

'You don't need to tell us that, my dear.' Fowl laughed. 'I've dedicated my whole life to it. My wife's left me 'cause I wouldn't stop chasing mystery cats. And I keep telling you – it is not a lynx. See?'

The man in a smart jacket snatched the microphone.

'Has anyone actually spoken to Mrs Cat? Because isn't this

her fault? Marching around like she owns the place. We should be suing for damage. As a community. She set them loose, and they've obviously been mating with god knows what.'

Next to me, Mumma's face suddenly dragged long.

'What? Like wolves or summat—'

'We don't have wolves in the West Country—'

'We are civilised people—'

'We are, but Batleigh's a shithole—'

'Listen.' The ranger, looked ill. 'Whatever it is, it had a beating heart like the rest of us, a'right? We got a shot in, so it's probably dead. Any questions.'

Almost every hand in the room raised.

'Eh, it's their fault—' The smart man was pointing at Mumma. 'If the lad doesn't pull through the old cat-lady should be done for manslaughter this time.'

The whole hall breathed out. *Oooh.*

Mumma pulled my arm, dragging me after her, running across the road.

Someone on the pavement shouted. '*Stop.*'

Tyres squealed.

I yanked Mumma back as a van swerved to avoid us.

The village hall was silent. Everyone had come to the door, to stare. Mumma's head was cradled into my chest, hiding from disaster.

'Come on.' I pushed her towards the car waiting to take us home.

⁂

I set the kettle above the aga, but it was cold. I opened the doors, but Mumma had switched it off. When I turned to ask her about it, she was drinking directly from the bottle of gin at the table, flicking through the estate agent's brochure. On the front was Nick Smith's photograph of a dirty, old house with a zoo nobody wanted. In it, I looked like a bald phantom haunting the window above its stairs.

'Sofia and Koshka wouldn't have survived in the wild,' she said. 'They'd never hunted a day in their lives. They would have starved to death, and, do you know, that is the worst way to go? But at least they were adults. I can't understand how Nella's cubs managed. Without their mother.'

'Mumma,' I said. 'Everything will be alright.'

'I'd always hoped they'd all drowned in the Vaults if she'd released them. They say drowning feels like dreaming.'

I took her head in my hands, charmed, because she said the same things over and over, like a child. I couldn't bear to correct her. I couldn't bear to tell her if you were found in a bog, you probably hadn't drowned. Across geography and history, bog bodies often shared similarities - lack of clothing, for example, and evidence of violence.

'Those men are not as good at tracking as they think they are,' I said.

'Shall we clean up? One last time?'

'Yes,' I smiled. 'Yes.'

'This is my fault. It's all my fault. But it'll be alright. We'll leave tomorrow, and get back to the way things were. Everything will be alright. You'll be alright.'

'Where will we go, Mumma?'

'You choose, darling.' She ran her fingers across my head. 'Anywhere. Anywhere but here.'

We covered each other's ears with our hands, so we couldn't hear properly.

'I love you.'

'I love you.'

We only saw each other's lips move, but it looked like we meant it.

※

Mumma packed her things, and left the suitcase open at the bottom of the stairs. She asked me to add anything I wanted to keep. I dropped my clothes and washbag and books onto the top of her clothes, washbag and books.

'Angel girl.' She kissed my cheek as she passed, checking every window, locking every room. 'One more night.'

⚜

From the library, I watched clouds smoking from the pines. The moor was a vague battlement, crenellated with rocks.

A tynx strolled past the house. Waiting. Too big for the deer park. Head like a battle axe. Chest like a shield. It sat and yawned, then looked at me with laser-eyes.

'Shall we have a last supper?' Mumma stood in the door, wringing her hands to warm them. Her face was flushed and her eyes were bright. I was so used to her face it came as a shock whenever I noticed how beautiful she was. She had been drinking all afternoon as she straightened and tweaked, Now she was finished, she gave me the keys, to lock the library.

When I looked back out of the window, the tynx was gone.

⚜

I lapped the last of my soup from the bowl, as Mumma pulled out a roll of bin bags. She ripped one off, caught it on the air and held it out.

'Will you do the honours, madam?' she said. I loved her very much.

Mumma was everything to me. Without her, the sun would gutter out and the ground would pucker, soaking up the rivers like a sponge. Although, that could be interesting, I thought. I dropped in the plastic pots of salt and pepper Digger had bought from the village on our second day here.

'Ta da!' she said.

'Ta da,' I said, knowing I would do anything for her.

There was noise of engines on the drive. Tractors, and cars, and quad bikes. Shouting.

'Shall I lock the doors, Mumma?' I saw the frightened look on her face.

'Thank you, darling, that would be kind.' She stared into the bin bag, empty but for the plastic pots.

'Stay here. Think about where we will go tomorrow.' At the front door, I turned the key in the lock, and drove the bolt home. At the back door, I did the same, knowing Mumma had already locked the rest of the house. I went to the window above the stairs.

On the drive, filthy four-by-fours parked at alarming angles to one another, wherever they found space. One hit a tree. In the flash of its hazard lights, drops of rain fell like embers. A tractor pulled onto the verge next to the drive, digging into the wet grass. I assumed quad bikes were queued behind it.

People slammed doors, and jumped from trailers.

'Get 'em to the door.' Someone shouted from the dark. A glass smashed on the gravel. 'Let's have some answers.'

They had carried on drinking, like Mumma, all afternoon.

Black figures lingered amongst the cars, perhaps not sure what to do now they were here, but someone in a boilersuit ran into the porch. There was a bang on the door.

A man in waterproofs followed more slowly. He looked twice when he saw me at the window. 'Eh, what d'you know about this my'stry cat?' he shouted. 'Where's Mrs Cat?'

'Is that the daughter?' Another man in waterproofs appeared behind him.

'No,' said the first man. 'The old one's the daughter.'

'Open the door.' Someone shouted from the tractor.

'You'd better open that door, right now,' said the second man, still pointing.

The door held fast in thick oak and loyal hinges as someone kicked it.

The man in the boilersuit appeared out on the drive, his back to the house.

'You lot just gonna sit there?' He shouted at everyone waiting amongst the vehicles. Bodies swam out of the darkness towards him, flitting in front of the headlights. 'Bring summat heavy.'

They brought nothing, except another farmer in a boilersuit, with a hay fork.

Mumma was still in the kitchen with her bin bag.

'Don't worry.' I took the bin bag and threw it to the floor. I led her into the hallway, where the front door thudded as something heavy was thrown against it. 'Look away.' I shielded her with my body to pass the window upstairs.

'Look.' There was a shout. 'There's someone else in there.'

Gravel hit the window behind us.

'You set that goddamn tynx on us? Is it a goddamn tynx?'

Something smashed through the window. A rock hit the stair.

I eased Mumma up the tower staircase, but gently, so she wouldn't trip and fall and break her neck.

'Come on,' I said. 'You can do it.'

She hesitated at the threshold, so I gave her a little push and she fell into the room, onto her hands and knees.

'Stay here.' I locked the door behind me so I knew she would.

⚜

I would have liked to staple my secret pictures together like one of Grandma's educational pamphlets – to pass it on to other girls trapped in towers. Because when you are a girl trapped in a tower, in a world made of boy, it is essential to understand how not to attract attention. I used my best skill. Research. The answer was hair. Some places you were supposed to have it, some places you weren't supposed to have it – unless you were very different, and very special, in which case, it would probably be OK to be very, very hairy indeed.

⚜

There was shattered glass below the window on the stairs. People had broken windows and climbed into the library and the drawing room and the dining room. Door handles rattled on the locked doors of the hallway. Voices demanded to be let further in.

There were more people on the driveway now. Perhaps they'd walked from the village. They lit cigarettes, shielding them from the rain with their hands, and swigged from cans. I saw the grocer, and the butcher, still in her checked trousers and bloody apron.

'Let us in,' said the butcher.

'My fucking farm is fucking done for,' someone else shouted. 'What's the fucking cat-lady got to say about that?'

'Did she set a mystery cat on us, or what?

'Is she mating cats and dogs?'

'I'm South-West Now, now. I'm South-West Now.'

The banging stopped in the house.

'A local boy is done for. He might as well be dead. What's Mrs Cat gotta say about that?'

A group gathered below the broken window. 'Where's the bloody cat-lady?'

Denny shouldered through them to stand beneath the broken window. 'Is the old woman around, sweetheart?' He took his hat on and off his head with a firm hand.

Peter Carter marched through. 'Where's the cat-lady, my love?'

'Dead,' I said.

'Well, this a right mess. That thing's attacked a boy and eaten half the livestock on Dartmoor. Angela Browning's lot are coming here next. So who's gonna deal with them?'

I shrugged. 'We've only been here a few weeks.'

And then, finally, they were quiet, looking at one another. Denny put his hands on his hips and stared at the ground. Peter Carter looked at Denny and the others, confused.

In the tower, Mumma was under my blankets, with her head in my pillow, rocking from side to side. She always said children were more resilient than adults. 'The things I dealt with as a child would send me mad if they happened now,' she would laugh.

I lay down, wove my arm around her waist.

'Better to be trapped in a cage with wings, than falling through the air with arms,' I whispered. 'Better to be a cat. Because if I'm not a cat, I might transform into something else. Something else I imagine too much and too long. Something worse than a cat. What if this isn't the last of my transformations? What if they never, ever end?'

She said nothing.

DAY 25

I T WAS EARLY. The house was cool and it had stopped raining.
I went through the boxes of medication in Grandma's bathroom, crushed four pills into powder between two spoons, dropped
the powder into a glass of gin.

In the tower, Mumma was still asleep. I watched her. Mumma
was excellent in many ways – she could find the end of the sellotape without even touching it – but she seemed trapped by her
straightening and tweaking. She deserved a nice break. I shook her
and offered her the drink. She took it, tasted it, surprised.

'It's alright,' I said. 'I'm tidying up.'

She closed her eyes. 'Don't go outside. Please, don't go out. God
knows, I've tried so hard to keep you in.'

'I'm safe,' I said.

'It's not you I'm worried for,' she said, sleep-talking. 'It's everyone
else.'

⁂

I unlocked the doors to sweep the broken glass and put it into a
crate. When the crate was full, I carried it through the zoo, to the
river, tipped it into the whirling pool – empty now the dead cats
had washed away – then returned to the house to do the same again.

I emptied the cardboard boxes Mumma had packed, dumping
linen and books and crockery onto the floor of the hallway. I carved
the boxes into pieces with a knife and fitted them to the broken
windows, sticking them in with heavy tape.

In the drawing room and library and dining room, wallpaper had been ripped away in places, revealing thriving mould where the moor side of the house took the full blast of the weather. I ran my finger along the furry black wall. Tasted it.

At lunchtime, I crushed four more pills and took them to Mumma.

Afterwards, I found a stiff brush, filled a bucket with soapy water and went outside to clean the walls where people had written obscenities.

A tynx lay on the path, eyes closed to the sun, paws resting on a ripped grey tiger mask. It purred like an engine as I passed, slowly, so as not to surprise it.

'Good guardcat,' I whispered.

⁂

Before I left, I crushed four pills, then another two, to last Mumma through the night. When she woke, she struggled a little, trying to sit up, so I held her nose until she drank it all, and sat with her head on my lap. I could hardly believe I'd once thought Mumma was a cat. She was a long puppet of oilcloth and stainless steel, veins stiff with beeswax polish.

I locked the door to the tower after me, and went hunting.

DAY 26

THE SUN WAS rising when I woke at the open door of the fridge surprised to be pushing a handful of raw mince into my mouth.

I swallowed. It was not good. But in some places, I thought, this might be a delicacy.

There was thudding from the tower, like Mumma was using her shoulder. Her weight. Like she was hitting her body against the door.

'Lowdy, please.' She was hoarse. She'd been shouting for a long time, and was becoming dramatic about it. 'I'll drown.'

In Grandma's bathroom, I ran the bath so high the water spilled over the top when I got in. The water turned pink as I cleaned myself.

When I came out, the house was quiet.

I was tired. I went into Grandma's room, empty except for the bed and mattress. There was a pale stain on Grandma's side of the mattress, so I lay on the other side. The bed had looked bigger with Grandma in it, than it felt now I was in it. The room felt as small as the tower, or a cupboard.

A tynx nudged the door open with its nose and jumped onto the bed, to sleep with its back pressed against me. I tried not to move. I didn't want to disturb it.

❧

When I woke it was mid-afternoon. The tynx had gone, leaving behind only shining hairs and a warm patch.

Mumma was shouting again. 'It's still going. We need to call someone.'

I went through a bin bag on the pile at the back door and found an old can of tomato soup. I heated it, crushed four pills into gin, and put it all onto the tray.

She rushed me as I opened the door to the tower.

I rushed her back, using the tray to push her onto the bed, splashing through water pooling across the floor. The soup spilled over her, and the saucepan under the bed stank.

'Now look,' I said.

She wiped soup from her face, and pointed up. 'The leak,' she said. 'The leak.'

Water streamed down the wall from the dark stain on the ceiling.

'It's the water tanks. The planks might be rotten. God knows how long it's been flooding.' She tried to push past me, but I put the tray in her way again, pressed it into her stomach, until she fell back onto the bed.

'Lowdy, darling, we have to go,' she said. 'This isn't safe.'

'Could you clear up that mess, please?' I said, of the gin and soup sinking into the bed clothes. 'I'll find you something else to eat.'

There was nothing edible in the first bin bag at the bag door. But I opened the second and found pieces of the cryptozoologist's leaflet. I ran my fingers through bits of ripped paper. The picture Digger had drawn. My newspaper clippings. The stories I had written. Mumma had torn up my mystery cat scrapbook, but she couldn't take away everything I'd watched and heard. I would get a new scrapbook.

But when I dug deeper, I found pieces of another picture I recognised. It was old, one of the very first I collected. I found most of the pieces of my first woman and placed them in the correct order on the doorstep next to me.

Sultry sixteen-year-old Sonya is sprucing up her garden now spring is on its way. She sat on her knees showing her breasts to an empty flowerbed. I looked at the photograph afresh, more open to the idea of someone my age interested in gardening now I owned a house and a zoo. I emptied the bin bag over the path, collecting the torn pieces of everything I had hidden so carefully - the thin paper I had folded and slipped behind family photographs in my project book. The ones I had hidden behind the cryptozoologist's leaflet and Digger's sketch of the lynx. I had stuck pages of my encyclopaedias together and dropped the women in between. They were always hiding, hiding, hiding, so you could only find them if you knew exactly where, and how, to look.

Mumma was screaming for help when I went into the house and unlocked the drawing room. I scattered every piece I could find on the floor. I found a roll of sellotape and sat cross-legged in the middle of a huge puzzle of shiny, hairless women, and tynxes.

When I had finished, I drank gin and arranged my new pictures like an exhibition on the floor. No one had their own head and limbs now. Each woman was a bunch of parts, skin-changers. I am, I thought, like this. Pieced together from the bits and pieces I found - a hole growing bigger and bigger needing to be filled - with fairy tales and glamour models, because there was nothing else in between.

When the boys woke to find me in their dormitory that night, did I mark my territory, or wet myself with fright?

⚭

ANIMAL BRIDES AND GROOMS

INTRODUCTION

In the fairy tales, some animal brides and grooms begin as animals, and some are cursed to be animals, but they only ever exist as their true selves temporarily, whether you consider the true self to be the animal, or the human. These shapeshifters go on journeys in order to become more socially acceptable than their animal form for the sake of their prospective marriage.

Sometimes when the animal self is destroyed, the story ends badly because the animal and human selves are not harmonized. Selkies, in particular, never deal well with their skins being stolen. But, regardless, the aim of these journeys, is for the animal shape to shift, ideally, into not only something acceptable to the new spouse, but to society, because the animal bride or groom marries a set of expectations, not a person.

❦

Before I went to bed, I sat outside the tower room door.

'Mumma?' I said, leaning my head against the door.

She said nothing, but there was movement inside.

'Mumma, I'm sorry to tell you, I go out now and you can't stop me,' I said.

There was no sound for a few moments, then there was a grunt and Mumma sobbed.

'Angel girl,' I said. I was glad she had taught me how to keep the ones we love safe. 'It's alright.'

DAY 27

THERE WAS A dull thunder. The house was quaking.

I woke in Grandma's bed, hungover and confused.

Glass smashed. There was a tide of noise, a splintery explosion, then everything went quiet.

I ran down the stairs.

A brown smog hissed under the library door and into the hallway.

❧

The stairs to the tower smelt damp and dusty.

I unlocked the door, and pieces of plaster dropped onto me as I pushed it open. The bed hung at a severe angle. I could see into the attic above, and through a hole into the empty library below. The floor had collapsed in, dragged by the weight of a water tank that had dropped through the roof above, and now balanced, still almost full, on the end of the mattress.

I crept along the wall to look into the sink room, but Mumma had climbed through the hole in the floor.

The bed slid further along the floor and as I reached out to grab the frame, it lost its grip and dived into the library. The water tank fell with it, bursting open as it hit the ground and flooding the room.

Most of the tower floor was ripped away. There was almost none of my room left.

Outside the doors, the corner of the house shuddered, and the balcony fell away, crashing to the ground.

I edged along the wall, around the hole, to where the cat yawned in its painting.

⚘

The painting swayed when I hung it on its hook above the stairs. I tweaked until the angle was perfect.

'Mumma?' I went into every bedroom, bathroom and the linen cupboard.

I searched the pantry, and even small kitchen cabinets she might have hidden in.

I looked in the library and dining room, but she was not in my house.

In the hallway, moss clung to the floorboards, creeping velvet over the hard wood.

I had left the door to the drawing room open and my pictures were messed about on the floor. Of course, she'd seen it all before. She was in the boarding house day and night – she'd seen the boys' walls. But she never mentioned them, perhaps she never even noticed them. Thankfully, she had no reason to suspect I had bitten off more than I could chew. If I *had* wet myself from fear in the boys dormitory, was it from fear of the boys? Or fear of Mumma?

The cardboard had been ripped from one window. I could see through broken glass to the rhododendrons.

On the path to the enclosure, Mumma slipped over in the wet tracks left by the convoy a few days earlier, muddying her feet, and leaving a round, brown smear on her behind. Her shirt was soaking and her arms were cut. I could see the scarlet of her bra, and her hair was a wet helmet to her head.

She was a mess.

What – I wondered kicking through my chimerical pictures – could have driven her to leave the drawing room so urgently?

I climbed out, following her into the woods where the river foamed in its cups, babbling on, filling the silences.

I looked at my bare feet, remembering the trail of broken glass I'd left along the paths and towards the moor. I hoped Mumma had noticed it too.

I heard her in the lynx enclosure.

Clicking and tutting. 'Come on. Come out. Where are you?' She was underneath the cat platform. She had her hand upon her brow to peer into the trees.

'I'm here, Mumma?'

'We need to find the tynx, Lowdy. If we don't give it to them, they'll never stop now. Look at the state of the house.' She dropped to her knees with her back to me, the soles of her feet glinting and bleeding.

'Mumma, come home,' I said.

'I need to find the tynx.' Mumma wiped muddy hands across her face, sniffing deep, trying to get control.

'I'm here,' I said.

'Loveday, stop it.' She ground her teeth and tugged her hands through her own fine, flyaway, thin, thin, thin hair. 'I wasn't too skinny to be pregnant. I had gestational diabetes.'

'Humans don't groom,' I said. 'Cats do.'

'The tumour wasn't cat hair. It was human hair, and you were pulling your hair out and eating it.' Mumma shook a little from the crying.

'What possible reason could I have had for tearing my hair out?' I knelt with her. 'When everything is so wonderful? Come home,' I said. 'What can I make you? What do you fancy?'

Her face was smeared with mud. 'Did you stab the Spring boy?' she said, sounding briefly like Mumma again.

'No.'

Her head swayed from side to side. 'We've got to find the tynx—' she said.

'I'm right here.'

She leaned into my face to scream. 'People cannot change into animals. Lick your own bum if you can reach it, pretend all you like, but you will not switch off 200 million years of cognitive evolution.' Her face was black purple, and her mouth was spitting like a snake. 'We've got to find the tynx, Loveday, because, if we don't, they'll come back again, and again, and eventually they'll find *you*.'

Sweet Mumma, I thought, worrying that I, a real skin-changer, would be found. She wouldn't want me in a cage. Or on the TV or in The Sun. She couldn't bear to see me a rug.

'Please, Lowdy. Repeat after me. People cannot change into animals.'

I stroked her face, grateful. She wanted me rehearsed and ready for when they came to find me. 'People cannot change into animals.' I winked slowly at our in-joke. 'Of course, Mumma, people cannot change into animals.'

She was still in my face, sweating and grey, shaking her head, lost for words.

Behind her, between the trees, a tynx sat tall, blinking slowly, like an old woman.

I held Mumma for a long time, and when I let go, she stood up onto four plush paws and trotted towards the other tynx. They reared and fell against each other, butting heads and sniffing each others' whiskers.

DAY 28

I TIDIED THE lynx enclosure.
   I tidied the old pump house.
I straightened and tweaked.

There was a wax jacket beneath the sunning platform in the enclosure. It was browned and greened from exposure, covered with moss and soil from the kick of heavy rain, but when I tried it on, it fitted perfectly.

The trichobezoar wasn't, necessarily, made of my hair. I heard the doctor confide this to Mumma in a lowered voice – cats have better hearing than humans, but also neither of them knew I was hiding behind the office door. 'She doesn't have any thin patches,' the doctor said. 'Her hair is thick and healthy. Can she be getting hair from somewhere else? Have you got cats at home?' 'No,' Mumma had said. 'No cats. It's just us. Us and five hundred harmless boys.'

DAY 1

THE SUN WAS a golden egg when I walked through the rhododendrons to see the broken windows and the bad words I hadn't been able to reach with the scrubbing brush. The balcony was in pieces across the lawn like a giant game of Kerplunk, but the roof was intact, wedged into the grass and now the moor was impaled on its tip.

I thought of the curtains and books lying in the moss in the hallway and sat down heavily in the long grass of the deer park, watching the clouds leap-frogging across the sky.

There were footsteps on the gravel.

Rosie threw a broken FOR SALE sign onto the grass.

'That was on the drive,' she said, walking towards me. 'Are you feeling better? You look like you've crawled out of a grave.'

I brushed dry red sphagnum from my feet. 'I've been clearing up,' I said.

Rosie stopped next to me, and followed my gaze to the house.

'Shit,' she said.

A patchwork of paper blew across the grass in the breeze.

Rosie looked down. I slowly placed my foot over it, but she bent, tugged it. I didn't move. But, she'd seen, so I lifted my foot.

She picked the grotesque woman up.

'Foxy,' she said, and turned it over, like there might be something of interest on the other side. There wasn't. She read my carefully printed handwriting.

'Loveday wants to do A Levels in English, Biology, Geography and History, and hopes one day to become a tynx.' She laughed out loud, but I think she got the joke regardless, whatever Mumma would say.

We sat and faced the view where Great Bat Tor was a black goblet, steaming with cloud.

'Sorry about your gran,' she said. 'That she died.'

I shrugged a nod.

'Is the house for sale, then?'

'Not anymore.'

The sun blinked. It was, at least, hot again.

'The moor used to be a sea,' I said, 'in cretaceous times.' A thin little tabby mewed and strolled over to us. 'Then it was a forest.'

'What is it now?' The cat threaded in and out of Rosie's arms.

'Rock. The sun and the rain and the wind are slowly stripping everything else away and one day there'll be nothing but rock from one side of the country to the other.'

'Cool.' Rosie smiled and rubbed her face into the tiny cat's neck. 'Did you eat the sheep? Did you eat all those sheep, poppet?' She let him go and he lay sphinxed between us. 'I love cats,' she said, picking clumps of his hair from her T-shirt. 'Some kid's found a massive skull near the coast. They've sent it off to London but they reckon someone killed the tynx and shoved it in the river so the grockles are going home. Absolute shitshow from start to finish. Where's your Mum?'

'Visiting my dad.' I turned and lay back.

'Oh.' She took something from her pocket, and folded my picture. 'Pass me that.'

I wiped the knife clean on the grass and gave it to her.

She paused, looking at it, then used it to score a line through the paper.

When she was finished, she lay back next to me. She nudged me with her elbow and offered me her joint.

'It's a home brew,' she said.

I took it, as a search and rescue helicopter shuttered over our heads.

'It's been out all morning over the Vaults,' Rosie said. 'Caitlin's gone missing. I keep telling them she was planning on leaving when she turned sixteen. No one listens to me.'

'Oh,' I said. 'Oh. Right.'

Rosie rolled onto her front, her head on one hand. 'I'll help you clear up,' she said.

I passed the joint back to her.

I smiled. 'Alright.'

A shadow probably moved, stealthy and balletic, in the rhododendrons below us, where the river carried on, thick-tongued through the valley, licking black boulders, and lisping away from the high and quiet places where no tracks or paths led but the rocks pressed out. Where the soaked land could eat a person whole and they might never be spoken of again.

Acknowledgements

With thanks to

Livia Franchini, Ben Pester, Hazel Barkworth, Paul Tremblay, Kate Caoimhe Arthur, Naomi Walmsley, Isla Gray, Chris Hamilton-Emery, Jen Hamilton-Emery, Kirsty Hamilton-Emery, Liza DeBlock

Paulette, Phil, Anne, Andrew, Doreen, Katie, Richard, Nicki, Hilary, Kate W, Kate VW

B, C, A

but most of all, Ben.

This book has been typeset by
SALT PUBLISHING LIMITED
using Neacademia, a font designed by Sergei Egorov for the
Rosetta Type Foundry in Czechia. It has been manufactured
using Holmen Book Cream 65gsm paper, and printed and
bound by Clays Limited in Bungay, Suffolk, Great Britain.

CROMER
GREAT BRITAIN
MMXXV